ABOUT THE AUTHOR

Peter Gray has been writing in various guises since he was twelve years old and he has never been able to stop. From plays to magazine articles Peter has produced a plethora of work.

His first 'Sam Series' book "A Certain Summer" has had excellent reviews, one from TV presenter and ex England soccer coach Bob Wilson who grew up in the same area and could easily identify with the character in the book.

With many short stories, articles and celebrated Mummers Plays plus many touring productions under his belt. Peter is always busy writing something or other. He has also acted in and directed some of those productions and one such production played at Warwick Castle for six full seasons. He has also written several scripts for advertisements, mostly with a humorous theme as well as several live shows for the stage. He has now embarked on a new series of Adventure Novels of which more details can be found on this website at www.petergrayauthor.co.uk.

He currently lives in the Highlands of Scotland.

ALSO BY PETER GRAY

A Certain Summer
Sam's Kingdom
With Feeling

FROM THE AVALON SERIES

The Drums of Drumnadrochit
Auld Clootie
The Brollachan
The Black Clan
Caledonian Flame

Caledonian Flame

by
Peter Gray

Tricky Imp Publishing

Caledonian Flame

First edition first published November 2019

Tricky Imp Publishers
Caithness, Scotland.
Email: books@trickyimppublishing.co.uk

A CIP catalogue record for this title is available from
The British Library.

ISBN 978-0-9572668-7-2

Cover design & artwork by the author.
Cover photography by Barbara Jane Gray

More Information at:
www.petergrayauthor.co.uk
www.trickyimppublishing.co.uk

Printed and bound in the UK by 4 Edge.

"Is God willing to prevent evil, but not able? Then he is not omnipotent.
Is he able, but not willing? Then he is malevolent.
Is he both able and willing? Then whence cometh evil?
Is he neither able nor willing? Then why call him God?"

David Hume on Epicurus.

Chapter One

The woman was in tears, she turned her head this way and that in a panic, wringing her hands that suggested she was about to break down completely. She really didn't think she was going mad, she thought what she had seen, what she had experienced, was real, but how could it be? She suspected her husband was not being truthful, after all, where did he go all day, and why wouldn't he tell her what he was doing? Or was she imagining that too? She stood and paced the room trying to wipe the tears from her face with an already damp handkerchief. In frustration, she sat again as she heard the door of the hall close. It would be her husband returning, how could she tell him that her symptoms had returned, and that she was believing her insanity herself?

Avalon leaned back in his seat, he had been in that same seat for almost an hour and he wasn't sure he wanted to remain there much longer. He watched the husband enter and saw the woman's eyes flit around the room, her hands still wringing, her tears now ceased, but her brow furrowed with despair. Avalon leaned on the arm of his chair and rested his chin in his cupped hand, watching the man slowly walk to his wife and ask her how she had been. She didn't reply, she played with the handkerchief, twisting it through her fingers keeping her eyes fixed on some random position on the floor. Avalon sighed. He knew that the man was trying to make her believe she was going insane, he knew he was trying to find hidden treasure in the apartment upstairs. He even knew that once the husband left to go wherever it was he went, a stranger would call on Mrs Manningham, and he would announce himself as Mr Rough. Avalon knew *exactly* what would happen, and that was probably why he was becoming so uncomfortable in the lightly padded seat. It was his own fault, he had seen the play *Gas Light* on two previous occasions and though he considered it a good play, it didn't really warrant a third viewing. The cast did a brilliant job of breathing new depth into it and the director had brought the whole drama to vivid life, but when you can almost mouth the words of the script it takes the edge off the spectacle as a piece of entertainment.

At the end of the second act, he left and walked the streets of the city to think of something else to do. He had tried the bars but when you are alone, the whole experience seems muted and pointless. Instead, he walked around aimlessly, taking in the sights and sounds of Edinburgh on a December afternoon. He felt at home in Edinburgh, he always had done, there was plenty to see and do, at least when you weren't alone. In more recent years, the city had lost something to the tourism industry but there were still the odd gems if you knew where to look. It was dark, it wasn't late, but the sun had gone down hours ago and the night was well and truly ensconced over the city. The weather had been mild and damp recently but Avalon considered as it wasn't raining

10

it was a good night for a stroll and reflection. He was on holiday but when the thought crossed his mind, he made an involuntary chuckle to himself.

'On holiday?' he thought. It was harder work than being at the office in Inverness. He just didn't know what to do. As he walked along the end of Lothian Road, he could hear music wafting towards him from one of the bars, so he headed off in its direction. The establishment was fairly busy but not overcrowded and so he entered and made his way to the bar. The music was a mix of styles, ideal for the way he felt and he ordered a drink and leaned on the wall to the side of the servery. He looked around, the ages of the customers were mixed but the over-riding impression he got was that he was the *only* person there on his own. He felt slightly ill at ease with this knowledge and once again wondered what it was about *him,* that made him choose this way of life. It wasn't natural, he would rather be there with someone else even if it was just an acquaintance, even if it was Ross. It had been a completely pointless act to go away, he could have relaxed just as much at home, at Inverness, taking the odd stroll down to the Castle Tavern. But no, he bent to the will of those around him who insisted that if he didn't go away, he would get called into work when it was busy. They had been correct of course, it had happened before, he had taken a few days off in a quiet patch to find out that it wasn't so quiet after all and the criminal fraternity hadn't wanted him to take a break. At least this way that wouldn't happen.

He soon found himself walking again, this time towards his hotel just as he had done on the two previous evenings, and he still had four days of this left to go. Yes, it had been quiet back at Inverness, it had been a fairly quiet year and as everyone had said, he hadn't had a proper break for almost eighteen months. He needed it, yes he certainly needed it, but not alone. The frustrations and the boredom were as stressful as being at work.

As he entered the hotel, he knew exactly what he would do, the same as he had done the night previous. He ordered a double, single-malt and a bottle of spring water from the bar and then returned to his room to open his laptop. In an effort to mitigate the boredom he was running through some old case files, nothing too serious but just trying to clear up some cold cases or new minor incidents. The problem was, he had no direct access to the case histories, just notes he had made and research on the internet. This could be as frustrating as doing nothing, and several times he looked over to the silent television fixed to the wall, resisting the urge to switch it on. He sipped at his whisky and scanned the internet for snippets of information. Several cases piqued his interest but for two of them, he was desperate for more details. The first was a missing person who had inherited a considerable amount of money. The odd part of the case was that several sightings of the person had been reported around Inverness. The other case, more accurately, a series of cases that seemed linked, were reports of breaking and entering over several months where nothing or very little of value had been removed. Usually, the perpetrator or perpetrators left a scene of destruction in their wake. In truth, that was the only aspect that seemed to link them. He was getting nowhere with the missing person, as even after plotting the locations of the sightings on a map, the whole thing seemed random. It was a similar tale for the breaking and entering, tenuous links can alter the view of what you perceive and Avalon knew that he needed more information. Several times he looked at his phone on the bed, the consideration of asking Frazer was tempting but he knew it was completely out of order. That damn phone had never been so quiet, for three days it hadn't made a peep. He even phoned his home number just to hear his recorded message to be sure it was working. He strolled the room looking out of the window now and then sipping the whisky to the point it was almost empty. He drained it and pulled on his jacket heading for the bar.

He ordered another double and noticed a woman seated on a tall stool at the end of the servery. She was the same woman he had seen the previous night. He nodded as he waited for the drink. She gave a smile and turned to her own drink. She was in her fifties, around five and a half feet tall, slim build, good make-up but not particularly attractive, dressed as if she was planning to go to a party but had changed her mind and stayed in the bar. Her blonde hair was piled up which seemed too showy for a quiet bar and the handbag and shoes were more nightclub than hotel foyer. Avalon redressed himself for his professional, analytical study of what was just another person. He took the drink from the barman and was about to say the number of his room but checked himself and just said,

'Put it on my account, please.' As he turned to leave, he gave the slightest smile to the woman who returned a similar gesture.

In his room, he placed the drink on the small dresser and pulled up the chair to where his laptop sat ready for action. He recapped on the cases he had reviewed previously but without the full access to the files, he could make no headway. He took a large swallow of the whisky before adding water and then slumped on the bed. He thought about the holidays he had taken in the past. He wasn't a holiday sort of chap if he thought deeply about it, what was the point? You spend thousands of pounds making your home exactly what you want and where you want to be, and then go off somewhere else. It made little sense. He remembered the holidays he had taken with his family when he was a child but even they had been an endless cycle of arguments between his parents. He even remembered on one particular occasion, a severe chiding over the amount of sweets he had eaten. There had been a few good ones with his ex-wife Carol. On one particular occasion, they had gone to the Norfolk coastal resort of Great Yarmouth and Carol being fond of fairgrounds had dragged him onto several rides, which he hated. Not for any reason except they just seem to start at one point and bring you back to the *same* point, and the ones that just go round and round seemed tediously boring. He had frequently insisted that a good blast on his bike was a lot more exciting. Carol had maintained he was a 'kill-joy' and dragged him onto yet another pointless ride. He smiled a little as he looked up to the ceiling remembering them kissing in a bus stop on Beach Parade.

He turned his head and glanced over to the phone, it was still very quiet and so he got up to make sure it was turned on. It was, and he sat on the edge of the bed and considered going back down to the bar but it was almost midnight so he went for a shower instead. As

14

he washed, he thought about the morning, at least he had something to do for the next two days. He was off south to Eyemouth to call in on Carol's parents, they were like an extended family to Avalon, he had always got on famously with them both. When he had phoned to arrange it earlier in the month, Carol's mother had insisted he stay the night and Avalon reluctantly agreed. Now he was glad of it as it was one night with something different to do. He had originally planned to go on the train but as he had come to Edinburgh in the car, he chose that as more convenient.

The morning was dull but Avalon was in an upbeat mood, he had slept well, probably because of the whisky and he felt reasonably refreshed. Living and working further north, where life seems to run more slowly than the rest of the world, he had forgotten quite what it was like to be on busy roads around cities such as Edinburgh and he began to regret driving down at all.

It was just after noon as he pulled up outside the bungalow, and Colin and Margaret were thrilled to see him again. As he sat with the first cup of tea, he wondered if either of them had phoned Carol about his trip.

'You're thinner,' announced Margaret in her gentle Scottish tones. She had a troubled frown and seemed to be visually analysing his whole body for signs of advanced emaciation. He didn't think he was thinner, but it had been some time since he had seen the pair of them, and then again, Margaret always thought anyone hovering under obesity must be on a starvation diet. A very odd concept for someone as petite as Margaret.

'No, he's not,' insisted Colin, 'he looks brilliant,'

and he turned to Avalon, 'you look well lad, take no notice of her.'

'That's the trouble with you English,' chided Margaret, 'you don't know how to eat,' and she cast the frown to her husband.

'That's big coming from a nation that invented the deep-fried Mars bar,' riposted Colin throwing back a playful frown too. Margaret turned to Avalon once more mumbling,

'Deep-fried Mars bar indeed, that's not at all what I was referring to,' and she flashed him a motherly smile. 'I think you look a little pinched anyway, and I bet there isn't a womanly hand looking after you is there?'

'Margaret!' interrupted Colin, 'let the lad drink his tea, he's only just sat down and you're trying to manage his life.'

'I'm just making observations,' she announced glancing at her husband for a split second, 'I'm just looking out for his welfare,' she added turning back to Avalon and smiling.

'I'm fine,' smiled Avalon, 'everything's fine and no,' he directed the next part to Margaret, 'there is no womanly hand involved in my appearance, it's all my own work.'

'So how's the job?' cut in Colin as if to prevent his wife asking any more embarrassing questions.

'Great,' he nodded, 'busy, but I like that, I have a good team too.'

'Carol told us she came up to see you earlier in the year,' continued Colin.

'Yes,' replied Avalon raising his eyebrows, 'unfortunately there was a big case on just as she arrived so it wasn't quite as easy-going as I would have liked, but it was nice to see her again.' He wasn't about to go into detail and the thoughtful look in his features made Colin change the subject yet again.

'So you're staying in Edinburgh?'

'Yes,' nodded Avalon, 'the plan was for me and one of the other chaps in the team to come down for a few days, but we realised we couldn't spare two of us away at the same time.'

'That's one good thing about rank I supposed,' grinned Colin.

'No, it wasn't that, I was the only one who hadn't taken any time of this year so it was my turn. Edinburgh seemed the obvious place as I could get back if I needed to.'

'Would they call you back from holiday then?' asked Margaret.

'Well yes,' he replied, 'if they need me I'll get a call.' Margaret made a disapproving sound but kept a smile on her face, then she stood and added, 'Well I'll leave you two to chat, I'll make something to eat.'

'I'm fine honestly,' demanded Avalon.

'Let her cook,' winked Colin, 'she'll not be happy until she sees you eat something.' After Margaret left the room, Colin and Avalon chatted for some time, mainly catching up, about the past and sometimes about the future but Colin never brought up anything about Carol. Avalon got the distinct feeling that Colin just didn't want to talk about her and that was puzzling, but he didn't pry. The evening was similar, they ate and then relaxed in the lounge with several drams and talked and laughed, but Carol didn't come into the conversation. Avalon was becoming suspicious and decided there was little harm in bringing the subject up, he had to decide

17

how best to introduce it.

'Carol told me she's moving to Merry Hill,' he decided.

'Yes,' nodded Colin, 'she told us, sharing a flat with a friend, apparently.' He gave nothing away in his face but the voice had a tinge of disappointment in it. 'Our little girl has made a few cock-ups of late,' he added raising his brows at the floor.

'Now, now,' put in Margaret, 'it's her life, you've said often enough yourself,' and she turned back to Avalon with a half-smile. So that was it, her parents thought Carol's recent relationship with the fireman had been a disappointment. Avalon didn't know the details of how much they knew or how Carol had explained it but personally, he didn't think it was all that serious a setback for her. Yes, it had cost her some money along the way and she was embarrassed about it from the point of view of telling her friends, but everyone made those mistakes. Except for Avalon of course, you had to have a life to make mistakes in it.

For the rest of the evening Carol's name cropped up again only once when Margaret informed him she was coming north for Christmas, and if he found himself at a loose end, it would be nice to see him too.

His stay there was pleasant but by the time he left the following day he was ready to return to his hotel room and his wearying existence there.

A storm blew over as he drove back, but on the streets of Edinburgh it wasn't all that bad, and after making a mediocre coffee bordering on undrinkable, he decided to have yet another look at the case files. Unfortunately, he saw nothing new and became bitterly frustrated. He decided that a quick call to the office wouldn't go amiss and then he drew breath and thought more deeply about it. It would be best to phone Megan Frazer's desk, she would be able to help him out without letting on that he had rung.

'*DC Boyd, C Section.*'

'Hello Alison, it's Avalon.'

'*Hello Boss, having a nice time?*' there was a little surprise in her voice.

'Yes, I am, is Megan there?' There was a pause.

'*Erm no, she's not at the mo.*' Avalon got suspicious straight away, there was something in the tone of her voice that put his instincts on high alert.

'Oh, okay, can you tell her to call me on my mobile when she gets back?'

'*Er, yeah, can do, erm…*' there was another pause, '*listen Boss, I'll call you back in a second.*' The phone went dead. Avalon looked at his phone like people do in the movies but never in real life. So many times he had seen it in films and always thought it looked ridiculous, and here he was staring at the damn thing as if he was in a cheap budget American mini-series. What had happened? Why did DC Boyd need to contact him in a few minutes if it wasn't so she could leave the office and speak privately? It worried him, he hadn't been out of the office for a full week yet and something had gone wrong. He quickly looked around the bedroom, how long would it take him to pack? The phone rang.

'Avalon.'

'*Hello Boss, it's Alison, sorry about that I just needed to speak privately.*' Inside Avalon winced.

'Problems?'

'*No, no, well nothing you need to worry about.*'

19

'I'm worrying,' he interrupted with a harsh voice.

'Really, there's nothing at all to fret over, I just didn't want DS Wilson to hear me, he told everyone not to tell you until you got back.'

'So you think this,' he paused for a split second, '*thing*, that is nothing to worry about is worth going against your superior officer's orders to tell me.'

'Well, you wanted to talk to Frazer, she's not here.'

'So where is she?' he asked losing a little patience.

'Having a couple of days off,' and he could almost hear Boyd move the phone from her ear and close her eyes ready for the onslaught. Avalon remained silent. He once again looked around the room and worked out what he needed to do. As DC Boyd was offering little information, he made himself plain.

'Alison, you need to tell me everything that has happened and if you leave anything out I'll make sure you spend the rest of your days back on the beat, is that clear?' His voice was calm but on the other end of the phone, Alison Boyd got the message.

'It was just a misunderstanding, that's' all.'

'Explain,' he said with a touch of anger in his voice. He heard her sigh, take a deep breath and then sigh again before she began.

'The other day, DC Frazer had just come into the office after returning from court with Rory, she came into the back end of a story that was being told by DS Ross.' Avalon somehow knew Ross would be involved and he nodded to himself. *'Rossy had been telling us he had been invited to join what he described as an intelligentsia club, and after the usual hat-full of jibes*

20

and insults had been cast his way, he admitted that he thought being in any club made him feel old. We were just having a few jokes at his expense as Frazer walked in with Rory.' She paused, probably trying to guess how Avalon was taking it so far, she continued.

'DC Rutherford just said Rory was probably the only one in present company who had the right to be in such a club. Rory asked what club and Rossy explained to Rory and Megan about his invite. Then Megan said the club being in Inverness must be struggling for members and particularly hard up inviting Rossy to join. Ross agreed that the club indeed had only around eight or so members and he counted them off on his fingers.' Boyd paused for breath, her speech had slowed and he suspected she was regretting the phone call.

'Go on,' he said trying to prompt her.

'Well,' she continued, 'Megan noticed that all the names Rossy had mentioned were men, and she said, 'They're all men, don't you think your club is somewhat sexist?' Rossy shrugged but said nothing and so Megan asked why there were no women in the club and Rossy smiled at her and said,' she paused again, it was clear that she was nearing the important part of the story as her voice seemed to go slightly dry and rasping. She began once more,

'He said it was because it's a club for intelligent people, and at that Megan sort of went purple,' Avalon anticipated another pause so he said,

'And?'

'She threw a paperweight at him,' there was another pause, 'it hit him,' pause, this time longer, 'on the head.' Avalon tried to think what Frazer's paperweight looked like, and if it was the same one he

21

remembered, it was a miniature millstone, the sort made of reconstituted stone you can buy from tourist shops. He then tried to think how far Ross would be away from her at the time, and what probable velocity the stone was travelling at when it struck Ross on the head. He exhaled deeply and was already packing his case as he asked,

'Do I want to hear the rest?'

'*Oh, he's all right, she threw it with her left hand as she had just taken a cup of coffee from Rory so it wasn't the best aim, and to be honest I felt like hitting him with something heavy too.*'

'I'm packing my things, I'll be back this evening and in the office early tomorrow.'

'*But Boss, it's all over with now, everything is fine and Megan is back in tomorrow,*' insisted Boyd with a hint of panic in her voice.

'And how's Ross?'

'*Fine now, he's back in tomorrow too, a few stitches and he's ready to go.*'

'So why have they had a couple of days off if they're both fine?' he asked raising his voice a little.

'*Well, DS Wilson went ballistic, he threatened to take them both off the cases they were working on and suspend them, I don't think I've ever seen him like that.*' This made sense, Wilson was a complex character and very little got to him, his fury such as that described by Boyd could just as easily be theatricals as much as real anger. He probably went home and had a laugh about it with his wife. Then again, he was a diligent officer and he would want to make sure they didn't get away without some repercussions.

'How is DS Wilson now?' he asked.

'*Fine, like nothing happened, the only weirdness*'

was that he wouldn't let anyone wash Rossy's blood away at first. He said it would remind us that arsing about can have dire consequences.'

'Has the blood gone now?' asked Avalon worried that something like this could drive the DS back into his previous gloom.

'Oh yeah,' said Boyd, *'he said it needed clearing up anyway, seeing as it was Rossy's blood it could be harbouring all manner of diseases.'* Avalon thought it was a strange jibe but then again when he was on form, Wilson had the driest humour he had ever come across, matched only by PC Dowd.

'Boss?' The voice was questioning and almost pleading.

'Go on,' growled Avalon.

'If you come running back now, DS Wilson is gonna know it was me that told you about it, and he was pretty adamant that no one should tell you.' He thought for a moment, would it matter, he could just as easily say he was bored?

'Okay, I'll set off in the morning, I'm homesick anyway,' he sighed.

'Homesick? I would have thought a single man in Edinburgh wouldn't get homesick easily.' She wondered if she had overstepped the mark but Avalon's voice had calmed a great deal.

'I like Edinburgh, but since I came to live in Inverness,' he paused trying to find words, 'well, I love the place.' There was a little silence at both ends of the line until Avalon added, 'I'll head off back first thing but I'll keep quiet about our conversation, I'll say I was bored.' It wasn't a lie, he was finding the whole thing very tedious. If it had been any other time than winter, he would have put a tent on his old bike and set off north into Sutherland.

He put the phone on the desk and wondered what the atmosphere was like in the office. It was bound to have repercussions, and he was going to have to put some thought into how he would react. He thought Frazer had finally sorted her life out, but then again, it wasn't that long ago that she had poured a drink over Ross in the Castle Tavern for suggesting they should get married and go on honeymoon to Dingwall. The town wasn't many people's first option on the list of honeymoon destinations, but it didn't warrant the loss of a perfectly good glass of wine. Maybe she would always be unpredictable, maybe she was simply a liability and he would eventually have to drop her from the team. But then again, Ross was just as bad, he had never really stopped giving her a hard time. Avalon looked at the clock on the radio alarm, it was three-thirty and the daylight was dropping fast. If he was going back in the morning, he wouldn't be able to drink himself silly but he would certainly sample a couple later. He decided to go for a short walk, have some food and then return for a shower before heading to a pub in the city. He was on his way back from a damp and windy stroll near the Grassmarket when his phone rang. It was such a surprise he even checked the number first, he normally just answered without looking who it was from, but he didn't recognise the number, anyway.

'Hello, Avalon.'

'Oh hello James, I didn't know if you would answer.' It was a woman's voice, he thought he recognised it but he wasn't sure.

'Er yes, yes I always answer unless I'm...' and

then the penny dropped, it was Sarah, Sarah Underwood, 'Sarah?' he asked.

'*Yes, I rang your office as there seemed to be some confusion about two of our reports that were filed about the arson at Invergordon.*' He knew of the case, but to his knowledge Alison Boyd was working on that. Sarah continued. '*I rang and asked to speak to you, to explain about the two reports but they said you were in Edinburgh so I had a word with DS Wilson.*

'DS Wilson is looking after things while I'm away,' explained Avalon thinking about the conversation he had earlier with DC Boyd.

'*But Edinburgh?*' she asked a little surprised.

'Why not, I like the place?' he insisted, 'I'm having a few days away and sampling the delights of a city in the stirrings of a storm,' he said as he glanced up at the scudding clouds.

'*Well, that's why I rang you on your mobile, I'm down here too, at a conference on forensics, quite a coincidence don't you think?*' Avalon's mouth went dry, okay she was down here in Edinburgh but what was the point in ringing him unless..?'

'Is it just for the day then?' he asked.

'*No, two nights, I go back Saturday morning,*' she explained. Avalon still wasn't sure why she had rung, if it was business why hadn't she got straight to the point and why the hell was he in such a panic just because Sarah Underwood had rung? '*the conference is pretty boring for the most part but there have been a few interesting developments, so it was worth coming.*' He didn't really take much notice of what she had said, he was thinking through the fact that her ex-fiancé lived in Edinburgh, was she going to see *him*?

25

'Same here really,' fixating on the only word he really heard, 'boring', 'I mean the city is a great place but, well you know…' and he trailed off hoping she did know because he really didn't want to explain to her that being so shallow and uninteresting, he was struggling to enjoy his time off.

'Yes, I suppose anywhere can be tedious when you're alone, that's why I don't particularly like these things.' She replied in an upbeat tone, or at least that's what Avalon thought. So even now, he still didn't quite know why she had rung. Avalon was silent, it wasn't intentional, but he had the distinct impression it should be him saying something at that moment. Nothing came but fortunately Sarah continued.

'So, I was thinking, if you have nothing planned?' There was enough of a pause for Avalon to get his hopes up, was she about to suggest that they meet up? *'I wondered if you fancy dinner? Not tonight because I'm going to be late finishing but, I thought…'* another pause, *'tomorrow evening?'*

'I'd love to,' was his instant reply, forgetting completely that he was leaving in the morning, 'what time and where?'

'I thought about seven-thirty? I know a great place to eat, if you're still okay with vegan food?'

'Yes, yes,' replied Avalon with a voice that sounded much too eager, he tried to calm himself down.

'I'll text you directions, assuming you're in the city,' she added.

'Yes, I am but it doesn't matter, I'll find it.'

When Avalon got back to the foyer of the hotel, the smile was still evident on his face. He nodded with that same smile to a man on his way out of the hotel and he walked all the way up the stairs still smiling. He showered, dressed, picked up his watch and phone and left the room with that smile still fixed on his face. He wanted to punch the air, but he was already so embarrassed due to his childishness that he prevented himself from further idiocy. He walked up to the bar and ordered a drink and once again the woman he had seen on two previous occasions had been seated at the end of the bar and once again smiled at him. This time her hair was down, she was wearing a tight-fitting red dress and matching shoes with quite an array of jewellery on her person. Somewhere in the back of his mind there was a voice asking him what the hell she was doing sitting in a hotel bar every evening, dressed to the nines and alone? He didn't know if it *was* every evening but Avalon tried to ignore that voice as the bartender placed his whisky on the small drinks mat and the bottle of water by its side.

'A man of habits I see,' said the woman. Her voice was deep and husky and for a moment Avalon had a suspicion she was actually a man. He had previously noted that she wasn't all that attractive but as he looked over to her, he would be surprised if she was indeed male. Her hands and arms were delicate, her legs were slim and long and her proportions were certainly female. True, back in Birmingham, Avalon and his partner at the time had arrested what they thought were two female prostitutes for fighting, only to find out they were both males. What had surprised him most about that ordeal wasn't that they turned out to be men, but that even in the grip of the altercation, they actually fought like women. Then it occurred to him, maybe this 'Woman in

Red' was a prostitute. He checked himself for being disingenuous and stereotyping. It was something he always chastised his team for and here he was doing it too, though he couldn't seriously reprimand himself, he was in too much of a good mood.

'Sorry?' he eventually asked raising his brows.

'A man of habits,' and the Woman in Red nodded towards the drink he was holding.

'Oh right, the whisky?' he smiled.

'Not just whisky,' she insisted, 'you order a double Dalmore and a bottle of spring water on each occasion. You then make your way back to your room glancing every time to the door before turning the other way and attempting to read the headlines on the newspaper in the rack even if it's upside down.' Her accent was English but he couldn't hear a localised dialect of any kind.

'Do I?' he questioned and then glanced into the middle distance before looking back to her, 'I don't recall reading those headlines, I certainly don't remember them.' He was standing with the glass in one hand and the bottle in the other as if about to go through those same rituals again so he checked himself and placed them on the bar. 'There, that's broken the cycle then,' and he flashed a quick smile. He leaned over slightly and held out his hand and began to say Avalon, but just as the first letter came from his lips he held it back and altered its sound slightly. 'Ah, my names James, Jim if you like,' and she took his hand. It wasn't so much as a shake as a clasp she gave him, soft and subtle and he once again felt himself making guesses at her background.

'Lucy, it's actually Lucinda but if you're Jim, I'm

Lucy,' and she gave another smile.

'You're pretty observant,' he began and nodded towards the newspaper rack across the room, 'I mean to notice all that.'

'Not really,' she sighed, 'when there are so few people coming and going through the bar this time of year you watch people a little too much.'

'So you come in here quite a bit then?'

'Only when I'm working around here, I usually stay in this hotel, it's not the best but I like the staff,' and he noticed her glance over to the bartender who didn't really react to the comment, he just continued washing glasses and replacing them on their shelves. She took a drink.

'So you're here working then, may I ask what you do?' That damn voice at the back of his mind got its way after all. The woman made a noise as if it was going to be a surprise and Avalon was now wishing he hadn't asked.

'If we were to sit here for a hundred years,' she said looking at herself through the mirror at the rear of the bar, 'you wouldn't guess what I do for a living.' In some ways that relieved him, his shallow side still thought she may be a woman of the night. She took a sip of her drink and turned back to him. 'I'll tell you what, unless you have somewhere more important to be,' and she gave a little smile again, 'let's play a game, you have a go at what I do and then I'll guess yours.' Avalon nodded, he would take the easy way out. She had said he wouldn't get it so he was free to come up with as many outlandish suggestions as he could.

'Well,' he looked her up and down, it allowed him to examine her more closely without making the

29

gesture seem rude. She had a good body, she looked fit under that dress and he suspected that she probably spent some serious time on her look. Her hands were fine and her nails were manicured but short with no nail polish that he could see. She was right, he would never guess it so he considered the fact that she must work away to be staying in a hotel. She was English but so was he, but then again she admitted she was staying at the hotel *due* to her work.

'You work in the theatre.' He eventually said, 'you're the person that designs the stage sets or something like that.'

'I wish,' she laughed. She took another sip of the drink and then said, 'You're not going to get it, so I'll tell you. I inspect elevators, or lifts as most people call them.'

'Oh,' said Avalon with little else he could think of to say.

'Yes boring isn't it,' she smiled taking another drink.

'Well, I'm guessing the money is good, it must be a responsible job,' he offered.

'The money is okay,' she shrugged, 'but the lifestyle stinks. I travel all over the UK, even out to those ridiculous windmills offshore and spend up to twelve hours every day dressed in overalls wearing a hard hat. So at night I put on my posh frock and come to the bar hoping there's someone to talk to, instead I end up getting steadily tipsy. I then leave, sleep, pick up my kit bag and go to work.' The smile had gone and Avalon could see something replacing it. That meant he would hear her life story. He didn't want that, he was in a good mood and he wanted no one bringing him down from that height, not even a lift inspector. 'Don't you think we live out our lives in a total spiral?' she concluded.

'Life is a spiral,' replied Avalon raising his brows, 'your turn,' he said. She looked at him as if she didn't understand the question but gradually she began to smile again as she looked him over.

'You're easy,' she grinned, 'the routine, the way you dress, casual and on the edge of being trendy, drinking double whisky and reading the newspaper headlines but not reading it. You're alone and you go back to your room quite early.' She paused for reaction but he didn't offer any. 'A rep, pharmaceuticals or something similar,' she concluded finishing off her drink.

'Yes,' he nodded, 'right on the button,' and he decided it was time to leave, there was something depressing coming over her and he didn't want anything to spoil his evening. 'Well, it's been nice talking but I have to get off, got loads of emails to get through, see you again though,' and he stood taking the glass and the bottle with him. She didn't reply, it was as if it was inevitable he would leave, as though she had expected it. He made sure he didn't read the newspapers on the rack or look towards the double-glazed doors.

As he walked up the stairs he considered it ironic that this hotel didn't have a lift, but that was probably the real reason she stayed there. Then he became slightly annoyed with himself. A woman working away, alone, constantly trying to connect to other people, someone just wanting to talk and he had refused her that. He was so wrapped up in his own world, his own petty life he had refused her the chance to chat, to engage with another person just for one evening. As he put the key in

31

the lock of his room and entered, he placed the now empty glass on the dresser along with the water bottle and slumped onto the bed. He laid back and looked at the ceiling and thought back to the conversation in the bar. Was he developing a duel personality because it seemed like it to him? He was different as a detective, he was a more compassionate person in his work than he was in his life, and that was probably the root of his problem. He had run away from someone who simply wanted to chat because he wanted nothing to take away his euphoria of having a dinner date with Miss Sarah Underwood. A woman he had admired and yet dare not pursue for some reason he couldn't quite fathom. The thought he was going to have dinner with her was pushing everything else aside. It had changed his attitude to the woman in the bar and he had even made a mental note about phoning the office in the morning to let DC Alison Boyd know that he wouldn't be coming back yet after all. He was changing all his decisions for dinner with Sarah. He sighed and pulled his phone from his pocket. If he rang her and told her something had cropped up and he couldn't get, he could kiss goodbye to getting a second chance and why would he do that, anyway? Self-chastisement? He put the phone down and looked back at the ceiling. No one would believe that the confident Detective Avalon would have these periods of doubt, these dark moments of inward assessment. He wondered why he turned into a schoolboy at those times and what triggered it, yet it was plain. Certainly, Miss Underwood was usually to blame, or some other woman. He sat bolt upright and wondered if he could make reparations, if he could appease his other side by just being the detective rather than the man, but then again the high moral side of that detective could sometimes impede enjoyment. He needed to blend the two sides of the person together, but then he wondered if what he really needed was a psychiatrist because these internal conflicts couldn't be normal, could they? He stood and placed the bottle and its remaining water on the bedside table and then looked at his watch. He had to sort his problems out, he needed to balance the two sides of his character and he decided that as he slept, that metamorphosis would take place, because it had to.

The morning broke much as it had done for the last few mornings, though the wind seemed to have dropped. Avalon showered and looked at himself in the mirror and decided against a shave. He dressed quickly and went downstairs for breakfast, something he rarely did in hotels. He ate toast, drank two cups of strong coffee and read the newspaper, something else he never did. The woman from the previous evening hadn't shown, and there were only four other people taking breakfast. Two middle-aged men, who looked like tourists on a walking holiday, and a young English couple who chatted about the Edinburgh Luckenbooths which also singled them out as tourists. He folded the paper and finished the dregs of the coffee and then climbed the stairs to his room. He then picked up his phone and called the office.

'Gordon, it's Avalon, everything all right?'

'*Oh aye Jim, fine an' dandy, how's life in the slow lane?*' The deep voice of DS Wilson had a hint of humour in its tone. Wilson was in charge as Avalon's second-in-command and he was an accomplished officer with a wealth of experience. Avalon's only doubt had been due to a period after a car accident the DS had been involved in, where a fellow detective had been seriously injured. DC MacDonald had since left the force and for some time after Wilson had not been himself which had worried Avalon for some months. He seemed over the incident however and the jovial tone of his voice showed that neither that, nor the recent incident with Ross and Frazer was causing him any worries.

'I'm a bit homesick if the truth's known, I was going to throw in the towel and come back,' replied Avalon.

'*Och man, get a grip. It's an age since y' had time off. Enjoy it, y' never know when the opportunity might crop up again.*' Wilson was from Inverness but his accent had a few other add-ons that he had picked up with his time in the police force.

'Yeah, you're probably right. I'll be back on Monday though whatever happens,' he replied and as an afterthought said, 'Everything alright there then?'

'*You mean apart from the boss being away and we are all tossing it off sat on our arses?*'

'Okay,' replied Avalon with a hint of a laugh, 'see you Monday… oh,' he slipped in, 'is Megan there?'

'*Aye,*' replied Wilson, '*dae y' want me to put her on?*'

'No, it's fine, I'll ring her.' Avalon ended the call and gave Wilson time to speak to Frazer, if he thought he needed to and then he rang.

'Megan, it's Avalon.'

'*Oh, Boss,*' there was a pause, '*how's it going?*'

'Fine,' he replied, he was going to ask her to find some information on the cases he was looking at but after hearing her voice he knew it wasn't a good idea. At some stage, he was going to have to deal with the incident between her and Ross. He now had to find an excuse for ringing her. The only thing he could think of was a complete fabrication, and that didn't sit well and so he struggled with something to say. The pause struck Frazer, she was beginning to wonder why he had called so she spoke first.

'*Boss, I need to talk, can I ring you later?*' Avalon knew what it was, she wanted to come clean about the incident with Ross but it wasn't something he could deal with over the phone.

'I'll be back Monday, we can talk then,' he insisted.

'*But I-*' she replied, but he cut her short, there was a slight overtone of anger when he said,

'Monday, we'll talk Monday,' and he ended the call. He needed time to think about his reaction to the incident and he also needed to get all the facts. At the other end of the phone, Frazer was realising the boss knew something, it put her on edge.

Avalon spent most of the morning cross-referencing what he had on the two cases once more until he realised he was wasting his time and was only pursuing it because he couldn't think of anything else to do. He decided he would leave it alone until he returned to work and looked out of the window. He was on the second floor and looking down he saw the Christmas decorations in the street and considered what his own Christmas would hold. He wanted to like Christmas, he really did but since joining the force he had found that almost every celebration that the year could bring would be interrupted by some issue. That meant he would be working and so he saw it was a time of celebration for other people, and he would just have to work. The Christmas fairy had a sick sense of humour it seemed. He looked back into the room and glanced at the clock, it was one-thirty and he considered taking some air and having a light lunch somewhere. He once again looked in the mirror and decided that he still didn't want to shave, though once he was on the street he felt as if he looked like a tramp. He didn't, he knew it was just the fact he was breaking a habit and in some ways, he felt liberated by it. In his work, he had to be spotlessly turned out, and that had become such a necessity that he had forgotten what it was like to feel stubble on his chin.

Through the afternoon he felt conscious about his look and found himself glancing in shop windows, checking his reflection, wondering if he was looking old. When it was time to go back to the hotel to get ready to meet Sarah, he pulled out his phone to check the instructions she had sent him. He wasn't anxious and to his surprise, he didn't feel nervous or worried as he expected to. Had his childishness and naivety finally departed? He hoped so and as he climbed the stairs to his room, he almost bumped into Lucy coming the other way.

'Oh,' she remarked not recognising him immediately. 'Oh,' she repeated but in a very different way, 'it's you, Jim,' and she broke into a weak smile. She wasn't so fussily dressed this time, just an expensive-looking blouse and casual but stylish slacks. Her hair was held up again and as usual, she had perfect make-up. 'Listen, I think I was a little tipsy last night, I'm sorry about that,' she began apologetically, 'I'm not usually that forward.'

'There's no need to apologise,' replied Avalon standing back a little as two elderly hotel guests walked past them in the corridor, 'I didn't think you were either forward or tipsy, that's not why I left.'

'Well, anyway,' she fumbled with the clasp on her small purse, 'I thought I was and so, I wondered,' she looked straight into his eyes, 'I wondered if I could treat you, to dinner.' For a moment he was stuck for words, there was no chance he was going to forgo the meeting with Sarah, but neither did he want to just say no.

'Well, it can't be this evening as I have a prior engagement, but...' he let the sentence run out of steam to see how she reacted.

'Oh, well another time then,' she smiled.

'Yes, of course, though as I say, there is no real need,' he smiled back.

'I'm leaving in the morning, I'm off to Aberdeen, some off-shore work,' this time the smile was weak and she let her eyes drop a little.

'Well, if I'm ever back down this way I'll make sure I come to this hotel,' he replied as casually as he could. She nodded, smiled and then said,

'Bye then,' and she turned and left. Avalon pulled out his key and made his way to his room and entered. In some ways, he was sorry that he was seeing Sarah that night. If things had been slightly different, he would have gone to dinner with Lucy and then he wouldn't have that final image of her turning, somewhat disappointed and not quite as confident as she had been the previous evening. As it was, he had to get ready, he had to prepare to meet Sarah Underwood at her vegan restaurant, he might even have a shave for the occasion.

Chapter Two

Sitting in the gloom of the small, square room, the man pushed away the book he was studying and pulled the old parchment towards him. He reached for the large magnifying glass and removed his pince-nez placing them by his side. He brought the candle closer to inspect the fading text found there. It was a scene that could have been witnessed two hundred years previously, an aging man with white unkempt hair, dressed as if it were the 1800s, perusing an ancient manuscript by the light of a candle. Even the glint of candlelight from the pince-nez was reminiscent of a Joseph Wright painting and yet this strange man who shunned all modernity was an expert in his field. He carefully read the ancient inscription at the top of the parchment following the script with the glass as he read. He then pulled back slightly and said aloud,

'Bullae originales per titulos et materias cliuisae quae in libris bullarum non sunt registratae sub Em: et Reu Domino Magro Fre Rugerio de Pinibus expeditae de annis.' He looked closely at the parchment and began to scratch gently at the surface with his long, tatty fingernail and then examined the nail with the glass. He

then touched the nail on the tip of his tongue and tasted it making a sound as if he was sampling an 1888 Chateaux Lafite Rothschild and not the scrapings of an old parchment.

'Humph,' he then exclaimed, 'fake.' He then looked closer at the parchment, this time without the glass and placing the pince-nez back onto his large and wrinkled nose. 'A good one, but a fake nonetheless,' he then added, and made a few more grunts and strange noises. He sat up straight and stared into the darkness beyond the realm of the candle and gave a little chuckle before rolling the parchment up once more and tying the ageing ribbon around it. For a second, he thought he heard a noise and felt a waft of cold air. He looked around towards the kitchen but it was dark and he saw nothing. He lifted the candle and twisted in his seat offering its light in the direction of the open kitchen door. Nothing, just long shadows and even the draft of air that had made the flame dance had gone.

'Humph,' he exclaimed again, like the principal character from a Dicken's novel, and then shrugged and placed the candle back on the table. As he watched the flame settle into its previous steady rhythm, he wondered why there had been a draft anyway and then he had second thoughts. He lifted the candle again and turned standing as he did and was shocked to see an immense dark figure behind him. Before he could register the danger, he had been lifted off his feet and felt himself flying through the air.

~~~~~~~

Avalon looked at his watch as he strolled down

the damp pavement, the streetlights and shop windows casting such a bright glow it was almost like daylight. He was exactly on time as he followed the directions to the restaurant to meet Sarah. He felt surprisingly calm as he opened the door and entered. He saw her immediately, she was sitting by the window at a table she had obviously reserved. She was dressed more casually than he had expected, black jeans and a knitted-style top. On the back of her chair was a tan, three-quarter camel coat, but he assumed it wasn't wool. Her make-up was different too, subtle, and it made her look younger. Maybe it was just a more modern approach, Avalon wouldn't know modern from modem and he knew it, so he ceased his initial appraisal.

'I'm not late am I?' he asked knowing he wasn't.

'No, early I think,' she smiled. Avalon sat and looked casually around the room before looking back at Sarah.

'I'm guessing you've been here before?' he said it as a question.

'Only once before, it's fairly new, but I enjoyed it last time I came.' Avalon wondered if that time was with her ex-fiancé, the doctor who obviously didn't see the unique charms of Miss Underwood.

'It looks nice too and busier than I expected.'

'Yes, if you don't book in advance, you're not going to get a seat, and it looks so sweet with the Christmas decorations,' she smiled. That confirmed it. Avalon then began to wonder if she had booked the table for someone else, and that person couldn't join her, or had she just managed to get the last place for them? He didn't really care, it was good to be sitting opposite her and he would just enjoy the evening for what it was.

'Have you written any more songs?' she asked with a smile. Avalon quickly thought back to that evening he had played his stupid song to her.

'No, I've given up on that,' he winced.

'Oh, why's that, I thought it was rather good?'

'Well,' explained Avalon, 'I played it to one of the lads who works with the probation office, he's been in a local rock band for years and though he was trying to be kind, I could tell he didn't rate it.'

'Well, I liked it but then again I haven't been in a local rock band for years,' she replied still smiling.

'Oh, it's no surprise to me,' admitted Avalon, 'when I lived in Wolverhampton they used to have a karaoke night at the local pub and I was once tipsy enough to get up and try to sing a version of 'A Little Bit More' by Dr Hook. The chap running the karaoke looked at me with a painful expression and said, 'Maybe it's an ear problem,' much to my disappointment.'

'I never know when you are being serious,' laughed Sarah.

'It's perfectly true I assure you,' added Avalon looking at her eyes as they wrinkled at the corners when she smiled.

'Well, let's try something more serious then, have you read any good poetry lately?' her smile was inquisitive rather than playful this time.

'I found an original copy of There was a young man of Toulouse,' he grinned, and she smiled more deeply, 'but yes, I've been revisiting Burns. I never got on all that well with most of his work but lately, probably because I better understand the language and the culture, it's starting to grow on me.'

'I don't know much poetry I'm ashamed to say,'

she replied, 'and the only Burns poem I ever read was To a Mouse and that was at school.'

'Were you at school in Scotland?'

'Yes, but I'm guessing Burns crops up in schools the world over,' she smiled.

'I was just wondering about your accent, it doesn't sound local and though I'm no expert, I can't place it,' he explained.

'That's no surprise,' she said as the waiter brought them a menu, 'I went to university in Southampton when I was nineteen and spent some years there,' she smiled and thanked the waiter. She then opened the menu and looked over it to Avalon. 'After that, I was at Durham University so I think I've taken on so many accents, it's sort of watered my own down.'

'You studied Forensics?'

'Yes,' she nodded, 'I didn't start out down that route though, I was originally going into Marine Biology.'

'What changed your mind?' asked Avalon taking a quick glance at the menu.

'Sherlock Holmes,' she grinned.

'Really?'

'Yes, really. I was two years into my degree and I read most of the Sherlock Holmes series back to back and it just clicked,' she shrugged, 'I just thought, why not?'

'Conan-Doyle was completely mad, you do know that?' smiled Avalon.

'He certainly had some odd traits to his character, but it was his characterisation of Holmes that pushed me towards police work,' she insisted.

'Police work?' asked Avalon raising his brows,

'not straight into Forensics then?'

'No, I was going to join the force,' she gave a slight nod.

'So what stopped you?'

'The uniform.'

'The uniform? I've never heard that cited as being a sticking point,' he laughed.

'I took one look at the baggy black tights and flat shoes and shuddered,' she smiled, laid the menu down and took a sip of her drink. It was only then that Avalon realised he didn't have a drink himself, he had been so intent on keeping the conversation going.

'Do you want another drink?' he asked pointing to the glass and half standing.

'Please, white wine,' she nodded. Avalon brought two drinks back to the table and sat. The waiter followed him and took their order before leaving and allowing them to continue.

'It's probably a good job you didn't like the uniform then, the forensics service would have missed out considerably,' Avalon continued.

'Well, I do feel it's what I was meant to do,' she nodded, 'but I don't think reading Sherlock Holmes was a good enough reason to join the police force do you?' Avalon just shrugged.

'Not everyone joins the police for the obvious reasons,' he insisted taking a drink.

'So what got you into police work then?' she asked. Avalon smiled a little.

'Case in point, for me it was those big bikes the cops used, the sort of thing I could only dream of owning.'

'Motorbikes?' she smiled.

'I'm afraid so,' nodded Avalon, 'nothing to do with helping the community or catching crooks, I just coveted the Norton Interpol and big Hondas. I mean there are some officers who joined for the right reasons of course.'

'What's the right reason?' asked Sarah with a more serious expression.

'That's a good question,' nodded Avalon looking down to the table, 'I suppose someone like DI Lasiter comes to mind.'

'So what was *his* right reason then?' she asked leaning back a little.

'Thunderbirds,' exclaimed Avalon.

'Excuse me?'

'Thunderbirds, International Rescue, that's what got DI Lasiter into the police.'

'You mean the Gerry Anderson thing, the puppet show?' and she laughed which subsided to a giggle.

'It was,' insisted Avalon with a serious glance, 'you ask him.'

'I don't believe you,' she said laughing louder this time.

'Well, it's completely true,' explained Avalon with a sincere look in his eyes, 'he told me when he was a child he fell in love with the program and watched every episode religiously. He thought that the way that they put their lives on the line to save others was something he could believe in and Scott Tracy became a hero and a role model. As he grew up, he realised there was no International Rescue and so he joined the police where he thought he could make a smaller but similar contribution.'

'That's quite an endearing story,' replied Sarah,

the laugh had abated but a genuine smile replaced it.

'Yes,' nodded Avalon staring into space for a moment, 'hard to believe it came from the grizzled soul of Lasiter though,' he looked back to her and gave a broad grin. She rested her left elbow on the table and cupped her chin with her thumb and forefinger.

'So were you a fan of Thunderbirds?' she asked with a playful smile.

'Oh yes, who wasn't? My favourite was Stingray, though I didn't rate many of the others, they were a bit...' he trailed off not quite knowing what the word was.

'My elder brother loved the Captain Scarlet series,' she announced.

'I didn't like that, it was like Superman.'

'How do you mean?' she asked.

'Well, think about it, why would you want to watch more than one episode? So Captain Scarlet walks into a building where a bomb is about to go off,' Avalon opened his arms a little with a shrug, 'and oh my god, the bomb goes bang sending a gush of flames into the sky and lo-and-behold, the building falls onto the scarlet captain. Is he dead? Is he hurt?' Avalon leaned forward as if he was about to tell her a secret. 'No, because there, in the rubble we can see his plastic hand moving, only it's not plastic because on the close-ups they used an actors hand,' and he leaned back in his seat and folded his arms as if it was the most serious subject in the world. She had a tight-lipped grin as if she was trying to contain a loud laugh, then she composed herself and raised her brows saying,

'But isn't that what keeps you on the edge of your seat?' Avalon shook his head slowly and replied.

'I know I'm a detective but the clue is in the title of the programme,' and he emphasised the first word, '*Indestructible*, Captain Scarlet. In that single word they are more or less taking out any ambiguity for the outcome, it's not worth watching because his survival is inevitable', like Superman.' His face remained implacable.

'Well, I never knew there was so much to learn about puppet shows,' she eventually said. He gave a slight smile and leaned forward again. She was still leaning on the table and their faces were just over a foot apart, he could smell her perfume. It wasn't strong, but it caught his nose and he almost forgot what he was going to say.

'Oh, that's nothing, wait until I get started on television cop shows.' She gave a slight nod and sat upright and for a moment, Avalon thought it was because they were too close but she had noticed the waiter bringing the food and she was making room on the table. Avalon noticed too and sat back.

'I think we'll leave that subject for another time, I don't want to get you overexcited,' she said opening her eyes a little wider. They began to eat and though some conversation passed between them, it was more akin to chit-chat than any formal subject.

When they had finished, Avalon asked if she wanted another drink but to his surprise, she suggested finding a pub or a bar to continue. It suited Avalon of course but as he didn't know in what sort of place she would be most comfortable, he feigned not knowing anywhere in particular and left the decision to her. As they walked, she chatted about some changes in the forensics labs and somehow the subject moved to her sister though neither of them knew why. By the time they reached the bar that Sarah had suggested the subject was exhausted and they ordered their drinks. The bar was quiet and well-furnished and they headed off to a raised area and sat at the table within a small booth.

'So, time off at last,' she smiled.

'Yes,' Avalon shrugged, 'it's an odd feeling really, I've spent so long with no real-time off, I don't know what to do with myself.' She sipped her drink but her eyes were watched him over the rim of the glass. 'I went to the theatre,' he continued, 'but it's not a great deal of fun on your own. Tried the bars, had a few conversations but everyone wants to talk about stuff I know nothing about like football or television.' She still watched him as she placed the glass back on the table. He noticed a playful look on her face but he couldn't read what she was thinking. 'I even went to see my ex-in-laws,' he added with a whiff of a grin.

'Really?' she asked with a little surprise, 'you still speak to them then?'

'Of course, I get on really well with them,' he admitted, but he felt it was an area of his life he didn't want to spend much time on and he tried to think of a subject change. 'What about you?' he said without really thinking about the next few lines.

'I don't have in-laws,' she smiled as she toyed with the stem of her glass.

'I don't mean that,' Avalon returned the smile, 'I meant about holidays, what do you like to do, where do you go?' He was pleased with the resulting question.

'Oh, it takes a bit of planning being vegan,' she gave a slight sigh, 'I have to plan anything around what and where I can eat. I went on a cruise on the Nile, I

47

enjoyed that but in recent years I have holidayed closer to home.'

'Still got family?' he then asked.

'Yes,' she nodded as if she was thinking about them, 'my parents live near Taynuilt on the west coast, when my father retired they moved over there,' her eyes flitted around as if she was wondering how much to tell him, 'my mum got religion though and in recent years she has been harder to talk to.' She looked down to her glass and Avalon saw this was probably something she thought about a great deal, then she looked up with a sunnier disposition and continued. 'My brother works for a big accountancy group in Glasgow, something to do with banking, my sister as you know does hair occasionally in Drumnadrochit and I poke around with dead bodies.' Her eyes flitted once again as she realised that she may have spoken a little too loudly for a quiet pub and made a theatrical embarrassed gesture to Avalon. He had a question at that point but decided against asking it, he wondered if her work had anything to do with her still being single. He then dismissed it as improbable, her work was honourable and important to the justice system, without the Sarah Underwood's of the world very few crimes would ever be solved. It still didn't completely rid him of the urge to know why she was single. He knew she had been engaged to be married recently, and he knew that was now water under the bridge and it had previously occurred to him that maybe she just didn't take relationships seriously. He also considered that after all these many months of wanting to spend a little time with her and wondering how to achieve that, he now happily chatted to her without the slightest hesitation.

'So the Underwood's are a mixed bunch as you see,' she eventually added, and she took a drink of her wine. Avalon decided that the time had come to delve deeper, his hunger for knowledge in all matters had risen its ugly head and he could feel a potentially problematic question being formed somewhere in the back of his mind. It developed quicker than he anticipated and he had little time to cushion the blow when it came. He took a sip of his drink as his mouth became a little dry.

'I was sorry to hear about you breaking off the engagement,' he began. Of course, it was almost a lie, he was sorry that it hadn't gone to plan for her but he wasn't sorry it was over. He looked into her eyes but couldn't read her reaction so he continued, 'and just tell me to mind my own if you like, but it seemed suddenly on, and then suddenly off.' To his surprise, she laughed. Not the sort of belly laugh that you have when a politician gets hit by a truck, but a sort of ironic laugh stifled and unfunny. She stopped, sighed and looked at her glass and then drained it in one. It was such an unladylike approach and with such a determined action that Avalon thought she was about to up and leave. She did stand however and Avalon stood too.

'I'll get them this time,' and she pointed to his glass. He almost breathed a sigh of relief.

'No, let me,' he insisted and took her glass.

'You don't have to buy all the drinks you know,' she said as she sat.

'Don't deny me the pleasure,' he smiled, 'I don't get to do this very often,' and he turned towards the bar. On his return, she looked contemplative, as if she had been thinking something over. She thanked him for the drink and said,

'Are you always so gallant?'

'It's who I am, I don't care if it looks old-fashioned, I don't even care when feminists swear at me for opening doors for them, I'll still keep doing it.' She looked into his eyes, in truth she looked from one eye to the other as if trying to see inside. Avalon knew that was a waste of time, he was in there and he didn't know what he was about.

'You're an odd one, for a detective I mean,' she eventually said but Avalon gave a shrug and a boyish smile. He didn't add anything to her comment, he was still waiting to see what she would say about his question, if anything. She leaned back in her chair, took an almost imperceptible look at her watch and then drew a large breath.

'I don't know why I'm telling you this,' she began, 'but yes, it was what people describe as a whirlwind romance except it wasn't a romance and neither was it much of a whirlwind.' She paused and looked down towards the table as if she was filtering out the subjects she didn't want to admit to. 'I met him during a birthday party of a friend of mine from university, we chatted, he seemed pleasant and later we went for a bit of a walk. I thought he talked a little too much about himself and his family but most people do. And that was it. I went home and forgot about it. Then the flowers began arriving,' and she looked back up to Avalon with a more belligerent glint in her eye. 'I'm not going to bore you with the details,' she continued, 'suffice to say that I eventually agreed to meet him, and we had dinner and chatted again. He came straight out with it. He wanted to marry me and I told him straight, no chance, but over the next month or so he kept up the

50

pressure and eventually I agreed to get engaged to see how it went.' She looked away from Avalon and towards the bar, he saw that she was thinking back to those days but her face gave nothing away. 'He told me he was happy to move to Inverness,' she suddenly said looking directly at him, 'and that was a lie. He was born in Edinburgh but his parents are Indian and they didn't like him moving away and he didn't have the independence you would expect a doctor to have, so that was it,' and she concluded by holding out her arms before folding them in, protectively. It may not have been a classic romance but he could see she was bitter about it. He wondered if it was a similar reaction to his ex-wife Carol, annoyed about the embarrassment of telling friends about her fireman friend rather than the actual collapse of the relationship. She then looked directly at Avalon and seemed to relax again. She unfolded her arms, reached for her glass and looked into it before adding, 'so there you have it, Sarah Underwood is happy to become an old maid and live her life as she was previously,' and she sipped the drink before replacing it back on the table and smiling to Avalon. 'It wouldn't have worked out anyway,' she concluded.

'Why not, I would think two professional people can still have a life together,' he regretted the words as soon as they had left his lips. It sounded like he was heading somewhere.

'Maybe,' she shrugged, 'but I don't think I'm the marrying kind, I like my own space, I like the way there is no one to tell me what I can and can't do. I've been this way for so long, I don't think I could change.'

'I can see that,' agreed Avalon, 'we all get into routines.'

'Is that how you see it,' she asked, 'a habit?'

'Humans are habitual animals, it's not necessarily a bad thing, well some habits are but you know what I mean,' he replied.

'Do you have that same habit?'

'Me?' laughed Avalon thinking of the best reply, 'no, I mean I have plenty of habits but living alone isn't one of them.'

'But you do live alone?' she asked as if she knew the answer.

'Yes,' he nodded, 'but I see it as a temporary situation, not as a way of life,' and he gave her a wry grin. 'I want to find the right partner to settle down with, get married, buy a house for the two of us and have two-point-four lawnmowers, I'm no hermit.' Sarah laughed, she was resting her elbows on the table and her chin was leaning gently on the back of her hands. Her eyes opened wider as if she was going to ask something but she once again glanced at her watch and sat upright.

'Well, as much as I have enjoyed myself I have to make a move,' and she finished her drink, 'early morning, unfortunately.' Avalon didn't want the evening to end, but he had been grateful for the time he had spent with her. He helped her on with her coat and they left the bar and stood on the pavement under the glow of the streetlights.

'I'll walk you back if you like,' Avalon said, and they set off the two streets to her hotel. They were all but silent on that short walk, Sarah said she had enjoyed the evening and Avalon admitted it had made the trip to Edinburgh worth it. Outside the hotel, she stopped and said,

'Here we are, and I really have enjoyed this

evening.'

'So have I, we must do it again sometime,' and he smiled. He thought it was the correct response, not too pushy but testing the water.

'Yes, why not?' she agreed, and she put her hand on his shoulder and reached up to kiss his cheek. With her so close he breathed in the whole scent of her, an intoxicating amalgam of womanly essence, soap and perfume. He wanted to grab hold of her and kiss her face clean off the front of her head, but instead, he smiled and said,

'Goodnight.' She smiled back and maybe it was in his imagination but he thought it was a different sort of smile as he watched her walk up two steps and open the door to the hotel.

~~~~~~~

Avalon entered the police station through the foyer rather than the back way, he didn't know why, maybe he had to re-establish a link with the place. On the desk were the two familiar faces of PC Olivia Kirk and PC Neil Dowd.

'They've got you on the desk again Neil?' smiled Avalon.

'Oh, DI Avalon, aye, I think et's punishment for not playing their silly game of promotion.'

'You're off yer heid,' announced Kirk, 'if they asked me tae be a sergeant I'd rip their arm off.'

'That's because you are shallow PC Kirk, you are one of those life-forms that suck happily on the teat of the cash cow,' said Dowd in a matter-of-fact way still manipulating the mouse of the computer to his side.

Avalon grinned, he liked Dowd, he liked Kirk too but together they were like chalk and cheese.

'What are y' on about?' came Kirk's broad accent, and she glanced over to Avalon, 'I think he's talking dirty sir, y' ought tae arrest him,' and she thrust her tiny thumb in Dowd's direction.

'You have to power to do that Ollie, you're a copper remember?' and she looked down at her uniform.

'Oh, I wondered what this was all about.'

'And she thinks I'm crazy,' added Dowd to Avalon nodding towards Kirk and then added, 'you don't have much o' a suntan there Inspector.'

'I've only been to Edinburgh,' replied Avalon as he moved off towards the stairs.

'Aye but et's south isn't et?' he asked, Avalon stopped at the doors and looked back.

'It would have to be a couple of continents further south to get a suntan,' he replied and disappeared through the door.

'An' there was me thinkin' that there was nothing beyond Berwick on Tweed,' said Dowd to himself.

'The Inspector looks like the break did him good,' said Kirk as the door swung closed.

'Aye,' replied Dowd, 'that'll change when he gets upstairs.'

~~~~~~

'Oh, shit!' were the first words that greeted Avalon as he opened the door to the Cave. 'The Cave' was the name given to a cramped office that C Section worked from. The words had come from the man currently in charge of the section, DS Wilson and he had made the comment from the glass booth that Avalon normally occupied. He was on the phone and his voice had been raised, for the moment he was silent as if he was listening to someone on the other end, staring down at the floor with a forlorn expression. Avalon looked around the office, he saw Rory first who looked up and smiled then called,

'Morning Boss, feeling refreshed?' Avalon didn't answer, the room was almost deserted and the only other face was Alison Boyd who raised her brows and gave a little wave.

'It's quiet in here,' he eventually said and then thought about the comment Wilson had just made, 'well, all except for the buffalo in the aquarium,' he added pointing backward with his thumb.

'Aye, it suddenly got busy, Rossy and Rutherford are out on a job but it sounds like there are problems. DC Frazer is at the control room looking at some CCTV footage.' Avalon nodded and turned to walk to the booth where Wilson noticed him and held up his hand as he still spoke with someone on the phone.

'Aye alright,' he sighed, 'but dunna get too wrapped up if y' can help et.' He concluded and dropped the phone on the desk.

'Problems?' asked Avalon as he sat in the spare chair.

'Mornin' boss,' he replied and then looked at the phone laying silent for a moment, 'oh y' know how et es, y' send two officers out to ask a few questions about a simple breaking and entering inquiry and then they get attacked by a man with a baseball bat.'

'Who've you sent?'

'Rossy and Rutherford,' replied Wilson sighing

again.

'Well, he picked on the wrong two there then.'

'Aye,' nodded Wilson, 'but they had tae arrest him and now they're not gonna get tae the other place until tomorrow.'

'Won't it wait?' asked Avalon.

'No, et's a break in with 'actual', the uniforms are there already,' he sighed again, 'I'll have tae go myself.'

'I'll go over, what it's about?' suggested Avalon.

'Er, no, sorry Boss I forgot I was in your seat,' he spluttered as he stood.

'Sit down Gordon, you're still in charge, at least until I get up to speed with what's on, now tell me about this, *Actual Bodily Harm.*' Wilson sat and pulled a notepad towards him and read a few details.

'Et's this old guy up on the moors, lives en the middle o' Christ knows where with no running water and no electricity. The only modern thing he has es an old truck tae get down into the village tae by his food.' He paused and sighed again before continuing. 'The postie found him, he was in a mess by all accounts, and the postie says he though a wild animal had attacked him,' and Wilson shrugged, 'I suppose there could be things runnin' about up there.'

'Well, it sounds like it's not going to be robbery,' suggested Avalon.

'Et could be, the guy es a bit eccentric, the postie described him as living en the past, whatever that means so he could be the sort to hide his money under the mattress.'

'I'm guessing he's been sent to the hospital?'

'Aye, they sent the chopper out for him but the

house es sealed off and the man tae talk to up there es…' he trailed off as he read the notepad again, 'Police Constable Fleming.'

'And where exactly is, up there?' asked Avalon thinking he might have some more travelling to do. Wilson checked the notepad for the last time and said,

'Et's near a place called Rogart,' and he began to jot the address down, 'from what I can gather et takes a bit o' finding.'

'I know where Rogart is,' said Avalon, 'but I've never heard of this place.' Avalon folded the paper and placed it in his wallet, then he stood and walked out of the booth.

'Oh, I didnae ask, did you have a good time?' asked Wilson as an afterthought.

'I didn't have as much fun as you by the sound of it,' frowned Avalon. Wilson looked at a loss to understand for a moment and then he realised.

'Oh, aye we had a moment but,' he shrugged, 'et's all sorted now.' Avalon held the stare for a moment without saying a thing, 'I'll try an' get en touch with PC Fleming and tell him you're on your way,' added Wilson trying to disarm the situation. Avalon nodded grimly and said,

'Yes, tell him it will take me at least an hour,' then he turned and left. He was angry, not angry with anyone in particular but more with the situation. He knew when he set off that morning it was going to be a difficult day and he was ready for it but now that had been put on hold and he was having to go into Sutherland to what sounded like an attack and he would have to psyche himself up all over again. Once he was in the car, he set the satnav with the address on the paper and set off.

The address was indeed difficult to find and the all-knowing satnav wasn't quite that all-knowing and twice he had to ask directions. When he found the house down a short track, he saw the police car parked in a pull-in at the side of the property. Avalon squeezed his vehicle behind the police car and as much off the single track as he could, he then strolled off to the house. The building was an old bothy with what looked like the original small windows still in place. It was grey and looked like it needed tidying up, fixed to the side was a small extension, built slightly lower and probably used as a store or a shed. The garden was littered with rusting metal, possibly remnants of old farming or crofting machinery and the remains of a further stone building stood at the border of the grounds. Avalon nodded to the PC.

'PC Fleming?' asked Avalon.

'Yes sir, you must be DI Avalon?' Avalon didn't answer, he looked around and he could smell the remaining odour of cigarette smoke in the air.

'Have SOCO been?' he eventually asked.

'Yes, they left about,' he checked his watch, 'thirty-five minutes ago,' he confirmed. Avalon nodded and moved to the door and pushed it open.

'So what do we know?' asked Avalon as he entered the gloomy room, it was a kitchen of sorts.

'The postman called this morning to drop off a packet, and he saw the door was open,' began the PC, 'so he called for Mr McKeith but got no answer. He stepped inside to leave the packet but noticed that the place was in a mess.' Avalon had been ready to ask how he knew, as the whole place seemed like a tip, but closer

58

inspection showed that the little house was clean, yes it was simple with the old ceramic sink standing on bricks and just a simple cupboard beside it, but apart from the obvious chaos that had been caused by the intruder, the place looked well cared for. Food tins and smashed crockery were strewn everywhere, just as if everything that had been sitting on a shelf had been swept from it by an unstoppable force.

'He called out again,' continued the PC, 'but with no answer, he decided to look in the main room, it was then he found the gentleman laid in a heap.' Avalon made a quick assessment of the kitchen and moved to the main room. Several bookcases had once been pressed to the wall but now they were tipped over with their contents strewn everywhere. There was a table in the centre of the small room and a chair pushed to its side, papers and manuscripts were everywhere, some torn, some still wrapped in old faded ribbons. It was gloomy and Avalon looked for a light but saw nothing. He saw candles and storm lanterns but no electricity.

'Are there no lights?' he asked the PC.

'No sir, I've got a torch in the car if you-'

'No, I'll manage,' interrupted Avalon. He checked the other doors, one to a small bedroom with an old-fashioned metal-framed bed, the other to a tiny bathroom. He looked back into the main room and examined the layout. 'I was told there was no running water,' he added.

'Running water? It has its own water supply from up the hill, it supplies a lot of houses here,' explained the PC. That explained the bath but how did he heat water? Avalon stepped over one of the bookcases and called to the PC,

'Give me a hand with this,' and they stood the bookcase back to the wall. Behind some papers was a small fireplace. There was no heat left in it but some papers were scorched which meant there had still been a glimmer of a fire when the papers landed there. He looked to the table and walked around to the chair.

'Do you know if the SOCO team put this chair back?' he pointed to the chair which was the right way up and close to the table.

'I'm not sure sir, I can try to find out if you want,' he offered.

'No matter,' he said shaking his head. He noticed that several papers on the table were stacked up which could be a result of the scenes of crimes people trying to tidy up a little, maybe so they could take photographs, then again... He sat on the chair, stood again and repositioned it, then he sat again. He lent his arms on the table and looked from the tiny fireplace to the kitchen door. Then he scanned the room and stood once more picking up one of the sheets from the table, they all looked old, some were on parchment or even vellum. He could just about read the one in his hand though it seemed to be in old English and was probably written with a quill. Others were in Latin and not a single one seemed to be younger than a couple of centuries old. He dropped the parchment on the table, sighed and looked at the ceiling which was coombed, no chance of a loft. He once again glanced around the room and then asked,

'What are your instructions after I leave?'

'Er, well,' stuttered the PC, 'I suppose I just secure the place and leave,' he shrugged. Avalon returned to the kitchen and checked the door to the outside. There was a lock but turning the key made no

60

effect on the mortice whatsoever. The door hadn't been locked previously by the look of it, there was a deadbolt but that was about it.

'You need to get someone up here to fit a hasp and a padlock, when you've done that, keep one key with you and send the other two to Inverness nick with my name on them, I'll get one to forensics in case they need to come back.' PC Fleming shrugged but after seeing Avalon's face nodded too. 'How's the man who was attacked?'

'Mr McKeith looked in a bad way but the paramedics had him conscious before they put him on the helicopter,' he replied.

'Where was he found?' The PC looked back into the room and pointed to a place under the window.

'He was found there, facing the wall on his side,' he explained. Avalon thrust his hands in his pockets and nodded.

'Okay, you can get off, but make sure the door gets secured, I think some of these rolls may be worth a great deal of money,' he insisted. When he heard the police car manoeuvring to get back onto the road, he looked over to where the man had been found. There were a few traces of blood there but nothing else. There were a few specs of blood on some parchments in that area too but that could have come from the intervention of the paramedics. He stood again and looked around the room once more, checked the windows and left, pulling the door closed behind him. He then walked over to an old Landrover which probably wasn't roadworthy but had been used recently by the tracks it had left in the mud. He looked inside the vehicle but found nothing of interest. Avalon then stood in the overgrown garden and looked out across the fields, it was a glum but dry day with a breeze coming up the field from the east. His mind moved from the incident in the bothy to what he would have to do when he got back to the station. He had to speak to DI Lasiter, he also needed to have a quick chat with Wilson and then he would have to do what he had hoped he would never have to do.

He felt himself becoming angry again, very angry and this time he knew who he was angry with. He strolled back to the car making sure the decision he had made was the right one. He knew there wasn't an option, well, not a better one that was for sure so he climbed into the seat and fastened his seat belt, closed the door, sighed and started the engine.

~~~~~~~~

Avalon leaned casually onto the bonnet of his car and looked out over the water, he could feel the tentacles of winter searching through his clothes and nipping at his skin. It was time to make a phone call. He pulled out his phone and dialled, listening for the tone.

'*DS Wilson C Section.*'

'Gordon, it's Avalon.'

'*Oh boss, how did y' go on up at Rogart?*'

'Fine, I'll be in later to type it up, I've just got a few things to do.'

'*Aye okay,*' replied Wilson.

'Oh,' added Avalon as if it was an afterthought, 'is Ross there?'

'*Aye, they've just got back in, shall I put him on?*'

'No,' I'll see him when I come in,' and he ended the call. He took another look out over the water and

62

rang another number.

'*DS Ross,*' came the voice.

'It's me,' said Avalon calmly, 'do you know the old ferry ticket office at the end of Kessock Road?'

'*Yeah,*' confirmed Ross in a flat tone.

'Meet me there,' and he ended the call. He then went to the back of his car and pulled out his overcoat, he could feel himself starting to shiver. He wasn't sure if it was the cold or the anger coming back. He leaned back on the car, blew on his cold fingers and then rang DI Lasiter.

'*DI Lasiter,*' growled the voice.

'Bob, it's Avalon, are you alone?'

'*Aye, all except four DCs, one DS and a whore's pile o' paperwork, why, what's on y'r mind?*'

The call didn't take that long as Avalon had caught Lasiter at an opportune moment, but the whole sorry mess was getting Avalon down and by the time Ross's BMW pulled into the parking place at the side of Avalon, he was furious. He valued Ross's friendship, it was something he had hoped would be a lasting thing, something that no matter what they moved on to do would still be part of their lives, but the job had to come first and if Ross couldn't see that too, then so be it.

'You find some odd places to go sightseeing,' said Ross as he looked out to where Avalon was gazing, the direction of the Kessock Bridge. Avalon looked at Ross. He had a small sticking plaster on his right temple and his eye was a black to purple colour towards the bridge of his nose.

'So how are you explaining that away?' asked Avalon in a flat tone. Ross glanced back to him and shrugged.

'I just tell people I did it at rugby,' and he looked back out towards the bridge, 'look, I know what you're going to say but it's all sorted, I mean, she even took me down to the hospital.' Avalon said nothing. He folded his arms and looked back over the water. Ross sighed, he could tell there was more to come from his boss and he could sense the anger. He leaned on Avalon's car and took a deep breath.

'It was my fault, and yes I shouldn't have wound her up. I accept the full blame for it so don't take it out on Frazer.'

'So did you get a promotion while I was away?' asked Avalon turning to face him.

'What?' asked Ross slightly puzzled.

'I was just wondering why you are presuming to tell me who I should, and who I shouldn't blame,' frowned Avalon the fury rising in his voice.

'No, course not,' insisted Ross, 'I just need you to know that it was all-'

'I have no interest how it happened,' spat Avalon, 'I just have to deal with the consequences, so don't even think about who was right or wrong because you were both wrong and now *I* have to make it right.' Ross kept quiet, it was obvious the DI had made his mind up and whatever was about to burst forth was no longer under his control. Avalon stood and paced towards a picnic table adjacent to the ferry slip and sat turning to face Ross. There was a glare emanating from his eyes that Ross had seen before, only once but now it was aimed at him. It was the look that had earned him his name of Auld Clootie.

'So what are you going to do?' asked Ross with

another sigh.

'For starters, you have to grow up, you know full well as a copper and particularly as a detective you have to take this life more serious.'

'I do damn well take it seriously,' now it was Ross who was angry, 'and you know I take it seriously, and while we are on the subject, this incident happened in the Cave, if it was outside our own environment I could understand your point but we have always been able to blow off some steam in there.'

'Not at the cost of driving someone to violence,' hissed Avalon standing again, 'can't you see the difference for Christ's sake. It's one thing pulling each other's leg now and then but this is unforgivable.' Ross looked at the floor, he was trying to keep the flak off Frazer but now he was bringing her back into it.

'Well, true, I didn't expect her to do that...' he said still looking at the floor, 'but-'

'No buts, you were both wrong, critically wrong,' he insisted, and that word made Ross wince, it meant Avalon would push this to its limit.

'Come on DI, it's the first time something like this has happened,' insisted Ross in a milder, almost pleading voice, 'it won't happen again.'

'I know it won't happen again because I'm going to make sure it doesn't,' replied Avalon walking back to the car, 'because you are going to stop being such a dickhead with what you trade for humour,' Avalon sounded like there were several points he wanted to make but as he gave a slight pause for breath Ross stepped in.

'We all use humour, it's what keeps us sane, you know it is,' he insisted, 'you do it, we all do it, if you take that out of the system then the system will collapse,' he added holding his arms out.

'Yes, we all use humour,' glared Avalon, 'but some of us think before we speak, you don't give a shit who you upset.'

'That's not fair, maybe I sometimes get it wrong but without being able to hide in humour this job would drive me round the bend,' insisted Ross raising his voice, 'all the beaten up faces, all the abused children, all the corpses I see would be swimming around in my sodding head all the time if I couldn't let off steam. It's not been a good time for me lately and this isn't making it easier.' The last words were almost shouted but Avalon raised the ante and he turned on Ross with such a fury that Ross stepped back half a pace. Ross was afraid of no man, he could look after himself, he even thought he could take Rutherford out if he had to but Avalon... At that moment something went off in Avalon's head that Ross didn't know how to explain.

'You think you have a monopoly on bad memories?' spat Avalon, 'you think that it's just *you* that see their faces?' The DI's eyes were glaring like a mad thing, spittle ejected itself with the venom of the words, 'do you think the rest of us get off that lightly, to live a normal life, to stay asleep rather than waking in a cold sweat, babbling like a madman to the point that your wife has enough of the miserable existence she suffers with you.' Avalon was so close Ross could feel his breath on his face and he knew it hadn't ended. 'Do you think I will ever stop seeing her face goddamit?' Avalon's nose was touching Ross's, and the DS felt his palms sweat and he was ready, no matter what, he was ready. Avalon ceased at that point. He pulled back, took a deep breath and wiped his mouth with the back of his hand. He glanced back at Ross with a slightly embarrassed look and turned from him to wipe the tears away that Ross had seen from in the detective's eyes. Avalon was visibly trying to calm himself as he faced the Kessock Bridge. Ross looked at the ground and leaned on the car. For the first time since he had met Avalon, through all the good and bad times they had shared together he saw that Avalon had a secret. Something that no one ever got to know about, like many other officers, but with Avalon it seemed obvious it still deeply troubled him. Ross also saw that the DI had now gone to another place and trying to alter the situation was pointless.

'So what now?' he eventually asked in a calm but careful tone. Avalon turned back and came a little closer.

'You were wrong when you said it was the first time,' he said as he leaned on the bonnet at the side of Ross.

'Meaning what?' asked Ross without looking at Avalon.

'The first time was when you tried to emasculate the gorilla at George Sands' house with a nineteen-seventies telephone, I should have clipped your wings then.'

'So am I suspended?' asked Ross quietly.

'No, we can't afford to lose two detectives.'

'So?' began Ross but he couldn't believe what he was hearing and he turned around to Avalon, 'so, you're gonna suspend Megan?'

'Like you, it isn't her first time,' was all he said. Ross shook his head, he stood up straight and looked out over the water for the last time and then back to Avalon.

'You know, I used to respect you, I thought you were the best thing that had happened to this nick,' he paused and thrust his hands into his pockets, 'I was wrong about that too,' and he walked to his car. Avalon kept his gaze towards the bridge as he heard Ross slam the door, start the engine and spin gravel from his wheels as he reversed, he then squealed the wheels as he set off at speed down Kessock Road. Avalon swallowed, the anger was still there, the difference was, he didn't know what or who he was angry about anymore.

Chapter Three

It's a strange thing about life, one-minute things can be running quite merrily and then, something comes along to make everything exactly opposite. You just begin to think everything in life is just right, the future looks bright and nothing can be better, then without reason or warning, everything changes and the whole house of cards comes tumbling down. It can happen the other way around too but it's the bad things that are remembered for the most part. Avalon was thinking through this phenomenon as he drove back to the Police Station. Sitting in a bar with Sarah Underwood, he had considered that things couldn't get much better, and of course they couldn't, everything had to change, everything would fall apart to leave him wondering if he had just been in some kind of emotional, atomic detonation. That was why he had decided that he didn't think he was in the mood to chastise Megan Frazer about her conduct while he was away. He decided that he would go to see DCI Croker and explain what he wanted to do and get his actions sanctioned by him. Then he would drive over to the hospital and see how the man from the bothy was doing.

It was an easy enough job to convince Croker that his plans were acceptable, the DCI left the running of the sections to their respective Detective Inspectors unless something went wrong, so by the late afternoon, he was on his way to the hospital without returning to the Cave. He was directed where the man was recuperating and he headed straight there noticing a male nurse filling in some forms by a desk.

'Hello, can I help?' asked the nurse looking up from the desk.

'Er yes,' replied Avalon, 'DI Avalon, you have a Mr McKeith here, he was admitted this morning I believe?'

'That's right,' answered the nurse, 'we're keeping him in for observation, he had quite a knock on the head.'

'Had he been beaten?'

'I have no idea, a broken arm, lacerations, heavy bruising and a severe cut to the head, probably where he fell,' replied the nurse and then added, 'the doctor seemed to think he may have fallen down some stairs.'

'Doubtful,' frowned Avalon thrusting his hands into his trouser pockets, 'he lived in a bothy.' The nurse shrugged.

'Then indeed, he could have suffered a beating,' he admitted.

'Can I see him?'

'I don't see why not but he's lightly sedated as he is still suffering some shock,' Avalon nodded understandingly, 'but don't tax him and be as brief as you can,' added the nurse and then he stood. 'He's in the last bed on the left,' he pointed with his biro. Avalon hated hospitals, every bed told a story and rarely a happy one. As the nurse had said the old man was tucked into the last bed and looked odd in the white surroundings after what he had seen of the house.

'Mr McKeith?' asked Avalon quietly as he closed in on the bed. The man had his eyelids closed but opened them when he heard his name. His light blue eyes searched around as if he was pinpointing Avalon's form and then he must have found the focus as his pupils seemed to settle on Avalon's features.

'Yes, who are you?' asked the frail voice.

'Detective Inspector Avalon, Inverness CID, I want to ask you a few questions if you feel up to it,' explained Avalon pulling a chair close to the bed.

'I didn't see what it was,' announced the man looking up towards the ceiling.

'What it was?' asked the DI.

'What attacked me, I only know it moved without making a sound and swept me aside,' there was an inevitability in his voice.

'So you didn't get a look at your attacker?'

'No,' replied the man shaking his head slightly, 'I just turned and this black shape lifted me up and threw me aside, after that, I don't remember a thing.' The man sighed and closed his eyes and then suddenly opened them glaring over to Avalon, raising himself off the pillow. 'My house,' he exclaimed, 'what happened to my house?'

'For the most part, it looks fine, it's untidy of course but I've had it secured.' The man seemed to settle at hearing this. Avalon gave him a moment and then asked,

'Have you any idea why someone would attack you?'

'Not at all,' replied the man after staring at the ceiling, 'I don't have anything and I keep myself to myself.' There was a slight Scottish lilt to his accent but Avalon considered in his younger years he probably lived elsewhere.

'Can you tell me what all the parchments and rolls are about?' The man turned his head to face Avalon, his straggling, long hair pushing up into his cheek.

'It's what I do, I collect and restore old manuscripts,' and though his focus looked vague, he seemed to search out Avalon's eyes, 'I also examine the providence of them for clients.'

'So there is money in it then?' asked Avalon considering a motive.

'Not really,' replied the man, 'well some are worth money to certain people, but generally there are better ways of investing money than in moulding parchments.'

'So did you have documents that would be worth stealing?' was Avalon's obvious question. The man returned his gaze to the ceiling and slowly shook his head.

'I just can't imagine someone thinking that anything I had there was worth the effort, it doesn't make sense.' Avalon gave a gentle sigh, if the man was telling the truth about the worth of the documents then it did seem an odd crime. Until the victim was more himself, it was obvious he would get little of any use from him. He thanked the man and said he would return when he was feeling better. In the mean-time, he needed some sort of expert to look over the documents at the house and as he reached his car, he pulled out his phone. For a fraction of a second, he considered contacting

Frazer and asking her to find someone who knew old manuscripts, but then he realised he couldn't do that. The incident in the Cave was going to have further ramifications than were obvious at first glance. He would have to do it himself as everyone in C Section seemed busy enough at the moment and in that case, it would have to wait. It was dark and as he slid into the driver's seat he glanced at his watch, there was nothing pressing and so he returned home to ready himself for what he had to do in the morning.

~~~~~~

Robert Gallagher looked at the large dial clock on the wall in his study. It was fifteen minutes past eleven at night and it was time for him to begin the final part of his daily ritual. He knew he did it, he didn't know quite why but almost every part of his day had become ritualistic and regimented to a point that he just couldn't bear to change. He closed the book he was reading and yawned, he considered that he probably always yawned at this time, so fixed were his ways. He had suffered from a mild form of obsessive-compulsive disorder, his doctor had diagnosed it as a double-faceted type consisting of both, 'checking and hoarding' as he had insisted but Robert hadn't agreed with the diagnosis. He wasn't a hoarder, he loved books, he was a collector, very different from being a hoarder and to Robert a person like a doctor would never be able to understand that. Yes, he checked everything, he knew that was a problem but having no faith in the words of the doctor he decided to contain the disorder himself. He was bright enough to know he could manage the problem himself by having a regimented day that ensured he couldn't check everything in the way he had done previously. It had worked to a degree but now he was so fixed to the new routine of the day, his new system had become compulsive instead. He didn't know how to go about changing that, it seemed impossible to alter the course of his day and even the thought of change brought a cold shiver down his spine. He didn't care that much. His lifestyle was good for the most part, he had his wonderful library and study on the first floor and that was his whole life. He didn't really agree with his friends who said that he was becoming a recluse, 'by default,' he had told them, 'if I was a recluse I wouldn't have friends and yet I have you.' If he thought about it, there weren't that many of them but that was because he was always busy, not because he shut himself away. As he placed the book back into its position in the glazed fronted bookcase, he looked around the room at all the other identical bookcases. Those shelves, the whole library, gave him a warm feeling, it had been his hobby in his early life and now it was his work and occupied the largest room in the house. As he continued the ritual of closing down the room, he switched off the three desk lamps in the order he always did and finally went to the large leaded window to pull the curtains against the darkness outside. He stopped with his arm extended, gripping the edge of the heavy curtain, his gaze fixed on a point down on the garden near the beech tree. For a second, he had seen movement and he considered switching off the last remaining lamp in the room, but that would mean leaving the window and removing his eyes from the spot he had seen the movement. It could have been a fox, but in Robert Gallagher's life, a fox not keeping to a schedule that fit with his own life could potentially ruin his day. He stood motionless realising that this inactivity could put his evening back by several minutes, he was clearly going to have to make his shower quicker than normal if he was to get back to... His thoughts ceased as he saw more movement, there was clearly something out there making its way along the edge of the shrubs and was about to enter into the space occupied by the lawn. It was a large, black shadow, clearly not a fox, maybe a person and as it reached the front door directly below the window it stopped. Robert expected to hear the doorbell but a caller at this time simply was unheard of, so he would ignore it and carry on but the shape below didn't ring the bell. It was coming nearer, how could that be? Unless it was... Yes, it was scaling the wall and Robert could feel his heart race, what could do that? What manner of beast could simply scale a wall? He finally let go of his iron grip of the curtain and moved to action. There was nothing else for it, he would by all necessity have to forgo his daily rituals and make himself scarce. As he descended the stairs to the rear door he heard the sickening sound of breaking glass.

'My books,' he said to himself in a panic. His hand was on the door handle now and he looked back up those stairs. 'My books,' he repeated with dismay.

~~~~~~~

Avalon looked at the bedside clock, it was just before three o'clock in the morning, it was still dark and he was still half asleep. He reached for his phone but couldn't find it in the dark so he switched on the lamp just as it stopped ringing. Then the main house phone rang, it was then he realised that being back after some time off, automatically put him on 'emergency duty' at the station. He picked up his mobile and made sure it was from the station, he then called back as he twisted himself from the sheets and sat on the edge of the bed.

'Avalon, it's DI Avalon.'

'*There's a shout Inspector*,' replied the duty officer.

'Any information?' asked Avalon reaching for his trousers.

'*Incident near Strathpeffer but I don't have anything else sir*,' replied the voice.

'Okay, there in ten,' replied Avalon and rushed his dressing.

At the station, it all seemed fairly quiet, so he knew it wasn't a major incident and he made his way to the front desk. A uniformed sergeant who he knew as Lamont looked up as he entered.

'Mornin' DI, DS Murrey is in the back room already,' said the sergeant pointing to the door behind him with his thumb. Avalon nodded, it was usual for the call-out roster to include officers from other departments, it was just a sliding scale of priority but it worked, it ensured there was less chance of being called out again if you had already been out recently. Avalon liked Tom Murrey, he was a good and capable detective.

'Morning,' announced Avalon as he entered the rear office, there were two other uniformed officers one of whom he knew only by sight, Tom Murrey was on the phone and as he ended the call he smiled at Avalon.

'Good morning DI, looks fairly straightforward,' announced the quietly spoken detective sergeant, 'we could be back in a couple of hours, breakfast and then back off to bed.'

'I'm never that lucky,' smiled back Avalon, 'it will turn out to be a long one I'm betting.' They set off two minutes later, Avalon driving and Murrey reading from the incident sheet putting Avalon in the picture.

'Mr Robert Gallagher, fifty-two years old, writer and lecturer. Lives alone, no children,' began Murrey but paused as the detective seemed to be drawing on a mental picture. He looked down at the paper once more by the light of a small flashlight and continued. 'He reported that he had been broken into and one of the local uniform officers managed to drag himself out of bed and eventually take a look.'

'Is that what it says on the report sheet?' smiled Avalon.

'Not quite but I've been there once upon a time,' sighed Murrey, 'roused out of bed in the middle of the night on an emergency, only to find that dear old Mrs Hendricks wants to report that her cat hasn't come home for his supper.' Avalon gave a knowing laugh and added,

'But I think you might find more to this one unless I'm very much mistaken.'

'You think it's more serious?' asked Murrey looking over to him. Avalon nodded slightly.

'I don't know but we've had quite a few break-ins lately where nothing seems to have been taken and yet the place is trashed.'

'Aye, I've seen the reports, I put it down to someone with a grudge rather than robbery,' suggested Murrey.

'That's more than likely but this arsehole doesn't seem to care who's in the house, it's just a matter of time before someone gets seriously hurt,' explained Avalon. 'Anything else on the report sheet?' he added.

'Not much, the address, the name of the reporting officer and a little note that says the officer at the site has called for an ambulance.'

'There you go, someone *is* hurt,' concluded Avalon as he turned off the A9 to head for Strathpeffer.

The house was on the far edge of the town at the opposite end and in the darkness, the streetlamps showed what must have once been a thriving spa resort. Avalon considered that all these spa destinations from the Victorian era looked virtually the same with similar architecture and layout. This was confirmed as they drove through the town and he smiled as he could easily imagine being in Buxton in Derbyshire, Woodhall Spa in Lincolnshire or any of the other English spa towns he had visited. As they closed in on the house, he could see two police cars and though they didn't have their blue lights flashing, several people could be seen at doors and windows trying to see what was going on.

'DI Avalon,' he announced as he walked up to the nearest uniformed officer, 'what's happened?' The young-looking officer replied in the local accent.

'A break in sir,' he pointed up to the large leaded window that nestled in the centre of the building but Avalon could see no detail in the dark, 'we haven't ascertained if anything was stolen yet.'

'How is the resident?'

'He seems okay, he's in the ambulance,' and he pointed to the vehicle where he could just about make out several people through the open rear door. Closer inspection showed another police officer talking to the man who looked as if he had a blanket around his

78

shoulders. Avalon turned to Murrey and nodded towards the ambulance.

'See what you can find out, I'll check the house,' and he strode off towards the front door. Another officer was standing just inside the house.

'Found anything?' he asked.

'Er, no,' hesitated the PC unsure who this new face was, but guessing he must be CID, 'I had a quick check to make sure the house was empty but that's all.'

'Good,' nodded Avalon, 'I'll have a quick peep,' and he looked for the stairs to take him to the room with the leaded windows. He soon found a door on a landing at the top of the stairs and realise he didn't have any gloves with him. He used a handkerchief to open the door and entered the dark room carefully. There was light from a distant streetlight but nothing else and so he went back to the car to get his flashlight. Murrey was heading towards him as he closed the boot of his car holding the flashlight and a pair of cotton gloves.

'How is he?' he asked.

'Seems fine, he's concerned about his books but more disturbing is that he seems to think that the intruder scaled a sheer wall.'

'Probably shock,' shrugged Avalon.

'Maybe but he seems to think that the figure just came straight up the wall as if gravity didn't exist.'

'Did he get a look at the intruder?'

'He says not,' replied Murrey frowning, 'he says as soon as he saw the figure coming up the wall he ran down the stairs and out of the back door. He then hid in a shed at the bottom of the garden until he thought the intruder had gone.'

'So he would have seen nothing?'

'Seems that way, the PC says he was freezing when they arrived, they had to warm him up in the car before he could talk. The paramedics are sorting him out.'

'So he probably *was* suffering from shock,' nodded Avalon, 'let's have a look at the wall where the gravity got turned off.' Murrey shrugged as Avalon headed back to the house, it was clear the DI didn't believe the details given by the victim. Avalon shone his torch up at the wall towards the leaded window, it was a triple window set back slightly from the roofline, which hung over it for about a foot or so. The panel to the right was clearly smashed in and there were a few shards of glass on the floor. He then shone his flashlight to the right wall and there in the corner was a cast iron drain pipe, glossy black against the white of the house.

'And that's where the magically levitating figure ascended the wall,' he said as Murrey stepped to his side.

'Are you always this cynical about witness statements,' laughed Murrey.

'Not cynical DS Murrey,' he smiled, 'just doubting, particularly when the statement defies logic and physics,' and he turned and began to walk to the rear door, 'come on, let's take a look upstairs.'

The beam of the flashlight showed the heap of broken glass and twisted lead where the whole panel had been broken and pushed in. It wasn't a surprise but what was odd was that this break-in seemed different from the previous one he had attended. Here, there was little of the chaos seen at the house near Rogart, and one cabinet was open and about half a dozen books were strewn on the floor below it, but that was it.

'Not much of a robbery, it looks like he was here

for some reading matter,' announced Murrey using his own flashlight to try to read the spines of the books on the floor. Avalon continued to scan the room but nothing else could be seen out of place.

'I'll get forensics up here in the morning,'

'You think it's worth it?' asked Murrey. Avalon understood what he was getting at, fingerprints would probably turn up nothing but if this was connected to the previous incident then there could be fibres in the room, particularly around the broken window. Maybe even a speck of blood.

'Maybe not but I don't want to leave anything to chance,' insisted Avalon, 'whoever this is, he doesn't give a damn about anyone, I mean, how much noise did he make smashing in that window?' Avalon shone his torch towards the pile of debris. He guessed Murrey had shrugged, the 'Hmm,' sound he made seemed to be something you would accompany a shrug with. They returned downstairs and informed the PC they would be sealing off the grounds and house and they should find out if the resident of the house had alternative accommodation. The PC looked questioningly at the detective.

'What is it?' asked Avalon.

'I was just wondering sir, do you think the intruder will return, I mean, from what PC Fisher said, it looked like the thief was disturbed in the act.'

'I don't think so,' frowned Avalon, 'I'm guessing he or she found what they were after, I wouldn't worry about a return visit.' He then looked over to Tom Murrey and raised his brows but he was unsure the DS would have seen the gesture in the poor light. 'Oh and,' Avalon looked back to the PC, 'will you ask Mr Gallagher if he'll come into the station tomorrow afternoon to make an official statement,' and then added, 'if he feels up to it of course.'

~~~~~~

DS Tom Murrey and DI Avalon did indeed have breakfast though Avalon didn't eat much.

'Not hungry?' asked Murrey wiping his plate with a last bit of bread.

'No, not all that hungry, it's a bit early for me.'

'It would be for me usually but when I get these early call outs I become ravenous,' replied the DS. Avalon smiled at him but then returned to a neutral gaze into the middle distance. 'You look deep in thought,' added Murrey.

'Not really, just tired and thinking about this robbery.'

'It's an odd one,' nodded Murrey, 'it looks like someone couldn't sleep and thought 'I know where I can find a book or two' and off he pops to the local library.' Avalon gave another ironic smile and said,

'It's not exactly bedtime reading anyway,' he then sighed, 'I took a look at some of the titles. I don't know about you Tom but 'The Lays of Ancient Greece' wouldn't be my first choice for a book at bedtime.'

'No probably not,' sighed Murrey and then added, 'I'm more of an Oor Wullie fan myself.' He then yawned and concluded with, 'Right, I'll get off and see my DI and then I'm off back to bed,' and he stood and left the room. Avalon had too much to do to go back to bed, he actually had a miserable day to go through which was why he had eaten so little.

He was already in his booth by the time C Section began arriving and when Wilson came in Avalon looked up as he entered the booth and said,

'Sorry Gordon, this is your seat for the rest of the week.' Wilson frowned a little and then said,

'You were out en the night I hear boss.'

'Yes,' nodded Avalon, and he pointed to the chair, 'another break-in.' Wilson puckered his bottom lip and sat down.

'An' ef this es connected t' the others, they're getting more frequent and closer together.'

'Yes,' nodded Avalon again, 'I think our intruder is getting more confidence as he goes on.' Wilson stared at Avalon with a blank expression but Avalon could see the fire behind those eyes, working the facts to come up with an appraisal of the situation.

'Do you think et's important?' he eventually asked.

'I don't know what the reasoning is behind it but he seems indifferent to the people who may be at home,' explained the DI, 'I think eventually someone will be seriously hurt or even killed.' Wilson looked down at the desk as Avalon sat in the spare seat and rubbed his chin with his fingers.

'Well, tae my way o' thinkin', he could indeed be getting confident, but equally,' and Wilson looked up at Avalon, 'he could be getting desperate, he could be running out of time.' It was an interesting theory but as they didn't yet know what he was taking from the scenes, if anything, it was a difficult problem to hypothesise.

'Your perspective on a case is invaluable, it

wasn't something I'd considered,' grinned Avalon but then his face turned more serious, 'but if you're correct, he certainly will become desperate.'

'So,' began Wilson with an inquisitive tone, 'why am I still sat en this chair and you're sat en that one?' Avalon returned his face to a smile and then he shrugged and leaned back. Fortunately, he couldn't see Frazer, having his back to the booth glass but he was well aware that he had to speak to her and he was dreading it. He sighed and then said,

'While I was away, I did a bit of searching through some of the old cases and I found a tenuous connection to the otherwise random forced entering.' Wilson frowned, that wasn't the question he had asked and unless his boss had a better explanation, he was going to think he was skirting around the issue. 'It's *very* tenuous though,' continued Avalon, 'and before we put resources into it I wanted to have a poke around with it. These two recent incidents however have altered things and if these are linked, I think we have a problem.'

'So what's the 'tenuous' link?' asked Wilson with emphasis on tenuous. Avalon drew a deep breath.

'Old artworks,' and then he shrugged, 'well, it was until he broke into two bibliophiles houses.'

'So instead of old artworks,' inquired Wilson, 'et's just old stuff?'

'Well, I suppose books and illuminated manuscripts can be grouped under artworks too,' added Avalon.

'I suppose there's a shitload o' cash tae be made en that quarter,' offered Wilson.

'I would agree,' nodded Avalon, 'but if our man is responsible for all these incidents, he rarely takes anything and when he does it's not particularly valuable,' and then he stood, 'anyway, you can man the guard towers while I dig a bit further into this, I need to find out if anything went missing at the last two incidents first.' Wilson nodded and then with a pained expression asked,

'Have you any plans to do anythin' about Ross and Frazer?' There was a pause and then he added, 'I mean, I didn't think it was my place to make anything of it and I told them you would sort it out when you got back.' Avalon gave a slow nod, Wilson was right, it was Avalon as the section head that had to reprimand the staff, not the DS who was standing in for him.

'I have plans, yes but it seems only right that I speak with them privately first,' he paused, 'and then I'll let everyone else know,' and he left the Cave without looking into the main room. It was this very subject he was now focused on, mainly talking to Frazer. He sat in his car and pulled out his phone and dialled Frazer's desk.

'It's me, don't say anything yet,' his voice was in a flat tone but he spoke steadily and precisely, 'just let DS Wilson know I've asked you to come and see me, then don't speak to anyone else, just get your coat and meet me in the car park.' Frazer just confirmed she would and two minutes later she was walking to his car with a very serious expression. She got in and Avalon drove off without saying a word so that the CCTV cameras wouldn't be on them and headed back out to the spot he had spoken to Ross, the old ferry slip.

'Boss, I-' began Frazer but Avalon stopped her.

'Wait,' he just said and the rest of the short journey was in silence. He parked up and turned off the engine. It was breezy outside and so he remained in the car.

'I don't need to tell you how stupid you have been,' he began, and he turned to face her, 'but unfortunately this time it's not so easy to pass over.' He watched her give out a deep sigh and look down at her hands on her lap. It was expected, she knew by the DIs actions that it was coming, she just wished she could turn back time. She waited a moment and glanced across to him and then back to her front.

'I suppose this es et for me then?' she said.

'If I was a better copper, I would have you disciplined and drummed out, but I'm not.' She looked around at him. 'The truth is, you're good at what you do but you have such a problem with anger management you're becoming a liability.' He paused and looked out of the windscreen over the water. There were a few other cars parked there so the Kessock Bridge was to Avalon's right, he thought back to his talk with Ross and made sure he wasn't about to repeat the outburst he had made. 'I shouldn't have to deal with this, you and Ross are supposed to be adults, you're coppers for Christ sakes,' and for the first time his voice rose in volume but he calmed before he continued. 'You are moving to B Section,' he caught her head snap around in the corner of his eye, he sensed she was about to speak but she resisted, 'and DI Lasiter knows why.'

'I suppose et's a fitting punishment,' she sighed. It was Avalon's turn to spin around and when he spoke there was obvious tension in his voice.

'I've told you before, DI Lasiter has a high regard for you, if not for him you would have been stacking shelves in a local shop some years ago so I think it's time both you and Ross grew up. You both need a reality check and start thinking about others and the consequences of your actions,' he remained reasonably calm but Frazer saw the anger in his features. She was visibly shocked, she had worked with the DI for so long that she knew all his moods but she had never seen Avalon this angry. It wasn't in his voice or his actions, it was something she just knew by instinct and she felt so sick inside that she had let him down, she wanted to scream. He looked back to her and his eyes were pools of fury. 'It's best not to say another thing because I'm so…' and he stopped speaking turning his head away from her, pressing his lips together to stop them saying what he felt. He took deep breaths and stared to his right and towards the bridge. Frazer left it a couple of minutes before she spoke.

'I'm so sorry boss, you're right tae be angry,' he didn't react, 'I can only say that we did make et up and had a talk about et after. We both knew et would come back to haunt us but et was all my fault, Rossy was just-'

'It's a pity,' he interrupted as he turned to face her again, 'that the two of you didn't do that before,' he turned back to the window, not able to look into her eyes any longer, 'but as it stands…' he trailed off and then after a pause said, 'Croker doesn't know, I arranged it with DI Lasiter so no one else knows why you are moving but C Section aren't stupid, *they* will know.'
In the back of her mind, Frazer was thinking that she would have to leave the job. She wouldn't get a transfer and going back to the beat didn't appeal. For now, she sat quietly until Avalon was ready to continue.

'So the story is, you're moving to B Section because DI Lasiter has need of a dedicated surveillance operative, we will be getting their newest face as a replacement.' He paused and then looked over to her again. 'If you so much as give anyone a sideways glance from now on, both I and DI Laster will wash our hands of you, do you understand?' Frazer looked calm considering the situation, but she just nodded slowly keeping her gaze through the windscreen. Avalon looked back to the bridge and then started the engine.

'When does this start?' she asked quietly.

'Monday morning, if you need to get your act together, take the rest of the week off.' Avalon knew she wouldn't, detectives rarely took unscheduled time off, it just meant more work for everyone else. They drove back in silence and once she had left the car Avalon headed back to the hospital but he was in a dark and thunderous mood.

Mr McKeith was looking much better, but he was very anxious about his house.

'You did say that you had it all locked up?' he asked sitting up in a chair by the side of the bed.

'Yes, the local PC made sure it was done, and I asked for the spare keys to be sent to me,' he looked around the ward, 'although it seems you'll probably be going home this evening from what I heard.'

'Good,' nodded the man, 'I can't stand it here, too light, too modern,' and he seemed to shiver slightly at his own description. Avalon explained that they would make sure a key got to him if he was to be sent home.

'Obviously, we don't know if anything is missing Mr McKeith, do you really have no idea what they might be after?'

'No,' replied the man shaking his head with a

puzzled look, 'there aren't any really worthwhile scrolls that would be any good to anyone but the most die-hard collector,' he seemed to search his memory for anything he could think of, 'there was an illumination of the Coronation of Mary from a book of hours,' he suddenly recalled, 'I was asked to repair some of the gold leaf but...' he paused, 'at the best auction house it would only raise a few thousand pounds.' Avalon nodded, it clearly wasn't worth the effort that had been put into the attack. 'Now if he had come last week, I still had a rare one I was validating,' nodded the man. Avalon sat up.

'Last week?' he enquired, 'what did you have last week?'

'Well, it wasn't heavily illuminated and probably not worth the sort of figures that paintings go for but...' he shrugged.

'So what was it?' repeated Avalon slightly agitated. The old man's blue eyes saw Avalon assuming it could be important, and he considered he maybe shouldn't have mentioned it.

'Have you heard of the Chinon Chart,' he said and immediately held up his free arm a little and continued, 'not that it was to do with that article.'

'No,' insisted Avalon shaking his head a single time.

'Oh, it's a long story then,' frowned the man then brightened as he considered the detective wouldn't see the significance if he had never heard of it. 'It was a parchment lost for seven-hundred years in the Vatican vaults, but when it surfaced some years ago, several other parchments were found, one of them has become known as,' he paused again and examined the face of the detective, he thought that the policeman wouldn't have

89

much of a clue what he was talking about so he continued, 'the Key Roll.'

'So what is it?'

'No one knows, it seems to be a list of names and words, some of which aren't even Latin words.'

'Ancient code words perhaps?'

'I don't know,' shrugged the man but winced as one of his wounds gave pain, 'no one does, but it's rare and I was asked to validate it.'

'And was it genuine?' asked Avalon.

'I couldn't see why it wouldn't be but I was suspicious about how the customer came about the document,' and he fell silent, he certainly had said too much but it was rare that he had an audience to talk about his manuscripts too.

'Go on,' said Avalon.

'Oh, I just thought, how do you find a document lost in the Vatican that apparently surfaces with something like the Chinon Chart and yet no one has heard of it?' He sighed, 'makes you think it's a fake does it not?' Avalon stared into the old man's face for some time, he knew a little more than he was saying but it was clear by his expression that for the time being at least, he would say little more. In the mood that Avalon found himself in at that moment, he was probably best leaving a full interview until a later date.

Avalon returned to the station and dragged himself up the stairs to the Cave. As he entered he saw Ross and Rutherford at their desks chatting about something they were working on and then he saw Wilson in the booth, yet again on the phone. Wilson was eternally busy and worked the section different to Avalon, he would make a great DI for sure. He seemed to drop into any role that was given him and he looked right doing the job too. There was the problem, Wilson was in *his* seat, at *his* desk so where would the DI actually work from? Rather than showing his indecision he walked to the booth and made an excuse up as he did.

'Ever heard of the Chinon Chart? asked Avalon as he entered.

'Nope, es et somethin' tae do with cameras?' shrugged Wilson.

'Clearly not a man that reads a great deal of Latin,' smiled Avalon as he sat in the spare seat. Wilson looked a little more serious as he said in a quieter voice,

'I'm assuming you've had words with Frazer?' Avalon nodded.

'Has she said something?'

'No, she didn't have to,' replied Wilson raising his eyebrows. Avalon frowned and looked at his watch then back up to Wilson.

'We're losing her, she's being moved.' For several seconds, Wilson stared at the DI without any expression until his eyes began to flit around and then he sighed. He looked back at Avalon and then said,

'From the station or...' the last word was dragged out.

'She's going to B Section, DI Lasiter needs a surveillance specialist but we're getting one of his crew.' Wilson was quiet again.

'Surveillance is it?' he asked without it being a question, his lips curled together, 'nothing to do with the little incident the other day then?' whispered Wilson raising his brows.

'I had to do something, she has a bit of history and though I thought she had overcome her problems...'

this time Avalon trailed off. Wilson nodded and leaned back in his chair.

'You know, I was here when it happened, it wasn't malicious, more playful than violent,' continued Wilson.

'It's not playful when one officer throws a kilo of reconstituted stone at another officer's hea-'

'And she was utterly beside herself after.'

'I don't care about that, it's the action I'm angry about. It may be stupid but it could happen with a...' he was going to say suspect, but it had already happened with a suspect and Avalon couldn't remember who knew about it. He knew a great deal about Frazer that Wilson didn't know and unless he put his foot down, he was going to have to explain himself. 'Anyway,' he continued with a sigh, 'I've made the decision and we're getting DC Angus Smith.'

'Smith?' exclaimed Wilson a little too loudly, and he repeated it more quietly, this time with a slight grin, 'Smith? The new boy from B Section?'

'Yes, and before you say anything, I'm aware that he doesn't get on well with the rest of the team,' explained Avalon raising a single eyebrow.

'That's a bloody understatement, I bet Lasiter es laughing his arse off,' said Wilson in mock laughter, 'he gets our most adaptable officer and we get his cast-off numpty collection.' Avalon just glared at Wilson, he was becoming tired of this. 'Do you know what they call him?' he added.

'No, and I don't want whatever nick-name they have branded him with-' for the second time in the conversation Wilson interrupted him.

'The Zombie, they call him The Zombie, doesnae

that tell you something about-' this time Avalon interrupted.

'Damn it Gordon, just accept it, she's gone and DC Smith is now in C Section,' and he stood and walked out of the booth noticing that the rest of the Cave had heard his comment, including Frazer. He left the room slamming the door behind him.

'Someone to see you DI Avalon,' announced the desk sergeant holding onto the door handle.

'Any name given?' asked Avalon sipping at his coffee.

'Mr Gallagher? He says you wanted to see him.'

'Oh yes,' agreed Avalon leaping out of his seat and finishing off the coffee, 'I'll be straight out,' and the sergeant closed the door of the little office behind him. Avalon placed his cup on the table and looked at the PC seated opposite.

'Thanks for the coffee,' he nodded and left the room for the foyer. He had been in the back office near the desk having a quiet chat with PC Dowd, nothing special, it was just a good place to get out of the way for a few minutes and Dowd was just ending his shift.

'I've told Ollie, I mean PC Kirk to put him in interview room two,' explained the current desk sergeant. Avalon nodded as he walked past and made his way to the little room down the corridor. Kirk was just coming out, and she smiled at Avalon.

'I've just taken him a cup o' tea from the machine, we call et 'liquid torture' so he'll be ready tae say anythin' by the time you get there inspector.'

'Thanks, Ollie,' he replied as he passed her and entered the room. He shook hands with Mr Gallagher and thanked him for coming in and then he sat opposite and began his questions.

'I assume you have no idea who is responsible for this?'

'No, none whatsoever and I can't imagine what it's about,' shrugged the man with a worried expression.

'I suppose some of your books are of some worth?'

'A few, but many are volumes I have had for years, they have no intrinsic value, more old friends than anything.' The man seemed to be uncomfortable and fidgeted constantly.

'Do you keep any other valuables in the house, I know some people use fake books to hide trinkets inside?'

'No detective,' the man afforded a slight smile, 'I know the items you describe but all I have are the books in that room, any money is in the bank,' explained the man.

'Any enemies, people you don't get on with?'

'No not at all,' replied Gallagher shaking his head, 'I keep my own company most of the time, I hardly go out these days.' Avalon sighed and tapped the table with his index finger in frustration.

'Well,' he continued, 'for the moment this one remains a mystery, all there is left to do is for us to see if anything went missing.'

'Then can I return home?' asked the man with a frown. Avalon noticed he seems to be trying to keep something at bay, the action people make when they are desperate to use the toilet.

'Forensics should be done up there by now but I'll make sure and then we can go and have a look around,' he hesitated before adding, 'to see if you can confirm that any of your items are not there.' Gallagher agreed and Avalon met him there later wondering why he was so uncomfortable at the station. It was dark once again, and they entered the house together. The man still seemed nervous, but that was to be expected and when they entered the room, it was very cold and Gallagher shook his head as he turned on the lights. The room had been heavily dusted for prints and the broken glass window was against the wall in a heap under the black plastic sheet that had been taped to the window frame. It was a temporary measure to keep the weather out but Avalon thought it was a nice gesture from whoever had done it.

'It's awful,' exclaimed the man holding his forehead and looking at the books strewn on the floor.

'Can you tell if anything is missing Mr Gallagher?' asked Avalon. The man looked around the room once more checking the glazed cases that hadn't been opened and then to the one that the books had been ejected from. He looked at a few of the titles and picked one up that had been slightly damaged.

'No, I don't think so,' he frowned, 'this is such a mindless act,' he then said. Avalon looked around the room himself and then over to the pile of wreckage that had once been a leaded window. He bent down as the man placed one of the books back onto its shelf and looked at the glass shards. He could see plenty of fibres so he was pleased that the forensics would have something to look through at least. He stood and placed his hands in his pockets from the cold of the room and had another glance around the bookcases. There were hundreds of books, some old, some not so old but a few looked ancient.

'Have you heard of the Chinon Chart?' he asked. The man looked over to him with a book in each hand and said,

'I don't recall it, is it a book?' and he looked at the spines before placing them onto the shelves.

'I think it's more of a document than a book,' added Avalon picking up one of the remaining volumes. It was entitled 'Discovering the Corbetts of the Highlands' and he handed it to the man.

'No, I can't say that I know of it,' repeated Gallagher as he examined the volume before placing it where he thought it should go.

'Fair enough, it was a long shot anyway,' sighed Avalon just as the man placed the final book onto the shelf. He looked worried, he took two books back out and slid a couple of others together, then he replaced the two books in his arms and put his hand on his forehead once more.

'I find that,' nodded Avalon, 'if you take a book from a cramped bookshelf, you can never get it back in.'

'No, that isn't the issue, they went in easily and they shouldn't,' announced the man putting his hands on his hips and looking very agitated, 'I think one is missing.'

'What was it called?' asked Avalon.

'I'm not sure,' he said turning and walking to a desk to find a notebook. He brought the notebook to the case and cross-referenced the books on the shelf with what he had in the notebook. Avalon waited for him to check them and check them again and then he said,

'Yes, it's missing,' and then 'oh my.'

'What's missing?' asked Avalon losing patience.

'The book is called, 'The Forming of the Forge',' he seemed unsure at first but Avalon put that down to an amount of shock.

'I'm guessing it's valuable from your comment?'

'Valuable? Yes, well no, it's not worth any monetary value,' stuttered the man, 'it's just rare, unique really.'

'Unique?' asked Avalon, 'what do you mean?'

'Erm,' he hesitated, 'well, it's probably the only copy in existence that is signed by the author, but utterly worthless to even a collector.'

'But it is rare?' asked Avalon.

'Not really, I believe copies can be found easily enough, as I say, no value on the market, if I was honest, I had forgotten I had it.'

'What's it about?' asked Avalon not sure he was telling the whole truth.

'It's an old mountaineering book, this entire shelf is mountaineering, but it's completely out of date, I can't understand why anyone would steal it,' announced Gallagher. Avalon pulled out his own notebook and said,

'Give me all the details you have on the book Mr Gallagher, this could be important.'

Chapter Four

The rest of the week was going to be uncomfortable in the Cave that was clear, but Avalon tried his best to put the problems aside and concentrate on catching up with the previous week's work and reviewing the cases that the rest of the team were working on. Wednesday was the hardest, he had to ask Frazer about a couple of issues with documentation on a particular case that she had worked on but he tried to be professional about it. Frazer on the other hand was sullen and withdrawn, Ross too was showing signs of his displeasure to the extent that he had little to say to anyone in the team. Not that it was a team any longer, the humour had departed the room, and it was quiet and subdued as everyone carried on but without the sense of belonging anymore. Rutherford was the only one who seemed unaffected by the change, probably because he was the last one to join the team, probably because he didn't give a damn about other people's mood swings over what he saw as a minor setback.

By Thursday Avalon had resigned himself to the fact that what he had built in C Section was now gone and he would have to start again to mould them into a cohesive and strong team. The issue wouldn't go away however whilst Frazer was still working from the Cave and it was likely that everyone including Avalon, was wishing she had taken the rest of the week off so that they could draw a line under the episode and carry on as normal. As it was, Frazer had been important to just about everyone in the section for many and varied reasons and she had become 'part of the furniture' in everyone's mind.

Friday was a little easier. Wilson was back working solely on his own cases with Alison Boyd and Avalon resumed his role from the glass booth at the end of the office where he felt even more isolated than he had done previously. He was however, expecting some results from the forensics team on the two recent break-ins and he was hopeful that he would glean some better information about the case. That would be after lunch though so in the morning he busied himself with the tedium of checking reports and the mountain of paperwork that seemed to grow by the hour. As he sat looking from his computer screen to the interior of the Cave he glanced now and then to the faces in that room, occasionally stopping on Frazer's face and then over to Ross. Something began nagging at his soul, like a little piranha of doubt gnawing at his organs from within. At first, he put it down to the regret of what he had been forced to do but then he realised he had been forced to do nothing, the decision had been his and his alone. *There* was the doubt, why had he actually done things the way he had done them? He stopped typing and looked into the room again. He saw Frazer, she was staring intently at her screen and occasionally blinked and looked up at the windows to her right. It was obvious her mind wasn't fully on her work. Avalon looked back to his screen and tried to answer his own question. He knew he had to react to a violent act within his own department but from what he could tell the act itself wasn't malicious, just hot-headed. Did that matter, it could have been more serious and would he have reacted so severely if it had been someone else, someone that didn't have any sort of history? He couldn't answer that. He *did* know Frazer's history and he had clearly made the decision based on that, fair or not, he couldn't un-know it. There was also the doubt in his mind that he was going through with this because he was following protocol, but there again, protocol demanded that the incident was reported to the DCI and Croker would meter out the punishment. There was another problem. Detectives were now under so much pressure to get results, to tick boxes and to do it cheaply, those protocols had become a nonsense. At the Wolverhampton station where Avalon had once worked, the detective chief inspector didn't even know Avalon existed, Avalon had never actually spoken to the man. Most regional bases had a single detective sergeant and a trainee so how would *they* deal with such a problem? They wouldn't have the luxury of a DCI to go to for sure. This made Avalon feel uncomfortable, he was starting to see that the real reason he had acted so harshly was the cycle of accountability that officers were forced into, the way that they were left to dig themselves out of the mire so that those above could deny any knowledge of a crisis. The Prime Minister, or the Witch of Westminster as most police officers were beginning to call her had stated that 'the police don't like me, but I don't care'. She had also told the police forces in the UK to 'stop scaremongering, there are more cuts coming so get used to it,' and Avalon had realised at that moment that the crisis in detective manpower was going to get worse due to the poor management from Westminster. He had been right. In London and other major cities, detectives were resigning after putting serious time and effort into a career that they believed in. That was how bad it had become, detectives who had been committed to the job were walking away from it because it was ruining their health, their sanity, and their private lives. In turn, that was due to a mountain of work that had become impossible to surmount. Avalon knew that some detectives sent out on cases were not trained enough or had too little experience to get results. He also knew that some detectives could be working on up to twenty cases at one time. Even in Inverness there were too many cases to give each one the time it needed to get a conviction. That was why the crime figures showed a down-turn, not because there was less crime, it was just that more crimes were going unreported because the public were beginning to realise there was no point. Getting an incident number from a voice on the end of a phone didn't equate to justice, it just meant that the public saw that the police were ineffective and maybe they would turn to their own system of law enforcement next time.

So why was he protective over it? Why was he protecting the system when the system didn't protect him or the people around him? Probably because he knew that a breakdown in the command structure would mean chaos, he knew if he wasn't seen to react to the problem that he would lose respect for his position. He leaned back in his chair and shook his head. He knew that was a nonsense too, he was losing respect anyway so was it just a pride issue? He sighed deeply and decided to take a walk downstairs to get some air.

'Oh, just the man,' announced Dowd as he saw Avalon. The DI just lifted his gaze a little but said nothing. 'There's a calendar here for the Cave,' continued Dowd, 'we all get one, surprise, surprise it's got coppers on it.'

'So what did you expect Neil, kittens?' asked Avalon glancing over to the PC.

'Well not exactly, but et would be nice if now and then there was something different from the propaganda shots of PC Perfect and Mrs Oldlady.' The word propaganda struck Avalon, it was a word that suited the police force quite well.

'Well, everything has to look like we live in a perfect world where there is a jovial copper at the end of every street and there is so little crime we have time to help old ladies across the road,' shrugged the DI.

'Really?' frowned Dowd, 'there was me thinkin' that this *was* the perfect job where the people at the top are looking after our welfare,' and he continued sorting through the pile of calendars for the various departments.

'So are you the station calendar monitor now?' asked Avalon.

'You know how et es Inspector, once you tell your immediate boss he can shove promotion where the conscientious officers lick, you're gonna get all the prime jobs,' replied Dowd lifting his eyebrows a little. Avalon smiled and nodded and then seemed to drift off somewhere. 'Es there anythin' I can do f'r you?' asked Dowd.

'Oh,' exclaimed Avalon blinking several times, 'sorry, I was just thinking on what you said, you may have something there Neil.' Dowd could see the DI's eyes reflecting a little of what he was thinking.

'I'm off for my break en a mo,' he asked at length, 'do you fancy a cuppa?' Avalon shrugged and then nodded.

'Yeah, why not?' smiled Avalon and he went to the little office in the backroom to wait for PC Dowd. As he waited he pulled out his phone and rang the man from Stathpeffer.

'Hello, Mr Gallagher, it's Detective Inspector Avalon, Inverness. I just need to ask you a couple of questions,' he said.

'*Oh yes detective, what is it?*' the man seemed less than pleased to hear his voice.

'There is one question I would particularly like to ask you Mr Gallagher, when you noticed that the book you called, The Forming of the Forge was missing, you seemed anxious.'

'*Did I, I suppose it was all a shock,*' replied the man but Avalon could hear he wasn't being truthful.

'I believe your words were, 'oh my,' Mr Gallagher.'

'*As I say Detective, I was in shock that anyone would steal from me,*' replied the man sounding very uncomfortable.

'So why do you think he would steal a worthless book from you, a book I can find no record of anywhere, not even on the internet?' asked Avalon.

'*I er,*' there was a pause, '*I'm not entirely sure, I wish I did understand.*'

'So do I Mr Gallagher, so do I, but I find it more

103

than a coincidence that you seemed taken aback knowing that book was the one he was after, and he was after that one Mr Gallagher because at all the other crime scenes he has been at, he left a great deal of destruction behind him.' Avalon made sure the man was aware that the DI knew he was keeping something from him.

'*Look Detective,*' said the man sounding impatient, '*I have told you all I know, you said there were a couple of questions.*'

'There were a couple Mr Gallagher,' Avalon looked up to the door as Dowd entered and filled the kettle, 'but I can't see the point in asking them if you are likely to tell me less than the truth,'

'*Really, inspector, I feel somewhat put out that you don't believe me,*' replied the man, Avalon could imagine the man fidgeting as he had done at the station.

'I'm sure you do Mr Gallagher, if you think of anything else, you know where to find me,' and he ended the call. Dowd reached over and handed him the piping hot tea and perched on a stool by the door and reached into a cupboard for a small packet. He unwrapped the packet to reveal several sandwiches.

'Sounds like problems,' he said as he sniffed the sandwiches.

'Oh, it's just that some people want you to help them but they don't give you the tools to do it,' replied Avalon pushing his hand through his hair.

'Do you fancy a Salmon sandwich?' Dowd offered, handing the packet towards Avalon.

'Not for me,' replied Avalon holding his hand up for a second, 'but thanks anyway,' he added then took a sip of the tea.

'Aye, probably best, et's not proper salmon

anyways, I think they put the wrong label on the tin, even our cat won't eat this shite,' he said but he still bit hungrily into the bread. He chewed for a moment and then said, 'I get this every day,' he announced holding up the bread, 'I once made the mistake o' telling the wifey I was sick o' corned beef. I said can I have somethin' different? She said, 'like what?' so I said, well you know, cheese or salmon, just somethin' different for a change. So now the condemned man has tae eat salmon paste for the next twenty years,' he concluded and took another bite.

'You could always make up your own sandwiches,' smiled Avalon.

'I did,' frowned Dowd, 'she's on shifts this week so *I* made these,' answered Dowd, 'I've eaten them for so long I'm not sure et would be safe for my digestion tae change now,' and he took another bite and then laid the remaining part on top of the packet. Avalon smiled at Dowd and shook his head. As he took another sip of the tea, he sensed Dowd was about to speak again as he ceased eating and left the sandwich on the table.

'You look a little down en the dumps ef y' don't mind me saying, is et just the general public holding back information or somethin' else?' he said quietly.

'Oh, some days are like that, sometimes you just wonder if you're going in the right direction,' replied Avalon raising his brows.

'I'm guessing this es mainly tae do with the three-rounder that DS Ross and DC Frazer had.'

'Well, I suppose the news was bound to reach this office first,' frowned Avalon, 'but yes, it isn't helping matters.'

'So you're doubting your decision?' asked Dowd

with a concerned look.

'How the hell do you know there *is* a decision, have you got electronic surveillance in the Cave?' asked Avalon with a frown.

'Not quite,' smiled Dowd, 'PC Robertson reads tea leaves, PC Kirk as you know is a witch and I used to have a booth in the railway station reading palms and throwing bones.' He took a sip of his tea and replaced the cup on the table before adding, 'Even Sergeant Gregory has a crystal ball en his locker.' Avalon shook his head once more, it seemed all information went straight to the front desk, there was nothing about Police Scotland that couldn't be found out from the staff of that department. Avalon stared at Dowd for a moment or two, it was so long that Dowd picked up the sandwich once more and continued to eat. Avalon eventually succumbed to Dowd's seemingly indifferent gaze and admitted he was regretting the whole episode.

'So what changed, did you just calm down or have you found more information?' asked Dowd between bites of the second sandwich.

'I just think I'm being too much of a company man, something you said outside made sense too,' replied Avalon as he leaned forward and rested his elbows on his legs.

'Well Inspector, I'd hate tae think that my words made any sense, what was it I said exactly?'

'About you refusing promotion,' replied Avalon.

'Surely this isn't the same thing is et?'

'It is in a way Neil,' nodded Avalon, 'I spend my whole career as a detective doing things my own way, even when it caused *me* problems, I still stuck with my morals and my own judgement.'

106

'So what changed?' asked Dowd.

'I'm not sure,' replied Avalon interlocking his fingers as he stared at the floor, 'maybe it's because I'm happier here than I have ever been and I don't want to compromise that, pretty selfish hey?' he added as he looked up into Dowds eyes.

'What ef et wasn't just that?' suggested Dowd, 'what ef et was also the fact that as a DI you're expected to react differently than you used to?' Avalon sat upright and sighed and said,

'I'm expecting something profound from you now, you realise that?'

'Nothing profound,' frowned Dowd as he reached for his cup, 'I refused promotion because I have nothing to lose if I don't take it, but I could lose plenty as a sergeant, *you* on the other hand,' he said pointing with the cup, 'do have something to lose if you get your decisions wrong.' He stopped to take a gulp of tea and then added, 'That's where you're really wrong however, et's your team, et's your world and your decisions are more important to the people you work with than they are to you.' He raised his brows and took another gulp of tea. Avalon looked at Dowd as he glanced down into his cup. He wasn't quite sure what Dowd meant but he thought through it. It wasn't Dowd's place to tell an inspector how to do his job but Avalon trusted the man and respected his opinion.

'I feel that I've just had a bollocking,' announced Avalon with a slight grin.

'Not at all,' replied Dowd looking back, 'en some ways you're a wee bit like me, you're from the old breed, the sort that think that being a copper es about helping people. These days that is'nae the case. The

107

modern copper es all about targets, ticking boxes and performance figures.' He stopped and gave a deep sigh then continued, 'you're either a copper or an accountant, y' cannea be both en my book,' and he looked directly at Avalon. 'After all, this es Scotland, not Scotland Yard and I doubt if anyone gives a flying fart how you choose t' run your section as long as you don't cause them any problems.'

'You're correct of course,' nodded Avalon, 'I don't think I've ever known you in error.'

'Oh, I was wrong once,' Dowd announced as he stood, 'I once thought I was en error, but et turned out I was right all along, so I was wrong tae think I was wrong,' and he drained his cup, 'Right, got t' get back to et, you'll sort et out Inspector, I know y' will,' and he winked and walked out dropping the used paper from his sandwiches in the bin by the door. Avalon felt as if he had been beaten up verbally, Dowd could do that to you. He watched the door of the little office close and then reopen, this time the PC who had been covering for Dowd came in. Avalon nodded to him, finished his tea and then he left too.

Outside he saw DI Lasiter going through the doors to the stairs.

'Bob!' called Avalon. Lasiter stopped and held the door open for him and then they both walked up the stairs.

'Don't tell me, you've had second thoughts,' growled Lasiter.

'What about?'

'About taking Angus White off my hands,' replied Lasiter looking at Avalon as he walked. 'I'm guessing you've seen his record?' he added before reaching the top.

'It's not about PC White, I want you to do me a favour.'

'Another one?' exclaimed Lasiter opening his eyes as wide as they could go, which wasn't all that much. 'What es et this time, you want me tae make a hit on someone you don't like, or maybe y' just want me tae redirect the Ness nearer to y'r house?'

'Nothing so bizarre, this is quite simple, well,' Avalon paused for a heartbeat, 'simple-ish.'

'Go on,' frowned Lasiter, 'but you're gonna have tae live t' be a hundred an' thirty t' get enough time tae pay me back all these favours.'

PC Kirk was walking down the corridor on the top floor, she was just returning from delivering some mail to the DCI's office and saw DI Lasiter and DI Avalon at the top of the stairs seemingly having a quiet conversation. As she got closer she heard DI Lasiter say with some surprise,

'You want me t' what?' and they both turned as one, nodded to her and then disappeared through the double doors into the section corridor.

~~~~~~

Avalon looked at the computer screen reading the main points of the two forensic accounts of the breaking and entering at both Rogart and Strathpeffer. There was very little to link them on paper, Avalon was looking for the slightest thing that might suggest the two incidents could be related. There was nothing. The report on the

Rogart incident stated that there was nothing of any significance found on the premises, the only clue that Avalon had was on one of the photographs it clearly showed the small pile of parchments that were stacked up on the table. He then went back to the Strathpeffer incident, here there were no traces of blood but there were fibres found and they had been analysed. They proved to be unusual in that the fabric contained something called UHMwPE. A little further the report explained that the initialism stood for 'ultra-high-molecular-weight polyethylene'. He didn't know exactly what that meant and though there was a short explanation he knew he would have to ring the forensics lab to get more information. It did however, state that the fabric is unusual and should be able to be traced. Other than that, there was nothing in the report of any significance.

'Hello, it's DI Avalon, Inverness CID, is Sarah Underwood there or,' Avalon hesitated, he had been told Hendry's first name but for a moment he couldn't find it in his memory, 'er, Mr Henrdy,' he eventually said.

'*They're both in*,' announced the female voice, '*any particular one?*'

'Not really,' admitted Avalon, 'whoever can explain something about the reports on the Rogart case and the Strathpeffer case.'

'*Just one moment*,' she replied and several seconds later he heard the phone picked up, it was Sarah.

'*Hello DI, I assume you got the report then?*'

'Yes,' he replied, 'have you got a moment to help me out with the second one?'

'*I'll try, though I realise there isn't much in there,*' she replied. As he listened to her voice he thought

110

back to their night out in Edinburgh, he began to think how she would look on the other end of the phone.

'It's just that I'm not sure what this…' he paused as he scrolled back up the report to find the wording, 'ultra-high-molecular-weight polyethylene is,' he eventually said, 'it's mentioned that it may be possible to trace it.'

'*Well yes, it should be but since then we've done some digging and it seems whoever this person was, he or she has probably been to America.*'

'America? Why America?'

'*There is a small piece of what looks like an unusual strand of Kevlar in there too, it makes it fairly unique to a manufacturing plant in the States.*' He heard her tapping some keys on a keyboard, '*I'm sending you an email with the information, it's likely they know who their outlets are so you should be able to find it easily.*' As the email arrived, he opened it and read a company name with some extra detailing about the fabric and particularly this new strand.

'So does your fabric expert have any ideas what this might be?' he eventually asked.

'*Not really, this UHMwPE is a sort of super fabric, it's strong, corrosion and impact resistant and self-lubricating, you can find out about it on the internet easily enough,*' she explained.

'It sounds like material a ballistic vest would be made from.

'*Exactly,*' she agreed, '*it is used as armour in some applications but in this case, it is just woven into the fabric, this item probably looks more like a fleece, or maybe a jacket.*'

'The strands I saw at the house looked black, is

111

that the colour we should be looking for?' he asked.

'*Yes, the Kevlar fibre is dark blue but the mainstay of the fabric is just ordinary black cotton.*'

'Anything else?' he asked expectantly.

'*Not really, except that as a clothing item it's probably expensive, it has to be unique I would think.*' That was it, that was all he was going to get on that one, he decided to ask if she knew if the images taken at the Rogart house were in an untampered state. She told him that they were, and he had the sudden impulse to mention their night out but he couldn't think of the words to use so he just ended the call by saying,

'Okay, thanks for that, at least we have a little more to go on,' and he put down the phone. He had another look through the images of both locations but it was clear there was nothing to link the two scenes together and he was going to have to treat them separately until something did, or didn't crop up.

It was Friday night and Avalon took a stroll down to the Castle Tavern as he usually did when the opportunity allowed but he sat alone on the raised part of the room usually occupied by him and Ross. Ross hadn't been in the pub since the little talk down at the old ferry slip and none of the regulars had seen him. Harry the Hat said he thought he had seen him with a 'lassie' but he admitted to being 'welted' at the time. Harry was usually hovering between welted and 'reekin' so that was no surprise. Avalon was more surprised how many Scottish phrases there were to describe being drunk. It depended greatly on where the person was originally from but his favourite was a predominantly Doric term from the Aberdeen area, 'stoatin' aboot'. There were many more he could think of but Avalon wasn't in the mood to be 'awa' wi' it', or 'minced' and so at around ten o'clock he drank up and returned home as sober as when he went out. For Ross it seemed, this difference of opinion was a permanent state of affairs, so much for Christmas cheer. Back at his house Avalon realised something was missing. After the festive feel at the Castle Tavern with their Christmas decorations adorning the place, Avalon's house looked positively morbid, and he wondered if he should make an effort for a change. He wasn't the sort of person to decorate the house, it always seemed pointless when you lived alone and usually worked through the Christmas period. Instead, he poured himself a drink, and slumped into his chair and listened to an audiobook. It was 'Under Milk Wood' and it had been a while since he had heard it but he gradually succumbed to the restful sound of the voice of Richard Burton and began to relax, or maybe it was the large tot of Glenmorangie. He finally took himself off to bed and as he dozed, he thought about the words of Neil Dowd and considered that the sage PC saw the world as it was, he never embellished it with a rose tint and he seemed to know the workings of the human mind as if he was he designer of it. If only he would take his detective examinations.

~~~~~~~

Detective Sergeant Ross sat on an uncomfortable dining room chair whilst his current working partner, DC Rutherford took a statement from a little old lady known as Mrs Doherty. Ross usually dealt with such matters as Rutherford could be rather imposing due to his size but Mrs Doherty had taken to Rutherford, she said he reminded her of her grandson, who didn't visit nearly enough but she loved him all the same. Ross had another try of the terrible tea she had made for them and considered that a Saturday morning could be a great deal worse than what he was doing right at that moment. The old lady had witnessed a hit and run and she was giving her statement, though she seemed to attach what she saw to anything connected to the television or the street where she lived. Fortunately, the victim of the hit and run wasn't badly injured, but it was thought that the car could have also been involved in a Road Traffic Incident in the city and so Rutherford tried to get the information from her.

'So you say he was a young man?' Rutherford had asked.

'Yes, yes he was young but then again everyone seems young to me,' she smiled.

'About what age would you say Mrs Doherty?' asked Rutherford in a loud voice as the old lady was a little hard of hearing.

'Oh, I don't know about that, he looked younger than my grandson but older than Mrs Taylor's oldest boy.'

'And what age would those two people be Mrs Doherty?'

'Well,' began the old lady looking slightly vague, 'Robert is forty-three this next June, or is it forty-four, my memory isn't what is once was.' She then paused and thought a little more as Rutherford looked back to Ross with an impatient expression. Ross just raised the teacup in a 'cheers' gesture and took a sip of its dubious contents. 'Now then,' she continued, 'Andrew, Mrs Taylors eldest, well let me see, he was born the same day

114

as that solar eclipse because I remember Mrs Taylor wondering if it would have any bad effects on the bairn, but as I told her, that's to do with a full moon not a solar eclipse. But then again she's not the brightest spark on the street and I was only telling-'

'So what age did you say the man driving the car was?' asked the exasperated Rutherford.

'Oh, I would think between twenty and forty, though my eyes are-'

'And what sort o' car was et Mrs Doherty?' asked Rutherford as he glanced back to Ross. Ross was having fun, he hadn't seen anyone get the better of Rutherford but this little old lady was managing quite well.

'I think it was one of those like that detective on television drives, erm that Jim Rockford.'

'But that's an American programme Mrs Doherty,' insisted Rutherford.

'Is it, oh well,' she sighed looking at the floor, 'it can't be him then can it?'

'Did you see what colour et was?' asked Rutherford deflecting her off the subject of the television programme.

'It might have been Detective Frost, I like David Jason,' she beamed.

'Colour Mrs Doherty, what colour was it?' insisted Rutherford.

'Colour, oh, I think it was red,' she frowned.

'You *think* et was red?' asked Rutherford trying to keep his patience.

'Well yes, I think it was, you have to remember that it was a few days ago now,' insisted the woman.

'This was yesterday Mrs Doherty,' explained Rutherford deciding it was pointless to ask more.

115

'Was it?' she asked, 'it seems longer ago than that.'

'Thank you Mrs Doherty,' interrupted Ross as he stood, 'you've been a great help and thanks for the tea.'

'Oh, is that it?' she asked with a puzzled look, 'I thought it would take much longer than that,' and Ross and Rutherford returned to the car.

'She *thinks* the car was red,' announced Rutherford shaking his head, 'I mean you could probably say you thought et was a Ford or a Vauxhall but the colour?'

'What you have to remember my friend,' said Ross as he started the engine, 'Mrs Doherty was probably doing things you couldn't imagine when you were still a rather ponderous sperm swimming along your mother's tubes.' Rutherford turned to Ross and frowned.

'I don't know why but that sound rather personal,' he insisted.

'Probably but it's the truth.'

'Aye et es but I'm no' sure I'm happy about you talking about my mother's tubes en such a casual way.'

'Get used to it,' replied Ross as he looked around and pulled out of a junction, 'women's tubes are a favourite subject of mine.'

'I think I'm going t' ask the boss t' work with someone else, I always feel so dirty after going out with you.' Rutherford then became aware that Ross had gone silent. That was worrying, it was so much out of character and then he realised what it was about.

'Oh, so you're still up yer' own arse about the boss then are you?' Ross didn't answer, he shrugged but he said nothing. 'Ef I didn't know better I would say you had somethin' goin' with DC Frazer.' This did make Ross react, he turned quickly and then just as quickly returned his view to the road.

'I don't give a toss what you or anybody else thinks, I think the DI is wrong, you were there and I was to blame,' he growled.

'That's shite and you know et, do the mathematics,' insisted Rutherford shaking his head.

'What do you mean?' asked Ross turning onto the main road.

'Et's a formula, how many days have you known Frazer divided by how many days you have taunted her over the days she threw a rock at you.'

'That's not the point,' insisted Ross.

'Of course et es,' demanded Rutherford, 'it's never happened before and so you couldn't know it would happen last week, ergo it's Frazer's fault and not yours.' Ross was quiet for a moment as he thought it through and then he asked,

'Wasn't that Jason's ship?'

'What?' asked Rutherford with a pained expression.

'Ergo, Jason's ship from Greek mythology?'

'That was the Argo you ill-educated Highlander,' sighed Rutherford shaking his head. Ross looked over to him for a second.

'And you're a dark horse,' he smiled 'who would think a gorilla like you would know anything about Greek mythology?'

'I know plenty, I just chose not tae let people know, et generally gets you more work,' the big man replied and then he turned to Ross, 'for instance,' he began as he turned back to look out of the windscreen, 'I

117

know *you* revert back tae humour when you know you're wrong.' Ross made an unintelligible noise and then remained quiet for the rest of the journey.

~~~~~~~

Avalon yawned heavily, the massive amount of administrative duties seemed to be getting no smaller and he was sick of the repetition to the degree he wasn't taking any of it in anymore. He decided to have a break to clear his mind and went into the main part of the Cave to speak with DS Wilson. Wilson and Boyd were the only ones left in the office, Rory Mackinnon was following up on a case that he and Frazer had worked on in Invergordon. Frazer was taking the weekend off before she was to start in B Section and Ross and Rutherford were investigating a hit and run near North Kessock.

'You two are off tomorrow I see,' he announced as he sat on the desk in front of Wilson.

'Aye, I'm thinking o' nippin' down to Rome tae do some Christmas shoppin',' nodded Wilson looking up from his desk.

'You could pop into Pierluigi's for a pizza before you fly home,' added Boyd without looking up from her computer. Avalon could see that even Alison Boyd had fit in with the humour of C Section, that made him feel even worse about the situation with Frazer and Ross, that 'esprit de corps' would probably no longer exist between the team.

'I don't even like spaghetti so there's no point in me coming,' said Avalon folding his arms.

'Is there anywhere you would like to go?' asked

118

Alison looking up to him at last, 'y' know, the bucket list sort of place?' Avalon shrugged.

'I always fancied Peru, there are so many inhospitable places, so many lost villages and areas where you can just walk and see no one for days,' he said.

'Sounds too much like the Isle o' Skye for my likin',' frowned Wilson looking back to his computer. There was a moment's silence and then Avalon asked a question directed at Alison.

'Have you heard of the Chinon Chart?' She looked at him and frowned, Wilson cut in.

'That's the thing you asked me about the other day.'

'The same,' nodded Avalon, 'I've done my research, and it seems it's the record of the absolution of the Templar Knights in 1308 but that is pretty irrelevant to my inquiry. I have been lead to believe that another parchment was found with when it was discovered in the Vatican vaults in 2006.'

'I didn't know what it was called but I do remember something about it,' replied Alison squinting her eyes, 'I don't recall any details about it though.'

'So what's the significance o' the second scroll?' asked Wilson.

'The guy who was attacked seemed to struggle to find a reason why he would be a target but he let it slip that he had been asked to check the provenance of a document called the Key Scrolls which was reputedly found at the same time.'

'But like you said before,' replied Wilson, 'even ef he was after this scroll, et has no connection with any o' the other break-ins.'

119

'I realise that but,' Avalon gave a deep sigh, 'I had the forensics report and there is nothing at all to link the crimes together, and yet I feel...' he trailed off.

'Well, y' know it's starting to look like a duck,' admitted Wilson raising his brows.

'You're probably right,' nodded Avalon, 'it's just my instinct telling me there's a connection.'

'But you're famous instinct is usually right boss,' added Boyd as she turned back to her screen.

'Not every time,' said Avalon getting up and walking back to his booth. Wilson and Boyd glanced over to each other but said nothing.

Sunday promised to be equally tedious for Avalon so he had decided to break up his time between the administration of the section and a little more digging into the break-ins to see if he could find any other past cases that might fit the bill. The Cave was quiet, with three of the staff off and Ross and Rutherford out on a case, there was only Mackinnon and Avalon in the office.

'How many cases are you working on at the moment Rory?' asked Avalon sitting in Frazer's seat. Rory shrugged and thought for a moment.

'Not including the bits I'm doing for DS Ross, five.' Avalon nodded.

'Do you think that's an average in this section?'

'I don't know boss,' shrugged Rory again, 'I know DS Ross and DC Rutherford have at least that number and though two have run dry I would say they have eight or nine current cases.' Avalon nodded once more. 'Any reason for the question Boss?' added Rory.

'No not really, there's something I could do with

passing on but I suppose I could find time for it.'

'I could give it a go if you like,' smiled the young DC.

'You've got enough on, particularly if Ross is putting on you too,' said Avalon as he stood.

'It's not that bad, he just wants a vehicle description cross-referencing,' insisted Rory.

'It all takes time though doesn't it,' frowned Avalon thrusting his hands into his pockets, 'a couple of vehicle checks is a meal with a young lady, taking a witness statement, an overdue visit to see an old friend, yes they all take time,' and he wandered off back to the booth. Mackinnon was just thinking what a sullen mood his boss was in when his desk phone rang.

'DC Mackinnon, C Section.' As he listened to the phone his eyes glanced up to the booth and then in a whisper he said, 'yes he is.' He saw Avalon glance momentarily towards him and he tried to look casual about the call. 'Yes, okay, bye,' and he put the phone down. He looked up to Avalon who glanced towards him again and though Rory fixed a thin smile to his lips, Avalon ignored it and looked back to his computer screen. Rory was becoming irritated by the attitude of Ross towards the boss and he was thinking of having it out with the detective sergeant though the irritation was probably motivated more by the sour atmosphere that pervaded the section at the moment than Ross. He was looking at his computer screen but wasn't seeing what was on it, his eyes were reading the emails but his brain wasn't registering their content. He was miles away, thinking how lucky he had thought himself to find a job like the one he had. He was so deep in thought that he didn't hear or see Avalon approach.

'What is it?' asked the DI.

'Boss?' was Mackinnon's questioning reply.

'You've got something on your mind and you seem agitated,' explained Avalon. Rory looked down to his desk for a moment then back up to Avalon.

'It's just this thing with Ross and Frazer,' he sighed, Avalon knew the lad was upset as he always used the formal titles when speaking to his boss, 'it's...' he seemed stuck for words, 'well,' he continued, 'I know the official line is that Frazer is moving to B Section but...' he trailed off again. Avalon leaned his backside on the small table that housed one of the office printers and folded his arms.

'C Section has been operating for many years now,' began Avalon, 'it's had it's up and downs and different personnel just like B section and others like it. People come and people go. This is about Ross and me at the moment,' Avalon paused for a second, 'and that will eventually settle down when DS Ross calms down. No single person makes things work in a section, it's about everyone and they have to continue to work together and get the job done, that's all there is,' he shrugged.

'I know that boss,' replied Rory with a slightly pained expression, 'but being in this section, well, it's been a pleasure to come to work.' Avalon unfolded his arms and stood up.

'Then you need to find another job,' he smiled, 'you're not supposed to enjoy your work,' and he turned to head back to his booth but stopped and turned to Mackinnon. 'Oh, and don't let it get to the DCI or he'll cut your wages,' and he returned to his desk in the booth. Rory smiled but in his heart, Avalon hadn't comforted him, he had just reinforced that there was no controlling how a team ran. No matter what the boss said, the individuals *did* matter, it was *they*, that could turn everything on its head.

Chapter Five

DC Frazer hauled herself up the stairs towards the corridor that accessed both C Section and B Section of Inverness CID. She made that trip several times each day but today, it felt as if someone had spread glue on the steps. She walked past the door that was the normal route into the Cave and around the corner to a similar door some way down the corridor. She opened it and walked in. Never in such a long time had a Monday morning seemed so dreadful. Inside the room, it was very different from the Cave. It was untidy and warm, the Cave was always fairly cool but here in Lasiter's lair, the place was very different. The DI didn't have a booth, he occupied his own office at the end of the room where the door was always open. Inside, he sat at a large desk to one side of the small office with another desk to his side full of box files and a second computer screen. There was no rich smell of fresh coffee to hide the smell of warm humanity. To Frazer, men smelled sour, even if they poured bottles of deodorant over themselves and B Section had no female representative to keep them in check. It was a slightly larger section usually running with more people than Avalon's team and those people were generally the longest-serving of the detectives. In the past, you had to do your time in C Section to get into this exalted company but fortunately, those days were gone. The only reason there were more personnel in the section was that B Section usually served the city and its environs while C Section went further afield.

The main room wasn't full by any means and only four desks were occupied. As she approached his desk within the office, Lasiter looked up.

'Oh, Megan,' he said with a little surprise, 'I'd almost forgotten you were here this mornin',' she didn't react, she just stood there with a small box of her desk items which included a particular paperweight. Lasiter looked uncomfortable as she glared at him. 'Right,' he began as he stood, 'before we get you settled en, there es something I need you tae sort out for me,' but he seemed uncomfortable. 'Nip over to the forensics lab and ask for Sarah Underwood, she'll fill you en with the details.'

'So where shall I put this?' she asked nodding down to her box.

'Er, right, your box o' stuff,' he said hesitantly, 'keep et with you for the moment, I havenae got your place sorted yet, we'll sort et when ye' come back.' Frazer was suspicious, this all seemed wrong, and she felt like dropping the box on the floor and walking out. Instead, knowing she had to be on her best behaviour she turned and left the room feeling like she no longer had a place, as though no one wanted her anywhere in the nick. She plodded all the way back down the stairs carrying her box and out to the car park where she dumped the box into the tiny boot of the car.

For several minutes she just sat there looking aimlessly into space, feeling for the first time for an age she wanted to cry. She resisted it by switching on the radio and starting the engine but the Christmas music coming over the airwaves made her angry and she switched it off again. She drove out of the gates and headed off towards the forensics lab not believing there was any reason for it and considering what she would do if Lasiter was stringing her along. Twice she looked at her herself in the rear-view mirror, craning her head to see her reflection and seeing eyes she didn't recognise. Why had it all gone wrong and why couldn't she get over it? A third look in the mirror showed she was being followed by a police patrol car and when it failed to turn off onto the main road, she began to wonder where it might be going. It was then the blue lights came on and the headlights flashed signalling her to pull over.

'Oh, come on you arse wipes, surely you have checked my number?' she called out to the reflection in her mirrors. She pulled up in a parking space and looked back to the mirror but the police car turned off its lights and pulled out to overtake her. As it passed, the officer in the passenger seat put his hand up and mouthed 'sorry' as they drove off. Frazer saluted him with her middle finger and called out,

'Merry Christmas wanker!' Suddenly the passenger door opened and Frazer physically jumped at the shock as someone slipped into the passenger seat.

'You shouldn't stop just anywhere, anyone could get in,' he said, it was Avalon, 'drive,' he continued.

'Are you trying tae give me a friggin' heart attack or what you stupid arsehole,' she spat as she covered her chest with her hand.

'Oh, and Merry Christmas to you too, I'm guessing the 'wanker' was aimed at me, I could hear it out there.'

'No, I was aiming it at the bloody stupid bastards that pulled me up, I know who they are and I'll…' she trailed off, 'et was you,' she said turning towards him, 'you set this up didn't you?'

'Like I said, drive,' insisted Avalon.

'Where to?' she asked.

'Where were you going?'

'Forensics but I'm guessing-'

'There then, let's go to forensics,' he nodded and pointed his finger towards the road. Frazer set off in the direction she had previously been heading but as they were close to the forensics lab, Avalon was surprised when Frazer turned off the main road and doubled back down a side street.

'Then we won't go to forensics,' he shrugged looking across to her. She looked livid and Avalon could understand that, but he was becoming unsure what she was up to. He looked at the street names as they wound their way through the edge of the city but he still had no idea where they were going. The car suddenly screeched to a halt and Frazer shouted,

'I don't know where I'm going or why damn it!' and she banged both hands on the steering wheel and got out of the car. Avalon jumped out too and walked over to her.

'Come on, I'll drive, I'll explain on the way,' but as she turned to look at him her face was like thunder and he thought she was going to strike him. Fortunately, she just blew out air and stomped off back to the car. As Avalon drove, he could see her right leg bouncing up and down with nervous frustration and he just hoped she could contain her anger until they had time to find somewhere they could talk. They ended up driving down Clachnaharry Road toward Lentran until he found a pull-in and brought the car to a stop. She was sitting with her arms folded and her leg was still bouncing up and down as if she was tapping away to some song that only she could hear.

'You have exactly two minutes to explain,' she suddenly began, 'or I swear I will drive off and leave you here.' Avalon looked at her and nodded slowly.

'Okay, two minutes is good,' and he composed himself for what he had decided to tell her, what he *had* to tell her. He took a deep breath and began. 'I'm not going to pretend that I wasn't in the wrong, but on the other hand, neither am I going to admit that anyone else is to blame but yourself.' Her expression was rigid and he could see more anger welling up inside. 'What happened in the Cave was completely out of order and in any other nick you would have probably have got your marching orders, but that said, this isn't any other nick and I think I must shoulder some of the blame for the way things turned out.' He paused and looked at her but there was still nothing but fury in her expression. He shrugged and turned to face forward resting his arms on the steering wheel. 'I just got it wrong, I should have chastised you but my actions were based on some knowledge about your past that you don't know I am aware of, and in that respect, I apologise.' He glanced over to her and saw that the expression was changed, she now just wore a deep frown.

'What the hell are you talking about, have I got a job or no? 'cause if I have, I'd just rather go back tae B Section and get on wi' et rather than listen to this shite.' Avalon was beginning to wonder if he had blundered yet again, maybe he shouldn't have tried to change things.

'Yes, you have a job but let me finish because this is difficult enough without-'

'So et's difficult for you es et? Well, just spare a thought for-' she interrupted but Avalon was getting angry now and he shouted at her.

'Megan, shut up!' and she did but her features became stiff once more, 'just reign in that temper before it gets you into more trouble,' and he waited a moment before continuing. 'Your reaction towards Ross had some justification, his comment was bigoted and sexist and as you know, I don't stand for that kind of attitude even when it is in humour, but you resorted to violence which given your job, deeply troubles me,' and he paused again to see her reaction. She just stared at him. He sighed with the thoughts of the next part of the conversation, he wasn't looking forward to it.

'After all, it isn't the first time it has happened and I know about your past,' once again he gave her a chance to think about it. She blinked as if she was thinking it through, obviously, she knew that her boss was aware of the incident with a witness, the one where she attacked the man, so what was he getting at? She looked away from him and through the windscreen trying to think what else he would know about her, the only thing she could think of was impossible for him to know about.

'I'm not with you on this,' she insisted with a furrowed brow, 'I still don't know what you're talking about,' she replied.

'You used to work for Detective Inspector Logan,' was all Avalon said. Frazer went pale, her angry expression turned to one of shock. She swallowed and

129

slumped back into the seat. 'You worked down in Aberdeen with him didn't you?' he added, but for a few seconds, she just sat motionlessly. Eventually, she asked a question without looking at him.

'Did you know him?'

'No,' said Avalon, 'but I hear he was a good copper.'

'So, why have you brought this up?' she then asked, her glazed eyes still looking forward.

'I know what happened to you in Aberdeen.' That was all he said, and he watched her for a reaction not sure what to expect.

'Who told you?' she asked with a quiet voice.

'That doesn't matter, only he and I know, but that's why I'm sorry, I should have told you somehow,' sighed Avalon but even now he wasn't sure how he could have done that. Her head slowly bowed and Avalon wanted to take her pain away but he couldn't, he just needed to get this out of the way so he could begin to help her get back on track, or that's how he saw it. She was silent and still, her leg had stopped bouncing and with her arms still folded she stared unfocused into the floor-well of the car. Avalon felt totally out of his depth, he was a decent detective but he had no idea how to proceed with this situation and he was beginning to see that being in charge of a section was beyond him. He had made so many mistakes and got so much wrong that he felt utterly miserable and sorry for Frazer. Eventually, she lifted her head and as she looked straight out of the window, she began to speak but then stopped. She seemed unable to find words.

'I'm sorry but I didn't think it was right for you not to know,' he said softly, just to break the horrific silence in the car.

'That's me done then,' she eventually said.

'I don't see why, you still have a lot to offer, you have skills that help the section run smoothly and no one I know of has the surveillance training that you have,' began the DI, 'the work you were doing in C Section was-'

'I can't go on knowing that people know about...' she paused and swallowed, 'my past.'

'The only people who know are the same two who knew before, nothing has changed and no one else will ever know,' he insisted.

'Who es et?' she asked calmly.

'Knowing that, won't help,' he replied.

'Who es et?' she repeated but this time looked at him. Her eyes were red-rimmed as if she had been crying and yet not a single tear could be seen.

'DI Lasiter,' Avalon sighed, 'I told him I was going to tell you, and I said I might have to mention his name.' Frazer looked back to the windscreen and seemed to be thinking through it all.

'How did *he* know?' she asked.

'Through DI Logan, it was Lasiter who got you the posting to Inverness, he pulled strings because he and Logan were close friends.' Her head shook slowly, just perceptibly. 'Robert Lasiter has watched over you all these years and you thought he didn't like you. He covered everything up over the incident in the interview room too, he only told me about your past because I threatened to expose him over it. He was ready to give his career up to keep it quiet, only when I pointed out that you would suffer too, did he relent.' Frazer looked slowly round to Avalon.

131

'And you would have done that?' she asked in a severe but calm tone.

'Yes, I thought he was covering something illegal up,' explained Avalon, 'after he explained, I dropped it. It's been weighing on my conscience ever since.'

'So why tell me now?'

'Because unless you know, I can't put this right. I have been a complete idiot, you can't do things by the book in this job, I knew that but I forgot about it because I didn't want to compromise what I had here.' Avalon looked through the windscreen now, he felt like he was coming to the end of the line himself. After this, everything was going to change anyway.

He turned back to her. 'I know it's not going to be how it was but I want you back in C Section...' he paused, 'if you want to of course, I have straightened it out with DI Lasiter, though I suppose I'll owe him until the day I die.'

'You're right about that, et can't be the same, not for me anyway,' she said and looked out into the woodland to their left. Avalon's phone rang, he stopped it ringing and put it back in his pocket.

'It can't for any of us I suppose but C Section has become more than the sum of its people, it's a fantastic team and the last few days have shown that.'

'So how are you gonna explain all this crap, tell me that?' she suddenly hissed, the venom resurfacing. She looked angry once more, but that lifted Avalon a little, Frazer wasn't Frazer unless she was angry.

'Honestly? I don't know but I've got from here to the station to dream something up,' he said with an open expression. The phone rang again, he cut it off yet again.

'And what does Lasiter think?' she then asked.

132

'He thinks I'm a dickhead,' shrugged Avalon, 'well his actual words were much more flowery, but he basically suggested that I should take a job I would be more suited to, like traffic warden.' Avalon paused for a moment looking around outside the car and then added, 'He was livid when I told him my plans but I think he felt relieved, I think he wanted to tell you earlier but didn't know how.' He turned to look at her. 'I know how that feels, it's not good having those sorts of secrets.'

'I suppose I can understand that,' she said a little less angrily, 'I mean, how do you put et? 'Would you go and take a witness statement DC Frazer, oh and by the way, I know you were gang-raped by four..." and at this point, she broke down. Avalon almost cried himself. He was confused, had it been anyone else he would have embraced them and tried to console them, but this was Frazer, she was not like other people. He threw caution to the wind and placed his hand softly on her sobbing head but she knocked his arm away. Seconds later, she leaned towards him and he held her as she cried. His phone rang again. He wound down the window with his right hand, removed the phone, and threw it into the woodland.

~~~~~~

'Does anyone know where the boss is?' asked a confused Mackinnon.

'No idea,' announced Wilson pulling on his jacket, 'me and Alison are off out,' he added. It was usual to have a meeting on Monday mornings but Avalon had left word that there wouldn't be one and so everyone was going about their normal business, all except Rory who had been tasked with following something up for the boss. He nodded to Wilson but as the DS and Alison Boyd reached the door, it opened and in walked a thin young man with a blank expression.

'Mornin',' nodded Wilson as he and Alison swept past him and out of the room. As the door closed, the young man looked at Rory as the only other occupant of the office.

'Hello,' nodded the man in an English accent, 'is DI Avalon about?'

'No, I'm after him myself, can I help?'

'I'm Angus White,' he explained but Rory was none the wiser and shrugged.

'So, Mr White, what can I do for you?'

'Erm, DC Angus White.'

'So, DC Angus White, how can I help?' repeated Mackinnon.

'I'm supposed to be in C Section this morning,' explained the man with a puzzled look.

'Oh,' smiled Rory with an amount of realisation, 'you're The Z...' he quickly checked himself, 'the new chap, well I'm sorry but the boss is out and I don't know when he'll be back.' The man just nodded and looked around the room. 'If I were you,' suggested Rory, 'I would go and get a coffee or something and try later.' Mackinnon had been part of C Section long enough now for pride to be an issue, and like most of the team didn't take all that kindly to new arrivals, particularly to someone who had earned himself the nickname of 'The Zombie'.

'I'll wait here,' he said pointing to a chair and tentatively he sat. Mackinnon watched as he sat down so carefully it seemed he didn't trust the chair to hold his weight. Rory wanted to tell the man that he shouldn't be sitting there as it was someone's seat but in a totally empty room it would sound like a cliché line from a television comedy show. Rory went back to his work but kept an eye on the silent DC White until the strain of the quiet was broken as Ross and Rutherford came through the door. Ross was telling Rutherford the punch line of some story he had probably made up as Rutherford nodded and grinned.

'The thing was,' added Ross with a broad grin, 'he didn't even *then* realise he was her father,' and he looked down at the new face in the chair, the smile evaporating. He nodded at first and then guessed who this must be. 'You must be the new boy,' he then said as Rutherford nodded to him and went to sit in his seat.

'Yes, DC White, Angus White.'

'Aye, I know,' replied Ross and then ignored the DC and went to sit in his own chair continuing as if the new arrival wasn't there. Rory began to feel a little embarrassed, he remembered the first time he had come into the Cave, it was daunting and he had been eager to impress but the team had taken to him and made him feel welcome. There were a few jokes about him coming from an island but that had been it, and yet this new face was replacing someone who had been a key member of C Section, and *that* would make *his* life difficult. Rory decided to ignore him too, it wasn't his job to babysit the new member of the section, the boss would deal with it when he returned... from wherever he was and he tried Avalon's phone yet again.

'Do you two know where the boss is?' he asked. Ross shrugged, and it was left to Rutherford to reply.

'No idea but his car is in the car park.' Rory

considered this, it was likely he was in a meeting with the DCI and if that was the case he may have turned his phone off, but then he discounted that. The boss never turned his phone off.

'Anyone know his personal number?' asked Rory knowing Ross had it but they both shook their heads. That was all Rory could do, he continued with his work and decided to forget about it, just as Avalon came through the door. As the DI closed the door, he noticed the new chap.

'Aah,' he exclaimed as he saw him, the reaction was one of irritation, as if Avalon had stepped in something nasty and Rory couldn't help thinking it was odd for Avalon to react in such a way. 'DC White,' he added and the young man stood as if to shake the DI's hand. 'Follow me,' he said and walked to the booth. Rory considered that if he was quick, he could tell the DI what he had found out before he engaged in further conversation with the new face. Avalon sat and pointed to the spare seat as Rory followed in.

'Boss,' he said apologetically.

'Morning Rory, what is it?'

'It's afternoon Boss, and I did what you asked and it seems the old fellow has taken a turn for the worse,' explained Mackinnon. Avalon seemed to be trying to remember what he'd asked him to do and then it twigged.

'Mr McKeith, what's happened?' Avalon looked questioningly at Mackinnon.

'The chap was about to be sent home but he complained of severe headaches so they checked him over again and kept him in for further checks. Yesterday afternoon he collapsed and he's now in a coma.' Avalon sighed and began to nod slowly. 'I tried to ring you but you didn't answer,' added Mackinnon. Avalon felt to his jacket pocket.

'Ahh, I seem to have misplaced my phone,' he frowned deeper, 'well thanks for letting me know, I'll check on that in a moment or two,' and Rory nodded and left Avalon to it. The DI looked over to White, he was fairly thin and gaunt with an ill-fitting suit and a modern hairstyle that Avalon wasn't happy about, the sort that comes to a point in the centre. On closer inspection he realised it wasn't actually the case, the lad was just untidy, and that was how his hair actually defaulted. Avalon found his record on the computer but decided not to read it, he couldn't see the point.

'DC White, I'm DI Avalon and I will tell you now that things have changed slightly.' White opened his eyes a little wider at this. Avalon leaned back and looked into the DC's eyes. 'Your stay in C Section will probably not be a permanent one, DI Lasiter wants you to work with us because we...' Avalon trailed off as he tried to think of a plausible explanation of why he *was* actually there, 'we attend slightly different cases than B Section, more rural as a general rule.' Avalon thought that was a reasonable-sounding explanation, even if it still didn't make any sense.

'Sir, with respect,' began the DC, 'I know why I'm here, there's no need to try to make me feel better about it.'

'So why are you here?' asked Avalon thinking the lad may be cocky as well as untidy.

'Because I'm not liked in B Section, because I'm new and B Section don't like change. There is also something to do with a DC Frazer too but I can't quite work out what that has to do with me being here.' White had an English accent, there was a regional dialect too, maybe Nottinghamshire or South Yorkshire but either way, Avalon was seeing why B Section didn't like him.

'Is there any other reason they don't like you?' asked Avalon casually.

'I've never been able to understand social prejudices sir, but I'm guessing that the fact that I'm English has something to do with it.'

'You couldn't be more wrong DC White, I'm English and yet they saw fit to give me a very good job here, and I'll tell you something now,' and he leaned over the desk with a certain amount of menace, 'there is no such attitude in this office, in B Section or in this nick whatsoever, I can't say that I have seen it in the Highlands while I've lived here either,' his eyes began to glare with a fire, 'so unless you change your attitude in that department you can pack your suitcase and take the next train to England, is-that-clear!' The last part was emphasised so powerfully that it was heard in the main room but to his credit, White wasn't all that moved by it. He nodded and said calmly,

'Yes sir.' At this point, Avalon looked at the computer screen to check on the records but again he wasn't really reading it, he was just skirting through the relevant points. Then he saw his training list, it seemed that DC White went for every possible training that was going, just for the sake of it.

'So you did four years as a uniform in Sheffield,' began Avalon reading from the screen. The DC nodded and replied,

'Yes sir, I was born there and lived in the Sheffield area.'

'And then you took your exams after moving to Glasgow,' continued Avalon and then, 'why Glasgow and why come to Inverness?' White shrugged a little and then said,

'My family are originally from Glasgow and I heard they wanted people for the CID.'

'Everywhere does, not just Glasgow,' frowned Avalon.

'Well, I knew there was no chance of getting a decent post in Glasgow so I asked around for the best location,' he ended looking blankly at the DI.

'And you were told this was it?'

'Yes, sir.'

'Well, it's not, so they were wrong on that account, it's too quiet if it's promotion you're after.'

'Yes sir.' Avalon frowned again, yes, he was beginning to see why he wasn't liked, his manner seemed ambivalent or even slightly tinged with a degree of insubordination.

'Well, C Section is smaller than B Section,' began Avalon but he then considered that the disparity in numbers was falling, 'so we haven't got time to hold your hand,'

'Smaller sir, but a higher solve rate,' insisted White taking Avalon by surprise.

'What?'

'C Section has a higher solve rate than B Section,' repeated the DC. Avalon stared at him for a moment.

'Who says?' asked Avalon.

'The figures show it sir, B Section had a seventy-two percent solve rate and C Section is on eighty-nine.'

'But B Section has more robberies and violent

crime than we do, they are harder to solve being so many of them,' insisted Avalon.

'There aren't that many more sir, look at the figures, they tell the story,' explained White. Avalon shrugged, he wasn't one for taking notice of figures, as one high-ranking police officer had said quoting Aaron Levenstein, 'statistics are like bikinis, what they reveal is suggestive but what they hide is vital'. Yet he had to admit to himself, it was an interesting fact if indeed it *was* a fact. He knew that in Scotland the CID had a one hundred percent solve rate in murders, but he also knew that the solve rate for other crimes was woefully poor.

'Does DI Lasiter know about this?' asked Avalon squinting his eyes and speaking in a friendlier tone.

'Yes sir.' Avalon gave a slight smile but ceased when he noticed White watching him. He jumped to his feet and said abruptly,

'Come with me DC White.' Avalon walked into the main office and gave a little cough before adding, 'this is DC White, he's…' Avalon paused for a moment, he had to be careful what he said next, 'on loan to C Section for a few weeks,' and several unenthusiastic faces looked up. 'Rory,' show him the ropes and… well, you know,' and he returned to the booth. Avalon looked up towards Rory a few times and he could see that the body language showed Rory would rather just get on with his job. Ross and Rutherford totally ignored the newcomer, but it was early days.

~~~~~~~

Avalon began his Tuesday in a sour mood. The previous afternoon he had visited the hospital to find out what the outcome with the Rogart victim Mr McKeith was. It seemed the blow to the head had caused some complications and after a full scan, the doctor had decided that they would keep the patient in a coma until they had made a full assessment. Avalon saw that the investigation into an odd breaking and entering with assault could become a murder. It meant that he could justifiably put resources into the investigation but he didn't have resources going spare. It wasn't the only reason he was in a foul temper, he had spent the end of the evening at home chastising himself for his utter incompetence in dealing with the problems within his own team. To move Frazer out only to ask her back was unforgivable, and it irked him from every single angle he could think of. It hurt his pride, damaged his reputation and eroded his confidence, he was a second-rate copper doing a third-rate job of running a section. Dowd was right on the money when he said, as a normal officer he had nothing to lose and promotion was great for those who were competent to deal with it. DI Lasiter had a lesser solve rate, but Lasiter was everything Avalon was not and under these circumstances, it showed. Lasiter had even berated Avalon in private for his poor dealings of the issue with Ross and Frazer and that hurt, he was embarrassed about it and he had to either deal with it or get out of the kitchen.

As he climbed into the car, he vowed he would have a conclusion by the end of the day, a conclusion he would stick with whatever it was. He drove half a mile or so and pulled into a public car park just off the Old Edinburgh Road and turned on the radio with very low volume. The passenger door opened and a slim figure slid into the seat. The door closed and Avalon drove off

141

to find the A9 and head north. The two occupants said nothing until they were over the Kessock Bridge when Avalon spoke without looking to his left.

'Are you sure you want this?' There was a pause of several seconds and then Frazer replied.

'Aye, I'm sure...' and then another few seconds of silence, 'but ef you ever tell anyone, I'll do for you.'

'If I could keep it a secret for this long, why should I-'

'I'm not on about my past, I'm talking about the tears,' she interrupted. Avalon gave a hint of a smile. Frazer was more concerned about people knowing she shed tears than anything else in her life, she just didn't want anyone to think she wasn't as hard as she made out.

'It's a deal,' replied Avalon, 'as long as we can go back to me being the boss and you being a lowly DC?'

'Deal,' she replied.

For the rest of the journey north, Avalon explained to Frazer about the attack on Mr McKeith and he also told her the basics of the Strathpeffer attack and the background on two other cases that he thought were connected. She gave little back, but that was to be expected, it was probably going to take some time for Frazer to get back into her swing as a detective constable and later as he turned off the A9 towards Rogart, she made the first real conversation.

'Et's really odd, there are so many places I haven't seen that are so close by, I mean, I can count on one hand the times I have been north of Tain.'

'I've been up here quite a bit, but I suppose you go where the job takes you,' replied Avalon.

'I don't mean that, not the job,' she said as she

142

looked up at the hills, 'et's so...' she paused to find the words, 'wild I suppose up here and yet beautiful.'

'I like it, but I thought I was the only one, Ross hates it, Gordon says petrol cost too much to bother and Neil Dowd says the coastline's okay but he 'wouldna want tae have tae walk et',' replied Avalon doing his best impression of a Scottish accent.

'All this time I have known PC Dowd, and I didn't realise he had an Irish accent,' commented Frazer still taking in the sights.

'That was my unfortunate take on Dowd's cross-pollinated accent,' smiled Avalon, 'come to think of it, that's my generic Scottish accent,' and he indicated to the right and drove up a small track. When they reached the little house, Avalon tucked the car slightly off the road and they got out and walked to the door that had been locked as Avalon had asked. He took the key from his pocket and opened the door. He peered inside and was struck by a smell of dampness, a sort of fusty, old smell. He looked around for the storm lanterns he had seen on his previous visit and set about supplementing the poor natural light with the lanterns.

'Et's a bit minimalist,' commented Frazer from the kitchen.

'Yes, but I imagine it could be made cosy with a little thought,' agreed Avalon setting two chairs to the table.

'So what are we supposed to be looking for exactly?' asked Frazer scanning the chaos of the main room.

'How's your Latin?' he asked.

'Carpe diem, and then I'm done,' she shrugged as Avalon sat to the table. The pile of manuscripts was still neatly stacked on one side and he reached over for them.

'Hmm, not a bad phrase considering our job, but these are what I'm concerned with,' he explained, placing his hand gently on the parchments. He then took out his little notepad and pencil, and opened it ready to take notes. 'For some reason,' he began as Frazer sat on the other seat after brushing it with a rag she assumed was a tea towel, 'the attacker looked through these. It was he who piled them here so we know he was looking for something specific. Did he find it? Probably,' and he gave a nod.

'And what makes you conclude that?' asked Frazer looking over one of the sheets.

'They were neatly stacked for one, if he hadn't found what he was looking for, it's likely he would have created more damage and I think this pile would have been knocked over.' Frazer shrugged, she obviously didn't totally agree but she was keeping her thoughts to herself.

'But ef neither of us can read Latin, what are you expecting tae find?'

'I'm not sure,' frowned Avalon looking over the first sheet, 'anything that will give us a clue to why these scrolls are put neatly aside, placed as if they were read but not cast aside to be mixed in with the others.' For ten minutes or so they silently looked through the sheets and scrolls but there were so many Latin words that bore no similarity with anything either of them knew. Avalon tossed the last roll onto the table and looked around the room at the other scattered parchments and read through a few of them too.

'Many of the others are in old English or some other language,' said Avalon more to himself than Frazer.

'But that doesn't mean much, I'm guessing that there are loads of Latin ones too,' she answered. Avalon thought that was true but out of the twenty or so parchments and rolls on the table, all of them were written in Latin.

'There must be a clue to what he was searching for though and I'm guessing he piled up all the ones with Latin until he found the one he was looking for,' he insisted.

'Have you any idea at all what et might be?' she asked looking at a parchment she picked from the floor.

'Not really, the old man spoke of the Key Rolls as I explained earlier, but he says that went back to its owner.'

'And you think whoever did this didn't know that?' she asked.

'I did,' nodded Avalon, 'until I thought about these piled up on the table. Whoever this is, he is calculating and psychotic and probably has a short temper, I think if he hadn't found what he was looking for he would have burned this place to the ground.'

'Maybe we need t' get these t' some sort of expert then,' suggested Frazer picking up one of the parchments. Avalon nodded.

'I'll get a couple of bin liners from the car,' he said, 'we'll put the ones on the table in one bag and a random selection of the other stuff in the other.'

When they got back to the station, they walked up the stairs to the door of the Cave and Avalon stopped and looked at Frazer.

'Ready?' he asked, she nodded twice but looked far from ready, there was a doubt behind her eyes that wasn't usually there. Probably the same doubt Avalon had, but he surged forward into the room with the DC in tow and walked straight to the booth. The questioning faces that looked to the glass box weren't lost on the two of them but they stuck to their plan and sat each side of the desk and began to talk about their morning. Now and then, Avalon would surreptitiously steal a glance into the room to see the odd puzzled look and murmured comments. Inside the booth, the two of them had decided that there wasn't anything further that could be done on the Rogart case until a Latin language expert had studied the parchments that they had in two bin liners.

'Okay,' said Avalon raising his brows, 'time to tell the others,' and he stood and walked into the main office. He looked down at Angus White and said,

'DC White, there are two black bin liners downstairs being processed as evidence, will you see if they are ready and when they are, bring them up here?' White nodded and left the room as Frazer sat in her old seat. Wilson and Boyd had arrived shortly before Avalon and Frazer and so the whole of C Section, with the exception of the new boy, were present.

'I want a quick word while our newest recruit is out,' announced Avalon as he leaned on the table that held one of the printers. 'DC Frazer will not now be moving to B Section,' he gave a slight pause but there was no comment or reaction. 'She will remain here with us, but due to a... misunderstanding with DI Lasiter, we will retain DC White for at least a few weeks,' there were some subtle reactions to this, but he continued, 'so long as the DCI has no objections of course, so I hope you'll all try to help DC White fit in and yes I know he hasn't been popular with B Section, but this isn't B

Section,' and he raised his brows. He then gave a short pause and glanced out of the windows as he continued.

'I have to admit that I made errors in judgement over the incident with DS Ross and DC Frazer, I apologise for that and assure you it won't happen again.' He then looked back into the room and his eyes moved around the faces gathered. 'There is however to be a change of policy in C Section. I will no longer tolerate the idea that this is a green room where the professionalism and good behaviour of the section can be disregarded. We will all conduct ourselves in the Cave as we would outside this room.' Avalon noticed the body language of several of the team showed a certain displeasure to the announcement. 'I want this to be an end to this incident,' he paused and took a deep breath before continuing. 'On a separate note, we have a new case that will need resources injecting into it...' but he paused as the door opened, it was DC White carrying the two bags. He was about to ask what to do with them when Avalon continued with, 'DC White, drop the bags by my office and take a seat. As I was saying,' he continued turning back to the room, 'this new case needs resources and I know everyone has enough work for the rest of the decade, but the way things are going this could turn into a murder inquiry.' He looked over to Frazer and then back to the room. 'For the time being, myself and Frazer will begin on the case as I want Rory to get DC White up to speed with how we do things here,' and he noticed Mackinnon's shoulders sink slightly. 'Any questions?' he then asked. Not surprisingly, Ross was the only one to speak.

'Aye, I have a question, how does this new policy manifest itself exactly?' and he looked over to Frazer, 'I mean, do we all have to become the teacher's pet now or can we still speak to each other?' Avalon sighed, but it was Rory who answered.

'What is it with you Rossy?' he spat, 'one minute you don't want Megan out and when the boss brings her back you're still not happy?' Avalon was so taken aback with Rory's outburst he failed to speak.

'When I want an opinion from the Islands, I'll ask for it,' growled Ross. Avalon strode casually to Ross's desk and leaned down placing the palms of his hands on its top.

'If you have a problem with my systems, come and see me privately DS Ross, and let me remind you, DI Lasiter is still looking for a replacement,' he insisted with a glare. For several seconds Ross glared back and then announced,

'Aye, that's not a bad idea,' and he stood and walked out of the room closing the door behind him.

'Any more questions?' asked Avalon as if the previous one had been answered satisfactorily.

'I have one,' announced Rutherford.

'Go on Martin,' sighed Avalon beginning to think the whole section would revolt.

'Why is Ross such a knob?' For just a second there was a silence and then a few murmured sounds were heard.

'If I knew that DC Rutherford, I would be working on Harley Street instead of Inverness,' smiled Avalon as he turned to walk to the booth. He looked at Frazer and added, 'we better make a start then,' and he picked up the bin liners and dropped them in the booth. Frazer sat opposite and Avalon looked at her expression. She seemed shell-shocked, not the usual Frazer of old.

148

'That went well,' said Avalon raising his brows.

'Et's all my fault this,' she announced.

'Forget it, Lasiter won't have Ross, he was glad to be rid of him.'

'Really, I thought they got on okay when DI Lasiter ran C Section.'

'The DI knew he was a good detective, he just didn't rate his attitude, he even apologised when he sent Ross to work with me when I first came up here,' grinned Avalon.

'Do you see him the same?' asked Frazer.

'No,' answered the DI with a deep sigh, 'I don't, I mean I do think he's a good officer and all that but I've seen a side to Ross that…' he paused thinking through some of the good times spent with him, 'well, I just don't think he's that bad.' He gave a forced smile to Frazer and then announced, 'right, the case.'

Chapter Six

It was Thursday 20th of December, just five days until Christmas and Avalon wanted to try to make some headway on the collection of incidents he was now calling the Break-In Case. He had spent Tuesday afternoon and all the previous day looking through the other breaking and entering cases for the past two years. Though there had been a spate of them early in the year which DS Wilson and DC Boyd had worked on, *they* were perpetrated by a gang of three teenagers and had nothing in common with the recent ones. Only three were really similar, the two that Avalon had been trying to get information on and another that Frazer had remembered that she dealt with when Avalon was investigating the Jason Buchanan case, back in April. The first two had been in the same week in the same village where two houses had been entered and searched. The first one had been left in a state of utter devastation but nothing had been removed, the second was not as chaotic but a small bronze statue of a stag had been stolen. The conclusion was that the intruder had mistaken the addresses as they were similar.

The one Frazer had dealt with was just outside

Dingwall and concerned the removal of what was considered a worthless painting. The irony there was all the other paintings in the property had been removed from their frames and scattered on the floor but left, they *were* worth money. Both Avalon and Frazer had worked on the minutia of the reports until late in the afternoon. There had been just one other incident which could have been attributed to the case, an unusual theft of a garden statue from a property on the outskirts of the city. It was an odd water ornament, probably dating from the early Victorian period of a cherub with an unfeasible amount of wings at a property at Scaniport. The only reason Avalon saw it as a possibility was that the statue wasn't in plain view and so the culprit had to know it was there. Ross had returned to the Cave late morning but was obviously going through some kind of soul-searching as he remained silent and withdrawn. Both he and Rutherford left as soon as they could and Wilson and Boyd were also out most of the time leaving Rory to make the best of a bad job with DC White. Neither Frazer nor Avalon had any contact with Ross.

So it was that the two of them continued on the case during the morning utilising the whiteboard on the wall for the details.

'This doesn't make any sense at all, you know that,' insisted Frazer looking at the notes and the photographs on the board. Avalon looked too, folding his arms but making no comment except for a deep frown. Avalon was keeping a careful eye on Frazer, she seemed fine if a little too relaxed. He turned to the windows on the other side of the room and looked outside for a moment. Then he shrugged and sat on the edge of Frazer's desk as she continued to look over the notes on

151

the board. To his right, Rory was going through a few procedures with DC White but there was little if any conversation emanating from their direction.

'So what, no comment?' asked Frazer eventually turning to her boss.

'What is there to say?' shrugged Avalon again, 'we're looking for some kind of random object kleptomaniac that has a sense of the ridiculous, his quarry has no pattern whatsoever.' Frazer turned back to the board and pointed to the pictures or descriptions of the objects as she related them back to herself.

'A bronze stag, a worthless picture of a loch, a book on mountaineering, a cherub water feature and maybe an old manuscript probably written en Latin,' she said. She sighed and then added, 'they couldn't be any more random ef he had tried.'

'It's not a cherub,' chirped up White. Frazer looked at the young DC with a little disdain.

'I apologise DC White but I'm no expert on garden décor,' frowned Frazer sarcastically. That was more like Frazer, maybe she was getting some blood back into her attitude.

'So how would you describe it?' asked Avalon.

'Is that photo of the actual fountain?' asked White nodding to the board.

'Yes, it's made of metal, painted with gilding on it,' nodded Avalon, 'it looks a little less shiny now by all accounts, the image was taken some years ago.'

'Well, shiny or not, what you have there is a Seraphim,' explained White.

'A what?' questioned Avalon widening his eyes.

'A Seraphim, to Christians, one of the higher angels tasked with the never-ending maintenance of

God's throne,' explained White as he began typing into the computer.

'You better not be winding me up DC White or I'll-'

'Here,' he interrupted and spun around the screen a little so Avalon could see it. 'A six-winged angel, sometimes associated with fire or heat I believe.'

'Are you religious DC White?' asked Avalon reading the internet explanation.

'No sir, but then again, I don't believe that Bilbo Baggins existed, but it didn't stop me reading Lord of the Rings.' White was obviously well-read but Avalon was having trouble holding back his temper. The young man seemed to be trying to wind him up. Instead of berating him, however, he turned to Frazer and said,

'Find the details of the owner of the statue and give them a call, see if they know what the statue is about,' and as she looked at the records, Avalon continued to read the explanation of the Seraphim, looking back over to the whiteboard when he had read enough. Frazer came back to his side.

'No one en, I've left a message so they should ring back,' explained Frazer.

'Could this be religious, or am I jumping to conclusions over one discovery?' asked Avalon to no one in particular.

'Well, ef a parchment did go missing from the house at Rogart, et's possible et had some religious connection but a stag and a book about mountaineering?' commented Frazer a little questioningly.

'Hmm,' sighed Avalon, 'the stag could be a pre-Christian icon but unless someone knows otherwise I wouldn't have thought climbing mountains was an

153

official religion yet,' then asked, 'what about the locations, are they connected at all?'

'No,' insisted Frazer, 'we went through that yesterday, on the face of et, there es nothin' to connect these crimes.'

'Except for the fact that the perpetrator of each one is single-minded and stops at nothing to get what he's after,' replied Avalon, 'and that smacks of fanaticism.' Frazer shook her head slightly with frustration and returned to her desk where she sat and tapped her fingers on the table. The room had gone quiet, and the trail was cold.

'What about the Latin language expert,' asked Avalon suddenly, 'did we get anywhere with that?'

'There's a guy that lives en Edinburgh according to Sarah Underwood,' announced Frazer still looking at the whiteboard from her seat, 'but he can't get up here as he's working overseas at the moment.'

'There must be someone else?' said the DI with an amount of frustration.

'Aye there es but she says he's a wee bit...'

'A wee bit what?' asked Avalon as she trailed off.

'Well, she mentioned that he can 'go off on a tangent', in her words,' explained Frazer as she looked round to him.

'What's that mean?' asked the boss.

'He's a weird sort of nationalist from what I can gather,' Frazer wore a deep frown, 'she did say that his field isn't just Latin either.'

'You're not making a lot of sense,' said Avalon returning the frown with interest, 'can he help us or not?' Frazer hesitated for a moment and then said,

'Other words she used were, vague, evasive,

manipulative and odd.'

'But can he help us?' asked Avalon again.

'He's studied ancient Greece and Rome and lectured for eight years in Glasgow on...' she paused to type something into her computer, 'Chilieteris,' she eventually said and looked back to Avalon, 'which et seems es a contemporary history of Rome.'

'So I'm guessing he can read Latin?'

'Yes,' she nodded.

'And that DC Frazer was the answer I was looking for originally.' Avalon wasn't being facetious, he was just trying to inject a little light-heartedness into the tedium of the day.

'When I say yes,' then Frazer added, 'I haven't asked him, I suppose he would.' Avalon gave her a brief frown and then said,

'Well, you can find that out when you contact him then can't you?' She picked up her phone and set about arranging to meet the man who according to Sarah Underwood, 'could be a little difficult'. He had another cursory glance at the whiteboard and then returned to the booth where he continued a task he had begun earlier, taking the manuscripts from the bin bags and placing them carefully into evidence boxes. As he handled those ancient documents, he couldn't help thinking they were trying to tell him something, trying to give him a clue to what this was all about. If only he could read Latin. Something suddenly popped into the back of his mind, something to do with his phone. He instinctively felt his pocket and realised what it was. That damn phone was somewhere in a small copse of trees near Lentran and the weather was looking more like rain than ever. He strolled into the main office.

'I'm off out for an hour,' he began, 'keep me posted,' but it was a pointless addition to the statement, they couldn't keep him posted because he didn't have a phone.

~~~~~~~

Charles Oswald Keane was a man who always thought that he was just a pawn in the game of life, a game for three to six people played only by the gods when they became tired of wars and famine. Part of his reasoning was his name. He hated the name Charles, it couldn't be shortened to anything better either. His boss Sandra called him Charlie, his workmates called him Chaz and his wife called him Chonkers, but that wasn't a sobriquet he would generally admit to. Even his second name couldn't be brought into play either, who wanted to be called Oswald? His great uncle had seemed happy enough with the moniker but *he* was a product of the Victorian era.

The only nickname he had become happy with was one given to him by the two Englishmen that worked in his office. They called him 'Wag' but when asked why they both admitted they didn't know, they just called people with the name Charlie, Wag. Charles had researched the source on the internet but found no definitive answer, either way, 'Wagger Keane' sounded okay to him, less formal, more friendly. It had only gone so far to placate his hatred of the name as he still cursed his parents for giving him the initials that inevitably spelled out COK, this had gone down really well at school and even as an adult nearly everyone he came into contact with noticed it. As he sat in his car, parked in a lay-by just outside Inverness, he listened to his boss Sandra give him his 'to do list' for the week. He wasn't taking any notice however, instead, he was considering what name he would have preferred. He didn't really know but just as he was wondering if a traditional Scottish name would have been more to his liking, he noticed a black Audi drive slowly past and pull into the lay-by. He watched the single male occupant look into his rear-view mirror and then get out of the car. The man stood and closed the car door, buttoning up his jacket and tightening his tie against the cold and then casually nodded to Charles who gave the slightest nod in return. The man then looked into the copse of trees and headed towards them, obviously going to relieve himself. Charles considered that the fabric of the modern world was coming apart at the seams, he didn't blame the man for relieving himself by the road, what else was there to do?

The so-called servants of the populace, the civil servants grouped under the noun 'Council', had decreed that civilised society could go to hell and public toilets were a luxury that the proletariat would have to do without. After all, what concern was it of the hoi polloi? They just paid the Council employees' wages and provided them with some of the best pension packages available. Then it occurred to him that the man wasn't actually having a pee after all, he seemed to be rummaging around in the undergrowth and that disgusted Charles. It was a pull-in, at the side of the road where amorous couples probably indulged each other and there could be all manner of revolting items in that undergrowth. He felt ill and suddenly realised that Sandra was still rambling on at the other end of the phone. To be on the safe side he threw in the odd 'yes,' and 'that's right,' but his eyes watched the odd man in the undergrowth very carefully. When Charles forgot who he was talking to and reverted to 'wife' answers rather than 'boss' answers, he heard Sandra's voice ask,

'Are you being offhand with me?'

'Sorry, what?' asked Charles still watching the man.

'You just said 'yes dear','

'Did I?' he said, 'look, Sandra, there's this guy just pulled up in a car and he's started rummaging around in the lay-by, it's quite worrying, I think I'll have to go, I'll ring you later.'

'Is he a tramp or something?'

'No, as I said, he pulled up in a car, he's wearing a suit.'

'Maybe... he's picking wildflowers... for his wifie?' stammered Sandra, trying to think of a reasonable explanation and not managing it.

'Flowers? Have you seen some of these pull-ins, the only thing that will grow here is bacteria,' and then he changed his tone, 'he's now taken a notepad out of his pocket and he's writing something in it.'

'He could be doing a survey.'

'In a suit?' asked Charles raising the pitch of his voice, 'he'd be better off in hazmat protective clothing,' and then added in a quieter voice, 'oh my god, he's looking over to me now... shite, he's coming over, listen I have to go, I may have to make a quick getaway,' and the phone went dead.

The man smiled at Charles, a sort of embarrassed, puckered lip sort of smile and he raised his brows for a split second. Charles wondered about hitting the door locks but he didn't want to look too scared so he nodded slightly and wound the window down just an inch or so.

'Hello, I see you have a phone,' the man said, 'I wonder,' he continued bending down slightly, 'could you ring this number for me?' he asked holding out a small piece of paper he had ripped out of his notebook.

'Certainly not,' replied Charles, his finger hovering over the door lock button in the centre console.

'Oh, sorry,' replied the man, and he fumbled about in his jacket pocket. For the briefest second, Charles considered he was about to see the business end of a knife or even a gun but all he saw was a wallet, an open wallet, that seemed to contain the warrant card of a police officer. 'I'm Detective Inspector Avalon from Inverness, I'd be very grateful if you could help, I'm working on a very puzzling case.' Charles took the paper from the man through the tiny gap above the window and looked at the number. The man in the suit withdrew and returned to the spot he had previously been in the woodland. Charles dialled the number on the paper and listened. He could hear the ringtone down his phone but there was no reply, it just kept ringing. The strange man in the suit suddenly leaped into action and bent down into the grass to retrieve something. He then walked back to the car holding up one hand to Charles who heard his phone go dead. In the man's other hand, he was holding what looked like a mobile phone. As Charles slowly lowered the phone from his ear, he looked once again at the number on the scrap of paper as the black Audi started up and turned in the road heading off the way it had come. The driver once again raised his hand.

'What the hell was that about?' asked Charles to

159

himself, staring out of the window towards the trees. He then realised he was still holding the bit of paper. 'Ugh,' he cried as he cast it through the gap in the window with disgust.

~~~~~~~

As soon as Avalon returned to the Cave, he could see Frazer had something for him and he nodded to the booth, she followed.

'I found my phone by the way,' he smiled.

'I didn't know you had lost et,' replied Frazer

'Yes, I threw it out of the car window...' he paused looked directly at her, 'the other day... when you...' he stopped as he decided he had said enough.

'Oh,' she replied a little embarrassed, 'I didn't know,' and she looked down at the floor. As Avalon sat he saw how stupid they were both being, it was as if they had been having an affair or something, both seemed uncomfortable with the fact that Avalon had held her as she sobbed herself back to something resembling the old Frazer. She probably saw it as a weakness but Avalon saw it as proof that under Frazer's dark and insular exterior, there was a normal person that just wanted to hide that normality from herself.

'So I assume you have something for me?' he asked breaking the silence.

'Oh, yes,' she blinked, 'I have been en touch with this guy that Sarah told me about, to be honest, he seems fine on the phone, a little abrupt but as long as we go tae him he'll see us anytime.'

'Good, did you ask...' began Avalon but Frazer got the drift of what he was about to ask.

'He can read Latin but he said something about et not being a single language like English or French. He says en some ways et's more like Gaelic.'

'Fine, we'll sort out a good time to see him and call him back,' nodded the DI.

'Oh,' added Frazer, 'the people with the statue got back in touch, I think the woman thought we had found et, I asked her what the statue was supposed to be and she insisted et was an angel, when I asked her ef she knew what a Seraphim was she said she did.' Frazer paused, and a frown broke across her brow.

'What?' asked Avalon.

'Et may be my imagination but she seemed tae change after that, you know, the excitement en her voice thinking we had et and then...'

'I tend to go with womanly intuition but I think you may be overdoing it there,' smiled Avalon.

'I don't know boss,' replied Frazer frowning again, 'she just seemed less willing t' talk.' Avalon thought about this, what might be the reasons for that anyway? Could the statue be cultish, an icon of some sort with a more spiritual meaning than the angel of God's throne? It didn't seem likely, it was just a water feature after all.

'Well,' sighed Avalon, 'if you have doubt, take Rory and go and have a nosey around, I'll leave that with you.'

'And leave you with DC White?' She didn't smile but Avalon heard an element of playfulness in her voice.

'Well, maybe Rory could do with a break from it,' smiled the boss as he nodded in Mackinnon's general direction, 'I might have a trip to see this Latin expert.'

Frazer nodded, she stood and walked into the Cave and had words with Rory who seemed visibly relieved to be going out. Avalon smiled, Rory sometimes reminded him of a schoolboy, he had retained an element of boyish mischievousness and yet he was going to make an excellent detective. The smile soon left his face when he looked over to Ross. The DS was staring out of the window, it was something he was doing most of the time these days, Rutherford seemed affected by it too, Avalon knew from experience that if either one of the partnership was out of kilter with the other, a bad time would be had by all. The first opportunity Avalon had to speak with Rutherford came when Ross left the room without speaking to anyone.

'It looks like your friend is taking all this very seriously,' suggested Avalon as he perched on the edge of a desk and folded his arms. He had spoken quietly as White was still in the room but Rutherford had no reservations and spoke normally.

'Aye, the weepy wee bastard needs to grow up ef y' ask me, it's like working with a lassie who's just found out she's no' pregnant and might have tae work for a livin'.'

'I suppose he feels he's to blame,' shrugged Avalon.

'Enough tae pack et all en y' mean?' asked Rutherford looking straight at Avalon.

'What do you mean?'

'He handing his notice en, he's that friggin' weepy about et,' sighed the big man shaking his head.

'Is he serious?' asked the DI unfolding his arms.

'Tae be honest boss, I don't give a shite one way or the other, et don't matter what he does 'cos the sun

162

will still go down tonight and come up again en the morning'.' Rutherford then went back to his work but then thought about what he had said and looked back up to the boss. 'That about the sun was me just bein' figurative o' course, I would want you thinkin' you would wake up in the mornin' and find the sun somewhere en the sky.'

'No, I sort of understood that Martin,' smiled Avalon, but the smile was forced. He was worrying that Ross may be thinking of quitting the force over a disagreement. He made his way back to the booth, picked up his jacket and left directing his comment mainly to DC White.

'I'll be back in fifteen.'

Avalon knocked on the door and walked in. DCI Croker was at his desk, leaning over an open record file vigorously writing with his biro. The DI never understood that in these days of computers and electronic storage, why Croker seemed to be forever writing manually. Avalon liked working with the old fashion system but when it came to reports, the cut-and-paste method worked a great deal better than handwriting. Croker looked up over his spectacles and then immediately back down.

'Ah, DI Avalon, I wondered how long it would be before I saw you.'

'Sir?' questioned the DI.

'Well, I assume you have come about that little envelope on the corner of my desk,' replied the DCI without stopping his writing or looking up. Avalon saw the envelope, it looked like someone had dropped it off recently.

'Er, what is it sir?' asked Avalon quite shocked that Ross had gone through with it.

'Unless my many years in the force have been for nothing, I would assume that when a DS comes in here with an envelope, a DS who I have spoken to on no more than four occasions I might add, and asks me if I will accept an envelope, I assume it is something serious.'

'It's likely,' nodded Avalon looking at the envelope as if it were about to fly around the room. Croker finished writing and placed his pen to the side of the report. He sighed, removed his spectacles and looked up to Avalon.

'I told that DS what I'm about to tell you, I'm rather busy at the moment and any further paperwork will have to wait,' he paused momentarily, 'so is there something I should know about, DI Avalon?' Avalon put on a vague expression and shrugged.

'Err... nothing I'm aware of sir,' and he opened his eyes wider.

'So what have you come to see me about?' asked Croker leaning back in his seat and looking at the envelope.

'I can't remember sir, whatever it was has gone completely out of my mind,' replied Avalon.

'I think it's something that happens to us at a certain age DI, I sometimes forget things, I'm sure I'll forget about that DS coming to see me earlier.'

'Yes sir, you probably will,' nodded Avalon looking back to the envelope.

'Carry on then,' nodded Croker, and he replaced his spectacles and picked up the pen to continue with his work. As Avalon turned, he slid the envelope off the table and into his pocket. As he put his hand on the door handle, Croker added,

'Oh, and keep it safe,' Avalon turned but Croker was hard at his task again, yet he still managed to add, 'you can always cross out the name, and put your own on there when the time comes.' Avalon paused for a moment, was that the DCI showing a little humour, or did he mean it? Avalon left before there was time for the Detective Chief Inspector to change his mind.

Back in the Cave, Ross had returned but Avalon simply didn't quite know what to do with his new knowledge and for the time being decided to ignore it. He sat at his desk and looked at the note Frazer had left with the contact details of the man that may be able to read the Latin parchments. Avalon wondered if he ought to know more about him, and anyway, it gave him a chance to speak to Sarah.

'I don't suppose Sarah is about is she?' he asked the person who answered the phone at the forensics lab. After a few seconds, there was a crackle from the phone.

'*Hello, what can I do for you, Detective Avalon?*' Avalon wasn't sure, but he thought he could hear a note of a smile in her voice, a slight bubble in the way the words were mouthed.

'I'm sorry to bother you but I wondered if you could give me a little bit of information,' he said, testing the water.

'*It's no bother, and you know if I can help I will.*' The bubble seemed to have gone, maybe he was playing it *too* safe, maybe she wanted him to bubble back.

'It's about this Steven Kerr, you mentioned to DC Frazer, you told her that he can be a bit difficult,' he had read the name from his notes, 'I wondered if there was something about him that might win him over?'

'*I don't know him that well, I've met him through work but I do know I didn't much care for him,*' she replied, '*he's very knowledgeable and highly respected but...*' she ended without any conclusion.

'Oh well, it was just a thought,' replied Avalon and was about to change the subject when she thought of something.

'*I believe he likes whisky,*' she added, '*last time I saw him he was babbling on about tourism and the whisky industry.*'

'Well, it's not the sort of thing I was thinking of but it may be an ice-breaker,' laughed Avalon trying to lighten the conversation. There was a pause as he tried to pluck up the courage to ask her out again though previously it was she who had asked him. 'Are you going away for Christmas?' was the lame question he eventually tried, he thought it would ease them into personal chat rather than professional conversation.

'*Away? No,*' she replied, '*I'll probably end up working through most of the holiday anyway, I usually do.*'

'Yes, me too,' he laughed again, 'I just wondered if you would be seeing your family?'

'*Not at all,*' came the reply, '*my mother is not the sort of person I would want to be around at Christmas, I will probably spend it alone watching repeats on TV and wishing there was something better to do.*' There was a pause, '*what about you?*'

'Same for me,' replied Avalon trying to think of a way of making the conversation more upbeat, 'the difference is, I don't have a TV to watch repeats on.'

'*You'll have to come and watch mine,*' she laughed, '*you don't know what you're missing, watching*

166

programmes that were mediocre the first time around.'
He wanted to say, 'I'd love to,' but it sounded too cheesy and so, as usual, he ran out of other options. In desperation, he just threw some words together and hoped that his mouth could sort them out because his brain certainly couldn't.

'I know it's difficult given the fact that we both have no fixed working hours, but...' the pause wasn't great but he felt self-conscious about it, 'rather than the two of us sitting alone three miles distant, why don't we try to sort out something to do?' Before Avalon had time to elaborate she said,

'*I'd love that,*' and there was another pause, '*not that we can carve it in stone of course,*' she replied and Avalon realised for the first time, he wasn't the only one feeling a little uncomfortable in this situation.

'So,' began Avalon tentatively, 'we'll get our heads together and think of something to do... but if either of us has to work...' he paused but she offered no reply, 'we try to reschedule?' It sounded more like they were setting up a business meeting than a date but Sarah somehow got the gist of what he was trying to say.

'*I think that would work,*' she eventually agreed, '*so how does getting our heads together manifest itself?*' Avalon suddenly became more confident, maybe it was the fact that he felt he was close to ending the conversation without making any decisions. He laughed, it was fake but it lead into what he was about to say.

'I can't believe we are making a...' he was about to say 'pigs ear' but given that Sarah was a vegan he changed it to, 'hash of this, what if we go for a drink somewhere and have a chat about it?

'*Sounds like a plan.*'

'What about Friday evening, as things stand I should be able to make it?'

'*Tomorrow, yes that sounds good, when and where?*' Avalon hadn't realised it was that far down the week, it was flying by as usual but he didn't know where to suggest. It was just a drink so anywhere would do, or were drinks not vegan? It was so complicated working around this woman but he didn't ever doubt that it was worth it.

'I've really no idea where to go, any preferences?' She thought about it for a moment and though she admitted she rarely went into town to drink, she had suggested The Waterfront, and though Avalon had never been in it, he knew where it was. So that was it, he was meeting Sarah for the second evening out, this time in Inverness at a riverside pub at seven-thirty on Friday. That had been a productive phone call. He now knew something about Steven Kerr that might enable him to ease information from him and he also had another 'date' with Sarah Underwood. He decided to phone Mr Kerr and make an appointment to go over and see him but twenty minutes later, his upbeat mood was changed as Ross walked into the booth.

'Here's my report on the theft of garden equipment at Smithton,' he said abruptly tossing the sheet on Avalon's desk, as he turned to leave Avalon said,

'We need to talk.'

'Fire away,' replied Ross turning to look at Avalon. He looked bored and spiritless.

'Not here, not now,' explained the DI, 'somewhere quiet, a pub maybe.'

'I don't have the time,' said Ross with a blank

expression and turned to leave again.

'Fine, if that's the way you want it,' sighed Avalon, and he turned to his computer adding, 'I suppose it's easier to walk away from something rather than admit you were wrong.' Ross stopped by the doorway of the booth, at first he said nothing and Avalon assumed he was trying to calm himself before speaking. That's what Avalon was hoping, if Ross walked away now there was no more Avalon could do, but if he could keep his interest for just long enough…

'You know,' Ross began, and he slowly turned to face the boss, 'you always think it's you don't you, what if it isn't, what if it's something else?' Avalon pushed out his bottom lip and his eyes moved to one side as he thought about what Ross had said.

'Well,' he began as he looked back to Ross, 'I assumed it was just about me yes, but even more reason to have a talk if there is something else on your mind.'

'You can't solve everyone's problems DI Avalon, some of us have problems that can't *be* solved,' began Ross leaning casually on the door frame, 'you may see yourself as a crusader for the good guys, someone who can think through a problem and sort out their lives but-'

'I have never thought that and you know it,' interrupted Avalon rather more sharply than he intended, 'you're just talking for the sake of it. I can't sort out your problems or Megan's problems or anyone else's, I can't sort out my own problems for Christ's sake,' and he took a breath and leaned back in his chair. In a more calm tone, he added, 'I just don't want to throw everything up in the air that we've worked for here, I have admitted my mistakes and it's time for you to do the same and get on with it. I just thought that mulling it all over with a pint may help, clearly I was wrong again,' and he leaned forward and looked at his computer screen. Ross was silent and stationary, still leaning on the doorframe. He looked down at Avalon hardly blinking but showing no signs of leaving. Avalon looked back to him and thought about the phrase Croker had used as a dismissal.

'Carry on DS Ross,' he said with a slight frown. Ross looked at him for a moment, took a deep breath and returned to his desk.

~~~~~~~

Rory and Megan came straight to the booth when they returned, Frazer sat and Mackinnon stood at the door leaning on the frame in the same place Ross had stood over an hour ago.

'So what did you find?' asked Avalon.

'Not everythin' that's for sure,' replied Frazer folding her arms.

'What's that supposed to mean?'

'She's hiding something.'

'About her garden ornament?' asked Avalon questioningly, and with a deep frown, 'what's to hide except it's re-constituted stone and not real marble?'

'But et es marble and et's real gold on the decorations, she had et commissioned,' explained Frazer leaning forward a little.

'Go on,' insisted the DI still frowning.

'She was very matter-of-fact when we first started talking to her, she just told us that they used tae have a similar statue but et got broken when they moved house. That's why they had the new one made.'

'It must have cost a bob or two then,' nodded

170

Avalon.

'Aye,' agreed Frazer, 'but lookin' at the house they can well afford et.'

'Did she say what the significance was then?' asked the boss.

'Tae start with she wouldn't say, but smart arse here,' she nodded up to Rory who was smiling, 'had done some research, and he asked her ef she was religious, she admitted she was, and Rory asked her ef her family motto had anything to do with the statue. From there on she went a little pale.'

'What's her name and what's the family motto?'

'Sinclair, Rosemary Sinclair, and the motto es, *Commit thy works to god.*'

'So that all makes sense doesn't it, being religious and having a Christian motto lets her off the hook?' asked Avalon.

'Aye but get this, after some checking up, we found out that's her maiden name, her husband's name was Roger Bell but soon after they were married, he changed his name by deed poll and both the children are now called Sinclair.'

'It's not much of a revelation Miss Frazer,' questioned Avalon with a slight smirk, 'she's probably just proud of her Scottish name and she's probably the only child.'

'Aye, that's right, she es,' frowned Frazer folding her arms once more.

'So what is it you think she's hiding?' asked Avalon not wishing to crush totally, any theory she had.

'Rory asked her why the Seraphim and not an angel,' said Frazer.

'And?' asked the boss holding out his arms to

171

Mackinnon.

'Well boss,' answered Rory standing upright, surprised to be brought into the conversation, 'she got evasive and said 'is there that much of a difference between an angel and a Seraph?' and that surprised me, it's an older word and in some ways means something different, and we had never called it that,' explained Rory. 'I only knew the word because of the research I did and so it occurred to us that the choice of the Seraphim is not accidental and has a reasoning she's not willing to share with us.'

'I still think it's coincidental but check through all the other items on the case to see if anything else can be connected with Sinclair's or Seraphims,' insisted Avalon as he had a thought. 'Thinking about it, the man over at Strathpeffer became evasive after he knew he had a book missing,' the Boss looked thoughtful.

'You think the items taken might not be so random after all?' asked Rory, clearly thinking the same thing. Avalon shrugged and then nodded with a sigh.

'It's beginning to seem that way but until we find more out just keep at it,' he said. Rory nodded and went to his desk as Avalon spoke to Frazer. 'I contacted this Steven Kerr, and I have set up a meeting with him in the morning...' he paused, 'interested?'

'Yeah, o' course,' nodded Frazer, 'I want t' see exactly how 'difficult' this man es.'

Chapter Seven

For most normal people, the countdown to Christmas was on. For Avalon, he just wished the whole thing would be over so he didn't feel guilty about the staff in C Section with families having to bow to the commitment of their job. If they were lucky, nothing serious would crop up and the cover could be lessened slightly. Avalon, of course, would have to be content with a couple of days off if he was lucky but there was some consolation if Miss Underwood could manage a little R&R too, Christmas this year would be better than it normally was. He was reasonably optimistic as he reached the station and as he entered the Cave, he closed his eyes breathing in the gentle aroma of the fresh coffee. Ross and Rutherford were out, but he knew they would be as they were helping out B Section and the coastguard on a tip-off about a yacht that was about to sail down the Moray Firth. He didn't have any details and thankfully he wouldn't have to be involved but it meant that Ross and Rutherford would have to find time to make up the lost hours. Frazer came to the booth and sat opposite. She looked somewhat better than she had of late, there was a little makeup on her face too.

'We'll have to take the box of manuscripts with us,' he said nodding towards the evidence box in the corner.

'I'm looking forward to finding out what es actually en those documents,' she said looking at the box.

'Probably shopping lists made by twelfth-century monks knowing our luck,' replied Avalon giving a little grin. She shrugged as if ignoring the expression and asked,

'Have you got anything for DC White, he's up t' speed and I think Rory has had enough of him.'

'What do you make of him?' he asked.

'New face,' shrugged Frazer, 'probably another dick head.' She stopped and thought about her answer and attempted a more conservative opinion. 'He seems bright enough but doesn't say much and when he does ET's to usually t' correct someone, I'm guessing he's never going tae be liked.'

'He seems the sort that isn't looking to be liked,' replied Avalon checking that he had everything, then said, 'I suppose I ought to give him something but with no idea of what he's capable of...' he trailed off staring at the man through the glass partition. 'I know,' he suddenly said. He stood and walked into the main room with Frazer following carrying the evidence box.

'DC White.'

'Yes sir,' he replied.

'You don't need to keep up the 'yes sir' stuff,' frowned Avalon, 'I want you do look through the details of the case myself and DC Frazer are working on,' he turned to Mackinnon, 'pull him up what we have Rory.' Mackinnon nodded as if he didn't have enough to do. 'I

174

think we need a fresh pair of eyes on this,' he continued back towards White, 'we seem to have hit a brick wall. We're off to see someone about getting the scrolls translated, hopefully, we might have something new when we get back.'

Steven Kerr lived in Dingwall and as Avalon brought the car to a halt at the address, he looked round to Frazer.

'Well here goes, let's hope he knows his stuff.' A small woman in her fifties opened the door to the house. It was a double-fronted building just off the main road and had a walled garden. Each side of it stretched a terrace, a testament to the odd mix of architecture to be found in Dingwall. The little woman beckoned them in and showed them to a lounge, she didn't ask them to sit but she seemed to have a pleasant nature.

'I'll go and tell him you're here,' she said in a soft, Scottish voice but once she had returned to the corridor the two detectives heard her shout in a raucous manner,

'Archie, it's the filth, they're here to see you,' and then she returned and said politely,

'He'll be but a minute,' and she left mumbling something like 'what has the wee bastard been up tae now?' Avalon drew a breath and widened his eyes to Frazer who couldn't help a whiff of a smile across her mouth. A large man arrived seconds later, he was dressed very casually and had a mop of greying hair all except for the top where he was bald. He was probably in his late fifties but looked a little older, probably due to his pale skin.

'Detective Avalon?' he asked in a clear voice

175

with a very slight Scottish accent.

'Yes, this is Detective Constable Frazer.' The man nodded.

'Don't mind Irene, she's harmless, she's a little…' and he made a circular motion to the side of his head with his index finger, 'you better come to the study,' and he lead them down the hall to a side door.

'Is she your wife, Mr Kerr?' asked Avalon.

'Irene? No, my sister, I never married,' and he showed them into the study. It was a room that was probably fifteen by twenty feet with a large bay window at one end but there were so many books that it seemed like a very small space where his desk and computer sat. Several bookshelves went this way and that, like a maze made from publications rather than hedging. Even the window was half obscured by books and Kerr pointed to a pile of books shaped like a chair. 'Take a seat,' he said. Avalon realised it was made of wood but fashioned to look like books. 'Oh, I'm sorry,' he said looking at Frazer and realising there was only one seat, 'you can fetch a chair from the dining room if you wish.

'I'll be fine thank you Mr Kerr,' nodded Frazer, and she casually looked around the room with her hands clasped behind her back.

'Oh, the chair,' commented Kerr noticing Avalon looking at it, 'it was made by a friend but honestly, I think I'd rather have real books.'

'It's very unusual,' nodded Avalon and then looked up to the man adding, 'your sister called you Archie.'

'Yes,' nodded the man, 'it was her husband's name, she has some goods days but not many.' He gave a slight cough and then turned to his computer screen. 'I

Googled your name before you arrived,' began the man, 'but to my surprise, it came up with a man who made soft porn movies, did you know about that?' Avalon noticed Frazer look towards him.

'Yes, I did Mr Kerr but I assure you, I'm a very different James Avalon,' and he resisted any sort of smile.

'So,' said Kerr clapping his hands together, 'you said this is to do with Latin parchments, I have to admit I'm not the best equipped for this kind of work, Latin is a very odd language and changes somewhat through the millennia.'

'I realise that Mr Kerr but we are short on time and anything you can give us would help,' explained Avalon.

'You are not the only ones short on time detective, I too have a very busy schedule and if I were to spend any significant...' as he spoke, Avalon slowly took a half bottle of whisky out and placed it on the edge of his desk. It was a single malt and its amber glow was increased by the light from a small desk lamp that stood close by, '...time on this... it would seriously...' the man eventually trailed off.

'What's this, a bribe of some sort?' asked the man with a hint of a grin.

'Not at all, Mr Kerr, I heard it was your birthday, and I thought I would bring you a gift,' announced Avalon looking at the bottle. Frazer had been craning her neck reading the spines of some of the many books but she looked over when she saw the bottle.

'I wonder why it is Detective,' asked Kerr, 'that when a man such as myself who can afford to purchase many bottles of single malt as he would wish, feels duty-bound to accept a gift of this sort with good humour?'

'Maybe because when such a gift is given, the recipient knows that someone spent the time to find out what that person would want for their birthday,' offered Avalon. Kerr raised his eyebrows.

'My birthday was in August but I did notice that there wasn't a gift from you,' smiled Kerr and Avalon nodded in deference, 'but this more than makes up for that omission,' concluded Kerr lifting the bottle and placing it by his side.

'So why are these documents significant' began Kerr, 'and what are you expecting to find?' he asked.

'We believe that a suspect in a crime singled out these documents and we are just wondering why,' explained Avalon, 'anything that links them together would be extremely useful.'

'I see, do you have them with you?'

'Yes, they're in the car,' and Avalon made to move but Frazer beat him to it.

'I'll get them Boss,' and he handed her the keys. While Frazer went to fetch the box, Kerr gave a frown and said,

'There's a chap lives out in the wilds further north, you know he would probably do a better job that I could, he's a great deal more-'

'A man by the name of McKeith?'

'Yes, the very same, how...' but Kerr ceased speaking, he could see a stern look in the detective's eyes that told him something was wrong.

'These documents are from the home of Mr McKeith, he was attacked some days ago and is now in a coma.'

'Oh,' swallowed the man, 'I'm sorry about that,

he's an odd little man but very knowledgeable.' Frazer returned with the box and placed it on a small pile of books close to the man.

'Well, I better take a look,' and he pulled the lid off the box and picked out the first parchment. He changed his spectacles dropping the ones he was wearing to his chest held to his person by a lanyard. He untied the ribbon from the roll and flattened it on his desk placing two glass paperweights on opposite corners to keep it in place. The man mumbled to himself and went to the next parchment. Avalon looked round to Frazer who simply raised her brows and continued looking through the books, pulling one out of its place now and then to skip through its pages. Avalon looked over at the bottle by Kerr's side and considered that although it was morning, a shot of the whisky wouldn't go amiss. Kerr stopped reading well before he had seen all the documents and removed his spectacles and turned to Avalon.

'I hate to say it Detective Avalon, but I can find no particular connection in these documents,' sighed the man, 'this one,' he singled out a parchment its dried fabric crackling with his touch, 'is a list of debtors to someone called Guilem de Ranville and this one over here are notes taken by a monk of Tewkesbury on the cost of a new grain store,' he paused, 'nothing of any significance I fear... except for the date of course but I'm sure you have noticed that.' Avalon glanced over to Frazer who looked slightly alarmed.

'The date Mr Kerr?' inquired Avalon.

'Yes,' frowned Kerr, 'you mean you haven't noticed the dates? They are mostly in Roman numerals, it's schoolboy stuff.' He noticed the look on Avalon's face and tried to soften the blow a little. 'I mean such as here,' and he chose a random parchment, 'you probably wouldn't be able to decipher the Latin that says, 'on the morrow of St Cuthbert' or maybe not the 'in anno dominus noster' but the MCCCX is as clear as day.' Avalon suddenly felt very foolish, and he tried to push the error aside.

'Are they all the same year and would the Julian calendar effect it?' he asked.

'They range in years but they all fall in a period of twenty years or so,' explained Kerr replacing his normal spectacles, 'and no, unless you are trying to track down a particular day, the calendar matters little.' Avalon was still stinging from the error but he tried to keep the momentum going, it was clear that the date was significant to the attacker, but how? Nothing else on his collection seemed to be from that date but then Avalon had an idea.

'I suppose you have heard of the Chinon Chart?' he asked.

'Of course,' nodded Kerr, 'and it is of a similar date but if this is leading where I think it is I have to warn you Inspector, I am very dismissive of the theories of the likes of Mr McKeith.'

'Theories?' asked Avalon.

'I suppose if the old man is in a coma he wasn't able to indoctrinate you with his moonstruck theories on the findings in the Vatican, but let us just say, there are people out there with too much time on their hands.'

'I did speak with Mr McKeith,' explained Avalon, 'before he deteriorated.'

'And I suspect he mentioned the Key Rolls?' asked Kerr raising his bushy grey brows.

'He did, but I still have no idea what they are.'

'Don't waste your time,' said Kerr shaking his head, 'I know for a fact that nothing else was found, there is no conspiracy and far too many very backward people think that the Di Vinci Code was a documentary.' Avalon sighed, he could see that this investigation had just opened up like the hole in the Möhne dam.

'You need to explain to me exactly what you are getting at Mr Kerr,' insisted Avalon, 'we were not able to interview Mr McKeith at length as he was ill and therefore the subject you are speaking of is unknown to us.'

'It's a nonsense Detective,' replied the man shaking his head slowly, 'borne through lack of facts and understanding of the subject. People want to believe there is more to the world than there is and if they can't find it they invent something. It's what comes of living simplistic lives and having too much time on-'

'Just the facts Mr Kerr,' insisted Avalon interrupting the man.

'But that's it, detective, there are no facts, the Key Rolls are well known about in scholarly circles and there are several copies all over the world but they were not found in the Vatican and they are worthless to anyone other than the people who wrote them.' He paused to catch his breath then added, 'no one with any intelligence believes in the stories and I would be disappointed if the police saw any truth in them.'

'What you are not seeing Mr Kerr,' began Avalon with a more powerful and determined tone, 'that this is nothing to do with you, I or the police in general believing or not believing, if the person or persons who are committing crimes believes it, then it is enough for us to investigate it, do you understand?' Kerr stared at the DI for a few moments and eventually nodded and sighed.

'Yes I understand,' he looked to the floor and brought his hands together, 'it isn't a short story thought detective,' he added a little more contrite.

'Then I suggest Mr Kerr,' though it sounded more like insistence, 'that we conclude this back at the station where we can be undisturbed and record your explanation.'

'Is that necessary?' Kerr asked.

'No, and you could refuse but then we would have to have a team come over here and I'm not sure that would be ideal for you or your sister.'

'No, quite,' nodded Kerr gathering his thoughts, 'when do you want me to do this then?'

'As soon as you can get everything together that you need, do you need to arrange something for your sister?' asked Avalon.

'No, not at all, she can manage on her own,' he said as he looked to Avalon, 'fortunately; she isn't quite that bad yet.'

'Then I'll leave it with you,' nodded Avalon.

'I could probably arrange to come over this afternoon.'

'I'll send a car for you,' nodded Avalon as he stood.

'There's no need, really,' replied Kerr.

'I just thought you may want to open your birthday present before you arrived,' added Avalon with a fake smile.

~~~~~~~

'Hello, it's Detective Inspector Avalon, Inverness CID, I'm just checking to see how one of your patients is doing, Mr Thomas McKeith.'

'*Just one moment*,' said the voice. As Avalon waited, listening to the phone, he looked through the glass partition of the booth at Ross. He and Rutherford had returned but there was no conversation passing between them. Rutherford looked irritated and Avalon thought that the time had come to do something about the problem. He was sick and tired of the issues within the section, yes, some of it had been his own fault but that now had to stop, it was time for a change in attitude before the rot began to attack the rest of the team. Avalon saw Rutherford look up, and he nodded for him to come to the booth, Ross was miles away looking through the windows again, chewing at the end of a biro.

As Rutherford approached, he saw Ross awaken from his dream and watch Rutherford until he noticed Avalon watching and then he buried his head in the computer screen. As Rutherford walked in the phone made a noise.

'*Hello Detective Avalon, it's Doctor Prentice*,' said a male voice.

'Oh, thanks for speaking to me doctor,' replied Avalon as he directed Rutherford, pointing to the spare seat, 'I was just inquiring if there is any news about Mr McKeith.'

'*I'm pleased to say I think he is stable and I suspect he will make a good recovery*,' explained the doctor.

'Oh, that's good, is he still unconscious?'

'*Well*,' explained the doctor, '*we're keeping him*

heavily sedated for at least another twenty-four hours and I doubt if you will be able to speak to him for some days if that's what you are asking.'

'That's fine, Doctor Prentice, thanks for your time,' and he ended the call. At least it wasn't a murder investigation, yet. He looked up to Rutherford. 'Any joy with your friend?'

'He's no friend o' mine,' frowned the big man, 'and frankly boss, I'd appreciate et ef you could put me with someone else, I'm working on my own at the moment anyway.' Avalon nodded.

'I was thinking that, but I didn't want to push it onto you.'

'Oh right, that sounds like I get the short straw.'

'DC Angus White,' nodded Avalon.

'Christ, from one zombie to another,' sighed Rutherford folding his arms, 'oh sorry boss, I shouldnae have said that,' he added.

'There isn't an option really, I need to put him with someone who can keep him working, and I need to find out what he's capable of,' explained Avalon.

'So is he staying?' asked Rutherford.

'That wasn't the plan,' sighed Avalon, 'but if Ross doesn't sort his act out, then we'll need him, and without another DS, you are the next best thing.' Rutherford was suddenly taken aback with the confidence that his boss was showing in him.

'But what about Megan, isn't she the next in line as DS?' Avalon didn't answer, he raised his brows but said nothing, he just let his eyes move to where Frazer was sitting, chatting now and then to Rory. He realised she must be telling the young DC about the bottle of whisky he had given to Kerr as she mimed the action to

184

him.

'So do y' want me to start with him now?' asked Rutherford eager to get back to work.

'Yes, find an excuse to get him out of the building and if Ross asks anything, tell him to come and see me.' Rutherford gave a single quick nod and heaved his massive bulk from the chair. He watched Rutherford pull his jacket from his chair and talk to White. White nodded, and he too stood. It was then that Ross spoke.

'Where're you off to?'

'I've got work t' do,' was all he said as he and White headed to the door.

'What work?' asked Ross but Rutherford just told him to 'take it up with the boss' as he left. Ross looked towards Avalon who just stared back at him showing a blank expression. Ross stood and walked to the booth.

'What's going on?' he asked standing by the desk.

'I'm taking you off your cases, Martin will take over for now.'

'Why?'

'Because sitting staring out of the window is not what you are getting paid to do, so you may as well take a holiday and work out what you need to do from here.'

'That's a bit unfair,' frowned Ross, 'just because I won't talk you're taking me off my work?'

'No,' hissed Avalon, 'not just because of that, mainly because unless every member of my team gives one hundred percent they have no business in C Section. I don't know where you are but you're not in here anymore.'

'I've always been dedicated to this section and you know it,' replied Ross in a fairly calm manner given

185

the circumstances.

'This dedicated?' Avalon replied tossing the small envelope on the table. Ross's eyes looked at the envelope and up to Avalon without any emotion. His lips were a stiff line on his face and he was clearly surprised by it.

'That's a personal note to the DCI, why has he given it to you?'

'He didn't, I took it,' insisted the DI, 'I thought it was just something you had to get out of your system, I thought you would come to your senses and regret it. Again, I was wrong. I suggest you go home and think about it, is this what you really want? If it is, drop that envelope back in with the chief on your way and go and see your mate, see if he still needs a driver for the minibus.' Avalon held the gaze for several seconds and then he looked back to his computer. Ross slowly picked up the envelope and tapped it on his other hand and then went for his coat and left. Avalon didn't even look up this time. Frazer did, she could see what had happened, and she watched Ross walk right across the room without a word or a glance to anyone.

The Detective Inspector had done his best to make the interview room a little more comfortable by providing drinks and biscuits for Mr Kerr. Avalon understood that the man had a reputation for being difficult and maybe he was more accommodating earlier because he was at home, either way, he needed the information that Kerr had, and he would go a little further to get it. He had considered that the restroom might be better but he couldn't guarantee they wouldn't be interrupted. As promised, a car had been sent to bring the man in and he duly arrived and was sent to the interview room. Avalon sat by the side of the table in a less formal way while Frazer sat to the table ready to take notes.

'I think the first thing we need to established,' began Avalon, 'is what was it that Mr McKeith was working on, you mentioned that he saw the documents known as the Key Scrolls as being important.'

'He did, but he wasn't the only one, there were plenty of supporters for the theory,' explained Kerr.

'And the theory was?' asked Avalon.

'There are people out there that have not even included these particular parchments into their research, mainly because they show nothing at all, but there are also those who think that they have been interpreted wrongly. I have brought copies…' he paused as he pulled out a few sheets of copier paper from the file on the desk and passed them to Avalon, 'which are reasonably easy to get from the right sources.' Avalon looked at the paper but it may as well been written by an alien as far as he could see. 'The only item of any significance on there,' continued Kerr, 'are the words 'factorum clavem' which translates to key maker but it doesn't say who or what the key maker is. It then becomes a list of words and names.'

'Can you give me an example?' asked Avalon.

'Errrm,' Kerr looked down to the paper, and ran his finger down the page, 'here for instance, it says, 'Avien de Craon, collis somniorum,' which roughly translates to, someone called Avien de Craon and then, hill of dreams,' he paused to find another one. 'Here's another, 'Sir Geoffrey Bannercote, de flumine saxa,' which means great stone from the river, or maybe even

187

river of rocks.' Kerr paused once more but Avalon had already got the idea.

'It sounds like a list of people and after their name a place,' he suggested.

'Yes, that's generally accepted, but that's *all* it is,' explained Kerr a little animated, 'just because it has the word 'key' in it, people think it's a treasure map, it isn't.'

'What makes you so sure Mr Kerr?' was Avalon's obvious question.

'Because, even a very learned man in the fifteenth century, couldn't work it out, and *he* had the benefit of living just a few hundred years after the event.'

'So let us assume for the moment that this *is* a treasure map,' suggested Avalon, 'and someone wanted to try to work out what it all meant, where would he start?' Kerr sighed, but he then nodded and took a deep breath.

'With the diaries of Bernard of Ravenscar, he's the very learned man of who I speak,' he explained.

'And who was he?'

'A monk who wrote about his travels and documented his search for what he called 'flamma de Caledonia',' shrugged Avalon.

'I'm guessing that translates to Flame of Scotland?' asked Avalon.

'Correct, but the problem is, not only don't we know what it was, we don't know how Bernard of Ravenscar came across it, as he never deigns to tell us that in his manuscript.'

'It sounds like it's going to be a gem or something,' shrugged Avalon.

'That has been suggested. One Italian scholar

insists that it was a giant ruby that adorned the Ark of the Covenant but most of these theories stem from ignorance rather than fact.'

'I can see how people would be attracted to such a story, treasure is always alluring, and it has a particular mystique to it.'

'It's all horse manure as far as I'm concerned inspector, like you I deal in facts, not myths or superstition,' insisted Kerr. Avalon rubbed his chin with his fingers and considered his next move. He picked up the copy of the document and read the top line but it made little sense, there were obviously several names and he saw the word 'leo' but that was about all he could figure out.

'The names are of little consequence I think, but can you list for DC Frazer all the items that look like place names?' The man nodded as if it was beneath him but he did as he was asked.

'Ab arce griseo,' he began, 'that's 'the grey castle',' he paused and looked up to see if the DC was writing it down, she was, 'lapis ab antiquis capella, which is something like, 'the ancient stone by the chapel.'

'Just the English translation will be fine Mr Kerr,' smiled Avalon. Kerr looked across to him and sighed again and began to list the translations. It seemed like random places and objects until he came to one particular description.

'This one is a hart,' and he looked up to Frazer, 'that's hart as in a deer, not the body organ.'

'As in a stag?' asked Avalon with a frown.

'Yes,' replied Kerr looking down and reading the entry again, '*cervum*, yes it means stag.' Avalon looked at Frazer but she was busy writing.

'Sorry, do carry on please,' insisted Avalon.

'I'm not sure how you want to write this next one down, the words are 'calculo seraphim' but I don't understand the correct meaning of this.

'Seraphim?' questioned Avalon.

'Yes,' nodded Kerr surprised the detective had heard of the word, 'but why the word 'calculation' is included I don't quite know.' This time Frazer was looking over, she knew quite well the implication of that word being included. Avalon looked back to Kerr and nodded and the man continued to translate. When he had done, he looked over to Avalon, but the DI was deep in thought, the shape of the case had changed that was for sure, whoever this person was who was breaking into people's houses, he was obviously looking for the Caledonian Flame, whatever that was. Avalon didn't have enough information yet, and it was going to take some considerable time to structure this case. He needed Steven Kerr on his side, he needed the man to spend much more time going through what he knew but he wasn't going to be happy about it that was for sure. For the second time, he rubbed his fingers over his chin and turned to Kerr with a very solemn expression.

'What I'm about to tell you Mr Kerr has to stay out of the public domain for now do you understand?' The man nodded but showed little interest, 'I think the person we are looking for in our case may be looking for this treasure. It remains a simple theory at the moment but I'd like to ask you much more on the subject... and it could take some time.'

'But Inspector, it doesn't exist, that's the point I've been trying to make,' he demanded. 'Even if it did,

Bernard of Ravenscar must have had other documents that he didn't mention, he freely tells us in his diaries that he read a line, 'qui excubant in custodiis claves Gulielmi la More' and that appears on no recorded documents,' he was clearly agitated but Avalon sat impassively.

'You have to realise Mr Kerr,' glared Avalon, 'I have no interest in whether this is real or not, my only interest is that whoever is breaking into homes and attacking people, clearly believes in this story of the Caledonian Flame, and it's my job to find him and stop him. I have to know where he will strike next, is that clear?' The man glared at Avalon for a moment but the DI hoped he would see sense, he couldn't make him help them and so he tried a different tack. 'I understand that you are busy,' he said in a friendlier tone, 'I understand that you think this is a waste of time, but we need your help, *I* need your help,' he emphasised, 'and I think the information that you can give us will directly stop this violent individual hurting innocent people.' Kerr looked from Avalon to Frazer and then leaned forward resting his arms on the table.

'I'll do what I can detective, but I'll have to ring Irene and let her know.'

'Will she be all right on her own?' asked Avalon.

'Oh yes,' nodded the man, 'she can look after herself but I don't want her to worry about me.'

'Of course,' said Avalon looking at his watch, 'I'll get DC Frazer to sort you out with a phone.'

'I've got a phone,' he said pulling the mobile from his pocket.

'Well, we'll give you a break to phone her and I'll arrange for some sandwiches to be brought down,' he

191

stood and looked at his watch once more, 'it's four-thirty, what if we continue around five?' he asked, 'is that okay?'

'Yes, that's fine,' nodded Kerr unenthusiastically, and he began to dial. Avalon nodded to Frazer, and they left leaving the door slightly ajar and he spoke with Frazer down the corridor.

'See if you can get someone to sort some sandwiches out, you better get some for us too, we could be here for a few hours.' Frazer nodded and walked off. Avalon could think of better places to be on a Friday evening but he needed anything this man could supply him with. As he turned to go to the toilets to freshen up, his heart sank like a stone in a loch. It was Friday, Friday evening, the same Friday evening he was supposed to be meeting Sarah Underwood at the Waterfront pub.

'Shit!' he hissed under his breath. He knew it was wrong of him but his immediate reaction was to try to backtrack on the interview but he knew that was impossible, he knew he could never do that. This was why detectives can't have personal relationships, this was why most of them had at least one failed marriage in their lives. He massaged his brows standing there in the corridor, thinking of the best way to explain to Sarah that he may be late, he may not be able to get at all. It was a phone call he just didn't want to make, would it mean she wouldn't rearrange? No, of course it wouldn't, she had already mentioned that her job was just like his with no set hours and horrible surprises waiting around every corner. He felt in his pocket for his phone.

'DI Avalon,' came a voice from behind him, it was PC Kirk and she was holding a tray with sandwiches on it. 'Where do y' want this?'

'Oh thanks, Ollie, that was quick,' he smiled dropping the phone back into his pocket, 'interview room two, oh and give a knock, Mr Kerr is in there making a call.' She nodded and walked past informing him that,

'DC Frazer's taken yours to the room at the back o' the desk.' He nodded and made his way there wondering if he was hungry or not.

~~~~~~

Michael Collis was a crook, he knew he was and made no pretence over it because to him, he was a crook in the old sense of the word. Yes, he broke into houses, barns and hotels but he didn't have a single violent bone in his body. To him, that made him feel heroic, a sort of 'Boy's Own' hero, a sort of Charlie Peace of the modern world, except that Peace was a convicted murderer. Michael couldn't kill that was for sure, he had been savaged by a dog during a break in because he didn't have the ability to maim or kill the beast as it attacked him. Collis just couldn't see why there was such a fuss or even a problem with him entering property that didn't belong to him, he saw those locations as his workplace like a baker or an estate agent. Those places were his office. His delusion went even further, he actually thought he was doing the owner a favour, lifting their property so they could claim it on their insurance and 'add a bit' in the process. He never considered the stress or the fear that his aftermath caused, simply because he didn't care as one copper that had brought him to book previously in his life had stated. That copper had called him a 'grubby little tea leaf' and that had hurt him more than the three-year sentence that he never had to serve, it hurt him because Collis was so deluded that he considered burglary as an honest profession. Yes, true, even when he was caught he just gave up without a struggle but that's why he got off so lightly every time. Things were about to change for Michael Collis though, he was about to have a life-changing experience. He only ever 'worked' at night, he had never thought of the dark as something to be feared, it wrapped him up warmly and made him feel secure. In the daylight, all the horrors of the world could be seen, and he didn't like that, it was too real, it wasn't at all as he wanted to see the world. His world was just the cone of light from his tiny flashlight, that was all he wanted to see. This particular dark evening, he found himself watching a large house in the Crown district of Inverness making sure there was no activity. He had seen nothing, no lights, no sound for a good two hours and he thought the time had come to get a little closer. The house was even larger as he closed in on it and after a few seconds checking the window for alarms with his flashlight, he opened his small pack of tools and began preparing to remove the glass to enter the room. He wasn't one of these, smash and grab amateurs, he did it properly, silently and cleanly. It took a little more time but it gave him more time once he was in. As he plopped onto the thick-pile carpet he dropped to the floor and listened. He always did this before continuing. He could hear nothing and so he made a quick assessment of the room and then he went straight upstairs checking for sounds along the way. He had the distinct feeling that this was his lucky night, he could feel a house as if it were alive, talking to him and this one was saying there was no one at home.

194

He grinned to himself as he thought this through, no one to disturb him and this large, rambling house to explore, yes it was certainly his lucky night. How wrong he was.

He found what he thought was the master bedroom, a large area with a balcony looking onto the drive, he could see the streetlights on the road and there was no one to be seen. As he moved around, he was careful to check for trips and triggers for the alarm system, not that it bothered him, most alarms were worse than useless to a professional like Michael. He found a dresser that looked promising and a locked drawer. Another small tool taken from his kit and the draw was open to reveal a host of trinkets, only one item was a fake and he left that. He looked around the room towards a sliding door that was either the en suite or a wardrobe and he was about to walk over to it when something caught his eye. Outside, on the balcony, he saw a glint of light, no not light, a reflection from the streetlights on a strand. It was as if a spider's thread was refracting the light from the street and it glistened now and then. He wondered what it was but as he approached it, he saw it was about a quarter of an inch thick, and it was vibrating. He held his breath thinking someone was coming down that line, someone had known he was here. Had he been set up? Impossible, he told no one was he was doing ever. He became shocked when someone came *up* the wire rather than down it and more to the point, came quickly up it as if they had been propelled. Michael darted back into the shadows and tried to glue himself to the wall behind the voluminous curtains at the side of the windows. He peered between the wall and the fabric to see what the new arrival was up to. The figure was on all fours, not quite like an animal but not like a human either. It was a completely black shape with no discernible features, but it had an oddly shaped head, which seemed a little out of proportion with its body. He thought that the outline reminded him of Spiderman from the old DC comics he had read as a child. The figure was close to the glass doors as if peering inside and then it withdrew only to return seconds later with an item he couldn't make out from where he was. The figure raised itself to full height and placed the item against the door and within seconds, Michael could hear what he thought were tiny cracking noises, few and distant to begin with but growing in speed and intensity. For a heartbeat, it went silent and then a sudden burst of sound broke forth as the whole door gave way and glass shattered onto the thick carpet. Michael was taken aback, he saw a tiny red light on the far wall begin to flash, it was as if it was Morse code and it was flashing, 'I'm the alarm so get the hell out of here.' He wanted to but if he moved, he knew the figure would spot him. His plan, if it could be called a plan, was to wait in the dark of the corner for the figure to move through the house and he would escape the way the intruder had made ingress. What if there was an accomplice at the other end of the wire? He didn't care, he had to get out and then he would run, he would run for all he was worth. The figure was on all fours again, looking around the room and Michael felt lucky he had chosen the dark spot he was in at that moment. He gave a quick look up at the flashing light of the silent alarm and then down to the feline figure, giving a whole new meaning to the term 'cat burglar'. Michael's heart raced even faster as he noticed the figure seemed to be looking straight at him.

'Oh sweet Jesus no,' thought Michael as he was

now sure the figure could see him, but how, he was in the darkest part of the room. The head was turned to him and he could see what looked to be a slight glow from the head, to be precise, from the forehead. It was a muted light, only just visible, but he was turned to him. The figure stood to its full height, and it was inches taller than he was, large too, its long arms slightly bent by its side. It approached slowly and for a second he thought about making a break for it but given the obvious agility of the intruder and a certain amount of fear, he just stayed rigid. The figure came right up to him, not in a threatening way, as if it was curious, it seemed to study him and then bent slightly to a few inches in front of his face. *It* had no face, it was a black morass, no mouth and no nose, just two, jet black shining eyes and a light blue glow from its forehead. Michael could move, he felt paralysed, and he was sure he was about to soil himself but he didn't get time. As the figure tilted its head in an inquiring manner, Michael felt a shudder go through his body, his ears screamed his tongue and teeth seemed to chatter at an unbelievable speed and his body seemed to explode in slow motion until his eyes were scorched by a blinding light, then total blackness.

Chapter Eight

Steven Kerr told what he knew as soon as Avalon and Frazer arrived back at the interview room.

'What do you know of the Knights Templar?' he asked. Avalon almost sighed, he could now see where this story was going and Kerr noticed his body language and gave a little smile, seeing that the detective may be coming over to his way of thinking.

'Religious order associated with the crusades,' replied Avalon with a sigh and a monotone voice, 'elite warriors not allowed to withdraw from battle unless overwhelmed by large numbers, probably the most overused religious order in films and literature.' Kerr smiled again and gave a slow nod.

'There are many aspects of the order that are misrepresented in the media, for instance, they were actually one of the most popular religious charities in the middle ages, many wealthy people thought that giving to the order would pave their way into heaven. They were not all knights either, there were support teams of men at arms and many skilled monks that worked for them, raising cash for equipment and weapons. Thousands of people donated to their cause including kings and princes, bestowing castles, lands and treasures.'

'So they were wealthy?' asked Avalon more of a statement than a question.

'Indeed,' nodded Kerr, 'the *Poor* Knights of Jerusalem were in fact, fabulously wealthy later in their history. They held lands in most Christian countries and fortresses throughout the holy lands. They were so wealthy that kings and emperors took loans from the order to finance their wars and armies. That was their ultimate downfall,' added Kerr raising his eyebrows.

'I remember something about the French king and the pope,' shrugged Avalon, 'but I was never really all that interested in their story.'

'Indeed, the French king, Phillip the fourth was deeply in debt to the order and it was this that spurred him on to be rid of them and thus his debt. As the pope was the king's puppet, he had all the French Templar knights arrested and tried for heresy.'

'It's not the first time in history and I don't suppose it will be the last,' insisted Avalon.

'That's true, King John did the same with the Jews, and we all know about Mr Hitler,' nodded Kerr. Avalon glanced down at his watch and Kerr saw the gesture. 'Well, to cut the story short,' he continued, 'it's likely that Pope Clement was convinced that while the Templars had committed some grave sins, they were not heretics. They had a weird initiation ceremony that may have included spitting at the cross and they may have practiced sodomy, all crimes in the Pope's eyes, but not heresy. He realised that they were committed to the ideals of the religion but living on the edge of the Muslim world they had to adjust to a different lifestyle. Yes, guilty of many other minor crimes, such as abuses, violence, and sinful acts, but not heresy. It didn't stop him ordering the disbandment of the order 'for the good of the church' however, and it's clear this was to placate the French king.'

'And this is what was found in the Chinon Parchment of course,' interrupted Avalon as much as to say, 'yes, yes, I know all this,' and Kerr saw the look on Avalon's face.

'I didn't know how much you knew about it,' apologised Kerr.

'I researched the Chinon Parchment but we need to get to the relevant part.'

'I think it's all relevant detective if I leave anything out…'

'Of course,' nodded Avalon with a little less impatience in his voice, 'continue Mr Kerr.' Kerr swallowed and gave a slight cough before continuing.

'Unfortunately, once we leave the facts of the Chinon Parchment we are sailing in uncharted waters as there is so much written in books, the internet and in films that most people don't see what is fact and what is fiction.' He paused for a moment. 'For instance,' he continued glancing towards Frazer who was jotting down notes, 'Many claim that the Templar fleet escaped en masse from the various ports in the Mediterranean and northern Europe, where they left for a mysterious destination to find political asylum and safety. The truth is, there is nothing written to give any facts of the matter, yes, it looks likely that on Thursday the twelfth of October 1307, the Templar fleet was in port but by the morning of Friday the thirteenth it was gone. What isn't widely known, is that the Templars didn't have many of their own ships, most were merchant vessels, hired or chartered for passage to here and there. They may have had as little as two or three ships of their own so when we talk of a fleet sailing away...' he shrugged at this and then added, 'they may have simply returned to their home ports when the arrests began.'

'Makes sense,' agreed Avalon, 'I suppose a merchant captain wouldn't want to get implicated in a papal witch-hunt.'

'Not at all,' nodded Kerr, 'the Catholic church at the time had an inquisition that would make the German Gestapo look like care workers.'

'So I assume this story is now going to follow the so-called fleet?' asked Avalon folding his arms.

'Sort of,' nodded Kerr, 'because if there were any ships coming out of the Mediterranean or other French ports along the Atlantic coast, they would have to converge somewhere to a safe haven. Portugal would seem the obvious choice as the Portuguese were very friendly with the Templars and the castle known as Almourol had been a Templar stronghold since 1171.'

'But you doubt the fleet sailed?' asked Avalon. Kerr nodded slowly.

'I do, the idea that every ship in use by the Templars in Europe could be sent to sea overnight after the arrests of Templars in France beggars belief, particularly considering the distances involved and the poor inland roads.'

'I see your point Mr Kerr,' nodded Avalon moving in his chair, 'but how does this relate to petty theft in Scotland?'

'Because there are many people who believe that this imaginary fleet sailed up the west coast of Ireland to the safe ports in Donegal and Ulster, where Templar properties were located and then on to Argyll.'

'So,' interrupted Avalon, 'the consensus of opinion of Mr McKeith and his friends is that the fleet sailed to Scotland with all their wealth and hid it somewhere?'

'That's pretty much the premise,' agreed Kerr folding his arms too.

'Et's probably en the cave that Robbie Bruce went spider watchin',' announced Frazer not meaning to speak aloud at all. Avalon spun around, he had almost forgotten she was there.

'That's another thing that backs up their weak theory Detective Frazer,' added Kerr unfolding his arms and pointing to her, 'Robert the Bruce was known to be a supporter of the Templars but he was probably in debt to them just like other monarchs.'

'So for those who believe in the story,' began Avalon leaning on the table, 'the records left by Bernard of Ravenscar give credence to the idea that the treasure is still on Scottish soil, and the Key Roll is the way to find it?'

'But,' shrugged Kerr, 'as I said earlier, the old monk must have had other documents or just made the whole thing up as there is little if anything in the Key Rolls. McKeith said that he had seen a document that had more details of the hiding of the treasure, but as usual, nothing was ever proven and McKeith never came up with the source of the manuscript,' Avalon could see that Kerr didn't have a high regard for Mr McKeith.

'But there could have been another set of clues, this so-called, 'Fly' is getting his information from somewhere,' insisted Avalon.

'Indeed, but I can't stress this enough,' insisted

Kerr, 'there is nothing, nothing as you would call evidence, to show that even if there is another document, the story is anything but one big hoax.'

'That's not exactly true Mr Kerr,' announced Avalon in a matter-of-fact way.

'Well, I know of nothing,' replied the man folding his arms.

'Nothing conclusive, but to my way of thinking,' continued Avalon, 'there is circumstantial evidence, for instance, the perpetrator of these break-ins almost always takes something away with him. Why is that?' he asked but didn't give Kerr time to think about it. 'Probably due to the item being a clue of some sort, which means, if there are clues, those clues probably point in a particular direction.' Kerr thought about this, the detective did have a point.

'It doesn't necessarily mean the treasure is real though does it?' frowned Kerr.

'No,' admitted the DI, 'but it would be a hell of a reason for someone to try to find it.' He let Kerr take in the information and then added, 'Mr McKeith did tell me that he had a version of the Key Roll to examine a few weeks ago and wondered if the intruder was looking for it,' explained the DI.

'That's nonsense,' frowned Kerr, 'I downloaded these copies from the internet before I came, why would anyone...' Kerr went quiet and then stared into space, 'Did he specifically mention the Key Rolls?' he asked still staring into nowhere.

'Yes, he did,' nodded Avalon. Kerr seemed to be considering something and then he made a noise like a snort and added,

'Well...' and the man leaned forward with some

animation, 'what if McKeith had been examining not the Key Rolls but some other parchment?'

'Such as?' asked Avalon widening his eyes, seeing that Kerr was beginning to see what Avalon was getting at.

'As I have said, copies of the Key Rolls can be found if you know where to look, and certainly they wouldn't point to any treasure. I'm thinking that Mr McKeith had something else, maybe this other document you think may exist. It could even the lost notes of Bernard of Ravenscar.'

'You think Mr McKeith may have been looking over them for a collector you mean?'

'Exactly, though I wouldn't call anyone who had those particular notes a collector,' replied Kerr squinting his eyes, 'more of a thief.'

'And the so-called Fly, found out somehow that he had them?' questioned Avalon but now Kerr had come to the same conclusion, he was thinking through the possible scenario.

'It's plausible,' nodded Kerr but Avalon was busy trying to decide if the Fly had actually found them, he was sure he had found something. He turned to Frazer.

'We need to know the moment that Mr McKeith can be interviewed,' and Frazer left to make a call. 'I'm guessing that if the document was taken we have no other way of tracking this man down?' Kerr just shrugged, he didn't know what to say. Avalon sighed and rested his elbows on the table.

'You know...' began Kerr but then went quiet, unsure whether to say anything.

'What is it Mr Kerr?'

'Well, McKeith is a very canny man and a very

good hand with a quill...' and he trailed off but Avalon got the gist of what he was about to say.

'You think he may have made a copy?'

'It's possible, it may indeed be the copy that has been taken.' Avalon thought about this. If the old man had copied it, he might remember what it was he copied down.

'You may be correct Mr Kerr but as it stands,' said Avalon, 'we don't know how this perpetrator is choosing his targets and therefore there is no way of knowing where he'll turn up next?'

'None that I know of,' insisted Kerr.

'So we really need Mr McKeith up and talking,' he said to himself. He thought about his options, there were so few but then something occurred to him.

'The clues to the places on the Key Rolls Mr Kerr?' asked Avalon, 'can you give me the names of the people that are associated with them, for instance, the Hart.' Kerr looked through his list and found the entry.

'Ranaulf De Hugeonson,' he said but Avalon just shrugged, then something at the back of his mind clicked. The name of the owner of the bronze statue was Hutchinson.

'And the Seraphim?' asked Avalon glaring at the man. Kerr quickly looked at the entry.

'Willelmus Saint Claire,' he announced.

'Sinclair!' said Avalon slapping his hand on the table, 'the key rolls *are* a clue Mr Kerr,' but he told him nothing more though the smile on his face showed he had found something important. He turned back to Kerr and said, 'Thank you so much for your time Mr Kerr,' and he held out his hand, 'if you think of anything else that may help please let us know but I think what you have given us is a great help.' He once again thanked the man and then asked the front desk to arrange a car to take him home. Avalon went back to the interview room and glanced through Frazer's notes, why did he get these weird cases? He sighed and leaned back in the seat, the truth was that it didn't warrant a great input of resources even now, in the scheme of things it was still a minor case and he would have to 'shelve' it until something more concrete fell into their collective laps or the crimes became more critical. Frazer came back into the room.

'Nothing we didn't already know then?' she said glancing quickly at her reflection in the two-way mirror.

'No,' agreed Avalon, 'nothing we couldn't find on the internet but he thinks that McKeith may have copied the parchment he was checking.'

'Oh,' she shrugged, 'not much good though ef the Fly has et.'

'We're just guessing that part,' said Avalon, 'but the best bit of information is the list that he calls the Key Rolls,' and he held up a list that Kerr had left them.

'Et doesn't make sense to me,' she frowned.

'No, I asked for the English translation of the places but just look on this sheet at the names at the side of the Hart and the Seraphim.'

'Bloody hell,' she said wide-eyed, 'the same family after seven hundred years?' and she looked at the other names, 'nothin' else rings a bell though.'

'No I realise that, but is this how the Fly is finding them?' asked Avalon.

'That's a lot of research,' she insisted, 'et took me six months on the internet tae find out my name was just a different way of spelling Fraser with an 'S'. I only got back as far my great grandfather who spelled it with an S *and* a Z.' Avalon smiled.

'Yes, I soon gave up with my name too, but we are getting somewhere now.'

'I didn't know about the Scottish connection with the Templar Knights though,' she added. Avalon raised his brows.

'Yeah,' he said, 'there's quite a great deal of it on the internet but as Kerr rightly said, most of it is crap. One armchair scholar actually writes that Bruce had no cavalry, and in his last battle with Longshanks he was getting his arse handed to him until a large cavalry contingent rode in and turned the tide of the battle.' Avalon sighed and raised his brows before adding, 'firstly he got the wrong king, it wasn't Longshanks, it was his son Edward the Second, secondly, it wasn't a large contingent and thirdly Bruce was never under the cosh at all, he seemed to have controlled the battle from day one. The premise of the armchair scholar is that these cavalry were Templar Knights, and yet once again, it is documented that the Scottish cavalry were few in number and wore very little armour, if any.'

'Was he an American?' asked Frazer leaning on the back of a chair.

'Who?'

'Your armchair scholar?'

'I've no idea, but I do think that Kerr is incorrect in saying that there is nothing in this story about the fleet, gradually there are tiny pieces coming together to suggest there may be something in this after all.'

'Well, the Fly certainly thinks so,' nodded Frazer, 'but et's odd tae think we could be the home of a vast treasure, we may even drive past et on the way to work.'

'That's the problem, everyone wants a mystery in

207

their life, if they can't see it, they'll invent it, and this story seems to have been cloaked in mystery,' sighed Avalon again. He glanced into the mirror and saw his reflection, he looked tired and worn, he needed a shower. 'Oh shit!' he suddenly exclaimed looking at his watch.

'What es et?' inquired Frazer slightly alarmed by his sudden outburst.

'I'm supposed to be...' he altered what he was about to say, 'I er, have an appointment at half seven and I have an hour and a bit to get this typed up, home for a shower and out.'

'I'll type et up,' Frazer gave a weak smile.

'It's okay, you get off home, I'll sort it,' replied Avalon standing up.

'That doesn't make sense,' insisted Frazer, 'you've got somewhere t' go, I haven't, I'll type et up,' she raised her brows and then added looking down at her notes, 'I doubt you'll be able tae read most o' this anyways.'

~~~~~~

Avalon was actually early at the Waterfront pub, Frazer had been kind enough to type up the details of the interview with Steven Kerr though it was all but worthless if they couldn't second guess where the Fly would strike next. To be fair, Kerr had certainly come up with some information, even if it hadn't turned out how he expected. For now though, he needed to relax, and he was here waiting for Sarah to arrive and looking forward to another pleasant evening. The pub was on the opposite bank on of the river down Huntley Street and so he had taken the car as the weather looked cold and cloudy. As he exited his vehicle, he had a quick look in the pub to find she hadn't arrived yet and then waited outside sitting on a convenient bench overlooking the river. It was cool but dry and across the water, he could see the many towers on the dark skyline of the city and the myriad of lights reflected in the polished surface of the Ness. He contemplated that it was a quiet city, even on a Friday night. There were a few Christmas office parties and certainly the drunks were still drunk but compared to other cities he knew and had worked in, it was quiet. Oh, he certainly knew that somewhere on those hidden streets, the law was being broken and it was likely that as the city grew, those misdemeanours would become more frequent and more serious. Where humanity gathered, crime flourished. He tried to recall the only part of John Milton's Paradise Lost that he ever remembered.

'The sun was sunk, and after him the star of Hesperus, whose office is to bring Twilight upon the earth,' he said softly to himself. There was to be no Hesperus that night, he looked up and saw only the looming roof of clouds, then he thought of another poem he couldn't remember. The Wreck of the Hesperus was one of the first poems he had read as a child but for the life of him, he couldn't remember a single line of it.

'A penny for them,' came a voice from behind, it was Sarah, back and side lit by the streetlights and looking somehow ethereal with a glow around her. The words of the poem suddenly came to him as he stood.

'Hello, I was a bit early, so I thought...' he pointed half-heartedly to the seat.

'You looked like you were still at work,' she smiled.

'No,' he laughed, 'I was actually trying to remember the words of a poem.'

'Which one?' she asked though she knew so little about poetry.

'The Wreck of the Hesperus by Longfellow.'

'What got you thinking about that?' she asked with both a smile and a frown.

'I don't know really, just a mix of thoughts, shall we go in?' he asked pointing to the pub.

It was what annoyingly to Avalon was called a 'gastro pub' but it seemed pleasant enough.

'I've never been here,' he announced as they took a seat each.

'I used to meet a friend here, she lived just around the corner, moved to Glasgow now though,' she smiled, 'so what do you think?' she then asked sipping on her drink.

'It seems pleasant enough though when I looked it up on the internet I noticed they had spelled whisky incorrectly.'

'Oh?'

'Yes, something to do with a whisky sauce but they had included an 'e' in the word,' he explained.

'Maybe they used American whiskey in the recipe rather than Scottish,' she suggested. Avalon shrugged, he hadn't thought of it but it was plausible.

'But logic says that being here in Scotland it would be Scottish whisky and not American whisk'ey,' he replied emphasising the e-y sound at the end of the word.

'Are you always such a stickler for the fine detail?' she asked with a grin.

'I'm a detective, it's my job.'

210

'It's my job too but I do clock off,' she replied widening her eyes.

'Point taken,' he nodded, and he took a sip of his orange juice. There was a little silence before Sarah spoke, Avalon had decided to be quiet as his first attempt at conversation hadn't gone too well.

'So this Longfellow poem, did you remember the words you were looking for?'

'No,' he smiled, 'I do struggle to remember many of them, just small passages that demand my attention.'

'I'm like that with song lyrics,' she added, 'they seem to be gone until you hear the tune, and then you realise they were not lost, just hiding.'

'Poems can be positively shy,' he smiled as he looked at the tiny features of her face. He couldn't quite work out why he was so fascinated by this woman, she was pretty, no, she was gorgeous but he couldn't have explained why he thought that. She was probably around his age and yet she looked younger and as he considered this further, he realised she must be the same age as Carol. He suddenly felt guilty for comparing them, but he couldn't help thinking how Carol was looking much older lately. He became aware he was staring at her.

'Sorry,' he said looking away.

'For what?'

'I thought I was staring.'

'I don't think you were, I thought that maybe you were still trying to remember the poem,' and though her face looked serious, she soon relented and laughed. Avalon smiled and nodded.

'You have a lovely smile,' he said, and he meant it but he hadn't quite meant to say it.

'Thank you,' she smiled back, 'I spend so much

of my day not smiling when I do there is plenty saved up, a sort of 'smile bank' you might say.' She leaned on the table with her elbows, interlocking her hands to the side of her face. Avalon decided it was time to make a suggestion.

'We were supposed to be arranging something for the Christmas period,' he began, 'and Christmas Eve is on Monday.'

'I thought about that,' she replied taking her arms from the table, 'I thought the best way to arrange anything would be for both of us to think of something based on days we think we might be available.'

'Sounds good,' nodded Avalon, taking another sip of juice, 'I'm guessing you have something in mind?'

'Sort of,' she nodded, 'I have been invited round to a small get-together with one of the team from the labs,' she looked for his reaction, there wasn't one, 'and I wondered if you would like to join me?'

'Yes, I'd love to,' he smiled, 'but I'm not much of a party animal.'

'Neither am I, but it will be fairly subdued anyway,' she admitted, 'it's on Thursday, around eight o'clock.' Avalon nodded, he had no idea if he would be able to make it or not, it seemed quiet at the office but you could never tell.

'Sounds good, shall I pick you up?'

'If you don't mind,' she hesitated, 'that would be lovely. 'Have you any ideas?' she then asked and then immediately said, 'oh sorry, you need time to give it some thought.'

'Not really, I was thinking of a quiet evening at mine, I'll cook something and then we can chat, if you think you could stand that.'

'No need to cook, I could bring something,' she cut in.

'It will be vegan...' he paused, 'honestly,' he added with a smile. She smiled back.

'Okay, your place, when?'

'The Saturday after, the twenty-ninth?' he widened his eyes, 'seems good for me at the moment,' he said it in an almost questioning manner. She nodded pursing her lips slightly.

'Saturday night it is then,' she agreed.

'If you can make it for around seven-thirty and...' he hesitated, he thought about the next question and then decided against it. There was more silence as he tried to think of something to say.

'And what?' she asked with a puzzled look.

'And... if you get bored with chat just say, I'll understand.'

'I'm fine with chat as long as it isn't about the correct spelling of beverages.' They both laughed, Avalon was glad, he had been about to suggest they she could stay over as he had a perfectly good spare room. It was utterly innocent but he considered it might not sound that way. The rest of the evening was spent chatting about Inverness mainly, a little about the environment but generally, it was just innocent conversation. When it was time for them both to leave they walked outside and over to the river bank.

'So...' she began pulling her coat closer to her, against the cold air, 'did you best Longfellow?'

'Sort of,' he replied, 'I remembered the first verse, no idea why I was thinking about it though.'

'So how does it go?' she asked. Avalon took a deep breath and began to recite the first verse.

'It was the schooner Hesperus,
That sailed the wintry sea,
And the skipper had taken his daughter,
 To bear him company.'

'I'm guessing it's a sad tale?' she asked.

'For the most part yes, but most good poetry *is* sad.'

'Hmm,' she nodded, 'maybe that's why I never got interested in it.' They both looked out over the river, he would have given her a lift home but she had already told him she had a cab booked and as he looked around he saw the vehicle pull up.

'This is me I think,' she smiled, 'so I'll see you on Thursday and she began walking slightly sideways towards the cab, she waved and mouthed the word, 'Bye'. No kiss, no peck on the cheek, just a little wave and 'bye'. He waved back and smiled and as the car left, he turned back to the river and turned up the collar of his coat, then thrust his hands into the pockets.

'Blue were her eyes as the fairy-flax,
Her cheeks like the dawn of day,
And her bosom white as the hawthorn buds,
That ope' in the month of May.'

~~~~~~~

Avalon pulled himself out of his car to a reasonable December morning and decided that the break-in case, would have to be side-lined until something more came in. It was the way of things, there were several more pressing cases that needed extra resources and he was aware that when the courts

214

resumed after the New Year, DS Wilson and DC Boyd would be tied up giving evidence on a previous case from earlier in the year. He stood and stretched with a little fatigue and noticed someone approaching in the corner of his eye as he locked the car. It was Ross.

'You lock your car even in the police yard?' he called as he walked.

'Of course, this place is full of criminals,' he replied nodding to the station building. Avalon took a few steps towards him and resisted the urge to make a joke about him being early. They both stopped a few feet apart. 'What is it?' asked Avalon. Ross pulled his hands from his trouser pockets and tightened his tie in a self-conscious manner.

'Two things,' he said, 'firstly, I just saw DI Lasiter in the corridor, he'd like a word when you have a mo.'

'What about?' asked the DI.

'No idea,' shrugged Ross, 'but knowing DI Lasiter it won't be an invitation to his Christmas Party.'

'And the second thing?' asked Avalon and Ross looked down again and began to shuffle his feet.

'I need to talk,' he said suddenly looking straight at Avalon. His expression wasn't belligerent, it was more a look of bemusement.

'Okay,' nodded Avalon, 'when?' Ross looked back to his feet.

'Not now and not here,' frowned Ross, 'I just wanted to catch you before you went up to the office.' Avalon couldn't read Ross, there seemed to be nothing in his expression to give a clue to the reason for the meeting. Maybe he wanted to recant on his decision to leave, then again, it could be to tell him he had made his mind up to jack it in. He had heard nothing more from DCI Croker but then again...

'What about this afternoon or this evening?' asked Avalon. Ross nodded and then seemed to remember something.

'It will have to be this evening, I might have to go out this afternoon,' and then added 'I have to pick the car up from the tyre company.' Avalon looked around the car park and noticed the BMW wasn't there.

'So you walked in?'

'Yeah,' shrugged Ross, 'I know, unheard of.'

'So anywhere in mind for the meeting?' asked Avalon.

'Not really, best not go to the pub, there'll be too many questions.'

'True,' nodded Avalon, then with an inspired idea he added, 'what about the Waterfront?' Ross frowned and shook his head.

'I was thinking somewhere quiet.'

'It's Saturday night,' explained Avalon, 'I doubt anywhere will be overly quiet.' Ross shrugged again and looked like he was losing interest in the idea. 'Okay, what about my place?' Avalon suggested. Ross thought for a moment and looked questioningly at the DI. 'I may have a single malt hanging around somewhere?' he added.

'Okay,' nodded Ross still without expression, 'what time?'

They arranged to meet at around eight and both Avalon and Ross returned to the building. Avalon shivered slightly, he hadn't felt the cold as he was talking to Ross but as he entered the building the warmth struck him. They spoke a little about the case Ross was working on and then they entered the Cave and parted company to their respective desks. Avalon left his jacket on until he had warmed a little and began to check his emails. There was an internal from Lasiter just to ask if they could talk. Avalon was guessing that it was about Frazer as Avalon hadn't seen him since his little argument with Lasiter. In truth, it wasn't an argument, Lasiter had berated him and Avalon had stayed quiet, he knew Lasiter was right but that was the last time anyone at the station would shoot him down, he vowed it.

Within the next twenty minutes or so, most of those expected had arrived at the Cave. Wilson and Boyd were having a much-needed weekend off and Mackinnon was on weekend cover so he wouldn't be in until later. Frazer, Ross, Rutherford, and White were all present however and as Avalon looked around the Cave from his booth, his gaze fell on White. Maybe that was what Lasiter wanted to see him about. Maybe he should get the visit over, at least he could settle down to the business of the day. As he was about to leave the office, he stopped at the door and looked down at Frazer.

'I think we'll have to shelve the break-in case, it's not really important enough for any further investigations.' Frazer looked up from her computer.

'Okay Boss, I've typed up the report, maybe somethin' else will crop up soon,' she replied.

'Maybe,' nodded Avalon, 'just as long as it's not a body,' and he left.

He was quite ready for confrontation as he walked the short distance to the large office that B Section worked from. He was ready for Lasiter too. As Avalon opened the door and strode in, he was like a

217

prize-fighter looking for his next opponent, resolute and hostile. The office seemed quiet, there were very few faces to look up at him and so he strode straight to Lasiter's office.

'Jim,' called DI Laister with a friendly smile that instantly disarmed Avalon, 'tak' a seat, thanks f'r poppin' over,' he was pointing to the chair by Laister's desk, nestled between box files, cardboard boxes, and other seemingly random office equipment.

'I got your message,' replied Avalon as he sat, 'what can I do for you?'

'Do y' want a cuppa?' asked Lasiter but Avalon shook his head.

'No ta, I've got a coffee waiting when I get back.'

'Aye o' course, how are you getting' on with White?' Avalon got the distinct feeling that Lasiter was softening him up for something, some sucker-punch to take the wind from his sails. He had an overtly friendly demeanour about him that Avalon was very suspicious of, he decided to tread carefully.

'Honestly, I've had little time to talk to DC White, I couldn't give a fair appraisal of him until he's settled in. I can't get the image of Sean Bean out of my head though when he speaks.' replied Avalon.

'Who?'

'Sean Bean, the actor,' explained Avalon with a frown as if to say, 'you must have heard of him', 'he's from Sheffield I think and White sounds just like him.'

'I bet he doesnae look like him,' said Lasiter considering the untidy-looking White.

'No not much,' smiled Avalon and then asked, 'do you want him back?'

'No, not at all,' replied Lasiter shaking his head and then he looked to Avalon and continued, 'he didnae fit en here, I don't know what et was about him but no one wanted t' work with him.'

'I'm not surprised by the nick-name you gave him,' put in Avalon widening his eyes. Lasiter shook his head.

'Nick-names have more or less died out en B Section, but the team seemed tae think that they were worth resurrecting for Angus White,' he shrugged and then said, 'but t' be fair, he got the name after. He just gets up people's noses, et's something about him. He just doesnae fit en.'

'Are you taking B Section back to the old days then?' asked Avalon leaning back and crossing his legs.

'What do y' mean, the elitism?' Avalon just gave a simple nod and Lasiter began to shake his head. 'Not at all, but neither do I want tae have a desk taken up with somebody that under-performs, gone are the days of useless mouths.' Avalon thought about this, he had given DC White the details of the case he had been working on and yet White hadn't given him any sort of report. Not even an acknowledgement that he had even read through them. Maybe Lasiter was right, maybe White *was* a 'useless mouth'.

'Okay John,' announced Avalon uncrossing his legs and leaning forward in his seat, 'I can't believe you wanted to chat about Angus White so what is it you really want to see me about.' Avalon had given Lasiter long enough, it was time for him to say his piece. Lasiter sighed and then picked up a biro and ran it through his fingers in a sort of apprehensive way.

'Well…' there was a pause, and he glanced

219

across to Avalon and then back to the biro, 'I wondered ef...' another pause and then he looked straight into Avalon's eyes, 'I wondered ef you had spoken tae DC Frazer yet?'

'I have,' replied Avalon, he now knew why Lasiter was on edge, he wanted to know the outcome of the conversation.

'And...' he paused once more, it was obviously weighing on his mind, 'did you mention me, I mean, did *my* name crop up?'

'It did,' replied Avalon calmly, 'I had no option, I had to explain the whole story to her.'

'How did she take et?' asked Lasiter putting the biro down.

'Have you heard the term 'ape shit'?' asked Avalon cruelly trying to make Lasiter's discomfort greater. DI Lasiter sighed.

'Tae be expected I suppose,' he said drawing in breath for another deep sigh.

'The thing is,' added Avalon, 'since then, she's not just calmed down, she actually seems relieved.' Lasiter's expression brightened, Avalon could see that the man didn't like the idea of Frazer being angry with him for trying to protect her.

'Well,' he nodded, 'I suppose having something like that as a secret must lay heavily on your soul.' Avalon raised his brows and then exaggeratedly raised his open hands and patted them onto his knees, a theatrical gesture to indicate he was about to leave.

'It must certainly wear you down,' he announced as he stood, 'but either way, we seem to have made our peace,' and he turned to exit Lasiter's office. Before he left, he turned and looked over to the DI who was visibly

220

feeling better about the affair and said,

'On the other hand, if I were you, I would stay out of her way for a few years,' and he strode across the main office and out of the door into the corridor. Outside, he stood for a moment wondering what Lasiter was making of his last comment, it made him smile as he returned to the Cave.

'You wanted to see me sir?' said the Sean Bean sound-alike standing in the doorway of Avalon's booth.

'Yes,' and he pointed to the spare seat, 'did you look through the details of the break-in case as I asked?'

'Yes sir?' replied White with no further comment.

'And?' asked Avalon a little sharply.

'I'm not sure what you want me to say, I suppose you're asking for something specific?' asked the DC. Avalon frowned and squinted his eyes at the man and as they opened a little the frown intensified.

'Do you understand what is involved being a detective DC White?' asked Avalon angrily.

'Of course sir, but as I say, you haven't asked me anything specific.'

'Specific?' growled Avalon, 'are you aware how universally disliked you are in B Section?' White puckered his lips a little as if he was giving it some thought.

'Yes sir, but what has that got to-'

'And was that your purpose DC White, to be as antagonistic and uncooperative as possible?'

'No sir, I can't be held responsible for other people's perception of what they consider normal behaviour,' insisted White flatly.

'Then why did you become a detective?' asked

Avalon leaning back. White didn't have to think about it, he told Avalon the answer straight away.

'It seemed the best employment to keep both my brain busy and my inquisitive nature satiated.' Avalon began shaking his head slowly.

'I find it difficult to imagine that your interpersonal skills are so poor DC White,' began Avalon, 'and I don't believe that you don't see how much you aggravate the people around you. Tell yourself lies by all means but I won't stand for them.' For a moment, White looked as if he was about to reply, but then he just looked blankly at the DI. 'I think,' added Avalon, 'you are just going to be moved from one department to another until there is nowhere else to go, but home DC White. I can't, no I will not try, to help someone to fit in who doesn't want to fit in.'

'Can I speak freely sir?' asked White with the first motive expression Avalon had witnessed on his face.

'This is the first and last time I will allow it,' nodded Avalon, 'go on.' White looked to his side for a second and then back to Avalon.

'Franky DI Avalon, I really don't care what people think about me, it isn't rebellious, and it isn't malignant, it's just irrelevant,' he began. He took a slight breath and then continued. 'I see no need to fit in, I don't wish to spend any time with other detectives and I don't want to be invited to any Christmas parties. Neither do I see any importance in having what people refer to as 'working relationships' and more than anything else, I can't see what any of that sort of bullshit has to do with me or anyone else being able to just get on with their jobs.' Avalon smiled and then the smile broke into a soft laugh.

'Okay Mr White,' nodded Avalon making a point of the 'mister', 'I understand your problem, I'll speak to DCI Croker later today,' and he leaned forward and typed something on his keyboard.

'I don't understand,' said White with a mite of a confused air about him.

'Oh, I know you don't understand and that's why I will make recommendations that you should be suspended from duty until a full evaluation of your personality can be made.'

'Based solely on the fact that you don't like who I am?' questioned White.

'Not at all,' replied Avalon pointedly, 'based on your unsuitability to be a detective. I can't even imagine how you got this far.' White gave a semblance of a sigh and folded his arms. 'That's all,' announced Avalon staring at the man.

'So what do you want me to do now?' he asked.

'That's up to you, frankly DC White,' said Avalon as a parody of White's own statement, 'I don't really care what you do, just ensure you close the door quietly on your way out.' And that's what he did. He stood and walked out closing the door quietly behind him. Frazer watched him leave and then glanced over to Avalon. He gave a slight nod to his side and then pointed to Rory and nodded towards him. Frazer understood he wanted them both in the booth.

'Boss?' said Frazer as a question as she sat. Rory leaned on the glass wall.

'I'm dropping DC White, I think DI Lasiter knew he was hopeless and so we may as well do without the...' Avalon thought of the term Lasiter had used,

223

'useless mouth' an old army term for those who had to be fed but couldn't fire a gun, but he actually said, 'hassle of having to babysit him.'

'Humph,' sighed Frazer, 'pity, I know he's a complete knob, but…' Frazer hesitated wondering if she should have said what she had, but Avalon sat impassively.

'But what?' he asked.

'Well earlier I asked him ef he'd found anything to link the break-ins, and he had.'

'He had?' asked Avalon confused to why he hadn't spoken of this during their conversation.

'Yeah, he did go on about how ef you dug deep enough you could always find a connection,' explained Frazer, 'but I didn't really understand what he was on about.'

'Molecular level,' interrupted Rory. Avalon looked up to him questioningly but said nothing. Rory seemed suddenly self-conscious and decided to explain. 'He said that if you looked close enough at everything on the planet, you could find a match at the molecular level so finding similarities didn't mean much.'

'If I want to listen to something I can't understand,' growled Avalon, 'I'll go and watch BBC Alba.' Rory shuffled his feet. Frazer bailed him out by explaining the other issues he had brought up.

'Rory's right boss, that's what he said, but he did bring up a point that we hadn't seen,' she paused but Avalon was still frowning so she continued. 'DC White said that all the homes attacked were residences of reasonably wealthy people. Rory pointed out that the fact itself wasn't surprising as most people who were poor had nothing worth stealing.' She paused for breath and to gauge Avalon's reaction, he still seemed to be listening so she continued. 'He then said that none of them seemed to have employment that went with such an income tae sustain their lifestyles, indeed some had no employment whatsoever.'

'And did you check that?' asked Avalon knowing the answer.

'Yes,' she nodded, 'and he was right all except for Mr McKeith who lives on the opposite side of the fence.'

'So there isn't a similarity after all,' insisted Avalon, 'because McKeith doesn't fit the criteria.

'Well...' said Frazer raising a single eyebrow, 'we thought about this,' and she looked round to Rory. Rory saw this as being his turn to explain.

'Well boss, the thing is with Mr McKeith, according to the local PC, he chooses that kind of lifestyle. As far as we know, he could be very well off indeed and as he owns quite a few old documents...'

'What Rory is saying,' added Frazer, 'some of those documents are probably worth money, so where did he get his money tae buy them?'

'I'm guessing from his work restoring them, it's got to be lucrative,' offered Avalon. Frazer sat with a blank face and without blinking. 'So you know something else I'm guessing?' Frazer nodded once but gave nothing away. 'So you have found out he has money?' he then asked. Frazer gave a single nod once more. 'And do I need to know how you found this information out?' Frazer shook her head a single time as Rory shuffled his feet again. Avalon raised his brows and leaned forward resting his elbows on the desk. 'So, your theory is,' offered Avalon going back through the information in his head, 'that all the people who have had their homes broken into, or as in the case of the Seraphim, had possessions stolen, have money but no visible means of making money.' Frazer nodded and once again glanced to Rory.

'We think they could possibly have hidden income,' he suggested.

'Which would probably be illegal, and so this could be retaliation?' added Avalon, and then after a moment's pause, 'tenuous to say the least. There are many explanations including a simple coincidence, more likely than gangland issues.' For several seconds no one said a thing, Avalon was mulling over this new-found theory and though it didn't warrant a full-blown investigation, he did think that it would benefit from a little more digging around.

'Okay,' he suddenly said, 'see what you can find out about these people and how they get their income. Do it discreetly but do it above board, is that clear?' The two DCs nodded and left the booth. Avalon sat for several minutes wondering what was wrong with Angus White. Why hadn't he just told him about his ideas? Maybe White was telling the truth, maybe he couldn't help being a complete knob as Frazer had said, or maybe there was more to White than the average eye could see. Whatever the reason, Avalon didn't have the time or the patience to deal with yet another problem within C Section. White was defective as far as he was concerned and that was an end to the matter, he would leave it in the hands of the DCI.

Two hours later, Avalon was back in Lasiter's office seated in the same chair, surrounded by the same random piles of paperwork and office equipment.

'What es et this time,' asked Lasiter, 'need advice on decorating your office?'

'I'll pass on that,' frowned Avalon making a show of examining the raffle that surrounded him, 'did you know we had an archive downstairs?'

'Och, most o' this stuff isnae archive-able anyways,' he grinned, 'so what can I do for you then?'

'I bumped into PC Dowd a few minutes ago and he was talking to one of the other PCs who went out on a call yesterday evening. I was just chatting with them and PC McColl said that they found a burglar, spark out on the floor of a house with glass all around him.'

'Aye that's right, I've just been reading DS Douglas's report, he was on call last night so he went out to et with two uniforms.'

'What time was that?' asked Avalon.

'About eight-thirty I recall, he went home about ten this mornin'.'

'So what was it about?' Lasiter squinted slightly and asked,

'Et looks like you heard about the oddball bits.'

'I just know it didn't make sense coming from the young PC downstairs, and it was made more complicated by the rambling rhetoric of Dowd.' Lasiter smiled at this and opened a file on his computer.

'I have to admit, et's a bloody strange tale ef et's true but with Micheal Collis involved you never know.'

'I've heard the name but never come across him.'

'He's a small-time crook with a gentlemanly sense o' fair play, ef y' can say that about a thief,' explained Lasiter as he found the file, 'he reckoned he didn't do the damage but admits tae being en the house

227

without permission.'

'How's that work?' asked Avalon with a hint of a grin.

'Do y' want tae read the report or would you rather me explain et?' asked Lasiter pointing to the screen.

'Ah, you tell me, I'm sick of seeing reports this week.' Lasiter nodded at this and made himself comfortable in his chair.

'Well, et goes like this,' he began, 'silent alarm goes off en one o' those big houses on Southside Road and the private security company who installed et reported et to us. One of the uniforms was sent round and radioed en that a large window on the second floor was broken and so backup was dispatched. The house was locked and they couldn't get an answer so they entered the house to see what the problem was. They found Micheal Collis en an upstairs bedroom unconscious with heaps of broken glass around him.'

'So I'm guessing he was faking it,' said Avalon, 'caught in the act but inventing some bullshit story to cover it.'

'No, et's not his style anyway,' insisted Lasiter, 'the response team entered the same way that Collis had done, he had removed a pane o' glass on a windae that wasn't alarmed.'

'So who broke the glass?'

'We don't know but after Collis was taken tae hospital for a check-up, he started t' tell a story about being attacked by an alien,' and Lasiter began to laugh. Avalon simply shook his head in disbelief.

'Does he drink?' he asked.

'No, not a drop from what I remember,' said

Lasiter still laughing. 'When Collis was given the all-clear, DS Douglas interviewed him and said that daft little shite told him that the alien zapped him with some kind o' ray gun, the irony es, the doctor says he was tazered.'

'So part of the story is true then?' asked Avalon.

'Aye, et seems so,' Lasiter was still finding it amusing. Avalon nodded, he had a much more serious face.

'The PC downstairs said the attacker came up on a wire.'

'That's what Collis reported but Douglas didnae find anythin',' insisted Lasiter, 'why the interest?'

'I think this perpetrator may be involved in several cases I'm looking at, everything fits.'

'Oh, I see,' said Lasiter raising his brows, 'd' y' want me to send DS Douglas tae see you on Monday?'

'Yeah, that would be good but I could do with seeing Mr Collis myself, do you think Douglas would mind?'

'I doubt et, but I can ring him t' find out ef y' like?' Avalon nodded and asked,

'Where is Collis now?'

'Still at Raigmore under observation but they should be releasing him t' our custody the night.'

'Okay,' nodded Avalon, 'he's not going anywhere, this can be done on Monday, I'll see DS Douglas then too.'

Chapter Nine

Ross was early. It didn't surprise Avalon, it just reinforced his theory that the DS wanted to get the meeting over with as soon as he could.

'Drink?' he asked as he made his way to the kitchen.

'Yeah, please,' nodded Ross with his hands casually thrust into his trouser pockets.

'What would you like?' asked Avalon stopping by the kitchen door.

'Whatever *you're* having,' replied Ross and then added, 'as long it's not one of those screw-top wines.' Avalon brought two glasses, a small jug of water and a half bottle of Old Poultney he had seen on offer in a shop somewhere.

'I thought we'd try this, I've not had it before,' suggested Avalon as he put the tray on the coffee table. Ross was still standing. 'Are we sitting or do you have to be somewhere?' asked Avalon. Ross raised his brows.

'Oh sorry,' he said and sat in the armchair. It was obvious there was something he was trying to work out, maybe how he was going to begin his conversation. Avalon poured two large drinks and handed one to Ross and then collapsed onto the sofa.

'Sludge!' he announced. Ross nodded.

'Cheers,' he replied and took a long pull on the neat whisky. He then sighed and leaned back in the chair. Avalon tasted the single malt and then added a little water taking another sip. He nodded to himself and then also sat back. Avalon wasn't in the mood for dallying and so looked over to Ross and asked,

'So what do you want to talk about?' Ross gave him a quick glance and then sat forward again cradling the glass between both hands.

'Nothing much, I just thought I ought to explain myself...' he paused for a second and looked back to Avalon self-consciously, 'the reason I have been difficult lately.' Avalon didn't answer, he thought any reply might put Ross off his stride. 'I mean... I was angry with you for taking it out on Megan and not me but... I didn't realise you were going to set her back on, and...' as Ross paused again, Avalon decided it was time to speak.

'Neither did I,' he said from under heavy eyelids, Ross frowned as if he didn't understand. 'It wasn't planned, I just realised I got it wrong, and then I got it wrong again, trying to put it right.'

'Oh,' replied Ross, still wearing a frown.

'Carry on, you were saying?' said Avalon taking a larger drink of the whisky. Ross thought for a moment and then he also took another drink from his glass.

'Well,' he said, 'I was already in a crappy mood but things went from bad to worse, a couple of things happened and I suddenly found myself staring into a dark void, I think it was some sort of whirlwind depression.'

'Did you get any medication, for the knock on

the head I mean?' asked Avalon making an attempt to point to the mark on Ross's head where the stitches had been placed.

'No, nothing, it wasn't medically induced,' insisted Ross, 'it was just a realisation, I suppose brought on by the anger I was feeling.'

'Well, it doesn't matter,' shrugged Avalon, 'what's done is done, we have to carry on and as far as I'm concerned it's forgotten.' Ross looked at Avalon and then down to his drink, there was obviously more on his mind. He nodded after a few seconds and took another gulp of the whisky finishing it off. Avalon leapt into action and passed him the bottle.

'The incident might be but I can't get that empty feeling that I had out of my head,' he explained as he refilled his glass.

'I'm all ears, tell me more about it.'

'No,' replied Ross shaking his head, 'in some ways it's embarrassing.'

'There's just the two of us here,' insisted Avalon, 'sometimes the only way of ridding yourself of these things is to talk. Bottling it up makes it worse.'

'With respect, Jim,' frowned Ross, 'you're not the one to preach about that subject, when we were in the pub with Carol she said…' Ross seemed to run out of energy. Avalon didn't know if he was more surprised that Ross looked tired or that he had called him 'Jim'.

'I remember, you probably thought I wasn't listening, but I heard her say *that*, was one of the things that damaged the marriage,' frowned Avalon, 'she was right, I did bottle everything up. I told no one about my nightmares, not even her and I regret that, but that means I know enough about it to be justified in telling you not to keep it to yourself.' Ross looked into Avalon's eyes for a second, he then shrugged and took another drink, this time taking enough of a gulp to make Avalon think about finding a second bottle. 'It doesn't have to be me you talk to,' he added, 'but you need to tell someone.'

'I think that's part of the problem,' laughed Ross, it wasn't an amused laugh, it was one of those ironic noises that is full of frustration and emotion, 'I don't have anyone who would listen.'

'I'll listen,' said Avalon flatly and Ross looked back into Avalon's gaze, it unnerved him but then comforted him in some way.

'Not likely, you'd have something on me then,' replied Ross trying to make light of it.

'Just tell me,' said Avalon in a calm voice, 'you know I would never make judgements either way, if it doesn't help, fine, what have you lost? Yeah, okay, I'll know you sleep in a baby doll nighty. But if it helps...?' Ross knew he was right, and he began to see sense in it. He took another couple of gulps and reached for the bottle, Avalon stood and fetched a nearly full bottle of Glenmorangie from the kitchen, finished his own drink and topped up his glass depositing the bottle on Ross's side of the table. Ross looked over to his boss as he slumped back in the sofa.

'A couple of questions first,' he then said, 'firstly, are you trying to get me drunk and secondly, who told you about the baby doll nighty?' Avalon feigned a shocked expression then replied with,

'You don't seem to need any assistance getting drunk and as for the second point, it cost me money so I can't reveal my source.' Ross nodded and leaned back for a moment as if he was thinking. He suddenly sat bolt upright and said,

'Okay, but if I show you mine, you show me yours.'

'My what?' frowned Avalon.

'When we were at the ferry slip, you almost spilled your guts about something, about a face,' Ross had spoken quietly but Avalon's expression showed a little anger for a few seconds but it soon passed.

'Not likely,' he eventually said shaking his head, 'that is the only thing I keep locked away these days, it caused me a broken marriage and a stalled career, I'm not giving it any room to manoeuvre.'

'So where's the difference then?' asked Ross, 'you try to make me believe it would be good for me to talk and yet you live by different rules. Isn't that somewhat hypocritical?' Avalon gave Ross a dark stare. 'Well, it is isn't it?' Ross added.

'Probably,' nodded Avalon eventually, 'but…' he was about to say, he wasn't the one needing to talk, but he thought it was an unreasonable comment given the situation. With a lack of anything else to add he just sighed and shrugged. Both men took another drink as they sat in contemplation until Avalon offered an option.

'Okay, you go first and I'll see how I feel, but I'm not promising, other than that we're at an impasse.' Ross looked at Avalon for a moment and then began to nod slowly.

'Right,' he said at length, 'but I think this isn't a good idea.' He stood and paced around the room a little trying to work up the courage to start. He held his glass in both hands as if his life depended on it. 'When that paperweight hit me on the head,' he began still pacing, 'it was as if it woke up my mind, I mean, for a second I

234

saw a few stars but I didn't pass out. I just slumped in a chair holding my head.' Avalon leaned back in the sofa and listened. 'There were people fussing around me and I knew I was bleeding but it was like a switch had been thrown and I was seeing everything with different eyes.' He took a sip from his glass and then decided to sit again. 'I thought about my marriage and the split up. I wondered why I had got over that so quickly, and at the time I thought it was just self-preservation but the truth is the whole episode had been a charade. We were never in love, we were never emotionally attached, we just got married because people did,' and Ross glanced over to Avalon.

'I don't think you're alone there, many people do the same thing.' Ross nodded and finished off his drink placing the glass on the table.

'But it made me think that if a person can walk around just going through the motions, what would happen if that person was totally honest with themselves? What if they let the heart rule the mind for a while?' He sighed and leaned back in the chair clasping his hands behind his head. He looked up to the ceiling and continued.

'So I let that happen. All the way to the hospital I let it happen and I began to cry, well no, that's wrong,' he corrected himself, 'weep would be a better explanation, all the way there, tears ran down my cheeks. When I got into Raigmore, Megan had followed and all she could say was, 'sorry', over and over again and that's what I felt too. I was sorry, but I didn't know what for. Then all the guilt came flooding in, it seemed everything I had ever regretted poured in and it overwhelmed me until suddenly, it lifted and I felt fine.'

He looked back over to Avalon for a second and then sat forward resting his elbows on his knees. 'As I sat in the hospital, as they patched me up, I saw everything so much clearer, to the point that I realised that one of the lies I had told myself had to be acted upon,' and for a moment he looked over to Avalon with a hesitation that was as noticeable as it was brief.

'And did you?' asked Avalon taking a sip of whisky.

'Yes,' nodded Ross but his expression looked dark, 'but it didn't go the way I expected. I knew I was in love with this woman, I hid it because I didn't think she was interested but at that moment I knew I had to act.' This surprised Avalon, he didn't know anything about it and wondered when Ross had ever had the time to meet anyone, never mind fall in love. There was a pause and Ross looked down towards the coffee table. 'She told me straight,' he continued in a flat tone, 'her job was worth more to her than any man.'

'Rejection can hurt, I know,' said Avalon, 'but it's not the end of the world,' he paused trying to find something better to say, 'and anyway, it probably took her by surprise too, particularly as you said, you had been hiding it.' Ross looked over to Avalon with a blank face and then leaned back into the chair once more. He was quiet for a few seconds.

'I told you it was embarrassing, it's so stupid when you look at it but my mind seems to be working on a different level. Things that were unimportant, now seem critical. I feel lost, empty and ineffectual. Nothing seems worth doing anymore.' Avalon took in a deep breath and exhaled slowly.

'I think that there are a few things going on here,'

he eventually began, 'I think you are exhausted, and if you don't do something about that, you'll end up like DI Davies.'

'A breakdown?' asked Ross opening his eyes wide, 'I always wondered what that would feel like.'

'I'm serious,' continued Avalon, 'this isn't something to ignore and I can see you are on the edge at the moment.' Ross just leaned his head back and stared up at the ceiling. 'I'm going to get you some downtime, I'll have a word with Croker on Monday. In the meantime, you can plan what you're going to do with your time off.' Ross sat up and looked over to Avalon with a worried expression.

'I don't want that, I don't want to be on my own with all these thoughts knocking together in my head.'

'But you're burning out man, I've seen it before, it never ends well if you ignore it.' Ross looked back to the coffee table, his breathing was laboured as if he had been walking briskly, but gradually he calmed it. He looked at his glass and then the bottle, he then started pouring another drink. 'I don't think you should be hitting that stuff either in this condition.' Ross ignored him and poured a good measure.

'Okay dad, I'll put some water in this one,' he said, and he dropped the smallest splash of water into the glass. They both sat in silence for some time, Ross sighed a couple of times but his breathing was now steady and he seemed to be calming down. Maybe it was the whisky but colour began to return to his washed-out complexion. 'So what about you?' he eventually asked.

'What do you mean?' asked Avalon not quite understanding.

'I've told you most of my nightmares, what about

237

yours?'

'You don't want to visit my dark place, this isn't the time, believe me,' said Avalon, and he emptied his glass.

'Can you remember when we stayed overnight at Golspie?' said Ross looking over to Avalon, 'we were with that woman you met, Julia?'

'I remember, why?'

'You called out in your sleep, I don't think you woke but it was quite loud,' added Ross and he looked back to the ceiling.

'Carol said I used to do that, she said it never made any sense though,' explained Avalon.

'It didn't make sense to me then, but it does now,' said Ross still leaning back and staring at the ceiling. Avalon wasn't sure he wanted any further elucidation on the subject, it was his turn to feel embarrassed. Ross took another mouthful of whisky and placed the glass back on the table before leaning back and closing his eyes.

'You called out 'Carol' first,' said Ross quietly, 'then 'I can't help her',' but Avalon couldn't recall any such line or anything else for that matter. He knew he had nightmares, but that was inside his head, he never knew what happened on the outside.

'We all have nightmares, it goes with the job I suppose,' offered Avalon, 'when I first started in the police I used to dream about riding my bike, speeding along an endless road, but that soon changed. By the time I entered the CID my dreams were about piles of paper, endless reports and a green suit that always seemed to be wet. Then as the years went by and my head filled with the grim sights of the job... well you know the rest,' and he looked over to Ross, but the DS was fast asleep. Carefully and quietly, Avalon got a blanket and covered him up. He then retreated to the kitchen so he wouldn't wake the sleeping policeman.

~~~~~~~

Not only was it Monday morning, it was Christmas Eve and C Section had a sort of tradition that predated Avalon and even Lasiter. The idea was, all those working would try their best to be around the Cave for lunchtime where a party took place. Party was probably not a correct description, a gathering would be closer but a few moments not working was a more accurate approximation. It was always muted, but the thing had gone on for such a time that no one had ever had the heart to stop it. The idea was that a Christmas tree that was kept in the stationary cupboard the rest of the year was brought out and ensconced on the large printer. The poor thing looked as old as Christmas itself and Avalon thought that some of the decorations must be collector's items. Bits of tinsel and Christmas cards had been appearing over the last month but when the tree came out on the last week, it meant that the festive season was truly upon them. Then there was the Christmas gift ritual. At random, a circle of names was made and everyone bought a gift for the person who was clockwise on the list, which ultimately meant everyone received a gift and everyone gave one, it was 'pot luck' however what you got. Avalon had drawn Alison Boyd and Rutherford had drawn Avalon so he wasn't expecting anything useful but he had found a suitable gift for Alison. As he entered the Cave, he was the second in, Megan being first and her gift was under the tree with Wilson's name on it already. Avalon put his with it and began to walk to the booth.

'What did you get her boss?' she said looking at the small packet he had left on the printer.

'Oh, just a couple of tickets, I heard her say she was into musicals so I got her two tickets to see Doctor Dolittle at Aberdeen in March.'

'Musicals?' said Frazer shaking her head with a deep frown, 'nice thought though.'

'Yeah, not into them either,' he frowned, 'it's ironic that they're called musicals when they're about as musical as a fire engine on a shout,' and he continued to the booth. He began to set out the day, not forgetting the gathering at lunch, as the rest of the team duly arrived. He had told Ross that he needed to stay home so he didn't expect him in. The DS was working himself into an early grave, he was exhausted and had taken little time off except for his couple of days forced on him by DS Wilson after the paperweight incident.

Avalon's first port of call was B Section to see DC Douglas about the Southside Road break-in. The atmosphere in their office was much more Christmassy than the Cave but there were fewer people present than he had expected. He nodded to DS Douglas as he walked to Lasiter's office, Douglas stood and followed him.

'Jim, good tae see you,' announced Lasiter with a smile, 'et's a wee bit early for a nip but we have mince pies.'

'No thanks,' smiled Avalon holding up his hand, 'I just want a word with DS Douglas if that's okay?'

'Aye, o' course et es,' and he looked past Avalon to Douglas, 'Kirk, tak' the DI tae see Collis will you?' In

B Section Tommy Douglas was known at Kirk due to the famous actor of that name. Douglas was short but well-built if a little plain. If you had to describe how he looked you would struggle. He was ordinary and forgettable but was a very capable detective with a much younger wife, who was reputed to have been a part-time model. By all accounts she was a real stunner and Ross had certainly waxed lyrical about her. Poor old Rossy, he was having a crisis and Avalon hoped he would recover before it went too deep. He was a very sensitive person as Avalon had discovered but even *he* hadn't realised how much Ross had been bottling up. When he had left on Sunday morning, he had seemed a little better but he was still walking around with a cloud over his head.

'Has Mr Collis recovered?' he asked Douglas as they walked to the cells.

'Oh aye, he a resilient little bastard I'll give him that,' laughed Douglas.

'So what did you find at the house, apart from Collis of course?'

'Nothing we didn't expect if that what you mean,' replied the DS, 'the 'Fly' as the press are calling him had a go at a wall safe that was hidden behind a picture.'

'The press, how did they get their hands on this?' asked Avalon with surprise.

'Through Collis I imagine, or his wife, maybe even the hospital. It's not going to compromise anything is it?'

'Not in this particular instance but if they put two and two together, it could impact on further investigations of the previous cases.'

'Well,' shrugged Douglas, 'at the time it just

241

looked like a bungled burglary, so no press blackout was issued.'

'Did he get in the safe?' asked Avalon.

'Aye,' nodded Douglas, 'angle grinder most likely, it wasn't a big safe but it was empty when we got to it.'

'So he knew what he was after?' asked Avalon but he was thinking aloud.

'I would think so, nothing else had been touched, or at least nothing other than what Collis had fingered. The little bag of trinkets that he lifted were still at the side of him when I arrived.' Avalon nodded slowly at this.

'DI Lasiter said that Collis mentioned the intruder used a wire to get in.' Douglas nodded but was frowning.

'That's what he said, but we saw nothing at the scene,' he explained, 'we let forensics do their stuff in the house but outside the uniforms had trampled anything that might have been there.'

'Hmm, it does sound like our man, I might have a look at the house if that's okay?'

'Yeah,' nodded Douglas, 'no problem, but the owners are away for Christmas, staying in Greece apparently,' he sighed, 'alright for some hey?' Avalon nodded but said nothing as they entered the small cell block. To his surprise, Michael Collis was seated in his cell reading the newspaper with the door wide open and what looked like an expired cup of tea and a mince pie tray, one of those tin foil containers that are usual.

'Michael, there's someone to see you,' announced Douglas. The small man folded the paper and removed his spectacles placing both at his side. 'This is

Detective Inspector Avalon from C Section, he wants to ask you about the break-in on Southside Road.' The man's face lit up, it was as if he recognised the DI.

'This is a pleasure,' smiled the man with such a deep voice, it seemed totally wrong for how he looked, 'I must be going up in the world if they send DI Avalon to see me.' The accent was as about as Invernessian as Avalon could imagine. He was about to tell him not to flatter himself but he needed answers. Instead, he sat on the bench opposite and leaned his forearms on his knees.

'I'll wait outside,' said Douglas, 'I'll see if I can get us a cuppa,' and he left.

'I'm sorry I can't offer you a mince pie Detective Avalon but they only brought me one.'

'You seem comfortable here Mr Collis.'

'Aye, not bad,' the man nodded.

'Have you fully recovered?'

'Enough to answer questions detective,' and he gave a brief smile. Avalon asked him to relate everything that had happened and describe what the other intruder was like in detail. Avalon wondered if he had exaggerated the story but he seemed to know police procedure so well it was doubtful if that was the case. He still described the intruder as moving like an animal, as having what seemed like alien technology and the misshapen head of a fly. Avalon didn't know what to make of that but Collis was adamant that he had seen a wire or line.

'Aye I saw it glint in the glow of the streetlights, I saw *it* before I saw him,' he insisted. Avalon thanked him and stood to leave.

'If this sort of thing can happen in Inverness,' announced Collis, 'I look like getting another job.'

Avalon frowned as he stared down at the man.

'Keep in mind Mr Collis that it isn't a job, it's a crime and a serious one at that.'

Outside, Avalon saw Douglas chatting to the officer in charge of the cells.

'What's with the open door?' asked Avalon, the two officers turned to him.

'He's been in here so often it feels like it belongs to him,' smiled Douglas and then added, 'Michael Collis is of the old school, he was once caught red-handed coming out of a house with a sack of stolen silverware by a beat bobby. As the officer was arresting him he got a call on the radio to a serious incident two streets away so he left Collis and went to attend the fellow officer who was in trouble. Later that day, Collis handed himself in at Burnet Road carrying the sack with all the loot still inside,' Douglas shrugged.

'Aye that's the way of Collis, he's a crook but he an honest one,' added the uniformed officer.

'I'm afraid I don't buy into all that crap about honest crooks,' frowned Avalon thrusting his hands into his pockets, 'Merry Christmas,' he growled and left.

As soon as he arrived back in the Cave, Frazer called over to him.

'The DCI wants t' see you Boss.' Avalon stopped, turned on his heels and went to see DCI Croker.

'Ah, DI Avalon, I'm glad you popped in,' announced Croker removing his spectacles and pointing to his second chair. Avalon sat. 'I believe you have had something to do with the break-in on Southside Road?'

'I've been looking at the details of it sir, just to

244

see if it has any similarity to a series of break-ins we are looking at.'

'And does it?' he asked. Avalon was cautious, he hadn't yet figured out what Croker's interest was in the incident.

'I'm not sure sir, the thing is, the break-ins are an annoyance but we have plenty of more serious cases to work on, so I'm going to have to shelve this one for the time being.'

'I see,' nodded Croker returning the spectacles to his head. He seemed to be looking at something on his computer screen but Avalon couldn't see what it was from the angle he was at. 'I had a call from the Chief Inspector this morning, it seems the house that was broken into was his brother-in-law's.' Avalon swallowed, he was never happy when there was a connection to the police and he suspected what was coming. 'He asked me if I would see who was assigned to the case.'

'That will be Detective Sergeant Douglas,' informed Avalon. Croker removed his spectacles again and looked over to Avalon.

'The notes say DS Douglas is dealing with a small-time thief called Michael Collis concerning his illegal entering of the property,' sighed Croker, 'it says that the safe was opened by an unknown party.'

'That's right sir, we have no idea who attacked Mr Collis and broke into the wall safe,' admitted Avalon in a matter-of-fact voice.

'And you think this could be the same perpetrator that is involved in a case you are currently thinking of shelving?'

'Yes sir, as I said.'

'Then I suggest to you DI Avalon, that you keep

the investigation open at least until the connection with the house at Southside Road has been cleared up,' and he gave a slight grin. Avalon didn't think he'd ever seen Croker have anything but a frown on his face.

'We don't have anyone spare at the moment sir,' frowned Avalon.

'I find that hard to believe detective, especially as you now have DC White on your team.' Avalon wondered how the DCI got his information, he was consistently to be found, sitting in his office all day and yet he seemed to pick up the slightest rumour or information about the workings of the station. He must have been a good detective in his day.

'The thing is,' hesitated Avalon unsure if it was the time to mention it, 'DC White is proving to be…' he tried to make it sound less damning but he couldn't think of the words, 'unsuitable,' and he cringed inside as he said it.

'Unsuitable?' mused Croker, as he began cleaning his spectacles with a small handkerchief, 'did you sort out the matter with the envelope?' he replaced the spectacles and tapped the edge of his desk with his index finger at the spot where it had laid.

'I think so sir,' frowned Avalon again.

'Good, then you can put DS Ross on the case then.'

'I've given him some time off, he's really overdue.'

'You surprise me DI Avalon,' said Croker in a more abrupt tone, 'when all this work is piling up that you suspend one officer and send another home. If I didn't know better I would think that you didn't have all that much work on after all.' Avalon got the gist of the statement and he knew anything further would be quite pointless so he bit his lip, stood, and said,

'I'm sure I can shuffle the team around a little,' and he was about to leave, then a thought occurred.

'I was wondering sir,' he began, 'would it be possible to find out what was in the wall safe?' he paused, 'the one that was broken into at the Chief Inspector's brother-in-law's house?' another pause, 'only it would be easier to track it down if we knew what we were looking for?' Croker nodded giving Avalon a quick glance.

'I'll see if I can find out,' then Avalon left.

As he entered the Cave, most of the team were standing near the Christmas tree looking at the various parcels that contained gifts. He couldn't see Frazer. DS Wilson had made some sort of punch in an old ice bucket, and plastic cups could be seen here and there with a brownish-orange liquid in them. Avalon wondered where you would find an ice bucket in a police station.

'Where's Megan?' he asked.

'Fetching some mince pies from downstairs,' said Rory. The team were chatting and seem to be getting into the Christmas spirit if only for a few minutes. The door opened and Avalon looked round, he was expecting Frazer but it was Ross.

'I thought I told you...' but he stopped as Ross pulled a parcel from his jacket and held it up.

'I had to bring this,' and he tossed what was probably a scarf or similar to Rory, 'Merry Christmas,' he called to him. Rory smiled and nodded. Avalon looked at the clock on the wall and gauged it by his watch, there was nothing else for it, it was lunchtime already and he would have to keep the C Section Christmas tradition. The job could wait. Rutherford handed him a plastic cup with the hastily made punch, it was revolting but strong and warming.

'What the hell is this?' he asked. Wilson smiled and held up his cup.

'A wee bit o' what I could scrounge from here and there,' he smiled, 'a drop o' Bells, a finger o' Rum, something called a Bacardi Breezer, oh and lashings of Ginger Beer…' he said the last part in an English accent, 'well Irn Bru actually,' he corrected himself.

'Ef y' can get past wanting to vomit,' began Rutherford, 'and then the urge to wash your lips in disinfectant… it's actually not that bad.'

'I call it C Sectioned,' laughed Wilson holding up the paper cup and toasting 'Slainte'. Several of the others returned the toast, Rory said something noticeably different and both Ross and Avalon said 'Sludge' just as Frazer came in with a large box of mince pies. Once everyone had a drink and a pie they opened their gifts and Alison Boyd was so impressed with hers, she planted a kiss on Avalon's lips and hugged him. There were various well thought out gifts, some humorous some just nice. Rutherford had bought Avalon a DVD about the history of Triumph Motorcycles, which surprised him, as Rutherford to his knowledge didn't know about Avalon's bike. Ross' gift to Rory was a specially made tee-shirt, which said in large letters on the front, 'Yes I'm from Mull, but I'm normal,' and immediately, Rory took off his jacket and pulled the garment over his shirt and tie. He turned around to reveal on the back, 'for Mull anyway!' There were several laughs and even Ross seemed a little more light-hearted.

They ate and drank and very soon they knew they would have to get back to work, Christmas had to be taken in small measures, just like the booze. There was plenty of chat and more laughing, after all, Avalon wouldn't spoil their fun but he sidled over to Frazer and told her that they would be keeping the break-in cases open.

'Oh, right,' she said with wide-open eyes, 'something cropped up?'

'I'll tell you later,' he smiled and sat on the edge of a desk.

As the frivolity subsided, and the Cave became a workplace again, Avalon returned to his booth but saw Ross was following him in there.

'Feeling better?' he asked as he sat. Ross sat opposite still holding his plastic cup with a few dregs left.

'Better, certainly,' he nodded, 'I don't need time off, I need to be here. I just aimlessly mooch around the flat and the weather isn't good enough to go out anywhere.'

'It's up to you but I still think you need some time off, we all do but it's ages since you had proper time off,' insisted Avalon but he knew what it was like, if you weren't there, someone else had to take up the slack for you. The pressure was overwhelming. Ross just stared at his boss and then raised his brows. 'And, you're out of uniform DS Ross.'

'You mean I'm wearing proper clothes rather than the cheap suit and crappy tie?'

'Yeah, you're making the rest of us look shoddy,' grinned Avalon.

'Hey, Rossy, what was et that old lady said t' you

249

a few weeks ago when you asked her if she recognised the man in the photograph?' that was Rutherford, he had been telling DS Wilson and DC Boyd an amusing anecdote and was trying to bring Ross into the conversation.

'Don't you tell it, you'll get it wrong,' called back Ross and then quieter to Avalon, 'looks like I'm required,' and he gave a weak smile.

'Well, if you're sure you're staying, I might have something for you, see me in a bit,' nodded Avalon and he returned to the booth to read the cover of his new DVD.

~~~~~~~

The rest of Monday had been what was loosely termed a 'free and easy' day, the Christmas feel of the afternoon making the conversation somewhat more easy-going than of late. There was still work to do however and Avalon had outlined his plans with Frazer; the talk he had with Croker, the ideas to further the investigation and a brief recap of what they knew. Frazer had new information too, she had tracked down the company who manufactured the fabric that they had found samples of at the Strathpeffer house. She had also received an email from the possible source of the garment.

'Et seems that this company makes military-style casual clothing,' she had told Avalon, 'so it has t' be somebody who has visited America.' The boss had pointed out that that wasn't necessarily the case, the garment could have been sent from the States, online or something like that. Frazer had checked that, they had no records of mail order to the UK. By the time everyone had gone home, C Section seemed a much happier place and Avalon was glad of that, would that remain? It was doubtful, there was still the problem of Angus White to overcome. He wasn't sure how he would go about that issue but he decided for the short term he would put White back with Rutherford and see if the big man could hammer some sense into the new DC. It was something he had to do, DCI Croker had made it plain by his comments that he was less than happy with Avalon lately, it hadn't been a direct criticism but Avalon was quite used to Croker's rhetoric to know he was displeased.

Most of the team were off on Christmas day, all except Avalon, Frazer and Ross but even they were resigned to the idea that they wouldn't be doing very much. The DI was relatively upbeat about the future, he now had another weird case to work, but at least he was justified in putting personnel and resources on it, if only due to the interest of the Chief Inspector. DCI Croker had informed Avalon by telephone that the wall safe at the house contained a 'family heirloom' but any other information wasn't forthcoming. That immediately seemed suspicious to Avalon. As he sat on the edge of Frazer's desk watching her explain to Ross the details of the case from the whiteboard, it gave him a chance to glance at the team. Ross seemed subdued and hardly gave Frazer any eye contact. Avalon then wondered about DC White who had seemed completely unmoved by either his suspension or the reinstatement soon after. Even when Avalon had explained that the DCI wished him to give the new DC another crack at the whip, White had just stared blankly as if he couldn't care less. Avalon

251

was growing to dislike the man intensely. He wasn't sure what Rutherford would make of him but he doubted the pairing would last for much more than a couple of days. He would deal with it after Christmas.

'So that's about et,' announced Frazer folding her arms.

'He's just a sophisticated cat burglar, should be easy to find him on record I would think,' announced Ross.

'Have you not been listening?' asked Frazer, 'this is not your run o' the mill burglar,' she pointed to the whiteboard as if to reinforce her point, 'this is meticulously planned, I'll bet this one's got no previous, not in this line o' work anyhow.'

'Megan's right,' nodded Avalon, 'this is different, he's done some painstaking research to get this far. I'm guessing there is a great deal at stake for him.' Avalon hesitated, 'look, if you don't feel up to it-'

'I'm fine,' insisted Ross as he stood and looked closer at the board, 'it's just a bit early for me at the moment.' Avalon noticed Frazer move out of his way and sit in her seat. There was something in the air as if she and Ross had not quite recovered from the previous debacle. He couldn't quite make it out... then it struck him. Ross hadn't made it plain on Saturday night exactly who the mysterious woman had been, Jesus, it was Frazer. Ross had fallen in love with Megan Frazer. Avalon almost laughed, he held it back as a cough. All this time Ross had been Frazer's arch-nemesis, he had been falling in love with her and then she had rejected him. Well-well, that was a turn up for the books. This potentially brought other problems but now Avalon was aware of it he could keep a check on things. He had to forget it, for now, there was a case to solve and it was by no means an easy feat.

'Okay,' announced Ross suddenly, 'I get it,' and he turned from the board and looked at Avalon, 'so we need to re-interview this McKeith I would think, has he recovered?' Avalon didn't answer directly, he looked down at Frazer.

'He's better than he was but the doctors are saying they need tae do more tests,' she explained.

'I'm not sure he'll give us anything anyway,' added Avalon, 'I was going to have a look around the house on Southside Road.'

'Expensive area,' nodded Ross, 'but a good place to start.'

'Nothing we can do until later in the week though,' shrugged Avalon, and he stood and walked into the booth. He came back with a carrier bag and that bag was chinking as if it contained glass. He brought out three bottles of lager and a bottle opener.

'For now, we take it easy,' he said handing them out, 'and unless there is an emergency, Merry Christmas.'

The following day Avalon called them into his booth.

'Right, let's get off, you drive,' said Avalon to Ross.

'Where to?' he asked leaning on the wall.

'Southside Road,' he answered picking up his phone and keys.

'What do y' want me tae do?' asked Frazer.

'You're coming with us,' smiled Avalon.

'Three of us?' she frowned.

'Call it my Christmas treat,' added Avalon.

The house on Southside Road was a large, detached stone property, very grand and very expensive. Ross pulled into the landscaped drive through large iron gates and parked alongside a double glazing van. Several workmen were busy replacing the large French windows on the balcony. There were a set of ladders up to the balcony where two men were manoeuvring the glass panel into place, another man was inside the room. Ross began checking the grounds for anything that may have been discarded, and Avalon began climbing the ladder.

'Morning,' he announced as he stepped onto the balcony. The three men more or less ignored him, they were busy securing the glass to the new door, but he thought they were less than happy having to go out to an emergency on Boxing Day. Frazer joined him and they waited for the men to complete their task. It gave Avalon a chance to examine the site, he looked down the way they had come and tried to imagine someone entering that way. Collis had said there had been a line or a wire, he looked over to the French window and then back to the balustrade atop the balcony and then up above him. The roof of the main house overhung the balcony at this point. He looked up and wondered if there was anything up there to loop a line around but he couldn't see anything.

'So what can we do for you?' asked one of the workmen once they had secured the glass in place. He was wiping his hands with a rag.

'Detective Inspector Avalon, this is DC Frazer,' Avalon looked at the other two men still sealing the glass to the frame, 'we're just checking over the site, I'd like to look inside when you've done.'

'We'll just be a couple of minutes before we can open the door fully,' nodded the man, and he went back to his work. Avalon looked up once more, he could see something, not that noticeable at first, but roughly in the centre of the eave, protruding from the timber planking he could see a dark object.

'Can you tell what that is?' he asked Frazer pointing up. Frazer covered her brow with her hand, it wasn't sunny but neither was it dull.

'Not sure,' she said, 'looks like a nail or somethin','

'It could be, we need to get up there,' he said quietly. He looked at the ladder leaning against the balcony, he was sure it was long enough to reach. He turned to the workmen and waited patiently. It wasn't long before the man opened the door as the others stood back.

'There you go, be my guest,' smiled the man and as they passed through onto the thick carpet of the bedroom he added, 'are you investigating the Fly?'

'The newspapers have a strange imagination,' he smiled, he had to keep the workmen onside as he needed a favour, 'but yes, we are investigating a series of break-ins.' The man bent down where a small bucket sat with a newspaper resting on it. He picked up the paper and found the article.

'It says here that he scales walls, it also says he's 'alien-like', is that right or is the paper pulling our collective pissers,' he paused glancing at Frazer, 'pardon my Italian,' he added.

'Alien-like?' laughed Avalon as he looked at the destroyed safe on the wall. The picture that once covered it had been pulled away and was now on the floor face down. The safe did indeed look as if an angle grinder had been involved. The space inside was small, ten inches long by about six inches deep and high. Whatever had been in there wasn't a large object.

'That's what it says in the paper,' shrugged the man calling through the open door.

'And what else does it say in the paper?' called Avalon, and he bent down and turned over the large framed painting.

'Er, it says, 'The Fly seems to be a great deal busier of late and is able to outfox the police at every turn',' the man paused and glanced over to the two detectives in the bedroom, 'and er, it says, 'he is reported to scale walls and has a large deformed head probably due to wearing a disguise in the shape of a fly.' He paused for a moment, 'and there's something about the polis not finding anything more,' he concluded and dropped the paper back on the bucket. Avalon hadn't been listening to very much of it, he was kneeling down staring at the painting. It was a print that showed a vast hall with flags and banners, and at the bottom, a solitary figure standing in full armour, a Templar Knight. The description printed on the mount announced, 'Tombs of the Knights Templar, by Alessandro Sanquirico,' and as he laid it down, he pulled out his notepad and jotted the details down. As he stood, he raised his brows to Frazer. Avalon walked past her and out through the doors to the balcony.

'Most papers say things like that,' smiled Avalon to the man, 'particularly when we don't tell them anything.' The man nodded. 'For instance, at this very moment, you can help us greatly with our investigation,' he announced pointing to the man. The workman folded his arms and grinned as if he was waiting for a punch line.

'Go on,' he said still grinning. Avalon looked at the ladder and then back to the man.

'A witness said the…' he wondered about using the term but he did anyway with an emphasis on the actual word, '*Fly*, is reported to have used a wire to enter the building, I wonder if you would help us to prove this by pulling up that ladder and reaching it up to the eave?' He pointed up, and it wasn't long before the man noticed the dark object fixed to the woodwork. By the time the man looked back to Avalon, his grin had disappeared.

'Yeah, course,' he said and jumped into action. They didn't use the ladder by the balcony, they fetched another section off the van and leaned it up towards the eave. One of the other men lashed the base to the balustrade and then they both held it as the first man climbed up.

'It's metal,' he called down, 'like a shaft with a small wheel inside it.'

'Will it come out?' asked Avalon but noticed the man about to take his gloves off, 'no, keep your gloves on,' he called.

'Oh right,' nodded the man, 'Jakey, throw me up a small chisel.' One of the men looked in his tool holder fastened to his belt and pulled out a chisel.

'Ten mil do?' asked Jakey. The man on the ladder was holding on with his left hand but held out his right as if ready to catch the tool.

'Aye, toss it up,' and Jakey did with a practiced throw that proved it wasn't the first time they had done the move. The man on the ladder deftly caught it and

257

began to gouge out some of the wood as Ross came up the first ladder and joined them on the balcony. He looked up at the man where small slivers of wood were falling as he quietly said,

'Nothing in the grounds.' Avalon nodded but kept his gaze on the man up the ladder. He seemed to have freed the object and casually tossed it down to Jakey who caught it in a small plastic bucket. He showed it to Avalon who removed it with his handkerchief as the man came down the ladder. The metal object was small and very light, a sort of dark, alloy shaft, circular in shape with a serrated, three-sided arrowhead. In the centre of the shaft there was a slot and in the slot was a small wheel.

'Not the sort of item you can buy from B and Q,' announced Avalon as the three detectives looked over it.

'So is it important?' asked the man who had been up the ladder.

'Oh yes,' nodded Avalon, 'it's important, and I think I know where I can find another one.'

Chapter Ten

Ross's car pulled slowly to a halt outside the large house at Strathpeffer and Avalon got out. He looked up at the windows at the side and then opened the gate to the garden.

'Do you want me to phone him again?' asked Ross leaning on the car by the driver's door.

'No, if he didn't answer before he's not likely to answer now,' explained Avalon, 'he's either out or ignoring his messages.' Frazer followed Avalon into the garden and they walked around to the main aspect of the house.

'Nice place,' commented Frazer but Avalon just nodded, he was looking up at the spot where the intruder had broken the leaded window to gain access. There was a sheet of Perspex over the area but that was all.

'I wonder why he hasn't repaired the glass?'

'I bet et's expensive t' get that sorted out,' suggested Frazer. Avalon looked over to her and raised his brows.

'Look at the house Megan, I can't see that he's broke can you?' She shrugged as Avalon looked up at the overhang that covered the large-windowed area.

'Bingo,' he pointed, 'there you are,' and he looked up to where a similar device to the one found at Southside Road was embedded into the timber. 'Get on to the contractors to see how long they'll be,' he asked turning to her, 'belay that,' he added, 'they're here now.' A white unmarked van had pulled up with a set of ladders on its roof. Frazer went to speak to them to explain what they wanted as Ross joined Avalon.

'This is a bit puzzling, I wonder what it's about?' he asked.

'Ancient treasure without a doubt but I'm starting to see that no one involved in this little escapade is telling the truth, they all have something to hide,' explained Avalon looking around the garden, 'even the Chief Inspector's brother-in-law too, as he hid his safe behind a Knights Templar print.'

By the time the ladders were secured and one of the contractors was at the top, Mr Gallagher arrived at the house and he looked somewhat put out by their activity.

'What in God's name?' he looked up at the man on the ladder, 'what are you doing?'

'Ah, Mr Gallagher, we did try to phone several times,' explained Avalon with the best smile he could muster.

'Oh, yes, it's you Detective, but what are you doing?' he looked quite flustered.

'We're searching for one of these?' explained Ross holding up a heavyweight evidence bag containing the gadget.

'But what is it?' asked the bemused man.

'The means to scale walls Mr Gallagher, the means to enter your house,' nodded Avalon.

'So,' he paused looking up to the man on the ladder and then back to Avalon, 'so there is one of these up there?'

'I believe so, and don't worry, the contractors work for the police on a regular basis, they will ensure the woodwork is as good as new before they leave.'

'Got it Detective Inspector,' called the man up the ladder and he handed it down on a line to the waiting hands of Megan Frazer. She brought is over already in a clear bag and they compared the two items.

'Perfect match,' smiled Avalon, and he turned to Gallagher, 'that was quite painless,' he smiled again. He let the smile subside and formed the beginning of a frown. 'My only issue now Mr Gallagher is getting the victims of the crimes to tell me the truth.'

'I hope you're not suggesting that I have been less than honest detective?' said the man with a little agitation.

'Then your hope is forlorn Mr Gallagher because I'm sure that even a collector as experienced as you would not fret over the loss of a book that has no intrinsic value and after our last telephone conversation, I doubt I have all the details.' Avalon ended with a questioning look.

'A collector such as I can get quite emotional about the loss of any part of our collection,' insisted the man, 'they are like children, I think of them even when I am not with them.'

'I have never come across anyone yet, even the worst of parents that forget that they *have* children Mr Gallagher.'

'I don't know what you mean?' frowned the man.

'I had even forgotten it was there, I think were

your exact words,' and Avalon frowned back with interest.

'Well, I suppose that was just a figure of speech,' sighed Gallagher.

'I see,' nodded Avalon, and he turned to Ross, 'let's get these to forensics,' he suggested and began to walk off, 'good-day Mr Gallagher.'

They dropped Frazer off at the station to do a little more digging into Mr Gallagher and his book, and then Ross and Avalon went to the forensic labs to drop off the items they had found. Ross had pointed out that as it was Boxing Day, it was likely that the forensics lab would be closed, Avalon said he knew that Miss Underwood was working. This prompted Ross to ask how he knew but Avalon just said he had checked earlier. As the two of them stood outside the labs waiting for Sarah to come to the door, each one of them looking at the objects and looking for any clues through the plastic, Ross was about to ask when it was, that Avalon had contacted Sarah.

'Hello,' announced Sarah with a big smile as she opened the security door, she glanced over to Ross and then back to Avalon, 'it must be important if they send two of you over, come in.' Ross thought he saw something in Miss Underwood that he hadn't noticed before, but then reconsidered it. He wasn't feeling quite himself at the moment and the sight of a very attractive woman was more likely to make him hungry rather than sexually aroused.

'Well, we've got two items for you,' smiled Avalon holding up both objects in plastic bags as if they were goldfish he had just won at the fair.

'My God, what are they?' she asked with a frown.

'I hope you can tell us,' shrugged Avalon passing the items to her, 'prints and metallurgy would be helpful but anything at all you can find about them.' She studied them and nodded.

'Most of this will take time until the team are back,' she said and then asked, 'have you got time for a cup of tea?' widening her eyes.

'Not really, but thanks anyway,' smiled Avalon, 'we still have a lot to do before the end of the day, oh and have you found anything at any of the break-in sites?'

'This thing they're calling the Fly?' she asked as Avalon nodded, even though he was sick of hearing the name, 'nothing yet but you would have to have the luck of the devil for this guy to make mistakes from what I've heard.'

'He has,' announced Ross, and he nodded towards his boss, 'the luck of the devil I mean.'

'Oh, he's made plenty of mistakes,' replied Avalon ignoring Ross's comment, 'it doesn't seem to bother him,' shrugged Avalon, 'and I'm hoping there are two more mistakes in those bags.'

Avalon had hardly got through the door to the Cave when Frazer called over to him.

'I've found out a few things about Mr Gallagher,' but her frown showed it wasn't game-changing information.

'And?' asked Avalon leaning on the wall by the coffee machine. Ross was pouring them both a cup.

'He's got no form, but he has previously had

treatment for addiction to prescription drugs and he probably suffers from OCD,' she explained.

'Is that what came before DVD?' asked Ross as he handed the cup to Avalon. The DI considered it wasn't the sort of thing that should be made fun of but he was just happy that Ross was getting his sense of humour back.

'How the hell did you get that sort of information without hacking his health records?' scowled Avalon.

'Facebook,' shrugged Frazer, 'he runs a book collectors page on there, all you need t' do es search through his posts.'

'It's weird what people put on that thing,' said Avalon sipping at the coffee.

'Well, I suppose it's better than images of what they had for tea or photos o' their mutant dog,' shrugged Frazer.

'It's not exactly breakthrough, but it does explain why he seems so uncomfortable all the time,' nodded Avalon and he looked over at the whiteboard once more. Ross stood by his side and asked,

'Shall we make arrangements to interview McKeith?'

'Yes, I need to ask Mr Keith some very searching questions,' answered Avalon and he turned to Frazer, 'contact the hospital Megan and see if Mr McKeith is well enough to be interviewed.' She got straight on the phone as Avalon looked back at the board.

'You know,' began Ross, 'if it wasn't for the fact that the Chief Inspector wants you to continue this, I would be forced to ask you why you are bothering with it?'

'Well,' nodded Avalon, 'I *was* about to shelve it,

but in the end, these are still serious crimes and this person could be dangerous.'

'But there isn't much to make a case out of it yet,' insisted Ross.

'There never is when you start, you know that,' replied the DI taking another sip from his cup.

'Is it your instinct again?'

'Probably,' smiled Avalon glancing around for a second, 'I can feel there is more to this than meets the eye. So much doesn't add up, not a single victim of the break-ins is telling the truth and there is the connection that DC White made about all the households being reasonably wealthy, and yet not having obvious income. They are hiding something and I would like to find out what.'

'There could be many reasons for that,' frowned Ross, 'and come to think of it, what was the theory putting White with Rutherford?'

'I didn't have any options,' shrugged the boss, 'White is a pain in the arse and Rutherford is a big brutal man who stands no crap.'

'I don't know who to feel sorrier for,' smiled Ross, 'Martin or DC White.' Frazer ended the call and the two men turned to face her.

'The nurse on his ward says he's much better, but the doctor wants tae see him again before he's sent home, an' et's not likely to be before the New Year.' Avalon nodded.

'But can we interview him?' he asked.

'The doctor says as long as et's brief and doesn't stress him.'

'Oh, I'm certainly planning to stress him,' replied Avalon with a forced chuckle. He would have to time the interview of the man carefully. 'There isn't a lot we can do until Miss Underwood has finished her work, so we better see if we can find anything like the gadgets we found at the house break-ins on the internet,' added Avalon directing the last portion of the sentence to Ross. The DS walked to his computer and began to search. 'See if you can find anything about the Chief Inspector's relations,' continued Avalon to Frazer, 'Mr and Mrs Davidson.' Frazer too went straight to work and Avalon continued to stare at the Whiteboard until he suddenly thought of something.

'I wonder why he takes these things?' he asked no one in particular.

'What do you mean?' asked Frazer.

'Well, it must take some pretty special resources to track his victims down, I mean, having to track down the families from the notes on the Key Rolls would take an age.' he frowned still looking at the board, 'and then when he finds them, he takes some pointless item and disappears.'

'Maybe there's some kind of clue contained in the item,' suggested Ross.

'That's what I thought but...' he paused, 'how does he know what he's looking for? Not all the clues on the list are items, some seem to be places.' No further answers or comments came from either Ross or Frazer and Avalon found himself glassy-eyed.

'How about cross-referencing the names and the items with them, we know a couple of them to start with,' suggested Ross.

'Some o' those names are French,' insisted Frazer, 'how do you track down the descendants of...' and she looked at her notepad for details, 'Tomat de

Avark,' she announced, 'and where the hell es the Grey Castle?' and she dropped the notepad on her desk.

'Hmm, point taken,' sighed Ross.

'As I recall, one clue was something like 'the ancient stone by the chapel' and that could be anywhere,' agreed the Boss and he shrugged and retreated to his booth. Once there, he knew it would now be a waiting game until something new cropped up. He busied himself with checking reports, it was a tedious task but in the long-run, it was better than having them sent back by the DCI because of errors or poor procedures.

~~~~~

Avalon thought about his day as he drove to work on Thursday morning, he was thinking that the worst of his problems in the section were over and there might even be some breakthrough with the 'Fly' case. He couldn't have been more wrong, his problems were just beginning, but the day began innocently enough. As he entered the building, he made his way to the front desk to see two uniformed officers escorting a man in a kilt from the foyer. He wasn't being restrained, but he looked dishevelled. Avalon paused by the desk to watch him leave and then turned around to see PC Dowd behind the desk.

'Morning Neil, anything for me?'

'No Inspector, were you waiting for something?' he asked checking the items in the record book.

'Just something from forensics but it was optimistic to expect it to be here this morning,' he smiled.

'I'll let you know ef anythin' comes en,' said

Dowd.

'Thanks,' and he pointed his thumb toward the main door where the kilted man had just walked out, 'late Christmas reveller?'

'Reveller? I don't know about that but he had certainly been helping Scotland's economy by the sound of et,' nodded Dowd, 'the lads that brought him in last night were on the verge of sending for armed officers from what I heard.'

'Oh,' said Avalon with a questioning look, 'and they're just letting him go?'

'Aye, et seems he was totally pished, and he just got a bit,' Dowd frowned trying to remember the word he had heard, 'emotional.'

'Well, I suppose we've all been there at some time or another,' smiled Avalon and began turning to leave for the Cave.

'I'm thinking that you never put a kilt on and piled all your furniture in the garden and made a bonfire though?' added Dowd as he continued sorting through the mail.

'Really?' asked Avalon with a grin, he stopped to hear the full story.

'Aye,' nodded Dowd glancing up from his task, 'then he began dancing around the bonfire swinging a bloody great sword and so the neighbours got the jitters and phoned et en.'

'I suppose that's natural, what was it about, did his wife leave him or something?' Avalon was smiling a little, it sounded like the night shift had something to stop the boredom anyway.

'I'm not sure,' shrugged Dowd, 'two local bobbies were the first out to him and they said he was shouting his head off in Gaelic and as they can't speak a word of et they didn't know what he was babbling on about,' he replied and ceased sorting the mail to tell the story. 'They reported he was foutered, but he was still able t' swing a bloody great Claymore, about with one hand,' Dowd paused and raised his brows, 'which to any English that might be en the building es a heavy two-handed sword and not a landmine.' He gave Avalon the semblance of a grin and continued. 'This guy was easily swinging the big sword with one hand and seemed tae know what he was doin' with et so they sent for backup and considered the firearms boys so they could introduce him tae thirty thousand volts.'

'Where was this?' asked Avalon.

'Somewhere near Munlochy from what Sergeant Gregory told me,' explained Dowd, 'he also said that when they got there, he was a little calmer and was sat cradling a deceased bottle of Grouse en his arms.'

'It sounds like another case of Christmas patriotism,' squinted Avalon, 'had he painted his face blue and taken to shouting, 'they may take away our lives, but they'll never take our freedom'?'

'So you're a devotee of Braveheart inspector?' smiled Dowd.

'Not really,' frowned the DI.

'Well, you should be, et was almost a documentary, et was so accurate,' and he winked and continued sorting his mail.

'Yes, about as accurate as Mel Gibson's accent,' smiled Avalon, and he continued to the stairs saying, 'well the poor man must have something on his mind to flip like that.'

'Probably,' called Dowd, 'when they got him in

the cells he was babbling on about the Pope being after him, and that would certainly make me flip,' and Avalon let the doors swing closed as he climbed the stairs smiling to himself. He was imagining the two uniformed officers thinking they would have a quiet post-Christmas evening, discussing how much the festive period cost these days, and wham, enter a drunken Highlander cursing them in a language they couldn't understand. So much for Christmas cheer. As he entered the Cave, he was still smiling and Frazer was once again already there.

'What are you so happy about Boss?' she asked.

'Morning Megan,' nodded Avalon, 'oh I've just heard about the incident up at Munlochy last night.'

'I haven't heard about et, anything serious?' she asked.

'No, just a drunken reveller, decided to get hammered and burn his furniture,' smiled Avalon turning to enter the booth.

'I'm guessing he's gonna be in deep regret this mornin',' she said thinking about the ramifications of such an act. Avalon sat and checked his emails then looked at his diary noticing the appointment with Sarah on Thursday night. He smiled once more at the thought, he was feeling excited about the prospect but he did think that even if nothing more than a friendship came from their time together, he would be content. To have some quality time with an attractive and intelligent woman was pleasure enough for him, though a passionate love affair would be pretty satisfying too. Then he thought about the professional side of his connection to Sarah, he was wondering how long it would take to get anything back from the two objects taken from the houses the previous day. It would just have to wait. Boyd and Wilson were having a few days break to be with their families for Christmas and Rutherford, White and Mackinnon's were also off until they might be needed later in the week. Avalon, Frazer, and Ross, however, were going to have to work through as they had all had some time off lately.

As Avalon sat in the booth, he thought back to a conversation with Rutherford a day or so ago. He had hung his head around the glass panel and called,

'Martin, you got a minute?' Rutherford had entered the booth and asked,

'What is et boss?' as he sat opposite the DI.

'How are you getting on with DC White?' Avalon had asked quietly, Rutherford shrugged.

'He's hard work t' be honest,' began Rutherford leaning back in the seat, 'he's got as much personality as a Calvinist minister and the humanity of a Dalek. I mean, he's bright, very bright but there's no conversation, no opinions, and no suggestions or ideas.' Avalon had nodded.

'Yes, the short time I spent with him I just felt like punching him in the face,' he said.

'I didn't realise that was allowed,' said Rutherford raising his brows.

'Normally I would say it wasn't but…' Avalon just shrugged. He didn't know what to do with the man. 'How the hell did he get this far?' Avalon had asked, but Rutherford just admitted he didn't know.

'Et's likely to be his work on paper,' suggested the big DC, 'he's got a high IQ I would say, but for some reason, that seems t' short circuit his rationality.'

'But what to do with him?' asked Avalon, not

271

really requiring an answer.

'I suppose I could hit him on the back o' the head and dump him in the canal,' suggested Rutherford.

'Okay, that sounds reasonable,' nodded Avalon, 'I'll have another word with the DCI but in the meantime stick with him.'

'Leave him with me a few days, maybe until after Christmas, I have a wee bit of an idea,' smiled Rutherford.

'The canal suggestion was a joke of course,' insisted Avalon raising his eyes.

Avalon was rescued from his thoughts as Frazer entered but as usual, Ross was a little late, but at least it meant he was getting back to normal. Avalon stood to speak to Frazer, but the telephone rang.

'Avalon!'

'*Hello, it's Sarah,*' the DI lost his severe frown as he heard her voice.

'Oh, hello,' he said in a softer tone.

'*I've finished preliminary tests on the two objects you brought in and I'm guessing you don't want to wait for the full report,*' she said.

'Not really, we have come to a solid wall on this one.'

'*Not much for you I'm afraid,*' she said in a flat tone, '*no prints and no distinguishing marks. Our metallurgist isn't back until after the Christmas break so we can't conduct in-depth tests until he returns, but I suspect it's a nickel alloy of some sort.*'

'Have you any thoughts about how it was projected through the air?' he asked.

'*Well, it certainly wasn't by a conventional gun,*'

high pressure compressed gas would be my guess,' explained Sarah.

'Okay,' he nodded to himself, 'I'll get someone to pick up one of the objects at some stage, you keep the other one for analysis,' he suggested.

'Will do,' she agreed and then said in a quieter voice, *'still on for tonight?'* Avalon had almost forgotten.

'Of course,' he said with a smile. They ended the call and Avalon held the smile much longer than he intended and wondered if Frazer was watching. She wasn't but the smile soon faded as he realised that the arrow-headed projectiles hadn't given him any clues.

For the rest of the morning, he went back through what they knew with Frazer and Ross until they were all becoming desensitised to what they had on the whiteboard.

'There is something I can't work out here,' said Ross eventually. Avalon had expected Frazer to make some comment about it not being unusual, but she didn't. He wondered if his warning to them had made a bigger impact than he had expected.

'Such as?' asked Avalon.

'This Fly character,' began Ross frowning towards the whiteboard, 'he seems to have some pretty high-tech kit for a housebreaker.'

'But we have considered he isn't just another house breaker,' sighed Avalon tired of covering the same points.

'Well, whatever he is, the kit he has goes far and above anything we have come across before,' he continued. 'For instance, the arrow projectiles, yes, I understand that looping a line over the tiny wheel and firing the thing into the building does the job, but then

273

you have to attach a stronger line and pull it through the wheel and then fit something to the line to pull you up.'

'If that's how he did it?' nodded Avalon.

'So is it just me that thinks this is a bit Mission Impossible?' asked Ross pointing to himself.

'Et did occur to me,' nodded Frazer, 'but I couldn't explain et so I kept quiet.' Avalon sat on one of the chairs and looked from one of them to the other.

'I know what you mean,' he eventually nodded, 'and if forensics are correct and a compressed gas gun is being used, then we do seem to be dealing with a remarkably well kitted out individual.'

'Indeed, not to mention a taser and probably some sophisticated night vision equipment,' added Ross.

'So what do we conclude from that?' asked Avalon raising his brows.

'That he's got plenty o' cash and he's doing this because he's bored?' suggested Frazer.

'Or it's a well booted and suited organisation,' suggested Ross.

'Either is possible,' agreed Avalon, 'if the Caledonian Flame is a treasure of some sort, then it may be worth a dedicated collector or even an organisation paying a specialist to find it.'

'Which begs the question,' added Ross, 'what are we getting ourselves into?' Avalon nodded. He had already considered that whoever this Fly was, he was comfortable going about his business and didn't doubt his abilities.

'Since the taser attack I have wondered about that myself,' confirmed Avalon, 'if we do manage to find out who he is and corner him, we will probably need backup including ARV officers.' Both Frazer and Ross nodded slowly, it was a sobering thought and none of them wished to dwell on it. Avalon knew that Frazer had her Tactical Care Officer training through her surveillance work but didn't take the Module D13 firearms course. This meant that none of the team could even officially use a taser, never mind a gun. The DI hated guns, it was a device for ending life, it had no other use and to him, it wasn't something he would ever consider. He had always maintained that you had to be mildly psychotic to take the training, never mind carry one. Either way, it was likely they would require at least one of those psychotics if they ever resolved the mystery.

'So does anyone *have* a theory,' began Frazer, trying to change the subject, 'what sort o' organisation might have the resources for this?'

'It's just a guess that it's an organisation,' shrugged Avalon, 'it's more likely to be an individual.'

'But ef et isn't, who would you suggest?' she asked. Avalon jutted out his bottom lip and shrugged again.

'Nor sure,' he admitted, 'but it could be one of these born again Knights Templar groups or even some sort of collectors syndicate.'

'The boss is right,' nodded Ross looking to Frazer, 'it's just speculation, it could be anyone. I admit though, from what we know of the people who were broken into, they seem to have enough in common to belong to an organisation themselves.' Avalon nodded at this but Frazer thought of something else.

'Could it be religious?' she asked, 'there es the connection t' the Seraphim and the Templars were a religious order?'

'You mean the Pope still wants his cut?' smiled

Ross. Avalon stared at him.

'What?' he asked. Ross was thinking that Avalon was about to chastise him. 'Pope?' he said still staring, 'where have I just heard that?' he stood and picked up Frazer's phone and dialled three numbers.

'Hello,' he said excitedly, 'is PC Dowd still there?' then a pause, 'if you would,' he then added. He covered the mouthpiece with his hand and then said to the two detectives, 'it was something Neil Dowd said to me this morning. It's only just struck but I need to find out...' he stopped talking as someone came back on the phone. 'Neil, you said this morning that the guy that burned his furniture said something about the Pope, were you joking or is that what he said?' Another pause as Avalon gave a few slight nods. 'Yes, yes, if you would, thanks,' and he replaced Frazer's phone on the cradle.

'You thinking of going to church then?' asked Ross.

'It's a long shot but two officers were sent out to a man last night who was steaming drunk, swinging a sword around his head and shouting in Gaelic. Dowd thinks that when they brought him in, he told the officers that the Pope was after him.'

'You're right, it is a long shot,' nodded Ross.

'It is, but Dowd said that the two officers couldn't speak Gaelic,' insisted Avalon.

'So what, I don't know anyone who can?' shrugged Ross.

'What if it wasn't Gaelic, what if it was Latin?' asked the DI raising an eyebrow. Ross squinted and then frowned.

'Look, I can't speak Latin or Gaelic but I could probably tell the difference by the sounds,' he said and then shook his head, 'I don't know.'

'Ef he was out o' his tree on the booze et would be slurred,' suggested Frazer. Ross looked back to her and nodded.

'Possibly, I'm not sure what slurred Latin sounds like though.' The phone in Avalon's booth began ringing.

'Avalon.'

'*James, you better come to my office straight away.*' It was DCI Croker and Avalon suddenly became aware of impending doom, the DCI rarely called him by his first name and what the hell was he doing in his office on Boxing Day? Avalon and his team had to be there, but Croker didn't.

When Avalon reached the office of the Detective Chief Inspector, he could hear voices in the small room and so he knocked and entered. There were two men besides Croker, one was seated and wearing a dark grey suit with a pink tie and Avalon had him down for CID immediately. The other man was harder to read. He was in his mid-forties but his hair was already quite thin and cut short. He had a neutral expression but looked casual, leaning on a filing cabinet with his arms folded.

'Ah, James,' said Croker as he entered, 'I have some bad news, unfortunately.' Many things zipped through Avalon's mind, one of the more upsetting thoughts was that something had happened to Carol. He stayed as calm as he could and with the hint of a frown said,

'Sir, what bad news?'

'You're going to have to open your notes up on the break-in case to these two officers.' Avalon breathed a sigh of relief inside, but on the outside, he looked impassive. His eyes glanced quickly down to the man with the pink tie assuming he was the cause of this dilemma

'Sir,' frowned Avalon, 'may I ask why?' Croker seemed highly agitated.

'To be truthful DI Avalon, I'm going to have to take you and your team off the case altogether,' and Croker looked very uncomfortable with the situation.

'Just the break-in case sir, or is it all of them? he asked giving himself time to think.

'The ones pertaining to what the press are calling 'The Fly',' frowned Croker. He was sitting with his hands interlocked on his desk with what Avalon thought was a funeral face, and that was saying something for Croker.

'So, as I said, why is that sir, we are just starting to make good progress?'

'Because the case is being investigated elsewhere,' explained Croker glancing over the man in the pink tie. The man was in his mid to late thirties and sat looking at Croker but never gave Avalon any eye contact. To Avalon this meant he might not be CID.

'Can I ask who by?' asked Avalon looking back to Croker. The CDI looked at the man in the pink tie who gave the slightest nod to him.

'This is Detective Inspector Dryden from the Metropolitan Police, he works in SDC7.'

'Flying Squad?' asked Avalon with surprise.

'Indeed,' nodded Croker looking quite apprehensive, Avalon still wondering why the DCI was seemingly under some pressure.

'I would have thought housebreaking in the Highlands wasn't in their remit sir,' and he looked over to the other man and wondered who he might be. He was dressed more casual, no tie and a bomber style jacket.

'It seems the person known as The Fly is someone they have been trying to track down for some time,' said Croker, but Avalon could tell he either wasn't telling the truth or he didn't believe what they had told him.

'So what's the story with this man Detective Inspector Dryden?' asked Avalon looking down at him.

'You don't need to know the details DI Avalon,' said the man, 'just that you can leave the investigation over to us.' He still hadn't looked up.

'It seems a little odd to me that you've only just started to take an interest in him, is it because he's appeared in the newspapers I wonder?'

'That's not quite true,' replied the man, 'we have been watching him for some time.'

'Then why is he still out there? asked Avalon relaxing a little more.

'We haven't brought him in because we need to watch him, and I can't say more than that.'

'So is it terrorism?' asked Avalon but the man neither answered nor looked at him. 'Then I'll ask you, DCI Croker, seeing as this person doesn't seem to want to converse or give me eye contact,' he said looking at Croker.

'I'll give you eye contact DI Avalon,' announced the man, and he did, his light blue eyes glued themselves on Avalon with no so much as a blink. Avalon held the stare, 'as I have said, I can say no more.' He continued looking up at Avalon. The DI looked to Croker as he spoke.

'With respect sir, we've put a great deal of time

into this, it doesn't seem right that someone can just waltz in and make that work totally pointless.'

'My hands are tied unfortunately DI Avalon,' and Avalon noticed that the James had gone and his title had become more formal, 'this has come from division and therefore-'

'At the very least,' interrupted Avalon, 'we need to be in on it.'

'That's not possible, this is way above what you are capable of dealing with and it needs a different kind of-'

'Don't patronise me,' interrupted Avalon, 'we do quite well up here without the help of the Heavy Mob, and neither do we cherry-pick cases like some forces I could mention,' the man folded his arms and broke the eye contact.'

'It's irrelevant what you think, this comes from the top, so step down or get pushed off the step,' said the man calmly.

'I don't work for you, and unless the system has changed overnight, *you* can't make that decision. Division or not, we can still appeal,' and Avalon looked to the DCI. This time it was Croker who broke the eye contact, 'oh I see,' said Avalon folding his arms, 'you've made your decision too.'

'As I say, my hands are tied on this matter,' shrugged Croker and Avalon was about to rip into him as the other man broke in.

'I think we need to calm down gentlemen,' he had an American accent and Avalon's eyes opened wide, 'I think Detective Avalon needs at least an explanation.'

'That's up to you,' murmured Dryden. The man with the American accent looked at Avalon and to his credit seemed easier going than Dryden.

'It's clear that you and your team have been busy on this case DI Avalon but we believe an agent has gone rogue,' explained the American.

'An agent?'

'From the States,' he explained.

'CIA?' asked Avalon with a frown, it was difficult to believe but then again there was all that expensive kit.

'Yes,' the man nodded, 'we lost track of him across the pond and so we spoke to some people over here and they told us our man might be in Scotland.'

'So are you with the CIA?' asked Avalon.

'I am,' he smiled, 'Agent Greg Warranden,' and he held out his hand. Avalon reached over and shook it, at least he had the decency to explain the situation which was more than the Flying Squad officer was going to do.

'So what's he done?' asked Avalon.

'Well, as you can imagine, some of the details are on a need-to-know basis but let's just say he's not playing for our team any longer.'

'I was thinking of here, what's he done here?' explained Avalon.

'As far as we know, just some housebreaking and I believe from what DCI Croker says,' the man smiled a little trying to make light of it glancing to Croker, 'he's made a mess in the Chief Inspector's house.'

'It was actually his brother-in-law's house,' frowned Avalon, he was beginning to think they didn't know anything about what The Fly had been up to. 'So you don't know what he's doing here?' he asked.

'Making a nuisance of himself,' smiled the American once more. Now Avalon thought *he* was being

281

patronising.

'So neither the CIA or the Flying Squad have any idea what he's doing here.'

'We'll find that out when we gather up all your reports and any evidence you have,' said Dryden without looking up.

'Sod that,' spat Avalon with exasperation, 'I want official documentation before that can happen.' Croker removed his spectacles as Dryden handed Avalon the paperwork from New Scotland Yard that had been sent from the Home Office. Avalon glanced over it.

'You got that cleared quickly,' and he tossed it on the desk and looked at Croker, 'and have you got nothing to say about this?'

'There is nothing I can say, I phoned division, and they have sanctioned it,' frowned Croker with a worried look, 'this seems all cut and dry, I don't see how it can be stopped.'

'It can't,' added Dryden, and he stood, 'get your team to have everything ready within the hour,' and he was about to leave, 'oh and anything you have at the forensics lab.' As Dryden left Avalon glared at Croker.

'I'm sorry,' said Warranden, 'I wish it could have been done differently,' and he turned and thanked Croker and left.

'There was nothing I could do,' sighed Croker interlocking his hands on the desk once more.

'There was plenty you could have done, what about going up the chain of command a little higher, what about an appeal to the Secretary of State for Scotland,' growled Avalon, 'anything to give us more time. You know the score DCI, you used to be this side of the desk remember?' Avalon had venom in his voice as he continued after a pause for breath. 'This is a bloody Scottish case, not English or American.'

'It wouldn't have made any difference, this is just a break-in case after all, how can I go to division and make a case, for God's sake Detective Inspector, they would laugh in my face.'

'So you just pull the rug from under me and my team, it doesn't matter to you that we've lost sweat over this does it, just so long that Division doesn't laugh in your face?'

'Detective Inspector Avalon, I'm still your superior officer and I think-'

'I can soon change that,' spat Avalon and turned and left, leaving the door wide open.

Back in the Cave, Frazer and Ross could see Avalon was troubled. He had gone back to his computer and worked furiously for a good ten minutes, then he came out and took his phone from his pocket.

'We've been taken off the case,' he said beginning to tear open the phone.

'Why for God's sake?' asked Ross.

'I don't have time to explain it, but they will be here to collect all the notes and reports we have, so be ready for it.'

'Who will?' asked Ross but Frazer was perturbed by the DI's frenetic actions and interrupted.

'What are you doing?' she asked watching Avalon fitting a new sim card to the phone.

'It's an old trick we used in Wolverhampton when we were on surveillance. It makes sure you only get calls from the people you want,' and he placed a scrap of paper on Frazer's desk. 'Put that number in your phone and name it 'Mother' or something innocuous.'

'What are you going to do?' asked Ross very puzzled by Avalon's actions.

'There's something not quite right about this, I've just spoken with a DI from the Flying Squad and a CIA agent. They reckon The Fly is a rogue CIA field operative, but I'm not convinced.'

'CIA?' frowned Frazer disbelievingly.

'So I'll ask again, what are you going to do?' repeated Ross. Avalon pulled out a sheet of paper from his pocket as soon as he snapped his phone back together.

'Croker wouldn't support us,' replied Avalon with that old fire back in his eyes, 'he's more concerned about his own position than the case so I'm out,' he announced holding up the sheet.

'That's crazy,' said Frazer with a deep frown, as Avalon took the scrap of paper with the phone number back from her, 'we're getting nowhere with the case anyway.'

'She's right,' agreed Ross, 'it's just a poxy break-in case.'

'Strange,' smiled Avalon, 'that's what Croker said,' and he stuffed the paper and the phone into his jacket pocket, 'but even if it had been a bigger case, the outcome would have been the same.' He looked at his watch and then up to the clock. 'Listen,' he insisted, 'I have a lot to do,' he was as frenzied as the two of them had ever seen, 'I have a few theories about this but I need some time, I also need to make some calls,' he gave a grin and winked at Frazer.

'He's loving this,' thought Ross not sure what it was all about.

'Right, I'm off, I'll be in touch, but don't phone me,' and he left quickly.

~~~~~~~

'You're doing what?' demanded Croker.

'Handing my resignation in, I have plenty of holidays due so I won't be back in. I'll leave my keys and cards on the desk downstairs with my ID.'

'But, this is stupid, you're taking this far too seriously,' stammered Croker, 'I understand you're angry but this isn't the way-'

'I can't work without support from my direct superior DCI, you let this go far too easily and that means I can't trust you to support me or the team, DS Wilson can manage the shop.'

'But, but for God's sake man...' It was too late, Avalon had left, and the door was wide open again.

He sat in his car still unsure what unseen force was driving him to do the things he was doing. The only thing he knew for certain, was that at least in the short term, it seemed like the right thing to do, and it felt good. He drove a few miles from the police station and parked in a supermarket car park then pulled out his phone and rung the station.

'Hello, is that Neil?'

'*Only my mother and a certain Detective Inspector calls me by that name and as my mother has a deeper voice I'm guessing that-*'

'Neil I need the contact details for the man who burned his furniture,' insisted Avalon abruptly. Dowd got the idea Avalon was somewhat flustered and so he got the details and gave them to him. 'Thanks Neil, oh and don't tell anyone I made this call.'

'*What call*?' asked Dowd. Avalon cut the connection and rang the number he had jotted down. He knew the man would probably be in because he was beginning to realise that anyone connected with the case, seemed to have some kind of hidden income so it was doubtful he would be working. It was Christmas anyway.

'What a bloody stupid way to spend your Christmas,' he said to himself as he listened to the phone dial out.

'*Hello*,' said the voice, it may have been Avalon's imagination, but the person seemed hesitant.

'Mr Greenaway, Mr Paul Greenaway?'

'*Yes, who is this*?'

'It's Detective Inspector Avalon from Inverness,' he announced, he had conveniently forgotten to hand in his keys and ID at the desk. He hadn't even left by the front door of the station. 'I wonder if I could have a word with you?'

'*Erm, what about*?' asked the man.

'It's just a follow-up call about the incident the other night, nothing serious, just a chat.' There was silence for a few seconds.

'*I suppose so, there's nothing I can add though, I was just a wee bit drunk.*'

'I understand that, it's just to clear things up, with you brandishing a weapon we just have to make sure that the matter is fully resolved.'

'*Oh, yes, right*,' he hesitated, '*it was just a reproduction sword*,' he added, '*but yes I suppose it would be okay.*'

'I'll be there in about an hour,' confirmed the DI.

'Have you got some ID?' asked the man from behind a chained door. The house was once again a large property surrounded by large trees and shrubs with immaculate gardens, all except for a patch of scorched earth and a pile of ashes, on what used to be a lawn. Avalon showed the man his ID through the gap and he opened the door fully. Avalon was shown into the kitchen where the man pulled out a chair for the detective and he sat at the opposite end of the table.

'I was just having one of those moments Detective,' explained Greenaway, 'I didn't mean anything by it.'

'Probably not but the local officers were concerned and were thinking of having you tasered,' explained Avalon raising his brows.

'Yes,' frowned the man looking down at his hands on the table, 'they told me that at the station.' He had an almost English accent with just a tiny residue of Scottish here and there along with some local phrases.

'Do you have the Gaelic'?' asked Avalon.

'Gaelic?' asked the man with surprise, 'no not at all, why?'

'Because the officers said you were shouting in Gaelic,' explained Avalon. Something seemed to flit across his eyes for a second and then he smiled, 'I know the words you see on touristy signs like 'failte' but that's all Inspector.'

'So I was correct then, it was Latin you were speaking,' said Avalon trying to make the man think he knew considerably more than he did. He saw doubt flood into the man's features, he suddenly looked pensive, like a little boy who had been found out, after looking at his

287

first dirty book.

'Latin?' he questioned with a false smile, 'why would I be speaking Latin?' Avalon sighed. He drummed his fingers on the table and casually looked around the room.

'You still seem to have plenty of furniture Mr Greenaway.'

'It was just some old stuff from out of the garage,' nodded the man.

'Which I also suspected,' said Avalon to add to the mystery he was trying to perpetrate. He looked for a long time into the face of the man without speaking. Greenaway was in his early sixties, strongly built with only a slight amount of extra weight. His hair was thinning a little but there was still plenty of it and it showed very little grey. His head was large like his frame and his eyes revealed little, except for what Avalon took to be doubt.

'I'm not going to beat about the bush Mr Greenaway,' Avalon eventually began, 'I don't have time for it, so I'll tell you straight.' He paused and took a deep breath then continued. 'I think you set up your little bonfire so it would get into the papers like the incidents perpetrated by the so-called Fly. I think you were trying to send someone a message. I also think that you are wrong on certain aspects such as who The Fly is.' He looked at the man who at first gave a little smile as if he didn't know what Avalon was talking about and then gradually it subsided. 'I think that you and all the people who have been victims of The Fly are connected, and that connection is the Caledonian Flame. I also think that you are convinced that The Fly is going after it and probably you too.' Avalon didn't believe the last part, he just wanted to fluster the man. 'Now tell me I'm mistaken Mr Greenaway so that we can get onto the next part.'

'I really have no idea what you are-'

'Yes, yes,' interrupted Avalon, 'now we go back to the serious part,' and he squinted his eyes at the man, 'what you don't know Mr Greenaway is that the man going after the Caledonian Flame is a professional, he's a man who doesn't care about anyone or anything. He is on a mission and he'll hurt or even kill to get what he's after. You sent him a message alright, and that message will be in the papers today. That message is who and where you are.' Avalon paused for effect and sat back in the dining chair. 'I don't know exactly what your part is in all this but I can tell you that you and your associates are in danger, and I'm your last chance before Satan comes knocking at your door.' Avalon sat and waited for a reaction. Avalon was guessing, he was more than guessing, he was gambling and that wasn't his usual style. If the man called his bluff, or Avalon was wrong... well, he would need to think about his own future then. The man looked at Avalon, then back down to his hands. He sighed a few times but said nothing. Avalon waited, he was beginning to feel nauseous, it wasn't going how he was hoping, though the man seemed to be thinking it through. That meant he *was* hiding something, but what? He had lost, the man was saying nothing, and he had nothing left to try. He slapped his hands lightly on the table causing the man to look over and then he stood saying,

'Well, I tried, I can't help you further,' and he stood and turned to leave. He opened the door and walked down the drive towards his car.

'Detective!' called the man from his door. Avalon turned and leaned with his arms on the roof of the car. 'You have most of it wrong, but I do realise there is danger.'

'Can we speak about it?' Avalon asked.

'Not here,' said the man looking around the grounds, Avalon got in his car and swung open the passenger door. The man reached back into the house and grabbed a coat and his scarf, and then locked the door. He then slid into the seat beside the DI.

Chapter Eleven

The Black Isle area was relatively unknown to Avalon, he had been on a couple of occasions during investigations of previous minor cases but that was it. As he drove from Munlochy with his passenger he was being directed by the man to find somewhere quiet. They were back on the A832 and heading west until Greenaway said,

'Here, take a left,' and Avalon did as he was told into a parking area within a wood. He noticed the sign saying 'Clootie Well' and saw the irony of it as he drew to a halt and turned off the engine. Avalon knew, that back at the station, some officers called him Auld Clootie behind his back. They got out of the car and Avalon reached in the rear for his overcoat. The weather was sunny with the occasional cloud, and it wasn't that cold but Avalon had been caught out before.

'Where are we going Mr Greenaway?' he asked pulling his coat around him.

'It's just somewhere I come to think,' he said and

he lead them from what seemed like a picnic area into the woods where strips of rag and cloth were tied to the branches of the trees.

'It looks like someone left their dustbin open during the winds,' commented Avalon, 'what is this place?'

'It's what they call a Clootie Well, a lingering relic of a forgotten religion,' frowned the man seemingly not happy with the DI's comment. Avalon had seen such places before, they were not that unusual but he couldn't help disliking them. They looked to his logical eye like the areas that are found near landfill sites where all manner of rubbish becomes blown into the undergrowth. There was no one else in the area and so Greenaway sat on a small bench and Avalon joined him.

'So, what do you have to tell me?' he asked pushing his hands deep into his coat pockets. The man looked around the place and seemed to be considering exactly how much to tell the detective.

'What do you know?' he eventually asked. Avalon looked to him and was about to tell him not to be so selective, but he knew if he wanted the man to tell him anything, he would need patience. He shrugged a little and then explained.

'That there is a treasure that once belonged to the Templar Knights that may have been hidden seven hundred years ago, that there is probably a professional on the trail of it, that he won't stop until he finds it, and that you and several other people are involved.' He then sighed, 'there's plenty more but some of it you probably wouldn't want to know about, but I do know about the Key Rolls and the monk called Bernard of Ravenscar,' he concluded. Greenaway nodded at this and sighed deeply.

'Do you want me to tell you the whole story, or do you just want me to tell you that the treasure can't be found anyway?'

'And can't it?' asked Avalon glancing round to the man.

'It hasn't been yet and I don't see how anything new could have cropped up,' explained the man but Avalon guessed there was more to that statement.

'Well, Mr Greenaway, that isn't my concern, I'm just worried that this person is likely to seriously harm someone whilst trying to find it, and he seems to have a great deal of information about those people.' The man nodded.

'He has, he has managed to track down quite a few clues already, but…' he paused, 'it will do him no good.'

'As I said,' insisted Avalon, 'that's of no interest, what I need to know is where he'll strike next.'

'I have no idea detective, his attacks are following no particular pattern as I can see,' replied the man leaning forward onto his lap.

'I need to know the details Mr Greenaway, we have some sketchy information but it isn't enough to work with at the moment.'

'That's clear,' nodded the man again, 'most of what you know is wrong but for me to tell you what I know goes against a pact that my ancestors entered into.'

'Franky,' said Avalon looking at him, 'I don't think you have the luxury of secrets any longer.'

'I think you're right, I think the time has come to end it. The clues to find the treasure are flawed anyway,' replied Greenaway.

'And knowing that is reason enough to tell me,' frowned Avalon, 'because if the person that is trying to track this down finds that out, I think you and your associates are going to be in some serious trouble.' The man stood and paced around as if he was giving it more thought, he took off his scarf and tied it to a bough of the nearest tree and then returned to the seat.

'Then I'll tell you, but it's a story that is seven hundred years old.' Avalon looked at his watch.

'I have an hour,' he said with the hint of a grin. The man nodded and began his story.

'When the Templar Knights in France were arrested in 1307, the Grandmaster was the one the French King was after. As soon as Jacques de Moley was arrested there was no chance of him leaving the cells alive and the French King planned to crush the order and absorb their vast wealth into his protection. The Grandmaster may have had information that this might happen and though at the time he didn't think that he would be found guilty of heresy, he did think that if the French Crown got hold of the treasure, they would never get it back. An order was given that the main fleet would sail if the information was received of any arrests. There were just seven ships of the order, all other ships were supply ships and vessels for carrying men, weapons, and horses. When de Moley was arrested, those seven ships sailed under the cover of darkness.'

'To Scotland?' asked Avalon.

'Not immediately,' continued Greenaway, 'they sailed to Portugal first and then they moved north to Ireland. Two of the ships sailed on to the Islands of Scotland to see if the Scottish king would allow them to land. He welcomed them, of course as they held land here and so the other five ships followed on and landed on the islands. One of the ships was lost in a storm and another badly damaged but it was decided to sail on to lands that the order had on the east coast. Their small force was split, most travelled across the land but the treasure would be sailed around the top of Scotland and down the coast.'

'So where was the place they were heading to?' asked Avalon wondering where the story was leading.

'Lands south of Inverness, the lands where Ardesier is now. They had been Templar lands for some years and it seemed to them the best place to stay until they could decide how to proceed.'

'And did they make it?' asked the DI.

'It seems so, and according to the scant records of the trip they stayed for some months but the treasure was a constant worry to them. It is said, that The Grandmaster of London came north as the Templar's were not hunted in Britain as they were in the rest of Europe and it is considered that the plan for the hiding of the treasure was his. We don't think that he actually devised it though, as he probably returned south as the trails in France became more serious.'

'So who did?' asked Avalon. Greenaway shook his head.

'Probably one of the monks with help of one of the higher ranking knights but it was so complex that even now we don't know where it lies.'

'So why make it so hard to find?' asked Avalon.

'You have to remember Detective,' said Greenaway looking around for the first time, 'these men were so devout, so dedicated to their god that they considered that if any man was worthy to find it, God would show them the way. They even had a banner made at the time which said, 'deus novit omne verum,' God knows the truth. It became their mantra, particularly after Jacques de Moley was burned at the stake sometime later. They felt betrayed by the pope, by the person that should have understood that they were not heretics, hence, 'God knows the truth','

'So in some ways,' said Avalon, 'they didn't care if it was lost or not?'

'Possibly true,' nodded Greenaway, 'either way, even Bernard of Ravenscar couldn't find it a few hundred years later.'

'So it must lie somewhere in Nairnshire then?' asked Avalon.

'No,' replied Greenaway shaking his head, 'the clues that have been deciphered point to it being in the Highlands, but that is as far as anyone has got.'

'I need more information,' said Avalon as he stood this time, 'it's all well and good telling me the story of how it started but this is getting me nowhere. Why is this so-called Fly breaking into the homes of these people?' asked Avalon and then he turned to the man and with a scowl added, 'and why is it that all of them are quite well off, and yet seem to have no visible income?'

'Are you deeply religious Detective?' asked Greenaway suddenly, Avalon opened his eyes wide and then laughed for a second.

'Not even slightly,' he replied still showing a smile on his lips.

'Then it's unlikely God will show you the way,' replied Greenaway looking to the floor.

'You think I'm chasing the treasure for myself?' asked Avalon incredulously.

'No, I don't,' said the man shaking his head, 'I think you intend to go after this man but for me to tell you what I know, particularly someone who is a detective, well…' he shrugged. Avalon pushed his hands back into his pockets. He sniffed the air. What the hell was he doing there anyway? He was no longer on duty and soon to be a civilian. He looked across to the man and returned to the seat.

'I have to tell you Mr Greenaway, I think that you could be in danger,' he said looking into the forest. 'The man looking for the treasure is probably an American and I'm not totally convinced yet, but I suspect that both the British and American governments know what he's looking for. Unfortunately,' he continued, 'I have no proof, it's just a feeling I get about this.'

'In some ways that doesn't surprise me,' nodded Greenaway, 'two documents went missing in the mid seventeen hundreds and it was suggested that they could have gone across the water.'

'This is complex to say the least, what do you say we go somewhere warmer to hear the rest of the story?' Avalon pulled his arms close in to show he was cold. Greenaway gave a slow nod and agreed that it was becoming colder. As they climbed into the car Avalon asked why he didn't want to talk at his home.

'I suppose I realised that I had attracted undue attention to myself,' answered the man, 'I was realising it was a mistake before you arrived and now…' he didn't finish, he simply shrugged and folded his arms. Avalon had started the engine to warm the car, and he decided to take a drive around the area as they talked.

'So what did you burn?' asked the Detective. Greenaway looked over to him. 'The bonfire?' added Avalon not taking his eyes off the road, 'you made a big show, enough of a show to get you noticed and I'm sure you did it to let this Fly know you had burned something.' Avalon drove back along the road heading deeper into the Black Isle and the man was about to answer, but as they passed the lane to Greenaway's house Avalon noticed a black four-by-four parked close by. He noticed Greenaway look at the vehicle and turn his head to see down the lane.

'Someone you know?' asked Avalon.

'No, not a vehicle I have seen before,' said the man still looking over the fields towards his house. Avalon pulled in, and turned the car around and headed off back. He turned down the lane and drove past the vehicle but there was no one inside, and no one to be seen in the gardens or by the house. He turned the car in a driveway and then closed in on the vehicle stopping fifty or so yards prior to it.

'Stay here,' he said and walked back up the lane to the vehicle. He noted down the number in his notebook and entered the garden of the house, he then walked carefully to the side of the property. He saw no one but as he returned to the gate, he saw a figure ahead moving to the four-by-four. Avalon noticed the figure was wearing a balaclava and his heart began to pick up the pace. The figure noticed him and quickly moved to the vehicle. Avalon called, but the figure started the engine and began to reverse. Avalon ran to his own car as he realised the four-by-four would have to reverse into a side lane to turn. He reached the car, started the engine and set off quickly in an attempt to block the vehicle in.

'Hold tight,' he said and then thought how stupid the move was seeing as he had a member of the public with him. He was too late anyway as the driver of the vehicle obviously knew what he was doing and he managed to spin the vehicle quickly to face the opposite way. Avalon set off after him and followed onto the main A832 back towards Inverness. As they raced after the vehicle Avalon said,

'Well, whatever it was you burned, this bastard doesn't believe you actually did it,' and he pulled on the steering wheel to steady the car through a tight right-hander. Greenaway was gripping his seat tightly as Avalon raced after the car. It suddenly occurred to him he wasn't able to call in the incident as the passenger wasn't a police officer. He managed to pull out his phone and hand it to Greenaway and called out,

'Find a saved number on here and ring it,' but the man struggled to find any numbers. Of course, he had swapped the sim card. 'Okay,' offered Avalon gritting his teeth as he pursued the four-by-four, 'ring this number and when it gets connects, hold it to my face,' and nervously the man did what he was asked. As Greenaway tried to put the phone to his ear Avalon did his best to speak, but it ended up as a shout.

'Megan, ten-eighty on A836 heading west to Tore,' he broke off as the phone moved away from his ear, 'believe a black SUV connected to the Fly.' On a straight bit of road, he grabbed the phone and continued, 'shit, he turned off before Tore, heading south,' and he tossed the phone back to the man as he tried to keep the vehicle in sight. Avalon heard the man talking on the phone but the four-by-four was pulling away and he had no idea where the road lead. He was thinking of giving up, there wasn't much he could do even if he could catch the vehicle and on these narrow lanes it was becoming unsafe for the public. The vehicle suddenly turned left just ahead onto what looked like an even narrower lane and so Avalon prepared to follow but as he turned the corner, the black vehicle was reversing towards him at a great rate of knots. Avalon braked on the junction but it was too late, the black four-by-four slammed into Avalon's car and the airbags were deployed as broken glass showered him. It was a tremendous bang, and the car had almost jumped into the air but as soon as he came to his senses, Avalon looked across to his passenger.

'Are you okay?' he asked. The man looked shaken, but he nodded. The black vehicle was drawing forward and Avalon wondered if it was preparing for another attack and so he shouted for the man to get out of the car and run across the field, towards a house that could be seen there. Avalon jumped out too and climbed over the fence but the vehicle was speeding off down the narrow lane. When he was sure it had gone, he jumped back over the fence and scrambled back into his car for his phone. Outside he could see the car was a write off with steam and fuel leaking out. He checked the ignition was off and then redialled his phone to explain what had happened. Frazer said she had put out a BOLO on the vehicle and Avalon was able to give her the registration. She said she would ring back. Greenaway was standing in the field looking completely lost, his face was deathly pale and there were several lines of blood running down it.

'How do you feel?' asked Avalon handing him

his handkerchief. The man puckered his lips still staring at the steaming car and blew out air.

'Not great,' he eventually sighed and began to dab the blood from his face. 'You probably need this,' he then said offering the handkerchief back to Avalon. The DI felt his face, there was blood there, but he refused it and wiped most of it on his sleeve.

'I get paid to bleed on the job, you don't,' and he gave the slightest hint of a smile.

'Did he…' began Greenaway but stopped to take a deeper breath, 'did he shoot at us?'

'No,' said Avalon shaking his head, 'the windscreen broke through the impact.'

'I could have sworn he shot at us, the windscreen seemed to break before he hit us.' Avalon shrugged, he had been so immersed in trying to avoid the vehicle he couldn't tell and so he began walking back to the car. Two other vehicles pulled up to see if they could help as Avalon reached the car. There was nothing left of the screen but the back window was shattered too and then he saw it. Stuck in the rear of the car roof, was one of the devices found at the houses that had been broken into. The arrow-head vanes of the object were poking through the top of the car, Greenaway was correct, they *had* been shot at. They had also been very lucky to escape with a few minor cuts.

As he sat in the rear of a police pool car being driven by Rory Mackinnon, Avalon remembered something he had to do. He pulled out his phone and dialled a number he now knew from memory.

'*Hello*,' said the female voice.

'Sarah, it's Avalon,'

'*Oh, DI, I'm guessing by the tone of your voice that tonight is off.*' Avalon was angry again, this time he was angry with the person everyone was referring to as The Fly. If Avalon was going to have to call him by that name he would change it to 'shit-fly' as that's what he thought of him at that moment.

'It looks like it and I'm really sorry,' he said making sure that no one could second guess who he was talking to, and about what.

'*Well, we did say that work might just be the culprit,*' she said.

'Yes and it is, at the moment my car is being taken back to the compound on a truck,' he explained. He noticed Rory's eyes look towards him in the rear-view mirror.

'*Oh, problems?*' she asked.

'Sort of, it's a write-off,' he said as calmly as he could.

'*Oh my god, are you all right?*' he thought she sounded genuinely concerned.

'Yeah, just a few cuts and bruises but I'll explain later.'

'*I'm guessing you had some sort of accident then?*' Avalon didn't reply straight away, he glanced back to the mirror but Rory's eyes were on the road.

'It's a bit more complicated than that but I'll try to ring later. I'm just sorry I have to call it off, I was looking forward to it.'

'*Don't worry, as long as you're safe, we'll still get together and you can tell me about it.*' Avalon was just happy she was feeling okay about the situation. As he slipped his phone back into his pocket, he turned to Greenaway by his side.

'Are you sure you feel okay?' he asked. The man nodded and said,

'Yes, I certainly don't want to go to the hospital.'

'And I think it best that you don't go home yet, it's pretty obvious this lunatic is after you now.' The man looked over to the DI with a worried face and swallowed. Avalon didn't quite know what to do next. If he came clean about the situation, then the Flying Squad officer would take over questioning Mr Greenaway but he couldn't really spirit the man away to question him alone. He needed to question Greenaway as soon as he could, he had to make out that the whole incident was unconnected with the Fly case.

'I think,' began Avalon, 'until we find this man we need to put you somewhere safe.' Greenaway nodded.

'I'm now wishing that I had thought this through a little better,' he said. Avalon nodded and then looked in the mirror as he spoke to Mackinnon.

'What's the story back at the office?' he asked he didn't want Greenaway to know he had tended his resignation yet.

'Oh, a bit of a panic to start with,' began Rory, 'no one knew what a ten-eighty was,' he smiled. 'Once we had established the vehicle was a hire truck DC Frazer got in touch with them for the details of the man but they are all fake. We tried to get the 'eye in the sky' over to you but it was dealing with some other incident so we were trying to get all the A9 unmarked cars on it, plus any local patrol cars.' Rory turned off the Kessock roundabout as he continued. 'DS Ross told me to get a pool car and pick you up but we still haven't heard anything about the four-by-four.'

'Who knows about this?' he asked.

'No one out of C section if that's what you mean?' smiled Rory.

'Good, we need to keep it that way,' nodded Avalon, 'drop us at the railway station,' he added.

'But I was supposed to take you back to the station,' insisted Mackinnon.

'Just do it Rory, I'm going to have to get Mr Greenaway somewhere safe before we do anything else.' Rory was about to say that he agreed and the usual way was from the police station, but he didn't. As Avalon and Greenaway got out of the car, Avalon walked around to the driver's side and spoke.

'Tell anyone that asks that you dropped us off here, and I didn't say where I was going.'

'Where are you going?' asked the DC but Avalon's blank expression told him to do as he was told.

'I'll be in touch when I'm ready, oh and you had better let someone know that Mr McKeith may need a guard, just to be on the safe side,' and Rory drove off. Avalon's then turned to Greenaway and said,

'We need to talk before we go any further,' and he entered the train station and took a seat facing the arrivals and departures board. Greenaway sat by his side. 'I have to tell you Mr Greenaway that I'm not going by the book with this,' and Greenaway nodded and said,

'I guessed that Detective, but I have also guessed that I'm in danger and in that respect, I have no idea what to do.'

'Do you live alone?'

'No,' replied the man, 'but luckily my wife is visiting her family in England.'

'Then you should contact her and tell her to

304

remain there until it's safe,' explained Avalon, 'then we must decide what our next move is.'

'Our next move?' asked the man slightly alarmed.

'As soon as I take you to the police station, you will probably be interviewed by two officers from out of the area,' explained the DI, 'but that could involve a trip to London.'

'I don't think so, I'd rather stay up here,' insisted the man.

'Then we have little time and to begin with, we can go to my house, it's close by and from there... well, we'll work on that once you have told me what you know.' Greenaway looked unsure at first but sitting there in the railway station he didn't feel particularly safe, so he nodded.

Avalon passed Greenaway a cup of coffee and sat on the sofa opposite. He had added a little whisky to both drinks as they needed a something 'extra' to set them up. As Avalon had been making the drinks, he was amazed how quickly the situation had moved on, it was as if he wasn't in control of what happened next. It seemed completely out of his hands and yet, it felt right. It felt as though he was operating as intended. What he couldn't quite grasp was what he should do from there. He knew he needed the information that Greenaway probably had, but what could he do with it? Officially, he was still a detective, but continuing with the case, any case was not considered proper and correct seeing as he had tendered his resignation and was taking his accrued holidays. He also wondered why he was so against handing the whole thing over to the Flying Squad officer and his American colleague. It was probably vanity, but then again, that instinct that Alison Boyd had mentioned was also involved somewhere along the way. Maybe it was just old-fashioned curiosity, but as curiosity was a fundamental attribute of a detective and not a variable, he doubted that was the case. Ultimately, it was Avalon's case and he was the only one who could shut down this Fly quickly. Anyone else would be starting from scratch, and from what he could gather, DI Dryden and Agent Warranden didn't have very much information on the Fly. Maybe they knew his real name but that wouldn't help catch him.

Avalon looked over to Greenaway as the man sipped slowly at his drink.

'I realise this must be a little stressful Mr Greenaway but at some stage, we need to know what this is about.' The man peered over his cup and then placed it on the coffee table with a thoughtful look.

'Stressful is an understatement,' he began, 'and ten years ago this position would be unthinkable.'

'I don't understand,' said Avalon. Greenaway shook his head slowly.

'Times change and situations change and in many ways I always knew that one day something like this would happen.'

'You'll have to be more specific Mr Greenaway, explained Avalon trying his best not to seem impatient, 'I'm not sure what you mean.'

'That's unimportant anyway,' announced the man suddenly looking at the DI, 'what matters now is that I give you enough information to stop anyone getting hurt.'

'Yes,' nodded Avalon, 'I would say that is a

priority but we also need to catch the person doing this.' Avalon paused for a moment for any reaction but the man just nodded. 'Do you know who the person is?' Greenaway shook his head.

'No, I have no idea but I'm sure that he had been working on this for some time, maybe several years and I'm guessing someone who has invested a good part of their life into this, will be single-minded enough to do their best to see it through.'

'We have considered that there is a great deal of research even to track down his victims,' Avalon was treading carefully, he didn't want to put the man off, 'but there is still a great deal we don't know about this case.' The man looked away and sighed, then picked up his drink. He gave another slow nod and sipped at his cup before replacing it back on the table.

'It's probably best if you tell me what you know, it will be quicker if I don't cover the things you have found out,' explained the man. Avalon told him most of what they knew, he left out any details he thought the man didn't need, and he embellished a little where they were speculating. When he had done, Greenaway glanced at him and raised his brows.

'You know so much but so little,' and he finished his drink. 'Most of the background is pretty close but there is so much you don't know.' He paused as if he was thinking about how to start. 'I can only tell you what is relevant and quite honestly there is still a great deal I don't know myself,' and he sat back in the chair. 'Earlier, you began to ask me what I was burning on my garden, well, I was burning my own notes on the subject. I didn't want this person to get his hands on them as I had too much information that could mean innocents could be implicated.' He was about to continue when Avalon's doorbell rang. The DI's heart jumped into his mouth and he held his hand up to Greenaway and motioned for him to stay silent. Avalon quickly leapt to his feet and headed to the front bedroom, then he peered very carefully around the curtains. He saw Ross standing at the door looking up and down the street. Avalon walked back to the lounge and reached for the phone. Fortunately, he knew Ross's number and rang it.

'*DS Ross*,' said the voice.

'What do you want?'

'*That's a nice welcome.*'

'Who's with you?'

'*No one why?*'

'How did you know where I was?'

'*The train station idea might fool Rory but I know you better*,' replied Ross. Avalon was now walking to the back door and he unlocked it.

'Come to the back,' replied Avalon, and he ended the call. Ross looked a little bemused as he entered.

'What's with the cloak and dagger stuff?' he asked.

'I've got Mr Greenaway with me and I wasn't sure...' he trailed off.

'Rory might be young but he knows the score, he only said what you told him to say.'

'So how did you know what I was up to?' asked Avalon.

'I didn't, I just knew you wouldn't leave Inverness,' smiled Ross. Avalon escorted Ross to the lounge and introduced the two men explaining to Greenaway that Ross knew the case. Ross then went to make them all another drink as Greenaway began to tell what he knew, some of it at least.

PC Tim McCulloch was just about to end his shift so when he got the call to a vehicle fire at Fortrose just two minutes after a vehicle theft at Rosemarkie, he realised the two incidents might be connected. You didn't have to be a detective to figure out that two-vehicle incidents within minutes of each other in an otherwise quiet area, in the middle of the Christmas period, were likely to be the same drunken teenagers causing mayhem. He phoned for some assistance just in case there was a patrol out on the A9 that could help track down the stolen vehicle. He already had the details, and they were given to the control and issued to all mobile units. He then decided to get straight out to the burning vehicle.

'Bloody hell,' he said as he jumped in the car. Ten minutes later and he would have been off and on his way home and someone else would have had to deal with it. He would phone his wife to let her know once he was at the incident site.

The vehicle was in a mess when he arrived but the fire tender was there and the remains of what looked like an SUV were still smouldering. The number plates looked like they had been removed prior to the fire being started, and so for the time being, all he could tell the control room was that it looked like a black Volkswagen Tiguan and it was probably a newer model. As he waited on the phone, he tried to imagine how many thousand pounds' worth of destruction sat there. He was surprised when the control announced that the vehicle was probably the very same hire vehicle that had a BOLO issued on it and that McCulloch should remain there

309

until someone arrived.

'Bloody hell,' he sighed again and began to dial his home number. At least he wouldn't have to go to the stolen vehicle incident, that was someone else's problem now.

Avalon and Ross listened to Paul Greenaway tell what he knew about the reasoning behind the break-in case and the man known as The Fly. Greenaway was adamant that he had no idea who the man was but he did know why it was happening.

'So ultimately,' interrupted Avalon, 'you are saying that the legend of the Caledonian Flame is true?'

'Absolutely,' nodded Greenaway, 'the Grandmaster in England at the time, Guillaume de la More is credited with devising the plan but it was more likely my ancestor, Aelfred de Verville. He was probably the man in overall command of the small fleet of ships.'

'So what was the reasoning behind the plan?' asked the DI.

'Once it was obvious that the Pope was going to allow the French king to have his way, it was clear that the Templars would be disbanded, some were already moving to the other orders, but what to do with the treasure?' He paused as if considering what they knew of the treasure side of the story. 'To say they felt let down by the Pope would be an understatement, these were all devout Christians and in their mind, the treasure belonged to God, not the Pope or the French king, and so they decided to hide it. I'm sure they didn't expect the haul to have to rest for over seven hundred years but they couldn't know how long their God would want it to stay hidden. So the plan was that the clues to find it

310

would be so obscure that the only way anyone would discover its location, was by the direct intervention of God.'

'Some plan,' smiled Avalon.

'It worked,' nodded Greenaway, 'but even some deeply religious people have wondered if God truly wanted it to remain hidden for so long. Some have wondered, like Bernard of Ravenscar, if God would see them as the chosen, and they have tested their piety by looking for the treasure, but to no avail.'

'Have you?' asked Avalon with wide eyes. The man smiled a little at this.

'Yes, hence my notes but though you probably won't believe me, even if I had found it, I wouldn't have brought it out of hiding.'

'So how did the plan work, and where do the victims of the break-ins come into all this?' asked Avalon. Ross was seated on a dining chair he had placed by the kitchen door and he shifted a little to try to get more comfortable.

'The victims as you call them are part of the plan. Twenty of the most trusted of the Templar monks were given the task to walk until they found something permanent on the landscape. A hill, a mountain or a church. They would then return and the place they found would be recorded. Once all the places were recorded they would be made into clues and the most trusted of the Templar Knights would protect those clues. In turn, they would be kept by the great wealth that the Templars held.'

'Is that how the clues are still maintained?' asked Avalon unsure if he was hearing correctly.

'Yes,' nodded Greenaway, 'but no one would

have imagined that they would need to maintain it for such an extended period. They still hold clues and in some cases unwittingly, but they are compensated for it.'

'How?' asked Avalon. The man looked a little uneasy at this and raised his brows for a split second.

'The treasure that came on those boats was vast,' he continued, 'so much so, that two more ships came after the first ones, there was so much wealth. For almost a year it was kept on the ships moving from place to place to keep it safe but one of the vessels was claimed by the sea and another was attacked by pirates, so it was taken north and landed on the east coast somewhere.'

'North from where?' asked Ross.

'The lands on the coast of Nairnshire were the most likely spot for anchorage, supplies could be brought in from Inverness so it was an ideal base.' Ross nodded and then the man continued. 'Someone, as I said, probably Aelfred de Verville devised a plan to hide the treasure. He found the ideal spot and then set about making a series of clues to secure it. It became a sort of small crusade and each part of it would be a pilgrimage for his followers. They even made a banner for it, a white cross on a black field with the words, '*deus scit omne verum*' written across the whole banner.'

'God knows the truth?' asked Avalon recalling what the man had said earlier.

'Yes,' nodded Greenaway and explained further, 'it's part of a dialogue that they devised, a sort of crusading hymn I would assume.'

'Do you know what that was too?' asked the DI.

'Yes, but over the years I expect it has changed a little,' and he began to recite it. '*Sapiens est Dominus Deus tuus, et scit omnia. Qui omnia videt, audit omnia, et ipse*

312

novit veritatem, et opera tua.' He paused and then looked directly at Avalon, 'It roughly translates to, *'Wisdom is thy God, and he knows everything. He who sees all things, hears all things, and he knows the truth, and the works of your hand.'*

'So it sounds like they were sending out a message to the Pope that God will judge him later?'

'Yes, I think that's an accurate assessment,' nodded Greenaway, 'but even though Templars were tolerated in Britain, after the decree by the Pope, they must have realised that their time was at an end. So the treasure was hidden and it was believed that God would point the way to a worthy soul when the time had come for it to be unearthed.'

'And the money has held out for seven hundred years?' asked Ross disbelievingly.

'Not exactly,' frowned the man, 'yes for a few hundred years that would be the case but these people and their offspring had no interest in great wealth, they did it for their faith. It wouldn't require huge amounts of money in the early years. Later, people needed more money to protect the keys, sometime in the late sixteen hundreds, some of the wealth was siphoned off to banks and some even invested. By 1720, a trust was established and most of the wealth was either banked or invested in large projects. This was to ensure that the Key Holders could be financially comfortable for their trouble, as by then, several families had fallen from grace and two had died out completely.'

'It must have been a great treasure to have lasted so long,' noted Avalon.

'Yes, but knowing that made some people greedy and by the 1830s, there was little contact between the trust and the Key Holders, they were paid but not kept informed about their purpose in the world. Many didn't even know what or why they were hiding. They just knew that they were paid, and to most that was as much as they really cared.' He paused for a breath and took a quick drink. 'Even the ones that could remember and still believed in the cause were unsure how it had all been achieved.'

'Do you know how it was done?' asked Avalon.

'We have a great deal of information that has come down to us in the written word and by word of mouth, but the full details remain a bit of a mystery,' admitted Greenaway, 'but over the last thirty years, I have spent my life researching it. That's why I destroyed my records.'

'So what information did you find?' asked Avalon.

'Well,' sighed the man, 'you know of the Key Rolls, there were many copies made of them, most of these copies were meant for the Key Holders, those chosen to keep the clues, but over the years they went astray to resurface over most of Europe. But there was another parchment that Bernard of Ravenscar had obviously seen. That was believed to be in a collection in Suffolk until it was stolen sometime in the seventeen or eighteen hundreds.'

'So how is this Fly finding these clues?'

'I'm not sure,' shrugged Greenaway, 'he must have found either the original copy of The Keeper of the Keys document or the notes of Bernard of Ravenscar. Both were said to have gone to the United States in collectors archives.' Avalon felt Ross glance towards him.

314

'Is there no other way to find them?' asked the DI.

'Just one,' nodded Greenaway, 'but I doubt God would speak to such a man.' Avalon nodded with a deep frown and looked across to Ross, the DS simply shrugged as if to say, 'I don't know what to suggest.' Avalon thought about the problem. He needed to know how to find out where The Fly was going to try to enter next. To do that, he would need to know how to find those places or people.

'Do you know who the Key Holders are?' he asked.

'Some of them,' nodded Greenaway, 'but I would doubt that any of them would admit to it.'

'Do they know you?' he then asked.

'Only two of them, we are a very secret group Detective.'

'So I'm guessing you are part of the trust that pays them?'

'Close,' smiled the man, 'I *am* the trust, I am all that is left. What little of the fund is left, is kept abroad in a bank.'

'Well, either way,' announced Avalon, 'for their protection and your peace of mind Mr Greenaway you will have to let us have their names so that we can put them on surveillance for their protection.'

'Couldn't we just remove the clues?' suggested Ross, 'to stop him going any further I mean.'

'That would mean changing the identities of these people to keep them safe from him,' answered Avalon.

'They would never agree to that,' insisted Greenaway, 'and in any case, the treasure *can't* be found.'

'I have heard that before Mr Greenaway,' frowned Avalon, 'why can't it be found?'

'Simply because,' answered Greenaway with a blank expression, 'most of the clues disappeared years ago.' The man saw Avalon's questioning gaze. 'After seven hundred years, several world wars, disease, accident and criminal activities, of the twenty original keys, there are only eight left, it's impossible to find the treasure now,' he explained. Avalon's face brightened.

'Then that makes our task easier,' he explained, 'we're not trying to find the treasure, we are just trying to figure out where he will try next.' Greenaway nodded at this.

'They were numbered,' he suddenly said.

'What was?' asked Avalon.

'The keys, each key and key-holder had a Roman numeral on the list.' Avalon glanced to Ross and then back to the man.

'We need to know those numbers,' he demanded.

'I would need a list, I would need the Key Roll,' he said, 'and that is just ash on my garden,' he frowned. Avalon stood and pulled out a sheet from his jacket pocket, he handed it to Greenaway and asked,

'Will this do?' the man nodded and began to read it. Ross's phone rang, and he retreated to the kitchen to answer it.

'The first one on the list that I know of,' began Greenaway, 'is number one ironically and was the theft of a goblet from Aberdeen.'

'We don't know about that one,' explained Avalon just as Ross returned.

'They've found the car,' he announced.

316

'What car?' asked Avalon.

'The SUV that gave you two a slapping earlier,' he explained, 'it was found burned out somewhere near Fortrose, it looks like the Fly has taken an old van, a white Vauxhall of some sort.' Avalon nodded and turned back to Greenaway.

'You were talking about the goblet,' he said prompting the man to continue.

'Yes, the goblet was gold and silver and was inscribed on the topmost circlet with, '*santorum regum throni,*' which means the throne of kings.' It is considered that it refers to Scone.'

'The coronation place of the old Scottish kings,' announced Ross as he sat once more.

'What is next on the list?' asked Avalon.

'Number four on the list, the theft of a painting.'

'We do know about that one, it was a print of Scottish landscape from what we are told,' said Avalon.

'It was a print of a well-known mountain Detective,' offered Greenaway with a sideways glance, '*ab arce griseo*', the Grey Castle.'

'Which mountain is that? asked Ross.

'Suilven, in the west of Sutherland, it was once called the grey castle because of its distinctive shape.' Avalon raised his brows and glanced at the list.

'The next one,' nodded Greenaway, 'number six in the list is a missing bronze stag,' and he noticed Avalon nod, 'the stag was unusual in that its antlers had a cross between them and represents the White Hart, or the legendary white stag of Edinburgh.' He paused. 'Then we have a statue of a Seraphim that was taken from a property at Scaniport, somewhere on the artifact it contained an inscription that at some stage was

317

changed from Latin to Gaelic. When it was replaced the key-holder had it converted back to Latin. Either way, we know it refers to the Clava Cairns near Culloden.'

'So if this list continues in order we should be seeing a parchment stolen from Rogart?' asked Avalon.

'No,' said Greenaway emphatically, 'I know of Mr McKeith but he is not a key-holder, the next one is also something you have dealt with I believe.' He looked into Avalon's eyes for recognition.

'A book, from Strathpeffer?'

'Yes,' nodded Greenaway, 'a book that contained in its fly sheet, 'a gift from Henry Abbot,' if I'm not mistaken.'

'That's very cryptic,' frowned Ross.

'Henry Abbot was the last in a family of key holders, he had no issue and the key was passed on in 1857 to a new key holder, the clue is in the title of the book, The Forming of the Forge. It refers to another mountain, An Tealach near Dundonnell.'

'So these are in order,' announced Avalon.

'They are only in order of the extant ones,' insisted Greenaway, 'there are several that are now lost.'

'These are the only ones of interest to us, Mr Greenaway,' insisted the DI, he then asked, 'do you know what was in the house of the Davidson's on Southside Road?' The man glanced at the list.

'I would say it was an ordinary stone, engraved into it were the words 'luna lapides' which means Moon Stones.'

'Do you know what that refers to?' asked Avalon.

'I'm not positive but I always thought it was the Camster Stones, the Hill of many Stanes as they call it, some people say it was an ancient lunar observatory.'

'Well that's not my interest at the moment,' smiled Avalon, 'but seeing as all the clues that exist have been visited by our Fly, then the next one on the list must be the one he is now planning.'

'That's a reasonable assumption,' agreed Greenaway, 'and according to the key on the list that would be…' he read from the list Avalon had provided, 'I suppose it just had to be,' said Greenaway.

'Explain please,' said Avalon. The man looked up, almost as if it had been inevitable.

'The next clue in line would be the one that has caused most doubt. '*Portum tutum*' and these days it is inscribed on a statue of Saint Erasmus. It means 'safe harbour' but that could refer to anywhere on the coast. It is generally considered to be the place they disembarked with the treasure.'

'And you don't know where that is?' asked Avalon.

'It had to have a castle as it was written that a castle overlooked the anchorage and so the most likely place would be Berriedale in Caithness.' Avalon nodded though he didn't know the place.

'Is the castle still in one piece?' he asked.

'No,' replied Greenaway shaking his head, 'there is virtually nothing left, but it's almost impossible to get to it.'

'Well, we don't have to, we just need to keep an eye on the person who holds the key to that clue,' said Avalon with a questioning glance.

'Ironically, that person lives in Berriedale,' smiled Greenaway.

'Hang on,' cut in Ross, 'if you say there is little of the treasure left, and what is left is in a bank offshore,

319

there isn't any treasure to find.' Ross wasn't frowning as such, it could only be described as a grimace.

'The Fly doesn't know that and I'm guessing that the Caledonian Flame is the real treasure?' asked Avalon looking from Ross to Greenaway. The man looked somewhat perturbed, like someone on a diet caught eating a cake.

'Not exactly,' he announced, 'that part of the legend comes from the notes of Bernard of Ravenscar. He wrote that he was trying to track down the last resting place of 'Flamma Caledonus,' the Caledonian Flame and those notes have been misinterpreted ever since. The Caledonian Flame isn't the treasure, it was the name of the ship that carried the treasure.' Avalon looked bemused, so the treasure didn't exist.

'The ship?' he questioned, 'so this is just a wild goose chase? There is no treasure!'

Chapter Twelve

Avalon poured himself a drink, he was now in the kitchen and staring out of the window yet seeing nothing. He looked around to Ross who was sitting by the door with his arms folded looking slightly anxious. Avalon walked back into the lounge and gave a passing glance to Greenaway who looked somewhat stressed.

'You'd better let us have the address of the person in Berriedale,' insisted Avalon as he sat back on the sofa, 'once the Fly finds out there is no treasure, he's going to be pretty angry and likely to go hunting the lot of you.'

'I didn't say there wasn't a treasure Detective Avalon,' replied Greenaway with a worried expression, 'I just said that the Caledonian Flame wasn't it.'

'But you don't want to explain further I understand?' added Avalon brusquely.

'It's been hidden all this time, I don't think it should be touched now,' explained the man.

'And why should it?' asked Avalon with exasperation, 'we have no interest in finding it, we just need to know what we are dealing with. We also need to know if the Fly knows what he's after?'

'I just think that once it is known what the treasure is…' the man trailed off and stared at the floor.

'So it's of a sensitive nature, then we can assure you that only myself and DS Ross need to know about it.' The man still sat silently. For a moment he looked like he was considering telling them, but he sighed and remained quiet.

'Then have it your way Mr Greenaway,' said Avalon as he stood once more, 'you can stay here tonight but we will have to drop you at the station in the morning so that you can be taken to a secure address.'

'What you have to realise Inspector,' said the man quite suddenly, 'is that the Templar Knights were more like monks than actual knights, they really didn't have any interest in money. They were more interested in their religion.' Avalon finished his drink as he stood and looked down to the man, then something occurred to him, something he remembered from the little research he had done on the religious order. He sat again, this time on the edge of his seat facing Greenaway.

'Is this treasure to do with the Templars fascination with relics?' he asked. The man just stared blankly but Ross asked,

'Are we talking about Holy Relics, the finger of this saint, the hair of another?' Avalon looked across to Ross.

'They were obsessed by them,' added Avalon, 'they even dug under Mosques in the Holy Land to rob the crypts under the old towns.'

'So this has suddenly become like an Indiana Jones plot?' asked Ross. Avalon just raised his brows then Greenaway added something.

'There was never anything known about what

was on the Caledonian Flame,' said Greenaway shaking his head, 'but it is very likely that there could be something in the collection that is so important, people would kill to get to it.' Avalon thought about this. Without telling the others his thoughts, he immediately considered the stories of saints heads preserved in golden caskets, the tales that he remembered from school and of course, the legend of the Holy Grail. He swallowed, he didn't even want to think about the items that could be hidden away, he just hoped after seven hundred years the site had been disturbed or even destroyed. It was safer that way.

'Well, let's not get into what might be there,' he insisted, 'let's concentrate on how we stop the Fly, he's proving to be as dangerous as he is elusive. We need to think about how we might catch him, and quickly.'

'I think we need to get a team watching the address in Berriedale,' suggested Ross, 'and we probably need some armed officers in that team by the sounds of it.' Avalon nodded at this.

'Yes, we'll start early in the morning and...' then Avalon stopped and frowned at Ross, 'hang on,' he said, 'what are you supposed to be doing?' Ross shrugged and then said,

'My orders are to see what you're up to.'

'Orders?' inquired Avalon.

'Yes,' nodded Ross, 'Croker told me to keep my eye on you, he reckons that seeing as we are both apt to hand our notice in at the drop of a hat, we would make a good team.'

'You've handed your notice in?' asked Greenaway looking puzzled.

'I didn't say we had handed them in,' replied

323

Ross with a stern expression, 'I said we were *apt* to.' This made Avalon smile, he knew it was a parody of what Greenaway had said earlier about the treasure.

'I'm surprised he gives a damn after the way I spoke to him,' he said with the remnants of the smile still playing in his features.

'He surprised me,' said Ross raising his brows, 'he's pulling all the stops out to keep your Flying Squad friend off this case.'

'It's a bit late for that I would think,' shrugged Avalon standing.

'From what I could make out,' explained Ross, 'he was already on it before they arrived at his office.' Avalon stopped and frowned at Ross, he didn't quite understand but at the end of the day, it didn't matter anymore. Avalon would keep at the Fly until something happened to stop that, but he still needed the back-up of the police force to carry it through. He outlined his plan to Ross, and the DC agreed that if he was sure he was going ahead with it, he would help out. They would spend the night at Avalon's house and get an early start in the morning so they could take Mr Greenaway to the station and some safety.

~~~~~~~

No police officer likes surveillance, it's one of the parts of the job that's necessary but is so utterly tedious that most would rather write out reports than undertake prolonged surveillance. On the television and movies, police officers are seen watching some location with binoculars or a camera, until suddenly, their quarry makes a move. In reality, they sit for days, sometimes weeks without so much as a sighting. More often than not, the mind-set of inactivity takes a toll on the thought patterns and when action is needed, the effort required is overwhelming to the point that mistakes can easily be made. Avalon had thought about the problem on many past occasions and he knew that the best way to overcome it, was to find something to do. Something to keep the mind active, but not unprepared, and to that end, he decided to purchase a cheap road map and study the locations of the previous break-ins. Reclined in the passenger seat of Ross's car, he plotted out all the sites of the break-ins and marked different symbols for the places where the clues pointed and then connected to ones he felt relevant with pencilled lines. Ross moved from his crumpled position behind the wheel and tried in vain to become more comfortable. He opened an eye and looked at Avalon.

'Isn't one of us supposed to be watching the house?' he asked still only allowing the use of a single eye.

'At least I'm still awake,' replied Avalon not looking up from the map book.

'So you think it's possible to sleep with you rustling paper and sighing every two minutes?' asked Ross.

'You must snore when you're awake then because you seemed asleep to me,' replied the DI. Ross decided to sit up, and he stretched as much as he could in the cramped area. He then yawned silently and looked around outside. Berriedale was the smallest of settlements nestled in a gorge on the river. They were parked off the main A9 down a lane towards the spot where the river flowed directly into the sea. An

325

enormous rock face blocked the actual view to the sea and to the right was a short row of houses. It was quiet, tucked away off the road and there was nothing to see or do. They just had to keep an eye out for anything unusual. Ross considered that it wasn't a place where 'unusual' came to visit very often so it would be easy to spot it if it arrived. It was made more difficult by the fact that several tourist types came down to the village from the café near the A9 bridge. Ross yawned again.

'Why don't you go back to sleep?' suggested Avalon still looking at the map book toying with the pencil, 'I'll wake you when I need a driver.'

'I've told you, I wasn't asleep, no one could sleep with you fidgeting anyway,' insisted Ross ending with yet another yawn. For several minutes they were silent, Avalon staring down at the map book and Ross looking around outside the car, rubbing his eyes occasionally. He glanced up to the top of the rocks at the front and noticed some stonework.

'Not much of the castle left is there?' he noted.

'No,' replied Avalon still not looking up at it. There was more silence and Ross was thinking of going back to sleep, not that he had been asleep of course. 'I can see why they abandoned it,' he added craning his neck to look up to the ruin. For the first time, Avalon looked away from his book and over to Ross. He saw he meant the castle and asked,

'Well, there's nowhere to park the wagon,' commented Avalon looking up to the top of the rock.

'You'd never get a window cleaner up there either,' added Ross. Avalon went back to his puzzle, picking up two sheets of notes he had made. Ross tapped his fingers on the steering wheel and looked around once more then he reached for the thermos flask in the rear foot-well.

'If you keep drinking, you'll have to keep getting out of the car,' was Avalon's advice. Ross didn't care, it was something to do, 'and that will draw attention to us,' added Avalon.

'Moot-point I would think,' replied Ross with a glassy stare, 'two guys dressed in cheap suits in a black BMW sat aimlessly in the village of the damned.' Avalon looked up.

'I think it's nice here.'

'Aye, if it was summer, and I was here with PC Middleton instead of you I would agree,' laughed Ross replacing the thermos in the rear.

'Who's PC Middleton?' asked the DI.

'Oh,' sighed Ross making light of it, 'a new woman PC from Aberdeen, doesn't look much in her uniform but by Christ, she more than makes up for it in civvies.' Avalon tightened his lips and gave a slight nod.

'Not seen her,' he said and looked back down to his book, then he thought about Ross's personal dilemma and his possible connection to Megan Frazer. 'How are you feeling by the way?' he suddenly asked looking over to the DS.

'What about?' asked Ross.

'The little chat we had last Saturday,' replied Avalon.

'Oh,' nodded Ross, and he looked back up at the rock for a moment, 'you know, we have to deal with all the things that kick us in the teeth,' he said, 'I'm sure as more disasters come to visit me in the future, this will seem like a bad sneezing fit.' Avalon put down his pencil and slid the map book by the side of his feet.

'Maybe, it's always problematic when we fall for someone we work closely with,' sighed Avalon.

'What?' questioned Ross.

'Well, I think I know who it was you fell in love with,' added Avalon with the most sympathetic face he could muster.

'Who?' frowned Ross but as he saw the look on the boss's face he understood and his eyes opened wide and his jaw dropped a little.

'You think...' he checked himself to be sure he had read it correctly, 'you think I fell in love with Megan?' and he began laughing, 'Jesus, I can see why you were sympathetic,' and the laughing continued. Avalon felt like a fool, he could see that Ross wasn't just covering it up, it really wasn't Megan but in a way, it made him angry that Ross thought it was so funny. He picked up his map book once more. Ross suddenly felt guilty. Avalon had cared, and that was obvious. 'No, it wasn't Megan,' he said and calmed the laughing, 'and I'm sorry for laughing but...' he didn't say any more, he still thought it was funny and decided to look out of the window. He watched a bird looking for scraps of food, he didn't know what sort of bird it was, there was so much about life he didn't know but he knew that Avalon cared and that made a difference to him. For the past week or so he had been angry with his boss, for no other reason than Avalon *did* care. That didn't make sense, but it was true and now he decided to tell him the full story.

'She's a nurse.'

'Oh,' said Avalon looking down at his notes.

'I first met her about seven years ago, before I got married,' he was still watching the bird and he reached for the packet of sandwiches he had. 'We met a few times for drinks and then she invited me to go to a party, and we went,' he pulled a tiny bit of crust from the bread and wound down the window. 'As usual, I got blind drunk and eventually, we found a bed in the house and that's all I remember.' He threw the crumbs outside, and the bird flew off, he thought about why the bird had flown off and decided the bird chose self-preservation over a meal. 'The next morning we left, and that was that, I mean I saw her twice after but it seemed strained somehow.' He paused and wondered if the bird was like him, even though someone was trying to help, the risk involved was too high, and it was easier to fly than risk the benefits that might come. 'Then, when I was in the hospital, she was the nurse that treated me, she didn't recognise me at first, or so she said, and so I reminded her.' Ross looked around for the bird but it had gone. He closed the window and looked at Avalon. 'She said she thought it was me but didn't like mentioning it seeing as I was a copper. I'm not sure what that had to do with it but I suppose Megan was with me too.' He looked back out of the windscreen. 'Later, I asked her how she was doing and she told me she was okay but being a single mother, times were hard. I asked about her family, she had a girl called Sherri, almost seven years old.' Ross paused. He looked back for the bird and then put the sandwiches away as he continued. 'I couldn't get it out of my head that Sherri might be my daughter,' he spun around to Avalon, 'and that felt odd, so damn odd, that I might have a child. I felt so different as if some overwhelming change had overtaken me.' He shrugged. 'As it turned out,' he continued, 'that night at the party, I was so drunk I couldn't even get it up, I just fell asleep and Sherri was the daughter of the man she later married

329

and then divorced.' Avalon swallowed, he didn't know what to say. This was way above anything he had experience of, there was nothing in *his* life that could even begin to allow him to understand what had happened to Ross, for those few hours he had thought he was a father.

'I'm sorry,' he said as he looked over to him.

'Nothing to be sorry for,' shrugged Ross looking back, 'just me getting mixed up about something that wasn't there,' and he looked outside once more. 'Let's change the subject,' he said after a moment's quiet.

'To what?' asked Avalon not sure where to go from there.

'What about your crossword puzzle?' asked Ross nodding towards the map book.

'Oh, it's just something to do to alleviate the boredom.'

'So have you found anything?' asked Ross.

'Not really,' Avalon admitted, 'but I don't know what I'm looking for, and without the other twelve clues, I think this is a puzzle beyond solving.'

'What are you trying to do, find the treasure?' asked Ross.

'Not as such, I thought that if we can't get the Fly here, we might get him if he makes a move to the treasure.'

'But as you said, not all the clues are there,' insisted Ross, 'and in any case, Mr Greenaway has now admitted that he also holds one of the clues, and the Fly doesn't have that one.'

'And hopefully, now we have Greenaway hidden away, that situation should remain,' nodded Avalon, 'but it hasn't stopped the Fly, not having all the keys hasn't slowed him yet, and I wondered if he knows something we don't. Like, can it still be found with the clues he has?' suggested Avalon. Ross looked at the map and shrugged, he slumped back into his seat.

'So what are all the lines?' he asked.

'What lines?'

'The ones on your map?' added Ross pointing to the map book.

'Oh, just a theory,' said Avalon looking down at his pencil marks, 'I just thought about Greenaway saying that the monks walked from the spot where the treasure was to be hidden, wondering off in straight lines looking for landmarks.'

'And you think that they did that at random?' asked Ross looking over to the house they were watching.

'Don't you?' inquired Avalon.

'Not really,' shrugged Ross, 'how difficult would that have been, I mean, I don't recall ever seeing a medieval compass do you?'

'No,' frowned Avalon, 'but it's easy enough to navigate over land fairly accurately, there are many ways to do that.'

'It just seems to hit-and-miss to me,' replied Ross sinking lower into his seat, 'what if you never bumped into anything worth mentioning, what if you ended up at the coast and that was it?'

'Then they would start again,' insisted Avalon, 'as Greenaway says, these were monks, they were used to hardship.'

'I feel sorry for the one that went all the way to Edinburgh then,' laughed Ross.

'I have to admit,' mused the DI, 'that did make

331

me wonder a little.'

'So what if some of these clues are red herrings then?' offered Ross.

'You mean like a bad whodunit novel?

'Sort of.'

'Then they should be easy to sift out,' admitted Avalon, 'the Edinburgh one for starters.'

'But it doesn't mean much if we don't have the other twelve does it?' insisted Ross sitting upright again, then he asked, 'are you sure they is no easy way into the back of this house?'

'Yes,' nodded Avalon looking across to the building, 'they would have to come down the steep hillside or walk past here.' Ross looked at his watch.

'It'll be dark in an hour,' he said.

'And then it will get really cold,' frowned Avalon.

'Yep,' replied Ross looking directly at Avalon, 'so how long are you planning to wait?' asked Ross. Avalon didn't answer, he looked at the house then up to the rock. 'I'll go for a pee while you think about it,' added Ross climbing out of the car and he went for a walk to find somewhere private. Avalon looked towards the house again and then opened the window. The weather wasn't at all bad, it was a little cool but the sun had shone all afternoon, there were still a few people about but they were making their way back towards the A9. He thought about taking a stroll himself when Ross returned, for now though, he had to content himself with watching the house and his puzzle, and considering exactly how long he would stay.

~~~~~~

A phone was ringing somewhere in the Cave and DC Frazer knew by its angry tone that it wasn't good news.

'Hello, C Section, DC Frazer.'

'*DC Frazer, is there any word from DS Ross or DI Avalon?*' it was DCI Croker.

'Er, no sir, not as yet, I was about to try to contact them.'

'*I see, well let me know what is happening as soon as you know anything,*' insisted the DCI. Oh, she would let him know, just as soon as she could work out what was going on herself. She was under the impression that he was with Ross up north on surveillance and that bothered her. Here was she, trained to the nines on surveillance work, stuck in the Cave trying to coordinate both the running of the office and two silent detectives almost eighty miles away. There was also an ARV on alert too plus the helicopter should it be needed, and yet no one was admitting to anything connected to the Fly or the spate of break-ins recently. This was all to do with some sort of road-rage incident and a weapon being discharged at a member of the public.

'Member of the public my arse,' Frazer had said when she was told the scant details, 'What are you up to Auld Clootie,' she thought to herself just as the door opened and in walked an unpleasant man with an English accent, it was DI Dryden.

'Where's DI Avalon?" he said as he looked around the empty office.

'As far as I know, he's gone,' she spat.

'Gone where?'

'Gone, finished, retired, whatever you want tae call et.'

'I've heard all that shit about him handing in his notice, where has he really gone?' growled Dryden. Frazer glared at him, she was in no mood to deal with the likes of this man or his American friend. Dryden almost grunted and smashed his hand down on the nearest desk.

'Temper, temper,' said Frazer, but the man began a tirade of swearing and insults that completely washed over the DC, all she could think was, 'it's a good job the boss isn't here.'

'I'll find him, mark my words and then I'm coming after you and your DCI,' spat Dryden, his face almost purple, his finger pointing just inches from Frazer's face. Any other time she would have caught hold of it and broken it in several places, but she promised the boss she would stay calm. So, she did. She just said quietly and with confidence,

'I can't speak for the Detective Chief Inspector but ef you want a piece o' me, you better come prepared.' Dryden dropped the serious look and smiled.

'You live in a different world up here,' and he leaned closer and lowered his voice, 'if I wanted to take you down, you wouldn't even know I'd done it,' and he smiled once more and turned to leave.

'Then we do live en a different world,' answered Frazer, 'because you sure as hell would know you'd tangled with me.' As he walked through the door, she was furious and so wound up, she needed some way to unwind her spring. She just couldn't think of any way of doing that, so she decided to ring Ross.

~~~~~~~

Ross's phone rang.

'Hello,'

'*What the hell es going on?,*' said the angry Scottish voice.

'I'm having a pee Miss Frazer, how can I help you?' said Ross.

'*The DCI wants some info and I've got Sweeney Plod giving me a hard time too.*'

'What does that bastard want?' asked Ross and then added, 'oh, just a mo, let me put this away.' Frazer heard a shuffling noise and then what sounded like a zip being operated.

'*Oh, Jees, you really were having a pee,*' she said in a disgusted tone.

'That's what I said I was doing,' insisted Ross, 'so I'm guessing that the DCI is about to go on the warpath?'

'*I don't know but I'm getting a bit sick o' havin' tae keep biting my lip rather than telling people what I think.*'

'We could have done with another team, it's going to wear us down if we're here for much longer, and the boss is less than forthcoming about how long he wants to hold out,' explained Ross.

'*Well, you can't stay there much longer, the DCI isn't going to allow it for sure,*' she insisted, '*ef you're both staying through the night I could come up for a few hours t' give you both a rest and bring some food and drinks.*'

'We have some supplies but a couple of hours' break would help,' admitted Ross, 'but I'll ask the DI,

335

he's not easy to read at the moment, I'll ring back.'

'Listen,' said Ross as he got back into the driver's seat, 'Croker isn't going to let us keep this up for long, if the Fly doesn't show tonight…'

'Is that what he told you?'

'Not in so many words but he's got Division on his back, that's a big weight to hold up for long.'

'I suppose so,' nodded Avalon, 'I'll just have to do it myself.'

'He's patient,' smiled Ross, 'but not that patient.'

'My resignation sticks,' frowned Avalon looking at Ross.

'You still don't get it do you?' insisted Ross, 'Croker wanted you out of his hair so he could deny knowledge of where you had gone.'

'I get it, I just don't believe it,' sighed Avalon.

'Megan just rang, she's getting flack back there. She wants to know if we need her up here tonight.'

'No,' replied Avalon shaking his head, 'I don't want to drag anyone into this.'

'But it was alright dragging me into it?'

'You invited yourself if I recall correctly,' replied Avalon glaring at Ross.

'Hmm, so I did,' agreed Ross, 'you better call her then and tell her.' The DI took out his phone and dialled Frazer.

'Megan, it's Avalon,'

'*Oh, Boss, I was just getting ready to set off I've got some things t' bring up-*' but Avalon cut her short.

'It's not worth it Megan, all you're going to achieve is a loss of much-needed sleep.'

'*Look Boss, ef you don't want me there, fine,*' she

said, '*but don't give me some shite excuse*,' and Avalon realised she was doing it for herself as much as for them.

'Okay,' he eventually said, 'if you want to freeze your arse off in the cold up here that's up to you.' As he ended the call, he turned to Ross and said,

'She's bringing up some hot coffee and some more food.'

'Good,' smiled Ross, 'we'll need it,' and he slid down in his seat pulling up the collar of his jacket. Avalon looked outside and then said,

'I'm off for a stroll before we bunk down for the night,' and he dragged his overcoat from the rear seat and pulled it on.

As he walked down to the house, he buttoned up the coat and tried to look as casual as he could, but in his heart, he knew that if the Fly was watching, he would be able to spot Avalon for what he was. He thrust his hands into his coat pockets and found the rolled-up notes he had made from Greenaway's story but decided to leave them there. He then walked past the house they were watching with just the slightest glance towards it and on towards the foot of the cliff that once held the castle. He then walked over the rope bridge that crossed the river, and up towards the beach and the row of cottages that faced the tiny cove. It was a lovely place and Avalon breathed in the air and looked to the sky set aglow by the setting sun behind the hills of Caithness and Sutherland beyond. He found a convenient bench and sat, glancing up at the ruin of the castle now and then, looking for any signs of movement. It was the ideal spot to view the area below and if Avalon had been more adventurous, he would have probably have chosen it to watch the house. The problem was, the castle was very difficult to get to

337

and getting back down in a hurry would be almost impossible. As it was, where Ross had parked the car, was the perfect strategic spot. Anyone entering this end of the settlement would have to pass by it and therefore make themselves known. Avalon saw that it would also be possible for a person to enter from the castle end too, they would have to walk across the fields but that wouldn't present any particular hurdle to the Fly. He sighed deeply and once again asked himself why he got the strange cases, the ones that didn't have the run-of-the-mill crook. He picked up a pebble and scanned the beach watching several seagulls swoop down over the water and up to the rock where the castle stood. Two of their cousins were perched on the edge of the precipice and Avalon wondered what the view was like up there, he also wondered why Croker was allowing Ross to help him out. Was he truly so clever that he was using Avalon's letter of resignation as an excuse to let him continue his investigation? On the face of it, he was off the hook if anything went wrong. The DCI was a constant surprise and not like any other Chief he had ever worked for.

It was becoming cold and Avalon shivered, he stood and walked back along the beach and on towards the bridge that crossed Berriedale Water. He stopped halfway to look down at the river rushing by, making its way around the corner to the sea where it would change from fresh to salt and once again become part of the oceans that covered the planet. As he passed the house again, he didn't look, but he listened. It was as quiet as he would expect, the owners staying at a hotel for the night, just to be on the safe side. He moved on towards the car and slid back into the passenger seat to find Ross looking through his notes and his map.

'It's bloody cold out there now,' he said keeping his overcoat on.

'It is and it'll get colder as the evening wears on,' frowned Ross giving him the quickest of glances. Avalon pulled out his phone again and brought up a number. He sat motionless looking at that number, wondering if he should phone it now or wait, not that waiting would alter the inevitable. There didn't seem any chance whatsoever that he would be able to keep his arrangement with Sarah, and he kept his eyes fixed on those numbers, burning them into his mind, knowing that another cancellation would seriously harm his chances of further contact with her.

'Your mother?' asked Ross peering over to the phone. Avalon cancelled the number and placed his phone back in his pocket as Ross put down Avalon's notes, it was too dark to read now anyway.

'Not quite,' said Avalon watching that darkness fall rapidly.

'It looked to me with the expression on your face that it was someone you need to call,' and there was a glimmer of a grin on his mouth.

'Don't jump to conclusions,' insisted Avalon, 'it could be quite innocent.'

'I don't think so,' added Ross. Avalon took a deep breath.

'Even if it had have been something like that, this job always gets in the way,' he said.

'You've quit, remember?' smiled Ross. Avalon took another deep breath, and this time sighed it out.

'I know,' he eventually said, 'and even that seems like an anti-climax.'

'That's because at the moment,' began Ross, 'you can't imagine what the future holds, you can't imagine what life will be like on the other side. Remember, I've been there and at the moment all that you can see is that your career is as dead as disco.'

'Not quite,' smiled Avalon, 'disco is never coming back, and he looked over to Ross but it was now so dark that Ross's features were difficult to see. 'I was thinking down there on the beach,' he continued, 'what are the minimum points of reference to find a particular spot on a map?'

'Four I suppose,' said Ross, 'or maybe three if you know about angles of triangles and some basic mathematics, why?'

'What you said about the clues to the treasure having several red herrings, what if they're all red herrings except four of them?'

'Possible,' agreed Ross, 'but without knowing which ones it could take time to link all the points together, that's a lot of possible options plus each one of those dissections would have to be checked on the ground…' Ross ceased as he thought his point was made.

'Unless there is another clue that tells us which of the clues *are* red herrings,' said Avalon.

'It's an idea, but I haven't seen anything to suggest that,' replied Ross. Avalon pulled his coat around him and reached for the last of the warm coffee and started on the final sandwich.

~~~~~~

Detective Constable Megan Frazer was tootling

along in her little car, heading north along the A9 trunk road to a destination she had never seen before. Spending most of her life between the Inverness area, Aberdeen and a short period in Edinburgh, she had never been north of the Sutherland border and all she knew of Berriedale was that it had the famous Braes, which she had neither seen nor driven through. She didn't expect to see much of it on this trip either as it was already dark when she set off after closing up the office. She had made several flasks of coffee and arranged a few sandwiches and other snacks to take with her, and though the thought of a long night after a long day, before another long day didn't appeal, she was optimistic that C Section was working pretty much as nature had intended. What she wasn't quite ready for, was the distance involved. Eighty miles doesn't seem much when spoken quickly but by road and in the dark, it felt like driving to the moon. It gave her time to think however and though there were plenty of bad thoughts in her head, there were a few good ones too. She had been honest with herself since the incident with Ross, she had looked inside her soul and addressed her problems and over the shock and changes of the last few days, she had been electrified into a new way of thinking about her future. In the past, she had stumbled from one relationship to another in the hope of finding something that she thought she needed. The truth was she now knew, there wasn't that much she actually wanted. She accepted that the feeling of being needed by someone was important but she now knew that it didn't have to be tied to a relationship, she could be content with the team needing her. Yes, she realised other people would see that as shallow, but she *was* shallow. In a relationship,

341

the partner wanted something in return and that was the part she didn't know how to give. She couldn't love back because she did not understand what love was. Other people said that love was when you couldn't live without someone, but that just didn't make sense to her, if you could live without them before you met them, why couldn't you go on if they went away? Maybe she just *couldn't* love. She sighed and turned on the radio but music wasn't something she invested a great deal of time in and so after a few miles, she turned it off and sat in silence trying to make out where she was. As she passed through Helmsdale, she knew there wasn't far to go, the little town twinkled in the dark as she drove over the bridge and then came the hill to where she saw the snow gates. To her, this meant she was going into the wild country, so wild and inhospitable that they had fitted gates to the road to stop people getting lost in the snow. There wasn't a great deal of snow to be seen that night, it was cold but the weather was fine and she could even see stars here and there. As the road wound this way and that, she passed a sign announcing she was now in Caithness and the road settled into long straights with gentle bends. She knew she must now be close to Berriedale, but then just up ahead, she saw a glow, it looked like a fire of some sort. As she closed in on it just beyond a sign advertising Berriedale Braes, she could see a vehicle was ablaze and several other cars had stopped to take a look. She jumped out of her vehicle and ran over to where three men and one woman were standing by the burning vehicle.

'Police,' she announced, 'what's going on?'

'Not sure,' explained one of the men, 'we found the van burning but we can't find the driver, we don't know if anyone is still in it,' and he pointed to the vehicle which was well and truly ablaze. She asked if a fire tender had been sent for and the woman said she had rung for fire and police. Frazer told them to stand well back and tried to see if she could get near the driver's side but the heat was intense now and if anyone was in the vehicle, there was nothing that could be done. She pulled out her phone and rang Ross, she still didn't know if Avalon's orders that she shouldn't ring still stood.

'Hello, Berriedale frog watchers group,' came Ross's bored voice.

'Rossy, et's Megan,' she looked around to get her bearings, 'I'm south o' Berriedale up on the hill, I've got a burning vehicle, not sure ef the driver got out.'

'Okay,' came Ross's voice with a snap, *'we'll be up in two minutes,'* and he ended the call. She put the phone away and began to look at the scene. From the bright light of the burning vehicle, she could see the area well enough. She asked two of the men to watch the north-bound entrance and the couple to make sure no one came from the opposite direction. The van was to the side of the road but the flames and heat were such that it wasn't safe to pass. She looked around but saw no other vehicle that could be involved and yet the van looked as though it had moved a little whilst it had been burning as there were a few signs of debris in the opposite carriageway. She did consider moving her own car to the south though, for when the fire tender arrived she wouldn't be able to get through. She drove quickly past the van and parked on the steep hill to the south just as Ross and Avalon arrived.

'Emergency services have been sent for so they should be here soon,' she explained. Ross and Avalon

343

looked at the van.

'Is there another vehicle?' asked Ross.

'No,' she replied, 'but I think the fire started as et came up the hill, et must have rolled back after. No sign o' the driver though.' Avalon looked at the vehicle and then to the spot that a little debris could still be seen, to the left was a private asphalt road snaking its way over the hill to the cliffs.

'Shit, shit shit!' he spat as he ran back to Ross's car, 'come on,' he called back. In the car, Ross slammed the vehicle into reverse and manoeuvred around the growing queue of traffic trying to head south.

'You think this is him?' asked Ross frantically making his way back in the direction they had come.

'Yes, he stole a Vauxhall van from the Black Isle,' he growled, 'I'm betting that is the van.' As they reached the turnoff to the main village, there were vehicles blocking the private road and so Avalon jumped out and ran down the lane. Ross angrily got the cars blocking the road to move so he could follow. As Avalon neared the row of houses, something twigged, they were being set up. This Fly had night vision equipment, he would see Avalon approach long before he could be seen himself. His heart was beating fast, and he was out of breath as he reached the house, not just because of the run, but he was afraid. He knew this man was a professional, maybe DI Dryden was right, maybe C Section *were* out of their depth, Avalon certainly felt that way as he quietly slid past the house and around the rear garden. He thought about the high-tech equipment this man had access to, he thought about the training he would have if he really was ex-CIA, he thought about the gun he probably had too. The rear garden was tiny and even in the swamping dark, he was close enough to the back door to see it was open. Either he was too late, or the man was still inside. He should now make the call to the ARV, it was now he needed the armed back-up, but he still didn't know if this *was* the Fly. He peered through the open door. Nothing, it was silent too, all he could hear was the muffled sound of the river cascading over rocks, and a siren in the distance, that would be the fire engine, not back-up. He looked down at the floor, it was far too dark to see footprints but the sparkle of broken glass could be seen in what little light there was. He then noticed the two smashed windows in the panelled door. Walking on that broken glass would make a sound. There was a decision to make, should he enter or not? Ross must have arrived in the car because the house interior lit up slightly and then he saw movement, just for a split second. Not in the house but on the hill, the lights of the car had just caught the movement of a dark figure trotting steadily along a path that seemed to lead up towards the castle on the rock. Avalon had no time to lose, he quickly took out his pencil and wrote on the floor by the broken glass, the word *castle*, and left his pencil there for Ross to see. He then climbed over the small picket fence and moved up to the path but it was slow going in the pitch black. As he reached the top of the rise, he looked back down the track but could see nothing in the dark. There was no light pollution whatsoever this far north and without a moon, there was just the faintest glow from the collective light of the stars. It was unnerving, the DI didn't know if Ross was following or not, he didn't know if the Fly was just over the crest watching him with his night goggles. He didn't know much except that he should have rung for back-up.

As he carefully reached the top of the crest, there was a breeze from the seaward side, and to his left was the peninsular of rock which held the ruin of the castle, to the right, a ridge climbing the rest of the hill up several hundred feet away to the south where a sort of tower had been visible earlier in the day. He began to wonder how the Fly would escape now he obviously had his clue. Ross had tried to convince Avalon that the clue should have been removed from the house, but Avalon had seen what the man did when he couldn't find what he was after. It was safer, and cheaper for the owners of the house to let him have the clue and try to catch him in the act. That had been the plan but this man was clever, he had distracted them by deliberately burning his vehicle, his means of escape, so what now were his plans. For just a glimmer of a moment, he wondered if the Fly was watching him and would make his way back and try to steal Ross's car. It would be an easy way to get out of the mess he was in. He could simply take the A9 north as there wouldn't be any traffic travelling that way until the fire was out. Then something obvious occurred to him. Why was he worried about using his little flashlight? It didn't make sense. If the Fly was watching him through sophisticated night vision equipment, switching on his flashlight wasn't going to give the man any further clues to his whereabouts. He saw a dip in the ground where a rock protruded from the cliff and bent down out of the cold air from the sea. He then pulled the torch from his pocket and switched it on just as he heard the hiss of what he took to be a shot from a silenced weapon.

Chapter Thirteen

Ross hurried towards the house to catch up with the boss but couldn't see him anywhere. He decided that it might be best to approach quietly just in case something was wrong. As he slid past the side of the house and peered around the corner of the building towards the back door, he could see the door was ajar. Slowly and quietly, he approached and glanced quickly inside the house. It was silent and he could see nothing. He looked to see if the clue, the statue of Saint Erasmus was still in its place but it was so dark he would have to simply enter into the gloom, or use his flashlight. Either option would give the game away. He decided to have the light at the ready and take a peep inside which he did and immediately heard the crunch under his feet. He could see that there was broken glass even before he shone the flashlight over the area, but he then saw the word *castle* and Avalon's pencil. That was it, off went the light, and he looked up to the rock as he climbed over the fence and scrambled up to find the path. It was then he heard a soft percussion, which sounded very much like a discharge of a firearm with a muzzle brake or a silencer. For a split second, he hesitated and then

347

surged ahead to make his way up the hill towards the castle. He didn't know if Avalon was injured or even if the shot was taken at him, but fortunately for Ross, he wasn't the sort of person who considered the possible outcomes until he had some facts. As he climbed, he noticed activity down by the houses, flashlight beams cut through the blackness and he assumed as least one of them was Frazer. As he neared the top of the first hill he could see the lighter hue of the sky, give way to the inky blackness of the sea and he was now presented with a choice, left to the castle or right to continue up the steep slope of the hill. He kept close to the ground though he didn't really know why for if the man they were after really did have night vision equipment he would be able to see him anyway. Ross felt cornered, he was now evaluating what he knew and was assessing the situation. This man had played them like a kitten with a new toy. He had seen them waiting for him earlier and he had waited for dark to fall. He had then crossed the fields to where he had hidden the stolen van on the private road Ross had noticed earlier. It was where the vehicle was burning, abandoned on the A9. Of course, he hadn't known another police officer was on their way, he had probably thought it would take time for someone to report it and the message to get back to the two surveillance officers. In that respect, he had miscalculated. He had almost been caught at the house and Avalon must have seen him escaping up the hill and followed. Now he was in control again, he was on that hill watching them climb up, waiting for them to be close enough before he… What if Avalon was lying injured, or even dead? Was he next? He had to move, the obvious direction was up the hill, that's where the Fly

348

would have gone, if he had moved to the castle he would be trapped there and so Ross considered a quick sprint up the hill to find cover. Towards the castle, he saw a rock, or at least it looked like a rock or was it a body. Back down the hill, flashlight beams were swinging this way and that and Ross could hear the distinctive sound of radio chatter, Frazer must have secured the help of at least one responder to the vehicle fire. Ross felt slightly more confident and went to check on the dark shape. It was a rock but there was also someone there. He switched on his torch and saw Avalon slumped at the far side of it, his face looked up but he was as pale as death.

'Are you all right?' he asked as he bent down, there was blood running down the DI's face.

'Christ, I thought you were him coming to finish me off,' hissed Avalon.

'Are you shot?' asked Ross not wanting to know the answer. Ross was a brute of a man to the untrained eye but he wasn't at all happy with the sight of blood. It didn't seem to bother him as much if the victim was dead, he just couldn't stand the sight of injuries.

'I thought I was at first but there's not much blood,' explained Avalon moving his arm from under his coat to show a red-stained hand.

'Where?' asked Ross.

'My chest, left side, it feels like I was kicked by a horse,' he explained.

'We need to get you off this hill,' said Ross in a pressing tone but to the rear, he heard voices, it looked like Frazer with two PCs and Ross flashed his torch towards them.

'Are you all right Boss,' asked Megan seeing him slumped by the rock with Ross helping him to his feet.

'We think he might have been shot, and the shooter is still about so let's make this quick,' insisted Ross. The four of them got Avalon off the crest of the hill and let him rest in a dip in the ground while Frazer checked his wound. Frazer had opened his coat and jacket and had pulled open his shirt to get at the wound.

'Et's stopped bleeding,' she said looking at it with a small flashlight, 'but we need to get you to the ambulance. One has been sent for to attend the car fire for some reason.'

'Any word from the ARV?' asked Ross, 'I did send the signal before I came up here.' It was one of the PCs who answered.

'I heard on the radio they are two minutes away, they should be here by now.' Ross nodded and looked back down to Frazer buttoning up the DI's coat.

'How do you feel?' she asked.

'Like I need a half bottle of whisky,' he replied, 'but apart from that like I'm ready for action.' He didn't look like he was but in the odd glow of flashlights, it was difficult to tell. By the time Frazer and the two PCs had Avalon back near the house, the DI was feeling groggy, he felt tired and cold but he didn't think he was about to die which was what he had felt on the hill behind that rock. The ambulance had nothing to do at the vehicle fire and had been sent down to attend Avalon who was soon made comfortable inside. By the time Ross had made sure the Fly had retreated he had made his way back there.

'How is he?' he asked the paramedic.

'Oh, he's comfortable, we don't think whatever was fired at him is in there, it looks worse than it is, but it must be quite painful so we've given him a little something for the pain.' Ross nodded and stepped into the ambulance.

'The doc says you're fine, just a bit of shock,' smiled Ross looking down at the Boss laid out on the couch. He was covered by a blanket but bandages could be seen over his shoulder. The blood on his face had been cleaned and showed a cut and a few grazes.

'Shock?' said Avalon, 'of course I'm in shock, they haven't got the half bottle of whisky I asked for,' and he smiled back. 'Is everyone all right?' he then asked in a more serious tone.

'Yeah,' nodded Ross, 'the ARV team are on-site and a specialist team are on their way to track him down. The chopper is in the air with thermal imaging kit, we should have him before dawn.'

'I don't know, this one is a crafty bastard,' said Avalon.

'We'll see,' smiled Ross again, and he turned and left. He walked down towards his car and he saw Frazer talking to someone on the phone. She ended the call and turned to Ross.

'Everyone's in place, there's nowhere for him t' run unless he jumps off the cliff,' she said, 'how's the Boss?'

'Fine,' nodded Ross, 'what a night?' he then added and walked off towards the river. He looked down at the water rushing by and pulled the collar of his coat up for the twentieth time and like the twenty times before it didn't make the cold go away. It was only now he thought about what had happened, only now did he feel the fear. It was odd that at the time, the danger hadn't registered for what it was. The thought that if the Fly hadn't been so determined to get away, he could have sat on that hill and taken them all out, one by one like a stall at the funfair. He shivered and turned towards Frazer.

'You all right?' she frowned.

'Course,' he smiled, 'if I can survive the wrath of Megan Frazer, what the hell can the Fly do to me?'

At the hospital, Ross found Avalon sitting up on a bed, bandages wrapped around his chest wearing nothing but some lightweight cotton trousers. He was holding his phone and seemed to be looking at it without doing anything.

'Have you got time to be sitting about?' asked Ross as he approached. Avalon looked at him and placed the phone on the bedside cabinet. 'There're reports to write out, Detective Chief Inspectors to grovel to and inquests to attend.'

'Any news?' was all Avalon asked.

'Yes,' nodded Ross, 'they cornered him on the clifftop and he gave in without a struggle.'

'So he's in custody?'

'For the time being.'

'What's that mean?' asked Avalon.

'Darren Mitchell Sumner, American national, an agent with the CIA for six years, more recently reported as missing in the States,' announced Ross in a matter-of-fact way as he paced around the bed with his hands in his trouser pockets.

'So you think they'll want him back?' asked Avalon.

'Yep,' nodded Ross, 'wanted in connection with the death of one Roger McClees, and possibly two other unsolved cases across the pond. I'm not sure how much of a diplomatic incident this has become but I have the feeling that wheels are in motion, wheels that we don't have the means to stop.' Avalon was silent, he stared down at his bare feet hanging by the side of the bed and then sighed. 'How are you feeling?' Ross then asked. Avalon looked up at him and placed his hand over the spot where the wound was.

'Not that bad, it's as sore as hell but the doctor says it was either a ricochet or a bit of the rock that broke off and hit me. Nothing left in there though, whatever it was, it went in about half an inch and then fell out.' He thought about shrugging but he knew that hurt so he raised his brows. 'The thing is, the cut on my head hurts more, and that was just a graze.' He pointed to the sticking plaster over his forehead.

'Well, you better leave the women alone for a bit, you look like shite,' smiled Ross, 'this new cut along with the cuts from the broken glass make you look more like a prize-fighter than a crime fighter.'

'Both of us,' nodded Avalon, 'you still have the mark of Frazer about you.' He did, the bruising had gone but the two of them walking into a pub would make the most hardened landlord question their motives. Avalon dropped the smile, Ross didn't know if it was the news about the case or the reason for him staring at his phone. He sat in the chair by the bed. Ross picked up Avalon's phone and tossed it onto the bed by his side.

'You need to ring her,' he said.

'Who?'

'I don't know, whoever's number it is you keep staring at,' shrugged Ross.

'How do you know the number belongs to a female?' asked Avalon. Ross simply raised his brows in a questioning look. 'Already done anyway?' explained

353

Avalon with a sour expression.

'Oh,' said Ross, 'sorry.' Ross could see that Avalon wasn't going to explain it and so he said no more about it. 'Ah, I was going to tell you,' he suddenly said, 'a few of us are going round to the pub on Sunday night, do you fancy it?' Avalon thought.

'That's New Year's Eve isn't it?'

'Aye, I think that's what some people call it,' nodded Ross.

'I'm not a fan of that particular evening I have to say,' replied Avalon with a thoughtful expression.

'Neither am I but just consider it another drinking session, Megan and Martin are going.'

'Oh,' exclaimed Avalon, 'I may pop in earlier in the evening,' he nodded, 'just for an hour or so.'

'It's nothing formal, just the sad git's club from the office,' smiled Ross.

'A gathering of people who had nothing better to do,' thought Avalon, but he just nodded. He wasn't in the most upbeat mood, he had just rung Sarah yet again, to call off their meeting, after he had done it he felt really bad. She had been sympathetic, and she even said she would come over and see him if he had to stay in the hospital but there was more to it. Something fatalistic had overcome him. Something he couldn't explain as if the Gods of Love had decided they wanted to taunt him. He could still continue with the meeting, but he really didn't think he would be up to it and he didn't want to make the evening a failure. Since making the call he had realised, he was a complete fool, and it angered him. At that moment he realised that no matter how hard he tried to change, he couldn't. He was who he was and he would have to live with it.

~~~~~~~

The house was quiet, Avalon sat in his conservatory hugging a cup of coffee and wondering what to do with himself. It was a couple of days since the events up at Berriedale and Avalon had heard nothing from anyone about the incident. In a fit of boredom, he had typed up his own report on the incident and emailed it to the station. His wound still hurt, but he had slept well and felt better for it, but moments of that night up on the hill still came back to him during moments of inactivity. He had been scared, he had thought that he was going to die, when he saw the shape approach that turned out to be Ross, he was sure it was the Fly about to fire his air cannon, and Avalon would face an excruciating death at the point of a multiple-barbed, high carbon steel harpoon. He now knew that the shock of it all had still been playing in his head when he phoned Sarah to call off their meeting. That had been stupid, and he regretted it. Twice he had disappointed her and he remembered something Ross had told him when he first came up to Scotland.

'Miss Underwood doesn't date police officers,' he had said, it wasn't difficult to see why. They were unpredictable, they had severe mood swings and ultimately they were unreliable. He didn't blame her one bit, in truth he thought she was wise to be that way. It didn't stop him wondering if he should phone her once again though. He knew she was off work for a few days and so what was stopping him? He didn't know, and so he picked up the phone and dialled.

'*Hello,*'

'It's me.'

'*Oh, how are you feeling?*' she sounded genuinely worried.

'Fine now thank you, I'm feeling much better,' he said as upbeat as he could sound.

'*I read something about it in the papers but it didn't really say much,*' she offered.

'Yes, there's a bit of a news blackout on this one,' he explained.

'*I rang Megan Frazer to see how you were,*' explained Sarah, '*she said you were shot, my God, you didn't mention that when you said you were in the hospital.*'

'Well, it's probably an exaggeration on Megan's part, I was hit by shards of rock, the projectile didn't actually hit me.'

'*That's not the point, you just said you had fallen, that's quite different.*'

'I suppose I was conscious that I looked a complete mess, I'm cut to ribbons and...' he trailed off, at that moment, he knew why he had called the whole thing off, vanity. It almost made him laugh.

'*You are an odd one Detective Avalon,*' she replied and Avalon wasn't about to dispute that fact, he was.

'Well, the reason I rang was,' he paused, 'well, I know it's New Year but I'm meeting a three of the people from the office down at the Tavern...' he paused again, 'it doesn't matter, you've probably got things planned...'

'*I haven't but...*' it was her turn to pause, '*it's not really my thing, I loathe the New Year's Eve scenario, I usually have a long hot bath through it all.*'

'That's okay,' said Avalon as he nodded, 'I'm not much into it myself, it's just that Megan and Ross will be there so I said I might pop in early before the rush starts,' and he gave a slight laugh.

'*We'll sort something out in the New Year,*' she said but Avalon could hear an amount of doubt in her voice.

'Yes, that would be great,' he said without enthusiasm.

He made another coffee, as the one he had was cold by the time he got to it and he sat at the dining table looking out of the window onto his tiny garden.

'Is this what retirement is like? Is this what ordinary people do?' he said to himself. The house was silent again. The only audible sound was the muffled noise of the road and even that wasn't loud or constant. He turned on the stereo but soon turned it off again, his music collection was looking and sounding shabby, he needed to find something new. In the summer, he would have taken the bike out of the shed. As it was, he had already been out to it twice and once even kicked it up to hear its own kind of music. Several minutes later he was back at the dining table but this time he took out the bundle of clothes he had been wearing that night, and placed them in the dustbin. Left on the table were the things from that evening, the notes that he had made and some of the scribbling he had done in the car. As he sipped the coffee, he opened one of the sheets and flattened it out. The top line was the so-called Hymn of the Templars that arrived with the treasure. He read through it and looked at another sheet that contained the clues. There was nothing obvious, but why had the clues been numbered, did it matter what order they were in?

He then counted the words in the Hymn.

'That's interesting,' he said and then he read through the words that were supposed to have appeared on their banner. 'Very interesting indeed.'

The pub was full to the doors by the time Avalon reached the Castle Tavern, he surfed the slow movement of those packed inside to reach the bar, but even as full as it was, Rutherford was easy to spot down the far end. The big man noticed Avalon, gave a big smile and made the motion that he was ordering him a drink. By the time Avalon had poured himself through the crowd, there was a single malt ready to be passed into his possession by Ross. The diminutive figure of Frazer was neatly placed to the side of Rutherford as a kind of protective barrier for her. Everyone toasted Avalon and asked how he was feeling and eventually, Avalon managed to find time to ask Ross a few questions above the loud noise within the bar. Ross had to put his mouth close to Avalon's ear to make himself heard.

'I was right, the bastard is being shipped back to America,' he tried to explain, 'it seems he was quite an embarrassment to the Yanks over here and they were worried he would go on some sort of killing spree.' Avalon nodded and then swapped positions leaning closer to Ross.

'So nothing was brought up about the Caledonian Flame issue?'

'No,' said Ross shaking his head, 'he killed a man in the states, well, actually tortured and killed him for some reason they couldn't work out,' explained Ross, 'I'm guessing for the information he had about the treasure.' This time Avalon nodded, he knew that would make sense.

'So did Dryden and Warranden know what he was up too?' asked Avalon having to shout a little.

'I'm sure of it,' called back Ross, 'that's why they hadn't brought him in, they wanted him to find what he was after then double-tap him and say he was killed trying to get away. I think that's why they want him back in the states.' Avalon nodded at this, it would be the easiest way to cover up their duplicity over the affair. 'I think that's what Croker thinks too from what little he said about it.' Avalon nodded again as Ross concluded.

'Has Croker said anything else?' asked Avalon but Ross struggled to hear and so Avalon nodded to the door. Ross turned back to Rutherford and Frazer who were busy in their own conversation and explained. They threaded their way back out of the bar and eventually reached the outer door, Harry the Hat was just coming up the stairs from the toilets.

'Jaysus Jimmy big man,' exclaimed Harry when he saw Avalon, 'you look like you've been through a car windscreen.'

'Funny you should say that Harry,' smiled Avalon as he stepped outside. There were several people in the beer garden now, some seated but the air was cold to say the least. Avalon moved over to the railing that overlooked the Ness.

'Did the DCI say anything else about the case?' asked Avalon again as he sipped the large measure from his glass.

'No, but he's not pleased, he wants an internal on how Division handled it, I reckon if he didn't hate the press so much there would have been a leak.'

'There might still be,' answered Avalon gazing out over the river.

'Well, it would be amusing to think that somewhere a press officer would be having a late night trying to explain what had happened,' smiled Ross. 'It wouldn't be good for the career though,' he added. Avalon turned to him.

'I'm sticking by it, I'm not coming back.'

'You will,' said Ross looking back at him, 'your lawn is too small to retire, and I can't see you becoming a bike dispatch rider any more than I can see me behind the wheel of a tour bus.' A large presence loomed over them.

'Do you two lassies want a drink?' asked Rutherford.

'Not for me thanks Martin,' said Avalon, and he pulled some notes out of his wallet, 'get everyone else one though.'

'Your money's no good tonight Jimmy boy, what do you want?' asked Rutherford turning to Ross.

'Lager please,' replied Ross emptying his glass.

'Why do y' drink that shyte when they sell craft beer?'

'Oh, don't start me on that word,' frowned Ross.

'What word?' asked Rutherford casting a quick grin to Avalon.

'Craft, the only thing craft about it is the people who use that word to sell substandard products. Craft my arse, what's that mean then?' he snapped.

'Et's used to describe something that is made in a traditional way using an age-old art,' insisted Rutherford.

'Pure bollocks,' growled Ross, 'most of your so-called real ale is put into conditioning tanks and then put in casks to send it out. It's no more real ale than the ubiquitous Tennant's rat urine,' explained Ross in full rant. 'And while we're on the subject, what is a craft baker, someone who makes bread in a clay oven? No is it arse. And what in the name of all that is holy is a craft butcher? Does he bring down his own wildebeest with a spear and cut it to shreds with a bronze knife? Pure bollocks.'

'Are you sure that you don't want one Boss? Something to numb you from the venom of Sarah Palin here?'

'No thanks Martin, I'll just take more of my medication for that,' replied Avalon and Rutherford went back to the bar, wading his way through the crowd, though he didn't seem to have as much of a problem as other people in that respect.

'So,' announced Ross calming himself down, 'what are you going to do?'

'I'm not sure yet, I might just sell up, move further north and walk up and down the beaches.'

'Sounds riveting,' said Ross leaning on the railings.

'I feel fine about it, I don't know what I want to do, I just know what I don't want to do.' He too leaned on the railings and watched the lights dancing on the water. 'Something happened crouched behind that rock up at Berriedale, I was crapping myself and I thought about the irony.'

'What irony?' asked Ross glancing around.

'I thought about my career, all the places I had worked including Wolverhampton where you got a free nine-millimetre semi-automatic with the Sunday supplement, but I had never been shot at in all that time.

I just thought how ironic it would be to be shot and killed working from Inverness in a village that no one except long-distance lorry drivers had ever heard of.'

'I see,' nodded Ross, 'you mean you wanted to be shot and killed somewhere more to your lifestyle, like the home of a famous poet?'

'You know what I mean.'

'I do,' nodded Ross, 'but you're safe and everything has worked out.'

'I don't see it that way,' said Avalon taking a deep breath, 'I've made so many stupid mistakes over the past few weeks, I'm just not cut out for it.'

'That's just your English side coming out,' smiled Ross, 'we're gradually curing you of that, you'll soon be a fully fledge Highlander,' he added looking back out over the Ness, 'then you'll truly know what it is to be confused.' They stood silent for a moment until Avalon suddenly said,

'I know where it is.'

'Where what is?' frowned Ross glancing over for a second.

'The treasure.' There was more silence as Ross glared at Avalon.

'How the hell...?' he began but then changed tack and added, 'no don't tell me, I don't want that kind of information in my head.' He looked back over the water and back to Avalon. 'How did you work it out?' The curiosity of the mystery was still intriguing him however.

'The Hymn was the cypher, it had twenty words, the same number as the clues, the banner had a shortened version of the Hymn, just four words. I just overlaid the banner against the Hymn and used those clues to plot

362

two lines that intersected on satellite images.'

'And do they intersect something obvious?' Avalon just nodded. 'So…' Ross paused and sighed deeply before he continued, 'are you going to…?'

'No,' said Avalon shaking his head, 'whatever came to Scotland on the Caledonian Flame has been hidden for seven hundred years and Scotland has done fine without it. I'm not about to alter that.'

'It's dangerous information to have,' nodded Ross sighing once more and looking out across the river.

'I know, that's why I'm going to burn all the maps and notes I have. As far as I'm concerned, it's lost forever.'

'Aye but don't use your furniture to get it going.' Avalon smiled and finished his drink placing the glass on the table behind him. He pulled out the bank notes once more.

'Make sure everyone gets a drink on me, I'm not good at goodbye's and so I'm gonna get off.' Ross took the money and looked at him.

'You don't have to go, I won't ask for a New Year's kiss,' smiled Ross.

'No,' laughed Avalon, 'but Martin might.' They stared at each other for a moment, until they both nodded, then Avalon turned and walked out of the beer garden and off down Castle Street. As he walked, he was aware of each of those footsteps, each one carrying him further away from a previous life, a previous job, and previous memories. On the other hand, they lead down a new route, towards a new life and new memories, and though he didn't know if it was a shiny new dawn, he knew that he would try his best to make it worthwhile. His time with the police force had been a bit of a rollercoaster ride, but his few years at Inverness had been the best. He didn't know what he would do certainly, but whatever it was, it would be in Scotland, no, the Highlands. He was a Scot now, right down to his insecurities. He looked over to the Caledonian Hotel, it had received a complete facelift in the last few years, from an old, black pitted building had come the shining example of fabulous, classical-style architecture. Avalon was sure he could do the same with his life. To take his scarred and pitted face and let it heal. Let it come back to life and be able to smile and believe that smile was genuine. He was never going to look quite as rejuvenated as the Caledonian Hotel, but as he stood across the road looking at it, he remembered a line of poetry. He waited for a group of young girls in fancy dress to pass behind him then he said quietly,

> *Now, of my threescore years and ten,*
> *Twenty will not come again,*
> *And take from seventy springs a score,*
> *It only leaves me fifty more.*

It was by A E Housman called 'The Loveliest of Trees, the Cherry now' and Avalon remembered its sentiment.

'And for me, just thirty-five,' he added, and he walked on with his head slightly bowed. Life was indeed rushing by, and here he was, still alone, walking back to an empty, silent house. Yes, it was good he was moving on. Was it, was it really? Then why did he feel so sad? Around him revellers were moving from pub to pub, already in the mood, already full to the brim of Hogmanay and here alone, Avalon walked on, going home to an empty house and what as he saw an empty life. For some reason that he couldn't fathom, he felt totally lost.

His phone vibrated in his pocket, he pulled it out and saw it was from Ross.

'Hello,' even that was different, gone was the abrupt, *Avalon*.

'*Where are you?*' asked Ross.

'Halfway home why?'

'There's someone here wants to know where you are.' Avalon wondered what Ross was talking about.

'What, there at the pub?' asked Avalon as he watched two young people arm in arm walk past.

'Yeah, where else?' and Ross must have taken the phone from his head because Avalon heard the background noise suddenly become louder.

'Tell me what you're on about Rossy 'cos I'm freezing my arse off here.'

'I said, someone wants to know where you are,' came his voice, picking out the words slowly over the noise of the pub.

'Who?' he asked impatiently.

'Sarah Underwood,' said Ross.

'Don't arse me about, I'm quite aware that having the eyesight of an eagle you could have seen the number on my phone but-'

'Just a minute, I can't hear you,' called Ross. Avalon heard shuffling as if Ross was holding the phone close to his chest. He could also hear lots of noise and muffled laughs. Avalon sighed and looked up and down the street, why was Ross doing this, it was so out of character.

'*James? James, it's Sarah...*' Avalon almost dropped the phone, he looked up to the sky, his eyes not quite knowing where to look. His stomach tightened and he felt strange. She was there, at the pub?

'Sarah…?' he said but could think of nothing else to say.

'*Where are you?*' she asked with concern. He tried to think of the words but it was as if language was no longer available to him. Then he said it. The only thing he could say.

'I'm on my way.'

The Avalon Series, by Peter Gray.

The Drums of Drumnadrochit

By Peter Gray.

Introducing Detective James Avalon, a man in turmoil. Both his
private and professional life is at an all-time low and to make things
worse he is seen as a liability to his senior officers. He has to make a
change in both aspects of his life, but how? Though he is still on
good terms with his ex-wife she is beginning to despair with his
lack of compromise in his life until a chance meeting with another
officer shows promise of opening new doors to his future.

Auld Clootie

By Peter Gray.

James Avalon faces a new menace in the second book in the Avalon
series. Change and upheaval within the police forces sees him
struggle with the problems of a reorganisation of the team. Trouble
visits once again in the shape of a major crime that seems to have no
clues or motives and Avalon has to work with limited resources to
solve a crime linked to religion, ritual and legend.

The Brollachan

By Peter Gray.

After just twelve months based in Inverness, Detective Inspector
James Avalon now feels more at home than any other time in his
career. With his personal life still a shambles, Avalon takes solace in
the landscape and his work, but when a woman disappears from her
car in plain sight, he wonders about the accuracy of the report.
When a body is found, the case becomes more serious. Is the
woman's disappearance linked to the body or does Avalon need to
reassess his methods?

The Black Clan
By Peter Gray.

When Avalon becomes embroiled in secret societies and Masonic rituals he soon finds out how far up the food chain the rot has climbed. Once again the Inverness detective is on the streets and this time he's angry.

Caledonian Flame
By Peter Gray.

Avalon is taking a much-needed rest, his first extended leave since being at Inverness. It gives him time to think, and for Avalon, that isn't necessarily a good thing.

Bored and kicking his heels in Edinburgh, he digs his way through old cases and uncovers much more than a crime, he stumbles on a whole culture of misdemeanours spreading oceans, continents and time.

Avalon scours the streets of Inverness in the last major case of this contemporary series. This time his life is on the line.

Also by Peter Gray

A Certain Summer

Sam's Kingdom

With Feeling

Please visit:

www.petergrayauthor.co.uk
www.acertainsummer.co.uk
www.avalon-series.co.uk

www.trickyimppublishing.co.uk